# LIGHTBORN

*For Aaro,*

*I love you,*

*C*

# PROLOGUE

In the late twentieth and early twenty-first centuries, we saw the beginning of our end. Though we missed it at the time, all the signs were there. The influx of magic to our TV's happened all at once but so quietly that we accepted it with ease.

Magic became a household form of entertainment. Magicians burst onto the scene performing magic in person and on our screens until we became almost numb to the phenomenon. Assuring ourselves that, although it looked like magic, it had to be something other. There was a logical explanation of how they read our minds, turned water into iced tea, and made it rain hundred-dollar bills.

We laughed and shrugged and moved on with our day, using reason and logic to overshadow the reality.

This need to be logical is why we missed it. The unusual events around the globe were explained away with just enough conviction that we accepted it as fact.

When a volcano erupted into a lightning storm that lasted more than a week, we looked on in awe at what Mother Nature was capable of.

When an entire plane full of people disappeared, we shrugged and cried and questioned how it could have happened…until we didn't anymore.

It took far longer than it should have for the truth to

shine through.

We were too cynical.

We just couldn't believe what our eyes and hearts were telling us. Until we had no choice.

# PART ONE

# CHAPTER 1

**After**

The second she was through, she snapped her fists shut, closing the portal. It cracked closed so close behind she could smell her burnt hair.

It was such a risk to run, but she hadn't been left with any other options. Being taken from her home and delivered to the Brotherhood was her worst nightmare.

Anya had always tried to be careful with her Light, knowing that if the Brotherhood found out what she was capable of, they would use her power to abandon the world to darkness and decay.

She was what they had been looking for, and she was their ticket out. So when they locked her in that room, she threw caution to the wind and ran.

Opening a portal without preparation was dangerous. Anya used to jump through with such ease, but these days, she really had to focus. She knew she couldn't wholly guarantee where she would end up, which would make getting back even more difficult. But it was worth the risk.

Anywhere away from the Brotherhood was safer right now.

She knew she would need to lie low for a little while and keep her Light under wraps to not to draw unwanted attention, but in her frantic state, there was no way to be sure of when or where she would land.

All she could hope was to get away and hide. Then she could focus and make it back to the safety of the Ludus. Mr Parks would know what to do.

Looking around, she had no idea where she was. She thought she was going somewhere her parents took her as a child, yet nothing looked familiar. Surrounded by trees, she could just make out some lights in the distance and decided to run. But she'd taken no more than a dozen steps when she heard a familiar sound piercing the quiet.

Afraid to turn back, Anya froze in place as the Light burned into the night behind her. Daring a glance, her mouth dropped open at the sight of the orange sparks. It was cutting into the air exactly where her own portal had been.

But that wasn't possible! Nobody could have traced her jump once her Light was out.

She'd purposely not jumped far to keep her Glimmer as small as possible.

And she was alone in the room! How did they even know she was gone?

With no time to think, she sprinted from the Light and towards the town. If she could just find a place to hide, maybe they wouldn't find her. Maybe she could slip away somehow and put some distance between them that they couldn't trace.

Behind her, the orange shimmer burned in the darkness, and a new portal opened in the same spot she'd come through. Brother Anwar stepped out slowly, looking around with a smile before following his prey toward the town.

As she ran, Anya tried to think of a plan. He was already hot on her heels and knew now what she could do. There was no way he would let her get away without a fight, but using her Light would draw too much attention if any other Lightborn were close by. They would come running at even the smallest spark, leaving her completely outnumbered.

But she was being chased by one of the Three, and her Light was all she had. If she could just catch him off guard, maybe she stood a fighting chance.

The town was getting closer, but Anya knew she wouldn't make it in time. The trees were too thick, and Anwar was likely to attack any minute. She was recklessly considering another jump when suddenly the lights in the distance went out, and the earth moved beneath her feet.

Anya fell, slipping across the ground as everything shifted. Her mind seemed to move with it, leaving her dizzy and nauseated. When she looked up, the trees in front were noticeably shorter and thicker.

"Just stop," his voice breathed from somewhere dangerously close. "You're not escaping. You're just wasting my time."

Anya covered her ears and stopped running.

Was he that close or just in her head?

She squinted into the darkness and felt a wave of confidence radiate from within. As she lifted her arms, she let out a steady breath and extended her fingers. The streaks and sparks of her Light bounced in the air, illuminating the forest in a blue-purple haze.

They progressed through the surrounding trees until they hit Anwar, standing on a hill behind her, hands on his hips. When her Lightwave passed over, he seemed to stumble back.

"Nice trick, but I can do better."

Before the last word was out of his mouth, a surge of fire flew from where he stood. Anya felt the heat before it reached her and had no choice but to protect herself.

With everything she had, she threw her hands around her body, feeling water and wind enveloping her like a blanket. When the flames hit, she heard the burst of heat hissing loudly around her.

Crouching low, Anya focussed on nothing but her protective shield. She wanted to look up and see if Anwar had moved but was afraid she would lose focus and burn.

"Stop!" She begged into the storm.

Her hair whipped around her face, and she couldn't see beyond her own reach.

"Enough!" She yelled again, only this time, she stood and stretched her arms wide.

Everything stopped, rushing back from where she stood in a wild dance of water and flame, each trying to overpower the other. The trees and grass were left both scorched and wet.

Anya looked up, searching for Anwar, but he was gone. She flinched when he spoke again.

"I'm impressed, Anya. The Nightless, indeed. You have more Light than I thought." His voice was a whisper in her ear, but she couldn't see him.

"I'm not here to impress you. Just leave me alone."

"You know that's not going to happen. Not now. Not after that."

He was at her side before she could react, his hands on her arms, pinning them to her side.

"So much Light. How?"

Anya turned her face and clenched her fist, but before

she could do anything, Anwar raised a hand and struck her across the face. She fell to the ground at his feet, blurry-eyed and defeated.

"It's over, Anya. Stop fighting." Brother Anwar, one of the Three, crouched down and lifted her chin to see her face. He saw the rage in her eyes and chuckled.

"I won't help you! Not ever!"

"You will. You'll help us do whatever we ask of you. Because if you don't, you and your family will burn with the rest of them."

# CHAPTER 2

**One month earlier - March 2091**

The TV came to life right on schedule. Nobody bothered to unplug it anymore - we knew the damn thing would turn on either way. The screen shone its red light around the room as the Brotherhood's logo pulsed big and bright in the middle.

"Brotherhood..." Uncle Mark mumbled to nobody in particular.

He always rolled his eyes or exhaled sharply when he saw that word. Having been a soldier, he 'knew what it really meant.'

We waited and watched as the image went from black to red and back again. The stupid emblem spun in the middle: some dumb star with flames around.

I really hate that thing. Nothing good ever comes from seeing it.

"I don't see why we have to just sit here," my sister said for the millionth time.

She got up and moved to the window, looking out as though she would actually see anybody. She knew better - we all did. The Brotherhood had something to say, and you better believe we were all going to hear it.

"How would they even know..."

Alexis turned toward the door, but Uncle Mark grabbed her wrist. They made eye contact for a second before she slumped forward and sat back down.

"They always know," my little cousin whispered, scared they would hear his every word.

Things had been quiet in the last few months. The most recent curfew was lifted, and we let ourselves fall back into a routine.

People went to work, dropped their kids at school, went on dates, and buried their loved ones. The Brotherhood stayed off our TVs and out of our radios, and it was almost as though they were gone.

Of course, nobody was going to forget about them. Their army of lackeys still patrolled the cities, and the Lightborn kept a close eye on their Townships.

We were all used to being watched by now. It was the standard way of life since The Blackout.

The Brotherhood calls it The Awakening but it has a lot of underground names: The Apocalypse nearing the top of the list.

I prefer to think of it as The Fall - our Fall from grace.

Mankind became so self-involved that we completely missed The Brotherhood's rise. Like a trojan horse, they snuck in with the gift of illusion and wonderment, but within was our downfall. These worldwide broadcasts were a slap in the face of all those who watched and laughed and ignored the power.

I like to think I would have been suspicious.

Did people really not see it?

Seventy years isn't a long time, not really. I just can't imagine the people of 2020 watching a man freeze a cup of tea with the touch of his finger or walk on water and not see the magic.

That's a tough word, even now. It's so much more than magic tricks and illusion. It's power. Real, big, evil power. The men who used to wander the streets reading minds and pulling cell phones out of watermelons are now the men who control it all. It was as though they woke up one day and realised what they were capable of.

But instead of choosing to do good, they chose to take over the world.

The Blackout began on June 23, 2023, when the whole world went dark. Every light, television, cellphone, and computer went out. Radios didn't work, elevators stopped, cars shut down, trains came to a screeching halt, and planes crashed out of the skies.

The chaos that followed was like nothing anyone had ever seen and raged worldwide. For seven days, people looted and caused destruction to cities, homes, and public property. From Tokyo to Paris to New York, the world was wholly unsafe.

Then on June 30, exactly a week after it began, every screen and television on the planet turned on to broadcast the same message to the world:

"Hello. We are The Brotherhood of Light. The Fathers of Power. The Lightborn. Exactly one week ago, we took control. We turned out the lights. We stopped the cars and trains and shut down your access to everything. We did this because we can no longer stand by and watch as the world runs itself into destruction. On June 23, our people removed the leaders of every single country around the globe. They are no longer in charge. We are. We let you destroy each other for the last seven days to show you the future you were blindly running towards. You were ignoring the signs of your own destruction. This was inevitable. Except now, you have us."

With this, lights came back on, and the broadcast showed footage of the carnage from the week.

People killing each other over bottled water.

Looters throwing Molotov cocktails into homes and stores.

Then in the blink of an eye, both on screen and in person, the destruction was gone. The Brotherhood raised their hands, speaking some kind of incantation. The streets were suddenly cleared, and the buildings were rebuilt. It was as if it never happened.

"This is what you became. This brought out the worst in you, and we are here to show you how to come back to the light. As of this moment, all looting and rioting will cease. We have eyes everywhere, and we will throw anyone caught breaking the rules in the same pit as the former world leaders. We will have order. We have placed one of our Brothers in command of every continent worldwide and will work to bring peace back to you. For now, all you need to know is that a change is coming, and you have little choice but to fall in line."

The message played simultaneously around the world, waking people up to the New World Order.

Naturally, people resisted.

Generals believed they could take back control with the force of their militaries but with communications still down, organising a revolt proved difficult.

When some five thousand strong tried to storm the White House, their guns turned to sand in their hands. They forced soldiers in Australia to turn their weapons on each other. Mercenaries in France went up in a cloud of smoke with the simple snap of the Brotherhood's fingers.

They broadcast all of this to the world in a 24/7 news cycle of carnage. The Brotherhood made it clear who was in charge and what would happen to those who defied them. It took six months of unsuccessful rebellions before the Brotherhood announced their total control. Militaries were now at their disposal, though they assured everyone they wouldn't be needed. The Brotherhood promised a new world, one without poverty or crime.

But their peace didn't last long. How could it?

Some people's hatred for the Lightborn outweighed their fear, and every so often, a show of power became necessary. Whispers and rumours of rebellions would spread, eventually reaching the Brotherhood's ears, forcing their hands.

A group of rebels was taken down in 2029 after trying to liberate a prison camp. Most of the group was executed live for all to see.

In 2034, the Brother of Canada rounded up the entire community of Toronto. He had them line the streets, and with nothing more than a sigh, froze every last one of them. They're still there, frozen statues for all to see and fear.

The whispers ceased after that for many years. Too many failed attempts to overthrow the most powerful men in the world had a way of keeping a resistance down.

Not that Alexis let it stop her...

"They can't keep watch over all of us all the time! There's only three of them, for Brother's sake!" Alexis hissed.

"Alexis, don't! Just...you always do this. Just stop. Complaining isn't going to change a thing, and you know it," I snapped.

Alexis always acted like she was ready to rebel but was all talk. Some nights I could let her go on, but tonight I just didn't have the patience for it. So we sat in silence, waiting for the Brotherhood to spew their nonsense.

When the emblem finally faded, and the Brothers came on the screen, I saw Uncle Mark stiffen and little Frankie flinch.

"Citizens, thank you for joining us tonight," Brother Anwar began.

He sat in the middle of the Three, hands open and welcoming. "We are honoured, as always, to have your attention."

Uncle Mark snorted and rolled his eyes. He downed the last of his drink and made to stand, before catching himself and sitting back in his chair.

Had we been outside somewhere when the announcement began, we would have had to scramble to find a screen. At least we had a little warning this time around.

During broadcasts, we've been shown what they do to people for missing an announcement, and it's not pretty.

I remember when I was very young watching a group of Lightborn age an entire family in the span of just a few minutes.

They stood in a row, all four of them, sad and sobbing. The Lightborn raised their hands, and the family grew old and frail before our eyes until they crumpled over, dead, grey, and lifeless. The youngest was no older than Alexis at the time, and it took far longer for him to go. Watching his little body wrinkle and fade haunts me to this day.

"Tonight, we have come to you to make a special announcement," Brother Oran continued. "As you know, in just a few short months, we will celebrate the thirtieth anniversary of our Ascension. Three decades ago, we won the Dark War and rose to become the most powerful Lightborn this world has ever seen. We defeated those who wanted to harm our way of life and brought peace to the world once more."

I tensed at the words. I may not have been alive for the Dark War, but I knew the history - the real history.

Oh, they won the war all right - the war they started! Millions of people died as the Lightborn fought their battles from the safety of their homes, and it took eleven and a half years of fighting before a 'truce' was finally called.

Trust me, nobody won anything that day.

Brother Uri took over now, nodding to his cohorts before he turned to the camera. His bright eyes always shocked me.

"For the last thirty years, you have seen what real peace looks like. We have given you bountiful crops, provided jobs for all, and kept you safe. Our Brotherhood has never been stronger. Every day, more Lightborn shine bright and are welcomed into the fold."

With this, the camera moved back to reveal the Great Hall. In front of the Brothers were rows of boyish men, standing to attention with their eyes cast down - the School of Light's newest graduates.

A few years after the Blackout, monthly tests were introduced to every school around the world. They took any young boy that showed even the slightest spark from his parents and put them into a new school, run solely by the Brotherhood.

For some unknown reason, all Lightborn are male and are expected to prove themselves worthy by working as security in local communities. After they gain enough experience, they're promoted and given control of a Township. Known as Leaders, these lackies act as the hands of the Brotherhood in the local areas. Senior to these men are the Lieutenants, higher-ranking members of the Brotherhood, in charge of multiple Townships at once.

On the screen, the young men held their arms in front of their chests, palms cupped around small glimmering orbs. They were the newest group of Lightborn to come of age and possibly the largest group so far.

"In the years following The Awakening, we saw so few Lightborn emerged. But since our Ascension, our numbers have more than doubled. We have installed senior Brothers in every major city around the globe, and our young men here will join the ranks in your Townships. Each man before us has taken a vow to uphold our laws and values and should be seen as our ambassadors."

The Three remained seated as the camera focused on their faces once more. Brother Anwar looked to his left and then his right. Brothers Uri and Oran nodded and returned their gaze to the camera, their eyes narrowing slightly as he spoke.

"Almost sixty-eight years ago, The Awakening brought our Light forward. The Brotherhood stood before you, twelve strong, united in their dream to bring this world out of the shadows. They shared their Light with you and gifted you with their wisdom and leadership. Although their courage and strength will never be forgotten, this Brotherhood is far different from its predecessor. We stand firm in our beliefs. We saw a better way for us all to progress and grow. We embraced our

Light in a way never before seen, and the world has been all the better for it."

"Elders...they talk as if they didn't start a war. They wanted to kill each other not so long ago, and now they talk like they're the best of friends!" Uncle Mark was fuming. He'd been part of the Dark War and still suffered the effects, as many others did.

Although the original Brotherhood, known as the Elders, initially stood shoulder to shoulder, behind the scenes, they were not quite the united front they appeared. As more, younger, Lightborn were brought into the fold, disagreements started.

The certainties of the Elders faltered as they differed in their approaches. Arguments would grow increasingly heated during gatherings, and factions soon formed. Some Brothers even began changing their communities against the rules of the Elders.

Tensions finally hit their peak in 2048 when a Brother in Sweden gathered all his Lightborn in an attempt to change the weather. Few had ever tried before, and anything more substantial than clearing a few clouds often spelled disaster.

But this Lightborn was sick of the cold and grey. He had his Lieutenants stand united as they tried to break through the heavy clouds and bring out the sun. It worked for a few days, and most people enjoyed the break from the cold. But on the fourth day, the temperature jumped, and over the next week continued to rise until the entire country was dry and exhausted.

A drought covered the land, fires broke out in the forests, and it took almost all the Brotherhood to bring normalcy back to the country. They called a hearing during which the council insisted this Brother be excommunicated from the Brotherhood.

To their great surprise, many disagreed. They felt - as the Swedish Brother felt - that their Light was not being used to its full potential. They wanted to use it and strengthen it. The Elders, however, knew how intoxicating the Light could be and how it could consume.

They demanded the rebellious Lightborn stand down and do as they were told, but arguments filled the Great Hall as the younger generations stood up, strong and organised.

When an earth splitting crack filled the room, everyone fell into silence.

Someone used their Light to attack an Elder, and one of the original members of the Brotherhood sat dead in his throne.

It was the straw that broke the camel's back.

Over the next decade, they fought, using their armies and local communities. They dragged men and women of fighting age from their homes to fight the men and women of neighbouring towns. Countries became divided as the Lightborn fractured into the Old and the New, using their Light to make the battlefields uneven.

A group of Lightborn from Beijing blinded Phuket soldiers, allowing their army to slaughter almost all the attackers.

A Brother in Sydney gave his army the ability to breathe underwater. They attacked the soldiers in Adelaide from the South, giving them little time to fight back.

Almost all of the soldiers were fighting against their will, following the lower ranking Leaders into battle.

Over the years, hundreds of Lightborn were killed, leaving their armies fighting with no leadership. But the ever-watchful Brothers punished any soldier that tried to step back.

This all culminated in three powerful Lightborn making an alliance and overpowering the Elders. In the end, the Lightborn left were vetted and either imprisoned or given limited power around the world.

Where there was once a council and a democracy, it was now three men controlling everything. It was their way or death.

I shuddered at the thought and struggled to keep my focus on the rubbish on the TV.

"Now, thirty years later, we have agreed that it is time to grow our number. Our combined Light," Brother Uri gestured to his sides, "is the greatest in existence. But we feel it is time to embrace new Light."

The Brothers smiled, and Oran took over, "In three months, on the thirtieth anniversary of our Ascension, we will hold The Tournament of Light two years early. As always, all Lightborn are encouraged to enter, and we will test them until two are proven the most worthy. Only this year it will be bigger and more spectacular than ever."

"We know how beloved these Tournaments have been, and you are all encouraged to attend and enjoy in the festivities - and they will be quite breathtaking! Naturally, it will be broadcast," Uri smiled and turned to his Brothers. "And at the end, instead of the normal celebration of a champion, we will bring two new Lightborn into our sacred Brotherhood."

My heart was pounding. This was bad. I knew exactly the kinds of tests they were talking about, and childhood stories of floods and bush fires came to mind.

The Tournaments were typically held every eight

years and were always followed by some kind of natural disaster.

"We are all looking forward to what the Tournaments bring and to welcoming two new Brothers into the fold. For now, thank you. May the Light shine upon you all."

The broadcast ended, the TV went dark once more, and we sat in silent fear until, eventually, Uncle Mark stood and walked to the window. He sighed and touched a hand to where a lightning bolt hit him, all those years ago.

"They're going to destroy us all."

# CHAPTER 3

"Get out." Anwar stood and moved from his Brothers.

They remained quiet as the Lightborn filed out through the enormous doors at the end of the hall.

"Relax," Uri called with a warning tone.

Anwar spun and pointed a finger at his Brother, "Don't you dare!"

"Dare what? We agreed."

"I didn't agree to anything!" Anwar turned his back and let out a rushed breath.

Uri stood and moved in front of the table, leaning back leisurely, crossing his arms and ankles. He shook his head in disappointment and glanced back at Oran, hoping for a little support. He tensed when he saw the beer.

"What?" Oran shrugged, taking a long draw. "He pushes me to it."

Uri uncrossed his arms and breathed out, knowing Oran had a point but that Anwar would be all the more upset.

"Are you really just going to stand there and drink yourself blind?"

Anwar was fuming. He hated when they were so calm and stood with his hands on his hips, a nasty vein popping out of his head.

"What do you want me to say? We took a vote, and it's been agreed. We need this Tournament. We need the Light. What else can we do?" Uri shrugged, keeping his tone light and even.

Anwar raised his hand, and as he closed his fist, the drink turning to ash in his Brother's mouth.

"Real mature, Anthony." Oran taunted.

Uri rolled his eyes and moved between his Brothers, knowing this could end badly.

"What did you just call me?" Anwar raged forward until Uri placed his hands on his chest, pushing him back.

"Really, Oran? Really?" Uri asked over his shoulder as Anwar shoved himself away.

Oran sighed and put the beer down, coming to stand by with the others. They'd had the same fight for years, and he was tired of it.

"Stop fighting us. We voted, and it's decided. You can huff and puff all you want, Anwar. This isn't a dictatorship. And you know as well as I do that without this Tournament, we're dead."

The pair locked eyes and Uri prepared himself, half expecting one of them to blow the other up. Instead, Oran shrugged and moved away, out the side door and into the rain. The two remaining Brothers stared at each other for a long time before either spoke.

"You know that we can't do it any other way. You're not strong enough-"

"The hell I'm not!"

"Anwar! We've been fighting this for almost 12 years. You've tried, what- how many times? Look around you! This world is dying, and if we don't find another Lightborn that can create a strong enough portal soon, we'll die along with it," Uri urged his Brother.

He knew Anwar was frustrated and tired. Being the only one of them capable of opening portals, it all fell to his shoulder. But he just wasn't strong enough to do what they needed. They'd abused their Light for too long and were out of options. They needed someone new.

"If we bring a new Lightborn to this council, everything will change. We will be putting all our trust in someone we don't know," Anwar warned for the millionth time.

He knew they needed more Light, but he hoped they could syphon enough from the Tournaments.

"Just let me try. A few days into the games, and I'll be able to absorb more Light than you can imagine! They'll be playing our stupid games, and they won't even realise their strength is diminishing. Not until it's too late. And by the-"

"You know we can't just have one plan!" Uri moved forward and put his hands on Anwar's shoulders. "I truly hope we can take in as much Light as possible. I do! I hope we can build up our strength and do this without the need for anyone else. You think I want to share our power? Of course not. But we have to be smart. And if we find a younger Lightborn with your ability to open portals, we must move forward with the second Ascension. It might be our only chance before the whole world crumbles around us."

Anwar shrugged his Brother away, crossing his arms like a petulant child.

"I can do it," he mumbled.

"Then prove it," Uri challenged.

Anwar gave his Brother one last glare before rushing

out the big doors, leaving Uri to his thoughts.

Uri was always the more level-headed of The Three, always had been. Oran had a vast amount of power. His Light had surprised them all, though he hid it behind humour and indifference. But it was deep and bright and the reason they won the war. Oran was as strong a Lightborn as Uri had ever seen. But he was a follower.

Anwar, on the other hand, felt himself to be an exceptional leader. His Light was great - that was not in question - but he was too emotional to keep it under complete control. He allowed himself to feel too much, and it was always his downfall. If he could just manage to control himself, Anwar would surely be as powerful as Oran. But his hot head prevailed.

Uri was never as powerful as his Brothers. His Light was bright but nothing compared to Oran. He couldn't open portals like Anwar or control the seas like the other two. But Uri was cool and calculating. He was one of the first to rebel against the Elders, laying seeds of doubt into the younger Lightborn and pushing and prodding until they stood up, on what they thought was their own accord. Uri's power came from his mind. His Light was the icing on the cake.

His name meant 'my light,' and he'd chosen it for its simplicity. Oran stuck with his Irish roots, adopting the title after the colour his Light appeared; green. Anwar went through a lot of names before deciding. Ultimately, his name meant 'brighter,' and he chose it to show his superiority. Their followers hadn't questioned their name changes when it came time to take over. But Uri was sure they preferred to follow Brother Oran than Brother Dave.

He left the Great Hall feeling defeated. They'd debated other options for years and had left Anwar with little choice but to go along with the plan. They were Three for a reason, and the majority won. Even so, they'd had to force him to join the broadcast. No way they could have done it without him.

They were now and would always need to at least appear united. Since their Ascension, nobody had dared to stand against them. That would change if they didn't make their plan work. Soon, their Light would fade and reveal the truth behind their power. The Cloaks would drop, and people would see how their Light had starved the world of its resources, causing irreparable damage.

The Great Hall was part of a vast, walled-in property. It stood alone, not too far from the gates, as a church might once have.

The original Brotherhood believed religion was nothing more than a violence-inducing cult, responsible for almost every great conflict humanity had ever seen.

So to keep the peace, every religion was wiped out entirely, and anyone caught practicing was removed from their community, never to be seen again. Today, religion was all but forgotten. But Uri read about it in the banned books and admired pictures of the old churches and temples. He liked their grandeur and had the Great Hall built in such an image.

The enormous doors were framed by columns, and the walls were lined with coloured windows. They painted the dome on top a golden red that shone when the light hit. He took the things he'd liked most from the past and put it in this building, and t was the first and only building that could be seen when passing the property.

He had no idea about God or Gods and honestly

didn't think of himself as such. But the idea of leaving people awestruck with this building was too tempting. They permitted people to enter every so often, and they would always stand, mouths open as they took it in.

Uri stood now, back to the gates, looking up at the large wooden doors that had been carved in fire and lightning. The scars and burns stood out in the moonlight, and he smiled at the beauty.

"You know he's not strong enough."

"I know," Uri sighed. "He knows it too. He just doesn't want to admit it."

"That last portal almost cut off his arm. He'd rather kill us all than admit he's weak." Oran rounded the corner, worry on his face.

"That's not going to happen. We won't let it."

Oran watched his Brother, trying to read his expression. The announcement had been a long time coming and was the fuel behind many explosive arguments.

Anwar even left the compound three years ago after such a fight and was gone for over four months. He came back looking weak but ready to talk. They didn't know what happened in his time away, but they had felt him using his Light. They didn't ask, and he didn't offer.

Still, it took another three years before they came up with their plan, and Anwar was still resistant.

"We may need to take the next step with Anwar," Uri warned, keeping his eyes up and his tone flat.

"That's...not going to be easy," Oran breathed, looking around.

The last thing they needed was for Anwar to be listening.

Uri sighed again and looked up to the stars.

"No, but it doesn't look like he's going to be giving us

a choice."

# CHAPTER 4

The Announcement was all anybody could talk about the next day, and as we made our way to the bus stop, people were prattling all around about the Tournament and the possibility of two new Brothers. Most people seemed excited about the idea. They wanted to see the Lightborn fight and show us their power.

Alexis' bus arrived first, and she got on without a look back. She attended the School for Performing Arts and was close to graduation. Early on, she proved she could sing and dance and was taken out of the regular. She said she didn't like it, but I knew she was excited to graduate and start performing in the real world. She was already looking at trying out for plays and movies.

Apparently, movie stars used to be a big deal. I heard that the none performers celebrated and practically worshipped them. Now, it's a job like any other.

Still, I used to be so jealous of her path. I wanted to be like her and begged my parents to let me go to her school. I didn't understand why I couldn't.

After the Awakening, the Brothers decided it would be better and more efficient to assess children to find their 'right path' and sending them to individual schools.

Alexis was a natural performer and was placed as

such. My friend Vinnie liked computers and was sent to a technology-based school where he learned about coding and could build a whole network from nothing.

If a child didn't show a particular aptitude for anything specific, they stayed in the public school where they usually ended up as a civil servant of some kind. Unless they had a growth spurt, in which case they almost always ended up working security.

I spent years afraid I would never make it out of the public school. I couldn't sing, fix things or speak another language. Alexis always made fun of me, saying I would end up being her driver. Until one day, we had a guest teacher who took a shine to me. She seemed to think I had a talent, and I was sent to the culinary school.

At first, I was angry. I didn't want them to pick my path. But after a couple of months, I found I actually enjoyed it. I was happy there, so when they asked me to come back and train to be a teacher, I jumped at the chance. I can relax in the kitchen and seem to know what I'm doing.

My little cousin was next, hopping on the bus with a spring in his step. He was too young to have a path and attended the public school close by. Thank the Elders he didn't have the Light.

The culinary school was a little further away, so I liked to bring a book. None of the other teachers from the school lived in Township 6, and I was content to sit and read.

Talk of the Tournaments followed me to class, and I heard people reliving the games from before. It seemed like the general feeling was excitement, and it took some time for the teacher to quiet everyone down.

"Now, today, we will be making Banoffee Pie!"

Miss Emberly loved her job, and I was happy to be learning with her. But she had a fondness for the Brotherhood that kept us as colleagues, rather than friends.

"Who can tell me which Brother has a particular fondness for this dessert?"

"Brother Anwar!" Someone shouted from the back.

"Good. And who can tell me what year Brother Anwar created the Banoffee?"

"2063!"

"That's right!" Miss Emberly squealed. "Before that, we used to have a yellow fruit called the banana. It was quite popular. People used to eat it on toast, in smoothies, or simply by itself. For this pie, a baker would boil up sugar until it bubbled and turned golden, then add cream and whisk as it steamed and spat at you. Can you imagine? The fuss! Brother Anwar wanted to simplify things, and thank goodness he did! The Banoffee is beloved worldwide!"

I scowled. Uncle Mark told me we used to have all kinds of fruits and vegetables until the Brothers decided they didn't like them. Admittedly, I do actually love a banoffee - when they're ripe, of course.

I still remember my first one. My Dad brought a bunch home, and we got to have one after dinner. I peeled back the yellow skin with such excitement and that first bite! Oh, it was heaven. The ooey gooey caramel core was everything I hoped for.

Now, I feel it leaves a bitter taste in my mouth. I wish I could have tried a banana.

The pies came out great, and I knew Uncle Mark would be excited to see me walk through the door. Miss

Emberly had me set the homework, and I asked the class to write up a new recipe combining two fruits, as Anwar had done.

I would demonstrate something in the next class and was leaning toward mango and strawberry. The Strawgo? The Mangberry?

The rest of the day went by like any other. We finished a batch of croissants from the day before, and I showed a younger class how to make pasta from scratch, having them make up their own sauces.

We spent lunch tasting everything, giddy and full of pasta. I blew a kiss to my perfectly marinaded pork shoulder in my last class of the day before placing it in the smoker, excited to taste it the next day.

On the bus home, my mind wandered back to the Announcement. It had been months since the last one, and that was just to congratulate the latest class from the Security school. Why would The Three want to bring in new members now? The Lightborn were all under their control anyway.

The Brothers personally oversaw the school and sat in during classes. I heard that sometimes they even taught themselves. And when the Lightborn came of age, they had to take a blood oath, vowing their allegiance to the Brotherhood.

The Three had total control. They could even sense when Light was being used. With all that power, why would they want to share their influence? I felt uneasy in my gut.

Only one thing came to mind.

I got off the bus a few stops before my own. Nobody seemed to notice, and I walked toward the fields drawing no one's eyes.

In the right light, I can see the Glimmer from afar. A Glimmer is a piece of magic that gets left behind after Light is used, like a magical residue that sparkles and shimmers.

Today the sun was hidden behind the clouds, but I could still feel it. I felt the warmth on my face as I got closer and looked back to make sure I wasn't being watched.

Sure I was alone; I held my breath and powered through. The Veil felt warm and wet against my skin, and when I came out the other side, my hair was a frizzy mess.

I wasn't even all the way through before my mouth dropped open. It was months since I last came here, and things had gotten so much worse. Like always, the darkness hit me first in the Veil. The sun couldn't break through the black smoke clouds, and the only light came from the flames that fell from the sky.

The trees were almost all burned up now, and the water in the lake had turned entirely black. The wind kicked up dirt from the ground, and it tasted like salt and sulphur. The only animals behind the Veil were those cast away by The Three.

Much like the banoffee, the Brothers tried to alter animals too. They sent some of their more nasty creations to roam the streets during times they set curfews. Here, I saw the dark things the Light had created, shuddering as they loomed in the distance.

Some looked like rabbits, only they were huge. Their teeth and ears hung unevenly, and their eyes drooped. They were deformed in such distinct ways - some with extra feet, others with humps on their backs.

Last time I'd seen what I think used to be a deer,

but their antlers were sharp and black. Their faces were twisted, and they had something growing out of their bellies.

When the wind became too much, I made my way back through the Veil. I was dusty and windswept, and my eyes watered from the sand and the sight of it all.

Sitting with my back to the Veil, I cried. Just like the first time I went through, and the second and third and every time since.

I was six the first time. Alexis and I had been riding our bikes to a sweet shop we both liked, and our parents let us go by ourselves since it was mostly grassed lands.

I felt the Veil before I saw anything. When we came over the hill, we both stopped. I could see the lights shining and feel the warmth on my skin. I remember looking at Alexis and grinning, excited and desperate to go see. But she turned to the side without a word and started riding away.

"What about the lights?" I called after her.

"There are no lights," she said, without looking back.

Reluctantly, I followed her. I wanted to see it, but I didn't want to go alone. On our way home, Alexis went the long way around, avoiding the lights and the warmth altogether. Whenever I asked her about it, she shrugged and brushed it off.

It took some time to build up my courage, but eventually, I went back without her. I remember raising my hand to the Glimmer and feeling the moisture on my fingers. Through the Veil, it was darker than outside but not too dark.

The trees were not burned but twisted and grey, with no leaves. The water in the lake looked murky, and I could see splashing. When I got closer, a group of deformed toads jumped out and chased me. I ran away, through the Veil, down the hill, and almost all the way back home before I collapsed.

Over the next month, I tried to get Alexis to come with me. I even tried with some of my school friends, but it was always the same. We would get close, and they would stop suddenly and turn away. I didn't understand why nobody else could see, until one day, my neighbour Will didn't get on the school bus.

I remember looking at his empty seat and wondering if he was sick. Then he didn't come the next day or the next. Eventually, enough of us got suspicious, and our teacher explained.

"William has been gifted with the Light. He won't be coming to class anymore."

I was still confused. I'd heard people talk about Light and magic before, but I never really understood it. I knew who the Three were and that they were powerful and in charge. But my six-year-old mind couldn't comprehend the reality of it all.

"Some boys are born special," my mother explained. "We don't know why or how, but they just are. In school, if a teacher sees signs of the Light, they can check with the men that have the badges."

"But where did Will go? I wanna see the Light!"

My mother sighed and looked sad, "William went to a special school with other boys just like him. He'll learn how to be special."

"How did they know he was special?"

"I don't know. Maybe your teacher saw him do something that nobody else can do."

I thought about the Veil and the creatures inside and panicked.

"What about me?"

"What about you?"

"Will they take me away too?" I started to cry.

Instead of bringing me into a hug, my mother grasped my arms and spoke in a harsh, angry tone, "Of course not. Only boys have the Light!"

But I knew better. I knew then, even in my naive way, that I was special too.

# CHAPTER 5

It was dark when I got home. The walk was slow and sad, and it wasn't until I walked through the door that I realised I'd left the pie outside the Veil. Poor Uncle Mark.

"Where the hell have you been?" Alexis demanded before the door could close. "Margot said you got off the bus early, but that was hours ago."

She was only a year older than me but still treated me like a child.

"I walked."

"Oh, you walked. Sure, ok. That's totally normal! Anya! Seriously?! Security is really cracking down, I've told you this! What if you-"

"Alexis, stop! It's fine. I'm nineteen, remember! I didn't even see any security, and it's barely dark. They wouldn't have stopped me, anyway."

"You don't know that, An. They're evil! They're mean bullies that get off on making us feel small. They work for the Brotherhood -they're the worst of them all!"

I waved my hands in surrender and apologised to my sister. I knew she was right, but she was overreacting just a little.

Alexis hated the Brothers and the Lightborn and anyone associated with them. After what happened to our parents, she'd developed a deep-seated need for rebellion. She toed the line in public and smiled like a dutiful girl, but she always looked for ways to break the rules at home. Of course, when I did anything like that, I got yelled at.

"Just don't give those jerks any excuses. We all know what happens-"

"I know, 'Lex!"

My neck flushed, and I could feel myself getting heated. I didn't want to think about it. I couldn't bear the wave of guilt always washed over me.

In my room, I sat staring at assignments that needed grading but not getting anything done. I just couldn't believe how much worse things looked behind the Veil. It was so much darker now.

Two years ago, I went looking for more spots like it, to no avail. But I knew they were out there. The Lightborn had been creating those monsters for years without people knowing.

Uncle Mark told us about the early days of the Brotherhood. How they had caused mass bush fires in Russia when they tried to make it snow in Thailand. They wanted to bring clean water to Africa and, in doing so, caused a massive drought in France and Germany.

They used their Light to suit themselves with no thoughts of consequences. And they masked those consequences behind the Veil so nobody would really know how dangerous things had gotten.

This was the real reason for the Tournament and the Ascension, I knew. Things were out of hand, and they needed more Light to try to fix it all. But the tests in the Tournament would surely only make things worse.

What if having a hundred Lightborn trying to make

a tree grow actually destroyed an entire forest? Why would they risk further destruction?

They owned the Lightborn. Why not just make them come together and fix things?

Unless...things had become unfixable?

“Anya? Dinner!” Frankie called from the kitchen, pulling me back to reality.

I joined my family at the table, though I didn’t eat much food. Uncle Mark was disappointed that I'd forgotten the pie, though he could see it was better to not ask why. He just shrugged and cleared his plate with a slight frown.

We moved in with Uncle Mark when I was seven. He and his wife agreed to take us in while our mother was...working. I remember good times with them and genuine happiness. But when Aunt Susanna died in childbirth, things were never quite the same. Of course, we all loved Frankie, but our loss, and now his, made the home a more solemn place.

Frankie was less subtle in showing his disappointment in me, and Alexis had to promise him a trip to the sweet shop the next day to calm him down. I didn’t answer when she asked if I wanted to come along, and she didn’t push me. I wasn’t sure if she remembered that day or if the power had simply erased the memory. Either way, she doesn’t ride that way anymore.

My dreams were filled with deformed dogs and burning buildings. The last image to run across my mind was of Brother Oran standing in the middle of a burning desert, arms raised as the sky fell down around him.

I woke with a start and knew I wouldn’t get back to sleep that night. My work sat out still, so I set about making my way through the recipes, all the while deciding to visit The Ludus that weekend.

# CHAPTER 6

**After**

Anya woke up back in the suite at the Brothers' compound. It was dark outside, she felt sick with hunger and had zero memory of how she got there. The last thing she remembered was him threatening her family. The smoke lingered on her clothes, and she flinched at the thought of his power.

She'd thought she was free.

She thought she'd jumped to safety, but he found her.

How could he follow so closely?

Quietly, Anya got up and tried the door. Locked, of course. An ear to the wood heard nothing outside, and she saw no shadows but was sure she wasn't alone. They wouldn't risk it.

Anya went to the window and looked out over the Brothers' land. She was on the corner, looking toward the Great Hall and further back into the compound. A house was lit up not too far, and further off, she thought she saw a few more lights and possibly a river or lake. It was beautiful, and it made her mad.

Why did they get all this when she was living so close to the decay?

Sitting on the bed, Anya could feel she wasn't strong enough to try anything close to opening a portal, not even to the next room. Her arms felt heavy, and she was finding it difficult to focus.

And then there was the hunger.

For almost her entire life, she'd hidden who she was. Held back when she didn't need to and played the normal, good girl for her family and the public.

What was happening to the earth - the decay under the Veil - she knew it was caused by the over-use of the Light. Nobody really knew where the magic came from, and since the Brotherhood came to power, there had been little they wouldn't allow.

When she was around ten or eleven, someone decided to make it rain white butterflies. This Lightborn was fresh out of school and trying to impress some girl he'd met.

The way it was told, the butterflies began to fall in a beautiful display of wings. More and more people came to see, dancing and laughing as the butterflies delicately flew amongst them, landing on dogs' noses and ears.

It wasn't long before things took a turn.

The wings started to change colour, pink and red seeping into their veins.

Then the blood began to pour.

Right in front of their eyes, the once elegant butterflies were now mere skeletons, dripping with blood before ultimately falling to their deaths.

The Lightborn responsible got a slap on the wrist.

The butterfly population was never quite the same.

Growing up, she'd heard all kinds of horror stories about the reckless use of magic and the way it once was. And after seeing the decay first hand, abusing her own Light felt wrong.

But her stomach was in knots, and she was starting to feel dizzy.

When had she last eaten?

Anya whispered an apology before holding out her hands. She smiled when a tray of tacos appeared, her appetite overriding her guilt. She had to eat, and they were spicy and delicious.

"I'm more a fish taco guy myself."

Anya coughed as the food caught in her throat. The voice had come from beside her, but the room was empty.

"May I come in?"

The door opened before she could answer. Anya saw the hallway was, in fact, empty, which surprised her. She'd assumed it would be lined with big, beefy Lightborn to keep little her under control.

In the doorway was Oran. He was eating ice cream, and she suddenly felt a surge of shame. She was no better than him and moved to put the tacos down, but he held up a hand.

"Eat. Please. I'm not one to deny anybody a good meal."

"Is my health so important to you? Elders forbid I lose a couple of pounds during my captivity."

"If we had done nothing other than make people skinny, they would have hailed us as Gods," he said with a sad smile.

Oran moved into the room and took a seat in an armchair by the window.

They ate in silence, making eye contact every so often. Despite it all, Anya felt at ease with Oran. But she wouldn't let her guard down. It was all an act.

Good cop, bad cop.

She'd seen enough movies and read enough to know this was what they did. They wanted her to feel safe, so she would tell them all her deepest and darkest secrets. She knew that the Three couldn't be trusted.

When they both finished, Oran sighed and looked out the window. Anya stayed where she was, hands in her lap, trying to decide what to do and say. Stuck between a rock and a hard place, she saw no way out.

"Have you always been gifted?" Oran asked eventually, still with his eyes in the distance.

She kept quiet. Why should she answer? She was a hostage, right? They kidnapped her from her home, and now he expected her to sit and have a civilised conversation?

"When can I go home?" She asked, instead.

"I think you're smart enough to know the answer to that."

"You can't just keep me here."

"You know we can. We can do anything we want. That's the whole point." He still wouldn't look at her, and it was infuriating. Because he felt bad? Or because he thought she wasn't worth his full attention?

"Anything you want. Like, destroy the world?"

That got his attention. He looked right at her, confused and impressed.

"Oh, you are something special, aren't you? How did we miss you all these years?"

"I guess you're not quite as all-powerful as you thought."

Oran stood and let out a seemingly genuine laugh. He walked to the door and turned back, motioning for Anya to follow. She hesitated but, knowing she had no choice, eventually followed.

He led her to the elevator and pressed the button for the top floor. They rode in silence, and she couldn't believe there didn't seem to be anyone around. The glass elevator showed the empty levels as they rose, and she started getting nervous.

No people meant no witnesses.

Was she about to meet the bad cop?

"I'm not going to hurt you. Neither is Anwar. We need you," Oran said unprompted. He took in her confused face and smiled before explaining, "Mind reading is easy after a little practice."

"So if I know you need me, then why would I do anything you want? Doesn't that mean I have all the power?"

"You tell me."

The glass doors opened to a long hallway with only three doors: one on the end and one each on the left and right, about halfway down. Anya stepped out and paused. Oran didn't move.

A door opening drew her attention, and Uri appeared. Anya looked back to Oran, but the elevator doors closed, and he left her. She watched him descend, and a sick feeling returned in her stomach.

"Come on." Uri turned and walked into the room, Anya following reluctantly.

From the doorway, the place looked like a fancy hotel suite. She saw a big bed and a living area. There was even a kitchen, and she could just about see a bathroom. The entire back wall was floor to ceiling windows. It was lovely. But it was a lie.

Once her foot touched the plush carpet over the threshold, the room changed.

Suddenly she was home. Uncle Mark was sitting with Frankie, watching some silly cartoons and laughing their heads off. Alexis came from the kitchen with snacks and joined them on the couch.

"Alexis!" Anya cried, rushing forward.

But as she reached out, her fingers went through her sister. They couldn't see or hear her. She wasn't there. This wasn't real.

"What is this?" She demanded.

"This is your family. Your weakness. This is how we know you'll do as your told." Uri sounded casual, almost bored.

Anya looked back to her family, and her heart sank as she watched their happiness, knowing she held it in her hands. Uri opened the door once more and touched her arm, pulling lightly.

"This way," he said gently.

She followed as he crossed to the opposite door. For the briefest moment, she thought she would walk into the Ludus - her other weakness. But she quickly put the thought out of her mind, looking to Uri to see if he'd picked up on it.

Could he read her too? She needed to do everything she could to guard her thoughts now. People's lives depended on it.

The second room looked much the same - slightly different decor, but a pleasant room nonetheless.

A chill ran up her back as Uri made eye contact. Did he know what she would see?

Anya didn't want to go inside, but she knew she had to. She took a breath and stepped onto the hardwood, the sudden brightness, making her turn away and cover her eyes.

They were outside this time, in a place she didn't know. The floor was dirt and gravel, and she could hear loud machines all around. When her eyes finally adjusted, confusion covered her face, and she knew Uri would read nothing helpful.

They were in some kind of quarry. People all around her were digging and shovelling in the stark heat. They were all wearing the same jumpsuit, and it didn't take Anya long to realise where she was.

“This is the prison? This is where they all go?”

She couldn’t believe it. Since the Great Blackout, the Lightborn arrested people for various so-called crimes, but nobody ever knew where they ended up. They just knew they never came home.

Rebellious generals in the early days, small rebel groups throughout the years, people that tried to keep practicing their religions - all of them taken away and never seen again.

“This is inhumane!” She cried, fuming and wanting nothing more than to engulf him in flames.

He must have read that in her and raised his hand. She immediately felt something inside and felt weaker than ever.

“Let’s not, hmmm?” He said simply, waving his hand again, so they were now alone in the dust. “Look around. Take it in. Is this what you really want for them?”

As he spoke, he turned toward some kind of tunnel under the rocks. Anya fell to her knees when she saw her family.

Alexis looked exhausted, her hair a mess, with tired eyes and scratches on her dry hands. To her side was little Frankie, trying desperately to pull a cart full of tools. Uncle Mark was behind, hunched over and pale.

“This is their future if you fight us. I need you to understand that.”

Anya reacted without a thought in her mind other than total disgust. She lunged at Uri, her hands and arms turning into armour as she reached.

She felt the metal connect with him as she punched into his chest, sending him flying back into the dirt.

At the last moment, he stopped his fall and hovered just inches above the ground. He stood quickly and sent Anya flying into the wall behind her. She'd used all the strength she had left, but it wasn't enough. She couldn't protect herself and fell to the floor, breathless and defeated.

"I'm going to let that go just once. It's an emotional time, I know. But next time, I won't be so gracious."

Uri looked down on Anya's family as they worked in the dust and heat. Frankie could hardly hold the shovel, and Alexis looked to be close to passing out.

Broken, exhausted, and utterly defeated, Anya dropped her head and let the tears fall.

Without a word, Uri walked by and left the room, leaving Anya on the floor, gasping for breath as her family worked the rocky ground.

# CHAPTER 7

**11 weeks to the Tournament**

Alexis and some friends were going into the city that weekend to see a play and look at places to live. Soon they would all be graduating and planned on moving to the city together.

Uncle Mark was taking Frankie to some ball game in the next Township, and I feigned illness. They wouldn't be gone long, but it would be enough time to get out with no one asking questions.

The buses ran on the same schedule, 24/7: every half hour, all day, every day.

It was, I'm told, one of the better things to come from the Awakening, providing jobs and much-needed transport to the smaller Townships.

The bus I needed was heading away from the city to one of the more remote Townships in our region. This meant it was a quiet ride, and I was one of only three people the entire way there.

I sat at the window, watching the fields go by in all their colours. Soon, there were no buildings, and the only other vehicles we passed were other buses running the same route with just as few people riding them.

In the beginning, the Elders spread themselves around the world to maximise their reach and influence. I can't remember when they did away with the old towns and cities, but I know it was all about power.

At first, one Elder was in charge of everything in their country - there were so few then. But as their numbers grew, they put Lieutenants at the head of all the major cities. When more and more Lightborn came of age, they soon realised they didn't have enough to go around. So, countries were divided up into smaller cities and Townships.

More Lightborn meant more Townships.

When the Three ascended, they stuck together, claiming unmatched power. What did they need to split up for? The UK was the birthplace of the Brotherhood, after all, and they had exceptionally loyal followers.

Their compound supposedly sat just south of the old capital. But even here, they didn't run the day to day. They had a Lieutenant in the South and one in the North.

Township 11 was right at the border.

I arrived in 11, a little before lunch. It was the last stop on the line before the bus turned, now empty, to head back to civilisation. The walk to the middle of town was only ten minutes, and I passed nobody on the way.

11 was tiny compared to other areas and home to only a hundred or so people, mostly farmers and their families. They provided the surrounding areas with most of the onions and potatoes we used and some other vegetables in smaller quantities. Nestled at the edge of our region, they kept mostly to themselves.

They tested their children like the rest of us but more often than not, the children wound up attending the local agricultural school in Township 9. If you were born in 11, you lived and died in 11.

One unusual thing, though, was a small cafe at its centre. It was the only place in town where the residents could eat out, so it was almost always full.

I managed to find a little table outside and ordered myself a sandwich. The locally grown stuff was as fresh as it could be, and it was always delicious. Today they had made fresh egg salad with pesto and crunchy red onions. My mouth watered before it even arrived.

I kept to myself, reading my book, and enjoying my food. I didn't want to be seen in a hurry. Didn't want to draw any attention.

It wasn't that unusual to have outsiders visit the small area. Alexis told me some people even came to stay in these more remote Townships. They said they wanted to 'disconnect.' I doubted the locals liked that too much, but the city folk had charge cards to spend generously, so they let it happen.

A small shop in town let you rent bicycles, and I made my way over, glancing in the store windows and smiling at the locals as I passed. I'd been there before, of course, and the owner smiled warmly, swiping my card just as she did every other time.

She never asked what I was doing there or where I was going. She just nodded and gave me the key to the little lock, told me to have fun and be back before dark.

I nodded and said, "Of course," with a laugh I had to force out.

Ok, so Township 11 sat almost at the edge of our region. The Brotherhood drew the lines when they mapped out territories and gave control to the Lightborn. Every few years, the lines had to be moved, and areas re-worked to accommodate the new Leaders.

Over the years, we've had our area divided just once,

but I know of other regions that have been split multiple times. The border between the North and south, however, always stayed the same.

We had our Community Leader in Township 6, and 11 had their own. The Lieutenant overseeing us both and the surrounding Townships was Jacobs. He had been appointed over fifteen years ago and lived in the city. Before him was Lieutenant Allan, whom the Three chose themselves after their Ascension.

Lieutenant Jacobs was young during the Dark War but made himself lots of friends over the years. He was very faithful to the Brotherhood. When Allan's time was over, Jacobs was an obvious and safe choice.

The border was made clear with a small fence running through the fields. Lieutenant Allan hadn't felt the need for anything more, as all regions were allies under the Brotherhood. Jacobs suggested something bigger upon his taking over but was met with negativity and soon relented.

So the small fence, which was short enough to climb over, ran quietly between the fields and around our region, and most people gave it very little thought.

You can't see the fence from Township 11. It was a bit of a hike, which is why I had the bike, and it usually took about a half-hour to get close enough to feel the power. Jacobs agreed to keep the fence minimal, but he secretly placed his own border around his domain. Any time a person or animal crossed the border, his Lightborn felt it and were dispatched.

Ordinary people weren't aware of this and felt nothing as they passed. But I could feel it as I got closer, and it felt very different from the Veil. This wasn't warm or moist. It felt sharp and electric. I could practically hear it buzzing as I stopped my bike and got off.

Standing around twenty feet from the fence, it was always tempting to get closer and see what it would feel like. But logic won over. I didn't need to be drawing any unwanted attention to myself, not here. Not so close.

So instead, I pushed the bike to the side, toward the giant willow tree. It stood alone, seemingly in the middle of nowhere. There were no houses or people in sight, and when I looked back toward Township 11, I saw nothing but fields.

As I neared the tree, I felt a different kind of power.

The tree moved slightly in the breeze, and I let the leaves brush over me, making my way to the middle. On the trunk, someone had carved initials into the bark - CP +AD. But the letters looked different somehow. Not normal, but not strange enough to draw any attention.

I pressed my hand lightly to the letters, and for the first time in a long time, let out a breath and felt my Light tingle in my fingertips. The initials lit slightly, and to my left, the ground opened. I raced down as quickly as I could, knowing the power would be felt and that the Lightborn would already be on their way.

As always, they would find nothing more than the willow tree blowing gently across the border.

As always, they would curse and tell themselves that they should get approval to cut the tree down.

As always, that wouldn't happen.

In ancient Rome, a Ludus was a school for young children. It was also the training grounds for gladiators. Given the purpose of our mission, the name was perfect.

Our Ludus was underground, spanning a cavern under the border of the two regions, hidden by Light. A safe place for people like me.

I walked the path in near silence, arriving at the entrance with my bike at my side. The old door was green today and had a smaller door in the middle. I knocked on both and waited.

The small door opened, and a little boy appeared, asking me who I was and what I wanted.

"I'm Anya. I'm here to see Mr Parks."

"Password!" He called with a mischievous smile.

I leaned down and whispered the password, making him laugh, "Farts!"

He fell back laughing, and the door swung open. Miss Turro was chuckling to herself as she ushered me in.

"All right, Robbie. Back to class!" She wagged a kind finger at him and watched him go with a smile before turning to me

"Farts?"

I shrugged and moved to lean my bike against the wall. "He liked it."

"Hmmm," she said. "It's been a while, Anya. Where've you been?" Miss Turro pulled me into a hug and squeezed. "You know we worry."

Her face got serious, and I tried to ease her mind.

"I've just been busy. I'm sorry."

We left my bike at the door and moved into the big open space. Even though we were underground, it looked like the sun was shining. There were trees down here, and the air was fresh. It never ceased to amaze me.

"New Light," Miss Turro whispered, gesturing to a small group of young boys nearby.

They couldn't have been over six or seven, and they sat on the grass, crossed legged, in awe as Mr Pihel made a bouquet bloom in front of their eyes.

"Looks like a lot of new Light," I said, looking around

and seeing more unfamiliar faces than I could count. "How many?"

"Almost fifty."

I stopped in my tracks and put a hand on her arm, "Fifty?"

Miss Turro nodded and smiled. She lifted her hands in a 'who knows' gesture.

"They're not all from here. Some have come from other countries, not just neighbouring Townships."

"Wait, what? Other countries? How is that even possible?"

"We have our ways," she began.

"But you're exposing yourselves. You're risking all-"

"We're safe. They're safe. You're safe." She put her hand in mine and squeezed.

"We started sending out envoys. They don't have the Light, so they can travel unimpeded. We have friends, Anya. Other teachers that want to protect these boys from the Brothers."

"But-"

"It's ok. We're discreet. We would never risk this place, you know that."

I did know that. I knew these people - these teachers - had already risked everything to protect these children and that they wouldn't do anything to jeopardise that. But I also knew that the more people that knew about the Ludus, the less secure it would become.

"Come on. I know he's going to be thrilled to see you."

We walked by more classes on our way. I saw young boys learning how to fill their glasses with water and older boys trying to levitate. I even saw a group of teen boys creating lightning in their hands. It was all so wonderful and exciting and terrifying to behold.

It had been a while since I visited. I used to come every weekend and then...I'm not really sure. Unlike these poor kids, I had the luxury of coming and going, and at some point, I think I got worried about being caught. I worried I would be seen, followed, and that we would all burn for our sins.

So I started making the trip less and less, using my Light less. Truth be told, I enjoyed feeling normal. As much as I loved learning what I was capable of, a small part of me always feared it. My father's face would flash in my mind, my stomach would churn, and I inevitably lost focus.

"You can't keep blaming yourself," they would tell me. "You have such power in you, but you need to embrace it, not fear it."

Easier said than done.

Beyond where the classes were taking place, we passed the regular lessons. Many families of the rescued boys came along, and they held classes for their siblings. These Lightless boys and girls sat listening as teachers and parents taught them how to add and subtract. I saw them learning about the world and the regions.

I wondered where they had all come from. I could see and hear that some were not from here. How many had come with their boys? How many had chosen not to? How many hadn't been given a choice?

"Anya?"

Mr Parks' grin lit up the room as he hustled towards us, pulling me into a hug, much like Miss Turro. He squeezed slightly and felt another twinge of guilt at my absence.

When he stepped back, he took my hands and smiled.

"We were worried."

"I know. I'm sorry," I repeated.

"The boys missed you and your cooking!" He said with a laugh, moving back the way he'd come from, waving at me to follow.

We walked through an archway and into the living area. To the left were couches and TVs. Some people sat reading, others watching a movie. In the far left corner was a kitchen with rows of tables and benches.

On the right side of the room, there were more couches and games and books. There was a smattering of people, old and young. I saw a group of what I assumed to be parents, talking, having a coffee, and holding the same book.

A group of teenage girls played a game on one of the TVs, and a smaller group of kids playing some board game. When they saw us, they jumped up and came hurrying over, all talking over each other and trying to be heard. Mr Parks calmed them and sent them back to their game with a kind, patient smile. We kept moving to the kitchen and sat at a table together, far enough from the others that we wouldn't be overheard.

"Will you have cake?" he asked, getting up without my answer.

I nodded, knowing I would get some either way, and we sat for a time, catching up on our lives, keeping things light.

But I was there for a reason, and it was time to be serious.

"We need to talk about the Veil," I said eventually, keeping my voice down so we weren't overheard. "It's gotten so much worse in there."

"How much worse?"

"Well, it's basically pitch black other than the flames falling from the skies."

"Flames?" Miss Turro gasped.

I nodded and took a bite of the cake, just for something to do.

"The announcement."

"Yes. Seemed odd to me," Mr Parks noted. "Why would they want to share their influence all of a sudden?"

"You think it's got to do with what's behind the Veil?" Miss Turro offered.

"Yes. I think it's gotten to a point where they can't deal with it alone anymore. I think they need help. They need someone younger and more powerful to stop the spread."

Mr Parks looked around the room at the young children. He cared so deeply for them all, not just the gifted ones. I knew that the idea of the Veil coming down scared him.

Miss Turro put her hand over his as if reading his mind and whispered, "If the Three can't fix it, neither can we."

"We haven't tried."

"What's happening there is because those monsters abused their Light. They did whatever they wanted for all those years and ignored all the consequences. Using your Light to fix this would only make things worse."

Mr Parks nodded and slumped in his seat. He pushed his cake away and looked long and hard at his hands.

"She's right, Mr Parks. The Light caused this. I don't think the Light can fix it now."

"So why the Tournament? Why the Ascension?" he asked, clearly upset.

"I don't know. Maybe they actually think they can fix it. They basically think they're gods, right. Why wouldn't they think they can fix the entire world?"

"We don't know that they can't..." Miss Turro started, not sounding convinced herself.

"I guess not," I admitted. "But what's behind that Veil is because The Three ignored all the rules.We know that our Light is not absolute. You can't just mess with the natural order and not see things balance out. I know I'm young, but I've heard all about the early days."

"Hmmm. Of course, you're right. I'm sorry, I just-" Miss Turro looked at her hands and went quiet.

I smiled at them both. They were so good. All they wanted was to help and protect. They started The Ludus for that very reason. Both had been teachers once and hated seeing boys taken away and brainwashed. They risked everything to create this place and rescue as many gifted boys as they could from the grasp of the Lightborn. Keeping this place safe was our top priority. But to do that, we needed to keep everywhere else safe too.

"I think we need a meeting."

Mr Parks looked at me for a long time with a sad but determined face.

"I think you're right."

He wasn't the first to start a place like this. He took the leap after meeting a teacher from Tokyo. They met at a conference, and after a couple of days, realised they were like-minded.

After the conference, Mr Ito took Mr Parks to his Ludus. It gave Mr Parks the push he needed back here, and he soon realised he was late to the party. Other places like this had been established since the Awakening. They were just very quiet and very secretive.

The Network of teachers around the world communicated through encrypted online chat rooms and never face to face. Getting the message out was dangerous and slow, and it was becoming increasingly difficult to know if people were truly anti-Brotherhood or spies.

For decades they had been using the dark web, which miraculously survived The Blackout. Apparently, taking away the livelihood of a bunch of hackers and developers wasn't the smartest idea the Elders had: idle hands and all that.

These tech wizards knew more about secret communication than anyone and always managed to get around the Lightborn. They set up the Network, making it possible for the teachers and rebels to communicate.

The downside was that teachers weren't exactly knowledgeable when it came to the Dark Web's inner workings.

Reaching out and making connections was slow. Finding other teachers wasn't easy, especially when using rotating chat rooms. This had been going on for decades, but the numbers had always been small.

But it was worth it to see these poor boys free.

Every boy they rescued was a risk, and it had to be done quietly enough so as not to draw attention.

Families leaving their homes in the middle of the night was always suspicious. Often, they would risk staying and drawing out their departure. Some parents made the hard choice to divorce. One would stay behind, and the other would leave with the children. Other parents sent their boys without them. A runaway is more believable, after all.

The Network grew slowly and eventually became a

global force. They figured out ways to bring in new boys without drawing attention and were expanding their numbers every day.

The most successful path was to alter the boys' test reports at the source and send them to an agricultural school. These schools were often in the middle of nowhere and barely ever monitored, the Lightborn in such regions being less powerful and unimportant.

These were not posts for the brightest of Lights, so they overlooked new families joining the small communities. They didn't see that most of the new students were boys right at the test age. It worked perfectly.

The Network's last meeting was well over five years ago and was called because a Leader near Paris was getting suspicious. They moved him into a new region and gave him a new Township. It wasn't long before he started questioning teachers about the number of boys being sent to the country. Though he was more concerned about their security force not getting as many junior men as he'd like, his sudden interest posed a threat.

Reluctantly, Mr Leandre called the meeting to discuss the future of his Ludus. With the Lightborn looking so closely, he couldn't move the gifted boys when he needed to. Miss Turro told me they all but shut down that chapter. They moved the boys and families to other Ludi until things calmed down.

"It's going to take time. We have to be careful."

"We don't have much time. The Tournament is only a couple of months away," I urged.

"We'll make it happen, I promise," Mr Parks said, taking my hand. "How have you been, really?" He asked, throwing me off.

"I'm…fine. I'm fine; why?"

"You just…it's just been so long since you visited." I wanted to apologise and make up some excuse, but they both knew me better than that.

"Things have just been…difficult, at home."

"How is your mother?" Miss Turro asked with an edge to her voice.

I took in a breath and tried to smile, "She's ok. Really. She's busy with work." Before they could say anything else, I stood up and announced, "I should be going."

"Already? Oh, please stay! I know the boys would love to see your Light!"

Mr Parks stood and smiled. Miss Turro stood beside me and put an arm around my waist.

"Come on, show them what real Light looks like!"

# CHAPTER 8

Oran woke to the sound of arguing. Blinking away his dreams, he sat up, trying to listen to the voices and decide if he needed to get involved. He stood, took two steps, glanced at the closet, and was dressed by the time his hand reached the door.

As it opened, the arguing got louder, and he sighed, knowing exactly what was happening. He half wanted to go out the back and avoid the headache, but he knew better.

"You can't just say 'no'! They said-"

"I know what they said! I was watching too. But you know as well as I do that they weren't talking about you!"

"I'm ready!"

"You're not!"

Oran lifted his hand and drank from the coffee that appeared. He stood on the stairs, listening, waiting for the best time to approach.

"Dad!!"

"All right, that's enough!" Oran bellowed, coming into the kitchen.

His son jumped out of his seat, and his husband spilled his coffee.

"For Brother's sake, Oran, can you not?!" Declan

groaned.

Oran walked around the kitchen island and kissed his husband, squeezing his arm in an apology.

"Dad, will you-"

"Listen to your father," was all he said.

He looked from his husband to their son, and the conversation was done. Tyler sighed, huffed, and left the room, slamming some door on his way past.

"Sorry," Oran said, taking Declan's hand. "I should've talked to you last night."

"A heads up might've been nice," Declan joked. "You know I hate these Tournaments. I mean, really? What is it, medieval days with knights and damsels?"

They both laughed, and Oran waved a hand over the table. French toast and fresh fruit appeared, and the pair sat for breakfast.

"You did say all Lightborn were welcome," Declan smirked.

"You sure that was me and not Uri? We do sort of look alike, ya know."

"Oh, I'm sure. Your son made sure I heard you!"

"He's not going anywhere. It wouldn't look right for him to take part," Oran sighed.

Declan focused on his breakfast and left Oran to his thoughts. They ate in silence, each thinking about their son but in very different ways. Declan worried that Tyler might get hurt. Oran worried he would humiliate himself.

After the Blackout, it became clear that the Light was not hereditary. It came to boys of all backgrounds and circumstances, but nobody knew how or why.

Tyler had not been born with the Light. But as a child, he was so upset he wasn't like his father that Oran gifted a tiny spark to his son. He never told Declan this truth, and he regretted it to this day. Tyler was weak. He was no Lightborn.

"He'll be fine," Oran said eventually. "He'll do as he's told, and he'll blame me, not you."

"Hmm."

Declan took his last bite of toast and pushed the plate back.

"I just don't understand why Oran. You and your Brothers have been in charge for so long. You're all so powerful. Why would you want to bring someone new in?"

Oran hesitated, having spoken nothing of this to his husband - Anwar and Uri forbade it. They didn't share matters of the Brotherhood with their families and disapproved of Oran doing any different. Nobody outside of the Three knew the truth about what was happening around them.

"We won't be the most powerful forever. New, strong boys are coming of age every day. It only makes sense that one - or five of them will have immense Light. It took less than a month for Uri to whisper thoughts of a coup into the younger Lightborn, and look how that turned out! We can't be so naïve as to think we can control them all forever."

It wasn't a lie, and he'd thought a great deal about this speech. He simply left out the part about the world crumbling around them.

"I don't like the idea of another Dark War, Oran."

"That's why we're doing this - to keep that from happening."

Declan sighed, kissed his husband's cheek, and left for the day. He'd worked at the School of Light as a teacher for over twenty years. It was how the two met. Declan did not have the Light, but he taught the boys about the history of the Brotherhood. He was a devout believer and had been a nervous wreck when he met Oran for the first time. But it didn't take long before he was standing by his side and challenging him in the best ways.

Oran stayed in the kitchen and listened to his husband's car leave. The house was empty and quiet, and where Oran would typically revel in the peace, today he couldn't stand the silence. He made his way to the back door and looked down at his side. A golden retriever sat patiently, looking up at his master, his head to one side.

"Aren't you handsome? You look like a Champ to me," he said, reaching down and scratching the dog behind the ears.

Champ reacted and got excited, ready to go out. They left the house, played fetch, and wandered the property for the better part of an hour.

Oran loved being able to roam with a dog at his side, but Tyler was allergic. When he was younger, Oran tried to cure his allergies, but it hadn't worked. Instead, it had made them exponentially worse. So as they reached the threshold, Oran took a knee to pet Champ for a few more minutes. When he turned to enter the house, his clothes changed, and the dog blew away in the wind.

His house was inside the same walled-in property as the Great Hall. The Three had chosen this land purposefully and built their community to their liking. Oran's house was the furthest east, near the river and overlooking hills and a small forest. It was a ten-minute walk to reach Uri's house, but the clouds were turning, so he took his car.

Uri's car wasn't in the drive, and Oran rolled his eyes, assuming he was late. Anwar's house was on the other side, much further back and out of sight.

As he made the turn to their office and pulled in beside the waiting cars, his assistant appeared at his window. Oran swore under his breath, exhausted by the kid's enthusiasm.

"You can wait inside," he suggested getting out of the car and moving past the boy to the doors.

"I have coffee for you, Sir," the boy offered.

Oran had already forgotten his name. They never lasted long enough to learn them.

He reached back and took the coffee, entering the building without waiting for his aide. Inside, the desk at the front was occupied by two other young men. They were Lightborn, all of them, and had been hand-selected to be the office faces. Each of them had proven to be bright and capable and, best of all, easily influenced. They made their allegiance to the Brotherhood clear and were delighted to be part of the inner circle.

"Where are they?" He asked, stopping at the desk.

"Brother Oran, good morning. Brothers Anwar and Uri are in the conference room, sir."

He'd hoped that they wouldn't be together so he and Uri could speak more about Anwar but was out of luck. Instead, he assumed he was walking into another argument.

For years they'd gone round and round, since they first noticed the sour spots around the world. At first, they ignored them, putting up powerful cloaks, and hiding them from view.

Out of sight, out of mind.

But in the years since, things had gotten too bad to

ignore.

Uri and Anwar sat at opposite ends of the table. The sheer size of it always brought a chuckle. There were only ever three of them, and he couldn't remember the last time anyone else joined.

It was about the show, of course. If anyone absolutely had to come to the Offices, they would be in awe of its greatness. Or something like that, anyway.

"Morning," Uri said without looking up.

Anwar grunted something and poked at his screen.

Taking his seat, Oran reached over and picked up his own tablet. He opened the files and began reading about fire-starters and ground-breakers. Each of them had the information for all the Lightborn that were of age and, therefore, eligible to Ascend.

They split the task evenly were looking for inexperienced men with bright Lights, though it was difficult to tell from the files. Most of the work they did at the school wasn't designed to bring out the boys' best. They learned to control their Light just enough to go out into the world, but they were never allowed to let their Light genuinely shine. The Brothers couldn't allow it.

What if someone shone so brightly that people questioned their power?

No, they had to keep the Lightborn subdued. Which meant the files gave very little away in terms of the power they were searching for.

Still, some boys had exceptional gifts, and they were usually difficult to hide. Oran raised his eyebrows as he read the file of a boy named Zachery. This boy had the power to heal, which was very rare. He went to the 'maybe' pile.

"This is getting us nowhere," Anwar complained

after an hour or so. "What are we supposed to look for? You know we need to actually see these boys in action."

"Which is why we are having the Tournament early, Anwar," Uri said impatiently and without looking up.

This wasn't the first time they had had the same argument, and it was wearing on them all.

"We need to decide the rules. Come up with tasks, games, etcetera. The normal schedule isn't going to cut it this time." Oran offered, trying to change the subject.

"I was thinking about that. We need some relatively simple tasks in the beginning. We can't make it too hard and be left with half a dozen at the end of the first day," Uri said, putting his screen down.

"So what? Walking on water? Creating fire? That kind of thing?"

Anwar grunted again and laughed, "If they can't even do that, then we don't want them!"

"Obviously, Anwar."

"We're going to get a lot of eager but inexperienced Lightborn. We need to eliminate the young ones early but keep in as many of the older ones as we can, for as long as we can. The longer they're in the arenas, the more time we'll have to syphon their Light."

"Yeah, yeah."

Anwar waved them away and stood. He walked to the window and ran a hand through his hair.

"Have you figured out the best way to do that? Without them noticing, I mean."

Uri looked to Oran and nodded. "The arenas will have barriers surrounding the properties. As soon as they walk through the gates, their Light will start to seep away. We figure that they won't really notice. They'll be tired from the excitement and the games. They will have been using their Light to try to beat each other, so of course, they'll feel a little less powerful. They'll just ignore it and assume they're tired."

"Exactly. And what are they going to do if they do think something is wrong? They'll come to us," Uri smiled.

It had been his plan to syphon the Light during a Tournament. He wanted to be as powerful as possible when (if) they made it through the portal and to another world.

"I want to try again," Anwar mumbled, keeping his gaze out the window.

"You're not serious?" Oran choked out as he tried to swallow a piece of a blueberry muffin.

"I told you I can do it."

"Last time you 'told us you could do it,' you nearly lost an arm," Uri pressed.

Anwar waved them off and walked to the end of the table. He pressed his knuckles into the wood until Oran could feel the vibrations.

"I'm getting closer. I just need more-"

"Time? We don't have it!" Uri shouted.

"Yes, time. And Light! We don't need this stupid Tournament. We control them, remember. If we tell them to come here and stand still, they will. If we tell them that their Brothers need their Light, they'll give it gladly."

Uri clicked his tongue and rolled his eyes.

"Do you really believe that? You think asking for their Light will paint us as anything but weak?"

"I won't be asking!" Anwar yelled.

Oran sat between his Brothers with his head in his hands. They'd been down this path before, more times than he could count. It was the same damn thing for almost a decade. Only now, it was worse. Now, they were at the point of no return.

"Enough!" Oran yelled above his Brothers, using his Light to shake the room. "We did this. Us. Nobody else. It was our arrogance and our refusal to see what was going on that's caused this. We saw what our Light was doing to the world all those years ago, and we ignored it. We knew what we were doing was wrong, but we just couldn't stop. And now, it will be our kids that pay the price."

"Oran-"

"No, Uri. No. You've had your head in the sand for too long. All of us have. It was so obvious. It was laid out in the simplest of terms: actions have consequences. But we didn't let ourselves see it. We put a bandaid on a crack in the earth, and we kept going and going, and the world is burning around us. This is where we are. I can feel the cloaks shifting. Soon they will fall altogether, and what we've done will be laid bare for all to see. They'll revolt. They will rise up and tear us down. But it will still be too late, and all they'll be able to do is watch as this world crumbles and dies around them."

The Brothers stayed quiet as Oran tried to calm himself. It was rare that he lost his temper, but after so long, he couldn't remain silent any longer.

"This Tournament will not only bring us more Light, but it might also bring us another Lightborn that can open a portal. If that happens, we can say whatever we need to get them to do just that. And yes, they'll do it gladly because their Brotherhood is asking." Oran looked from Uri to Anwar and sighed. "Anwar, you need to stop being stubborn and get on board."

"The minute the first day of games is done, I'm trying

again," he said, pointing a finger in his Brother's face. "The minute!"

Oran nodded, "Fine. You should try it again. Take in as much Light as possible, then try and try again. But know that you might fail, and we will have to go through with an Ascension."

Anwar sighed and closed his eyes. Oran could tell he was tired - they all were. When he finally opened them, he seemed to slump forward where he stood. He looked...defeated.

"You're right," he said, so quietly that Uri and Oran looked to each other for confirmation of what they each heard. "You're right. I want to try, but...I'm tired, Brothers. And this isn't just about me. So...Ok."

Uri opened his mouth to speak but couldn't get his words out. Oran stood and walked to Anwar, putting a hand on his shoulder and smiling.

"Ok," he said, feeling like true Brothers for the first time in over ten years.

# CHAPTER 9

The next week was nerve-wracking. People were still talking about the Tournament, and work had begun erecting a vast arena in the city. They were being built all over the world so the Lightborn could attend and we could all watch.

I had no intention of going, always steering clear of anyone that might see my Light at all costs.

Friday arrived, but it was dragging, and I had plans to go through the Veil again on my way home to have an up-to-date report the next day at the Ludus. I could only hope that a meeting had been set to discuss the future with the Network's other members. I just needed to make it to the end of the day.

"Anya? Are you with us?" Miss Emberly asked.

I was staring out the window, my mind focused on fire clouds and demonic bunnies.

"Yes, sorry, yes. I'm here," I stuttered.

She looked at me, waiting for an answer to the question that I'd missed.

"A sous vide," someone offered.

"Hmmm. Excellent Callie."

Miss Emberly smiled and told the class to get their ingredients prepped before turning to me with worried eyes.

"Anya, are you ok? You seem distracted."

I nodded and apologised, feigning a headache and trying to bring my focus back. The class was almost over, and we would be heading home soon. I tried to clear my head and be present, but my eyes kept wandering to the clock.

"Now, before you all go, I have an exciting announcement!" Miss Emberly sang her words and was buzzing with excitement. "We have been contacted by The Brotherhood and have been asked to provide our services for the Tournaments!"

She squealed and clapped, jumping up and down.

"Wait, what does that mean?" I asked.

"It means all the culinary schools around the world will get to show off our talented students by providing food and drinks to all the people attending the Games!"

The class erupted in cheers and hoots. I sank into my chair.

"Obviously, we won't be alone, and we can't possibly be making food for everyone every day. We will be given a schedule, but they have assured me we will have free rein to show off our talents!"

The class and Miss Emberly were elated.

I felt sick. How was I supposed to get out of this without looking suspicious?

The bell called for the end of the day, and I somehow managed to find my way out but was so distracted by Miss Emberly's announcement, I missed my stop. Shaking my head, I got off and walked back, hoping it would clear my mind.

A few students looked at me funny, but they went right where I went left. Nobody followed, and I didn't see anyone watching. It was still light out, so Security wasn't patrolling yet.

As I got closer to the Veil, a tiny part of me wondered if it could have gotten better. Maybe last week was just a fluke, and things weren't so bad. I knew I was wrong the second I rounded the corner.

The Veil was all but vibrating, and the Glimmer was shining as bright as ever. I could hear it, and the humidity reached me much further away than before. My skin was moist, and my hair stuck to my face.

When I finally reached the barrier, I closed my eyes, putting my hand up to the Light. It felt different somehow. It was warmer and thicker, and as I passed through, I felt like I was walking through water.

My hair hung heavy as I stood on the other side, my clothes clinging to my body like I'd stepped out of a pool.

It was as though they tried to put more layers of protection over a crumbling wall that was leaking from top to bottom. Like duct tape on a cracked roof in a rainstorm, it wouldn't hold much longer. I looked around and wondered if anything had escaped.

The sky was black, the flames fell faster, and I could see some creatures trying to hide from the fire under a burned-out tree to my right. I moved in a little further and noticed the lake was all but empty now. The waters had either evaporated or absorbed into the rotten earth.

A loud whooshing drew my attention beyond the lake, and I saw a trio of small tornadoes causing chaos as they got closer. The flames from the clouds made contact, and soon I was looking at three flaming tunnels of destruction. I watched in awe as they pulled trees and animals from the ground and spat them out, burned and dead.

When one neared the edge of the Veil, I flinched, terrified it would breakthrough. But the Light held, and the tornado bounced back onto an alternate path. As scary as it was, I was relieved to see the Veil was holding.

After a few minutes, I decided I'd seen enough. I pushed my way out and took multiple deep breaths once I got far enough away, and the air thinned out a little. What we'd said the week before was right; the Light couldn't fix this.

Looking back, and my heart sank. I knew this was because of The Brothers. I knew they were likely looking for younger, stronger Lightborn to help them fix their mess.

But I also knew that the Brothers weren't stupid. They would know exactly what caused this and that they wouldn't be able to fix it.

So what was their plan? How were they going to save us?

If the Veil, and likely Veils plural, dropped, we would all be done for. This decay would spread, and nobody would be able to stop it.

My feet took me the right way without my brain having to get involved. It got darker as I got closer to home, and I started o mentally prepare for another argument with Alexis.

"You! Where are you going?"

It took a minute for me to realise I was 'you.' The two Security guards coming my way looked inexperienced and angry. Unfortunately, it was much darker than I'd realised.

"We're talking to you."

"I'm going home," I said, still walking and not making eye contact.

"A little late, innit? Where you coming from?"

"Work. I work at the Culinary School," I replied, still not breaking stride.

One guard stepped in my path and held up a hand, "School finished hours ago."

"Yes, and I should really get started on checking over the students' work."

The guard put his hand on my shoulder and stopped me. He held firm, and I kept my eyes down, knowing it was better not to argue.

"This isn't the city. You don't get to just wander around."

"I wasn't just wandering around. I was-"

"Who said you could speak?"

"Hey! Hey! Knock it off!"

I looked up to see Alexis coming our way. I sighed in relief as the guard stepped back and let me go. There was only a year between us, but she stood taller and fiercer than I ever could.

"What do you think you're doing, putting your hands on my sister?"

I stepped back, shocked at her tone with these guys.

"She can't just-"

"She was at school doing extra work and ran late. Is that a crime?" Alexis challenged.

"She should have arranged-"

"A pickup? What do you think I'm doing? She got off the bus, and I'm meeting her."

"Well, you should've picked her up at the school!"

"Oh, right. I should've left my little cousin and gone to get my sister, who couldn't possibly take the bus alone. She's not a child."

The guards looked equally mad and embarrassed - Alexis had that effect on boys. Ever since we were kids, boys would fall at her feet and lose the ability to talk when she was around. These guys were no different. I envied and admired her power and the way she used it.

"We're going home. Go bother someone else," my sister snapped, taking my hand and turning on her heal.

She didn't wait for their response and waved her hand dismissively when they tried to call after her.

"Thanks, 'Lex-"

"Where were you?"

We made it into the lobby of our building, and I couldn't even thank her before she tore into me.

"I missed the bus and had to wait."

"Bull," she said, crossing her arms and staring me down.

I'd always wanted to tell Alexis the truth, but was scared. I was afraid she wouldn't understand. That she would blame me for what happened to our parents. That she would turn me in. Mostly I was scared of what might happen to her if I ever got caught, and they found out she knew.

"I'm sorry, 'Lex. Really."

She seemed to want to keep yelling at me, but bizarrely she gave me a hug and sighed.

"Mum's home," she breathed into my hair.

I froze. She wasn't due home for another few weeks. I thought she would be gone until the Tournaments started.

"She's...back early?"

"Hmmm."

"How is she?" I asked as we turned to walk up the stairs.

I dragged my feet.

"She's ok. You know how it is. She'll just need a few

days to get back to normal."

I hesitated at the door. My nerves rooted me to the spot as I ran my hands through my hair and looked to Alexis.

"I look ok?"

She smiled and tucked my hair behind my right ear.

"Beautiful," she said with a wink.

Alexis opened the door and walked through with all the confidence in the world. She tussled Frankie's hair as she passed the couch and tapped Uncle Mark on the shoulder, gesturing with her thumb toward me.

He turned and looked at me with a grimace, shaking his head and waving at me to come in.

I slowly stepped through the door and closed it behind me, taking my time as I took my shoes off and put them on the rack, keeping my eyes down while I hooked my coat up and turned to the living room. Frankie didn't acknowledge me, but Uncle Mark nodded to a plate of food he'd saved.

I could hear the water running from the kitchen. Alexis closed the curtains and joined Frankie on the couch. Uncle Mark took his seat in his chair as I sat at the table to eat dinner. It was cold, and I struggled to get it down, but I didn't want to go into the kitchen to heat it up.

I just cut and ate and cut and ate until my plate was clean. Part of me wanted to leave it right there and run to my room, but I took a breath and made my way to the kitchen.

My mother stood at the sink. The water was running as she slowly made her way through the dinner dishes. I watched as she moved the sponge over a plate, over and over, until I thought the pattern would come off. Then she carefully placed it on the rack to dry before picking up the next.

She still had her hair in the long braid down her back, but she'd changed out of her work clothes. That was usually the first thing she did when she got home. It surprised me to see the braid. It was longer than I remembered.

How long had it been this time? Two months? Three?

"Are you just going to watch?" She spat without looking back.

"Uh, no. Sorry."

I moved forward and put my plate into the too hot water. She didn't look at me as I stood beside her, pushing the plate into the water and continuing with the dish she'd been working on.

"I can help if you..."

"You probably have work." It wasn't a question, and I took it as my dismissal.

In my room, I sat on my bed and held back the tears. I wondered how long she would be home and swore at myself for hoping it wouldn't be long. I tried to put my mother and her cold shoulder out of my mind by going back to the big issue.

Nothing about the Tournament or the Ascension made sense.

My students had done a great job on their most recent assignment, and I tried to give their work my full attention. When I heard my family laughing, however, a tear came to my eye. I listened to my mother and pictured her on the couch with Alexis. They always sat snuggled together - two peas in a pod.

When she was home, I was left to the floor now that Frankie was too big to sit in anyone's lap.

Through the tears, I looked at the picture of our family from before we were torn apart. My father's face lit up the frame, and I cried at his memory. Even in his last moment with me, he managed a smile. I pictured it now, and it steadied me. I tried not to think about what came next.

The image of him being dragged away always broke my heart. I could feel the guilt seeping in, and I tried to push it away.

It wasn't your fault, I would try to convince myself. But I knew better. If I hadn't-wait!

Wait, wait, wait, wait, wait. My eyes cleared along with my mind. I thought back to that day when they took my father away, and I looked beyond the tragedy. I looked beyond my wailing mother and sobbing sister. I remembered back to what happened before they took him, and it hit me. I knew exactly what the Brothers were planning.

# CHAPTER 10

I left the house early before anyone else was up, not wanting to argue with Alexis about where I'd really been the night before.

Or lie to Uncle Mark about where I was going.

Or awkwardly sit at the breakfast table with my mother and her scowl.

Her being home always threw me. She was usually away for months at a time for work -though I'm not sure you can call it that if the only other option is prison.

Unsurprisingly, the bus was empty. Before the Brotherhood, there was no bus out here at all. People had their own personal cars, and if you lived out of the city, well, good luck getting anywhere without one. I've seen pictures of cars, and they're in the movies. I think it would have been exciting to drive one, but the Elders banned them not long after the Awakening. It was how the Brotherhood created so many jobs.

I looked to the driver and wondered what he felt about driving an empty bus back and forth to the countryside all day. Was he appreciative of the work?

This time I stopped in Township 9 for breakfast. I figured I shouldn't be seen at that little cafe in 11 too often, and Township 9 had a fantastic pancake place my parents used to take us to. They had all different kinds: blueberry, chocolate, banoffee, apple-cinnamon, and were big, fluffy, and delicious. I ate three before my jeans felt tight, and I had to stop. Savouring the time alone, I took my coffee without sugar and enjoyed the peace.

The place hadn't changed, and I looked over to the booth we used to sit at. My Dad always got the peaches and cream and would clap his hands when the waiter came. He was like a little kid, and my mother would jokingly admonish him for being silly. But I could tell she loved it.

He was fun and kind, and he was a wonderful father. She used to be warm and sweet and happy for the most part. She doted on Alexis, where I was a Daddy's girl. But I hadn't seen her like that since the day they took him away, and I was sure I would never see it again.

Even when she's with Alexis and doesn't know I'm there, she never quite lets herself smile. And then if she sees me, well…her walls go up.

I put thoughts of my mother out of my mind and focused on my task. I needed to explain everything in as much detail as possible and help come up with a plan to save the world.

No big deal. Everyday stuff.

My biggest worry was for the boys at the Ludus. If the Heads of the Network got involved, what would happen to the young Lightborn they were trying to save?

"Anya! We're so glad you're back!" Mr Parks always made me feel welcome and wanted.

"Well, we need to talk more. I think-"

"We will, we will. You should know that we've made arrangements for a meeting. The Heads of all the other

Ludi will meet to discuss the Veil and the Tournament. When I reached out, it was obvious nerves are running high."

"Wait, all the Heads?" I asked, incredulous.

"That's right. Once word got out, they all got in touch and want to be a part of a solution."

"They won't be coming here, will they?"

I looked around and got nervous. Bringing in that many people would require a lot of Light, which would draw much more attention than a tree branch.

"No, we've...come up with something safer. A middle ground where we can communicate without having to travel."

My mind was slow from the sugar, but I finally got there.

"You're going to astral project? But I thought-"

"It's ok. We will keep the vibrations low and calm. It won't be more than a flutter, a blip."

Mr Parks sounded sure, but I was immediately nervous. Astral projecting wasn't something your average Lightborn could do. It took time and patience to learn, and even longer to truly master. It also took a strict concentration of one's Light and usually left behind residue.

I'd heard of people being caught in the Astral world by the Brotherhood. Mr Parks told me this was how many of the Lightborn met to discuss their plans to bring down the original Brotherhood. Men like Brother Uri.

"I think I should be there too."

We'd left the boys to their activities and made our way to the couches near the kitchen. It was still early on a Saturday, so there weren't too many people around. Even Miss Turro had slept in.

"It's too dangerous, Anya."

"Mr Parks, I figured it out. I know what they're planning, and I need to be there to explain it to the others."

He looked confused and sat back in his seat. "What do you mean?"

I took a breath and exhaled slow and smooth. Last night I'd gone over and over everything in my mind, and now I was sure. But I wasn't sure that I wouldn't sound like a crazy person if I said it aloud.

"I think The Three have known about the decay for a long time, decades probably. How could they not? I think they saw the effects years and years ago, but instead of being responsible with their Light, they chose to just cover up the bad parts. And then it got worse. They got worse. I think what I've seen isn't the only place like it on earth. If we really went looking, I'm positive we would find countless more out there, all over the world. I went back yesterday, and it feels like the Veil is ready to fall. It's like they're just adding layers on top of broken layers and hoping it will keep everything sealed inside."

Mr Parks nodded with his brow furrowed and moved to speak, but I lifted a hand and asked him to wait.

"They know they've caused this. They know it's because they abused their Light. So why would they hold this huge Tournament two years early that could potentially rip the Veil open? All those Lightborn performing silly tricks and trying to out-do each other? It'll be chaos."

"Exactly. This is what we've-"

"They don't care about the Tournament!" I interrupted, getting a little too animated. "And they're not trying to fix what they broke. They're looking for something- or someone. Someone special that can help them."

I'd be talking too fast and needed to breathe. Trying to keep my train of thought on track, I closed my eyes and thought back to my Dad.

"We had to learn all about the Brothers in school. I know that Brother Uri is the smart one and was instrumental in bringing about the coup. I know that Brother Oran is the strongest of them all. They told us he single-handedly brought the sun back to Paris after a group of eight Lightborn cast it into darkness during the War. They also told us that Brother Anwar can open portals. He used this during the War to skip through time, watching for how the enemy would attack so that his army would be ready. Being able to go back and forth in time has given him an edge like no other. It's also probably one of the major reasons the world is dying around us."

"So...you're thinking, what? That Anwar is planning on going back in time to fix things?"

"No. No, I don't think so. To do that, he would have to go back to before any of this. Back to before the original Brotherhood and try to warn every single Lightborn of the effects of their powers. It would be impossible."

"Ok, so how?"

This was it; I had to let the crazy out.

"My mother read me a book when I was younger. It was about a young girl that falls down a rabbit hole and into another world. She met talking cats and singing flowers, and the whole place was unlike anything she had ever seen."

I tried to keep my thoughts in order, but I knew that what I was saying must've sounded like nonsense. To his credit, Mr Parks listened intently.

"I think...I think they're planning on having Anwar open a portal to a new world. I think they will use the Tournament to find a Lightborn that can open portals. With the extra power, they should be strong enough to not only find a new world but keep a portal open long enough to let through their people. They're not planning on saving us; they're planning on abandoning us."

Mr Parks let out a breath and took some time to sift through my insane theory. He got up, made us tea, and walked around with his brow furrowed, a hand on his cheek.

"Let's say you're right; we can't be sure of any of this, of course. But, if you are right, how would they even go about finding a 'new world'?"

"It's not as hard as you might think," I murmured with my eyes on my tea.

"Anya?"

I took another deep breath and tried not to babble.

"I can do it too. I found out when I was young, and I used to do it all the time. I would flitter in and out to different times and places. It was like an adventure."

His mouth fell open. We'd known each other for years, but I'd never shared this.

He started to speak and stopped a few times before asking, "Why didn't you tell us this?"

"I haven't done it in years..."

"Anya, if you can really do this...how weren't you caught? I mean, the amount of Light that must've..." He stopped when his mind caught up to his words.

"Yeah. All those stupid adventures I thought I was having. I didn't know I was leaving behind my Glimmer. I didn't know they could sense it. By the time they showed up, it was too late."

I blinked my eyes shut to stop the tears. This wasn't the time for self-pity.

Mr Parks sat back down and put his hands over mine. "That's why they took your father?"

I nodded. "When they came, my Dad pretended not to know what they were talking about. We didn't have any boys, so why would the Lightborn be looking at our house? He played dumb and tried to talk his way out of it. I don't remember exactly what happened. But when my Dad figured out that they weren't leaving without answers, he stepped forward and let them take him. He did it to protect me."

"Oh, Anya." He stood and moved to me, but I pushed back, not wanting to let myself get upset.

"It's not about me, Mr Parks. It's about all of us. I know what Anwar is capable of, and I know that this is their plan. We just need to figure out how to save the rest of us."

# CHAPTER 11

**After**

Anya woke up early the next day. With the curtains still open from the night before, the sun shone in her room, waking her from her nightmares. As she sat up in the bed, she kept her eyes closed, hoping it was all a terrible dream. It wasn't, of course. She was still in the suite in the Brothers' compound.

Her heart sank when she thought back to the night before. The image of her family in the dirt at the prison camp would likely stay with her forever. Even though she knew it hadn't been real, it so easily could be. She wondered what they were all doing now. Were they trying to find her?

After a hot shower, Anya used her Light to get dressed. The guilt at such liberal use of her magic was heavy, but since she hadn't been given time to pack a bag, she was left with little choice.

Surrounded by the Three and their people, she felt utterly alone. Anya briefly contemplated running again but knew she wouldn't. Instead, she waved a hand over the small table to her side. The tea was warm, and the bacon sandwich was crispy and delicious.

The truth was, as guilty as she felt for using her Light so frivolously, a small part of her couldn't deny the tingle of excitement. Since her father, she'd hidden her power deep down. At the Ludus, she was free to be herself, though she hadn't been visiting as much in recent years, and it scared her to use her Light outside of its safe walls.

But sitting in her prison and conjuring something as simple as a cup of tea felt so seductively wrong.

After an hour, Anya was feeling restless. She paced the room, banged on the door, and drank more tea than she should have.

Where were they?

How long was she supposed to just sit and wait?

Shouldn't they be doing something?

The end of the world wouldn't wait.

Fresh anger took over as she forced the door open. The hallway was still empty, leaving her free to walk to the elevator with her head held high. Selecting the ground floor, Anya tapped her fingers against the wall impatiently.

How were there no guards?

"Because we don't need them," a voice said from somewhere behind her.

She jumped and swore, embarrassed at her elevated heart.

"Get out of my head!" She hissed as the doors opened, taking to the lobby in a rush.

The three nervous Lightborn at the desk panicked when she flew by but hesitated - they didn't seem to know what to do, blocking the door and looking to each other for guidance.

"Don't make us hurt you," one threatened weakly.

"Hurt me? How do you think the Three would react to that?" She sniped, pushing by and gliding down the steps.

They didn't come after her.

Anya followed the road back the same way they'd driven in. The Great Hall was up ahead, and then it was the gates. She looked around and saw no-one but knew they were watching. Somehow they were following, and she knew she wouldn't make it off the property.

It wasn't easy keeping certain thoughts out of her head, and Anya stuck to what was in front of her eyes. She took in the grass, the flowers, and the wall surrounding the compound. Being naturally curious, and since they weren't keeping her locked up, she pushed her luck as much as she could.

As she approached the Great Hall, a dog's bark pulled her attention. A handsome Pitbull made his way over, happy and friendly. He was black with a white stripe between his kind eyes and a little white tip on his wagging tail.

He looked so glad to see her with his mouth open as he panted nudged up to her leg. Anya pulled some treats out of her pocket and brought a water bowl from behind her. The sweet-faced boy slurped and gobbled as he got close for pets, leaving her smiling and laughing, totally forgetting her circumstances.

"His name's Ozzie," Oran called.

Anya turned to see him leaning against the Great Hall.

"Funny how dogs have such an effect on us."

"We don't deserve them," Anya said, scratching him behind the ear.

"That's true. They're perfect creatures - much better than any of us."

It was surprising to see he was sincere, and Anya dropped her gaze, not wanting to let her guard down.

Ozzie licked her face and ran to his master, jumping up as Oran scratched his head, tossing treats in the air. The dog barked happily and ran around the corner toward the gates.

She watched him run down the path, a smile on her face. When Ozzie neglected to slow, she glanced to Oran, but it was too late. He quietly turned to dust in the wind before reaching the property line.

She gasped in horror and fell to her knees.

"He's fine. He was never really here anyway," Oran assured her.

"Why?" That was all she could get out.

"I like the companionship, but my boy is allergic. This way, we're all happy."

"You think that poor dog is hap-" she cut herself short as Ozzie reappeared on the road. He ran to Oran, jumped up for treats once again before coming back to her side, licking the tear that had escaped her right eye.

"He seems ok to me," Oran said, moving toward a small door on the side of the Great Hall. "Come in. Ozzie can come too if you'd like."

She wanted to stay outside, with Ozzie and the open land. She wanted to turn and run.

Like he knew she would, Anya stood and followed without a word. With Ozzie at her side, she felt more confident. He comforted her with his playful smile and sweet face, and she got the feeling he would try to protect her, even if he would never win against her enemy.

Inside, the Great Hall was like nothing Anya had ever seen. On TV, it always looked old. She'd seen similar halls in movies about knights and dragons, with great long tables made of thick, impressive, worn timber, adorned with goblets and feasts. The stone walls looked robust and solid, and the lights were usually candles and lamps.

The hall she now stood in differed vastly from what she had seen and expected. It was modern, white, and sparse. The walls were flat, plain white with absolutely nothing to break it up. At the opposite end from where she entered, near the big doors, was a workspace.

The enormous glass desk had three chairs and at least a dozen monitors. Uri and Anwar were sitting and working, not noticing Oran and Anya at all. They only looked up when Ozzie barked, the sound echoing around the vast room.

"Uhg, what's that doing in here?" Anwar said with the disgust of a cat lover.

"He's mine," Anya said defiantly.

She noticed Oran look at her in slight surprise and chuckle.

"Take it out-" Uri started but was cut short by Oran.

"Let her have the dog. She'll be more amenable with him at her side."

Anya felt a wave of gratitude for Oran, and she wondered if he'd brought Ozzie along with this in mind. She turned and pet his head as he sat patiently beside her. He made her feel at ease.

"What do you want? What is all this?" Anya demanded, moving further into the Hall.

"We needed an area to test you. This will work perfectly," Anwar answered without looking her in the eye.

"Test me?"

"You came here as nothing more than an anomaly - a girl with the Light. We were intrigued, but hey, the Light has always been gifted at random. It was bound to happen someday," Uri said with a shrug. "But then you ran. Not just ran, but jumped! Through a portal, no less! And wouldn't you know it: we've been looking for someone just like you. And now here you are - brought right to our doorstep! What luck!" Uri smirked, and Anya saw the malice in him.

She saw the treachery that caused the Uprising and the downfall of the Elders. It frightened her.

"You showed some significant power yesterday. Not just the jump - after, in the forest. How have you stayed out of our reach for so long?" Anwar seemed genuinely intrigued.

Afraid her thought would turn to her father, Anya panicked, picturing the flames in the forest and the fear she'd felt. If any of them were looking, they would only see her weakness.

"It was safer to not use my Light. I didn't want to be taken away from my family."

"Hmmm. I don't know that you're being sincere, Anya. But we don't have time for this. We need to see what you're capable of," Uri finished his sentence, and almost immediately, Anya was surrounded by Lightborn.

They knocked her down from behind and then from her left just as she stood again. Ozzie barked and snarled at the men, but Anya put a reassuring hand on his head. She closed her eyes, and Ozzie turned to dust at her side.

In the same breath, she blew purple flames across her palms, opening her arms and spreading the fire around the circle. Her attackers stumbled back, crying out in pain. She let them squirm for a few seconds before snapping her hands closed, putting out the flames. Standing tall in the centre, she made eye contact with Anwar. Was he impressed?

Before anyone could speak, two Lightborn charged from opposite sides. One went high, engulfing Anya in a wave of water. The other went low, wrapping her legs in chains, rooting her to the spot.

The most crucial thing she'd learned at the Ludus was how to remain calm under pressure. Their Light could be so fickle, and an erratic mind was hard to control. Though she felt the water in her throat, and her lungs were protesting, she stood still. If she panicked, whatever she tried to free herself, would likely go wrong.

So she stood. Anya held her breath and kept her balance, ignoring the shouts and jibes from the men watching. She counted to ten and pictured the water falling. In her mind, it fell to the ground, dissolving the chains and rushing to the edge of the room. She kept her eyes closed as she pictured the water rising up and over their heads.

When Anya opened her eyes, she was in the storm's eye. The wall of water was getting higher and higher, and the panicked Lightborn were stuck.

One had tried to conjure a raft, but in his frantic mind, he turned his arms into canoe paddles. Another was clutching at his chest as what looked like gills ripped into his flesh.

Anya looked to the Three, who were sitting behind a wall, perfectly dry. She couldn't tell if they were mad or impressed. It hadn't been her intention to show them her power, but they had forced her hand.

Once she was sure they'd learned their lesson, Anya clasped her hands into fists and let the water rush away, dropping the Lightborn to the ground. They hit the hard floor, none of them able to soften their falls.

Obviously, they didn't focus at the School of Light.

Around her, they stood slowly with enraged looks on their faces. She noticed one making a move, but before she could stop him, he appeared to freeze in his tracks. She looked up to see Oran standing with his arm stretched out and his fist tight.

"Enough. You're obviously no match for our new friend here." He waved his hand, and they all disappeared.

"Now, let's try a portal, shall we?" Anwar said, standing and coming to meet her in the middle of the room.

"I can't just-"

"Yes, you can." Anwar cut her off with a dismissive flick of the wrist. "You can, and you will."

Anya thought about opening a portal and leaving Anwar behind in some desolate world. But how to find one? When she was younger, she could easily imagine any number of beautiful worlds, and she would just… be there. She had the imagination and the fearlessness needed.

As an adult, it was harder to let her mind go. And she couldn't remember all the places she'd been when she was young.

"I need a minute," she said as she sat on the dry ground.

Ozzie appeared back at her side, but Anwar wasn't in the mood.

"Enough with the dog. Open a damn-"

"Anwar!" Oran shouted from behind the desk.

He stood and walked over, Uri close behind.

"You, of all people, know the toll this takes. You also know it's not just a matter of snapping your fingers. So let her do what she needs. Give her some damn space and leave the dog be. He's calming, and that's what she needs."

For a second, Anya thought his head would explode. Anwar looked red with rage and let out a frustrated breath, turning on his heel and walking away.

Oran nodded down at Anya and gave Ozzie a scratch. The Three took several steps back, their eyes never leaving her as Anya took deep, calming breaths. The truth was, she really did need this. After what she'd just done, she needed to re-focus.

She wasn't used to using her Light so freely and with such force and needed to gather herself and recenter so she could try to focus on a time and place to jump to.

It was difficult. In her young mind, all it took was an idea or an image of something that made her happy. These focal points grounded her subconscious and allowed her to jump.

But in that hall, she didn't want to think of anything they could use against her. She didn't want them to see anything that brought her happiness. That made it hard. Her mind was blank, and she couldn't think of anywhere to go outside of her comfort zone.

Too soon, Anya sensed Anwar pacing and growing increasingly annoyed. After a while, she also felt Uri trying to pry into her thoughts, making a mental note of how it felt so she could be ready the next time.

Then she found it.

It was an inoffensive place she could open a portal to that wouldn't put anyone she loved in harm's way. Her memory of this place was weak, but aspects were vivid enough to hold onto.

Anya stood and opened her eyes. She saw Anwar was about to blow, but before he could speak, the air in front of them tore open in a blaze of sparks.

Her Light ripped across the Hall in a purple-blue haze, and she could see the city on the other side. The arena stood tall and bright, and people were milling around trying to finish everything in time for the Tournament.

Anwar moved to her side, gazing at the opening, pure wonder on his face. He stepped forward and put his hand close, allowing her Light to touch his fingertips.

It felt oddly violating. She didn't want anyone, least of all, Anwar, feeling her power.

She hadn't moved in time but rather put her mind to the arena. They were looking at the present, her memory not quite strong enough to take her back there.

Anwar could jump in time at the drop of a hat and would not be impressed.

"Are you going?" She asked impatiently.

"No. You can close it now," he said, pulling his hand back.

His eyes remained on the tall buildings as Anya relaxed her shoulders, letting the Light return to her open palms. The Glimmer left behind was bright, and she felt a hint of pride.

The brighter the Glimmer, the stronger the Light.

"Why have me open a portal if you're not going through?"

"Oh, I'll go through. When it's the right portal. For all I know, you could move a hundred years from now and trap me there in a split second."

"Surely, you have enough Light to get yourself home?" Anya asked, not to be rude, but as a genuine question.

He was one of the Three, after all. But Anwar took her tone the wrong way and grabbed her. He squeezed his fingers into her upper arms until she cried out. Ozzie barked and snarled until Oran stepped forward and pried his Brother's hands away.

"That's enough for today," Uri sighed. "Take her back to her suite," he added as two Lightborn appeared by the door.

Anya didn't fight it, and she followed them out of the hall, Ozzie trotting along in front. She rubbed her arms where Anwar had grabbed her, and the pain went away. She would not let him leave a mark on her.

Above them, grey clouds seemed to roll in overhead, and the rain started pouring before they made it back. Anya didn't try to stop it, instead letting it drench her.

Back in her room, she took another hot shower before snuggling with Ozzie on the bed. She gave herself a TV and settled into a silly show that Frankie liked. Now more than ever, she needed to stay calm and think of a way out.

But she had to do it carefully, without Uri or the others seeing.

# CHAPTER 12

**8 1/2 weeks to the Tournament**

I don't like public speaking. Who does? I know.

But I especially hate it because I've always tried to stay under the radar. After they took away my father, I all but stopped using my Light outside of the Ludus. It terrified me that I would be caught, and his sacrifice would have been for nothing.

I once read about a young Lightborn who accidentally blinded a group of people during a speech because he was too nervous. And another who killed his own parents when some people tried to rob them.

So when it comes to public speaking, I don't like the idea of being the centre of attention when I'm nervous. I would already be in the Astral world and would need to focus on that. We would all be vulnerable, and just one slip could have us all in chains.

But I knew that speaking up at the meeting was critical.

"Just remember to breathe and keep your vibrations low," Miss Turro explained as she tucked me into the cocoon. "Don't force it, Anya. Let your body go when it's ready. Breathe in and out, and focus on yourself and only yourself. Flex your muscles and feel your presence. You'll know when it's time. Remember, there's no rush.

You know time moves much slower in the Astral Plane. Even if you take hours in here, it will only be minutes to them."

I nodded and smiled. This wasn't my first time, but it was the most important. And I hadn't done it in so long that I had forgotten how it felt.

The cocoon was a small pod that sealed shut in a room on its own. Mr Parks was in a similar pod next door - it was almost impossible to enter the Astral plane with someone beside you. We both needed to be alone with our minds to allow ourselves space and time to project.

But my mind wouldn't calm. I was too nervous that I would make waves and bring the Lightborn down on us all. Every time I closed my eyes and tried to breathe, I pictured the fire and destruction of the Veil and couldn't focus.

With Miss Turro's voice in my head, I allowed myself some to panic. Time was different over there; there was no rush. Cycling through sheer panic and deep breathing exercises, my mind cleared. I focussed on my toes, curling and stretching them out. Then my fingers. I flexed and released every muscle in my body until finally, I felt the vibrations.

They came as little tremors at first, and I held on, focusing with every brain cell I could muster until I knew where I needed my mind to go.

Before I knew it, I awoke in a chair in a compact room filled with people.

"Are you ok, Anya?" Mr Parks reached out and touched my hand, grounding me with him.

Although I couldn't actually feel his touch, I felt the warmth from his presence and relaxed. I looked around and noticed not all of the seats were taken. That meant I wasn't the last to arrive.

We sat quietly, waiting for the rest of our group. I saw a couple of familiar faces, but the rest were strangers - other people who risked everything for the boys in their charge. There were twenty-four seats, including mine and Mr Parks, and soon they were all full.

"Thank you all for being here," Mr Parks began. "I know that this is risky, so we need to get right to it. I'm not sure how many of you know about the Veil near our Township and what we've found beneath. But for those of you that aren't aware: we've found a spot on the earth that is dying. It's hidden under powerful Light and cannot be seen by the average eye. We're sure that this is not the only spot like it on earth. In fact, we believe it is one of a great many. The only explanation we can come up with is that the Brotherhood has been abusing their Light for too long, and the earth is fighting back." He paused and looked around, gauging the reactions. "But the power that holds it in is diminishing, and soon, the Veil will drop altogether."

"What do you mean 'the earth is fighting back'?" someone asked.

Mr Parks looked down at me and nodded. "This is Anya. She was one of my best students. She-"

"She's a girl!"

"That's right. And she has one of the brightest Lights I've ever seen. She found the Veil and saw what's beneath it. She came here to tell you."

Mr Parks sat down and nodded for me to stand. I took a breath and tried to keep calm.

"I found the Veil when I was younger. It started out bad, with deformed creatures and angry skies, but it's gotten so much worse. All those years of manipulating the weather and trying to create new animals has had consequences. The sky is black, the trees have burned to nothing, and the animals are hardly alive. And the Light that they've used to try to hide it is fading. I can tell. They keep trying to cover it up, but pretty soon that Veil will come crashing down, and the decay will spread."

Nobody spoke for what felt like an hour. I stood with their eyes on me and felt clammy - I hadn't even gotten to the bad part yet.

"And that's not all. I think the reason they're holding the Tournament early is to find a Lightborn that can open portals. I think they know they've caused irreversible damage, and now they want to jump ship."

"Portals?!"

"What do you mean 'open portals'?"

"Jump ship to where?"

"Brother Anwar can open portals," I shouted over the unfamiliar voices. "They taught us about him moving through time during the war. Well, now he wants to move through time and space to find a new world. A place unburdened by the Light. And they're not planning on taking us all with them."

It was quiet for a second, and then they all launched into arguments. I couldn't hear one over the other as they shouted their confusion across the table. Mr Parks tried to calm them, but it was no use. They either thought I was crazy or...well, just crazy. My mind wandered. I was losing control, but I needed them to hear me.

"You'll have time to scream and shout later, but right now, you need to listen! The Veil and what's beneath it is real. And the Brothers are planning on abandoning this world to that decay, sooner rather than later. I'm sure of it. It's the only reason they would bring the Lightborn together like this. They need a younger, stronger Anwar to help with the portal, and then they will pack their things and walk away without a second thought. But we can't let that happen. We need to fight back. We need to do whatever we can to protect the people on this planet - those with the Light and those without. So get on board quick because time is running out."

When I took my seat, I had to hold onto the table, my breath becoming ragged, and my vibrations hummed more than I was comfortable with. It wasn't easy to stay calm after losing my temper, but I managed to hold it together.

"I've seen it - the Veil? There's a place like that near my Township in Adelaide."

I looked up in shock. "Really? You've actually seen it?"

He nodded and stood.

"My name is Mr Barber. I run the Ludus in South Australia. Last year I was out trekking with my partner when we came across it. Chris doesn't have the Light, and I couldn't understand why he suddenly turned away. When I asked him, he just said-"

"There are no lights," we said together.

He nodded at me and hung his head.

"That's right. He walked away, but I went back. I went through, and what I saw... I'll never forget it. The sky wasn't a sky at all, but black water swirling overhead. The ground was crumbled and fractured, and there was a terrible shriek in the air, though no wind at all. I was only there for a few minutes, but that was more than enough."

"Well, that's two," Mr Parks said, "two we know of.

And even if those were the only two, without the Brothers' Light keeping it at bay, that same destruction will seep into our world. We all know that the Brothers and their Lightborn have abused their power. They've done whatever they want for decades, and now everything is out of balance."

"So maybe they'll fix it."

"You don't really believe that, do you?" I asked with a tone I immediately regretted. "Using Light to fix this is like using lighter fluid to try and put out a fire. The world needs to heal, and it won't do that if the Lightborn keep going on the way they have been. Keeping themselves young, stopping the rain - it's all going against Mother Nature. We might be responsible and respectful of our gifts, but their range is boundless. Their damage is worldwide."

"But we still can't know that their plan is to abandon us. Anwar could open portals to the past, not to new dimensions. How do we even know that's possible?"

I cleared my throat and looked him right in the eye, "Because I can do it too. I can open portals, and I've been to such places. Not just the past or the future, but to places that are wholly different from this one. I once got lost in a world that had absolutely no people. The animals ruled the land, and it was beautiful and unspoiled. These places exist. I've seen them. So I know that if I can do it, so can Anwar."

"How is this possible? How do you even have the Light?"

Mr Parks stood to my defence, "What does it matter how-"

"It's ok, Mr Parks. We're expecting them to trust me; they deserve answers." I looked up and tilted my head at the ceiling that wasn't there.

We didn't have time for too much detail, so I kept it short.

"My mother was originally pregnant with twins. I had a brother with me in the womb, and at some point, early on, I...absorbed him. It's very rare, but it happens. My brother must've had the Light, and...he gave it to me."

This was met with silence. I was expecting as much. It wasn't something I ever talked about or really thought about, even. Not that I felt guilty or sad. Neither of us were formed things yet, just sacks of cells. But it was still a weird thing that was usually met with strange looks and judgement. I only found out because I found an old sonogram that had two little peas instead of one.

"If all this is true, how are we supposed to fix things. We can't use our Light? If Anwar isn't strong enough to open a portal, then I doubt you are. How do we save the whole world?"

"That's what we're here to figure out," I said before taking my seat.

I looked up again and tried to think about how long we'd been here. Minutes in here could be hours out there, and Miss Turro was probably sick with worry. I smiled as my mind went to Alexis and the trouble I would be in later.

It went very quiet in the small room, each face deep in thought. I had no clue how we would fix things, and I was sure that the rest felt just as helpless. Our natural instinct would be to use our Light. But with that off the table, we had little left.

"You said you can open these portals. What if...what

if we align with the Brothers? You could join Anwar-"

"I really hope you're joking, Piesch!" Mr Parks snapped. "Join the Brotherhood? We've been hiding from them for years, and now you want to walk into the Great Hall and bow down?"

"Of course not. But we have to think of everyone else out there. If we go to them with conditions- tell them we won't help unless we bring everyone-"

"Everyone? You think I could open a portal that lets through the entire population? You're insane!"

"Well, what other option do we have?!"

They started shouting again, and I realised that we would not make any headway here. I'd said my peace, and we all needed to go away and think.

"What? What did you say?" Mr Parks said from beside me.

I looked to see him staring across the table.

"Say that again." He was speaking to a younger-looking Lightborn who had been mostly quiet.

"I said," he began in an almost whisper, "we should save ourselves. You said it yourself, we can't fix this with our power. It's that power that's caused the imbalance. The Brothers will take their people and leave, and we should all do the same."

Nobody spoke for a time. I looked at their eyes and didn't like the darkness there. Would they really just abandon the world? Were we no better than the Three?

"We can't just-" I began.

"Why not? We take our families and the people from our Ludi, and we go. What good will staying do? Dying with the rest of them?"

"Because we're better than that!" Mr Parks yelled. "We're better than them!"

"There might be another way..." Everyone looked at me, and I swallowed, trying to gather my thoughts.

I'd been thinking about it for a while but never felt confident enough to say it out loud. But their reactions frightened me, and I knew they needed another option.

"What if there was no Light anymore? What if we gave it back?"

"Back? Back to who?"

"To the earth. These gifts we have, they were given to us from somewhere. Conjuring a cup of coffee or a bouquet of flowers isn't the reason for the damage. We all know to keep our Light under control. We use it within reason out of respect. But the Three don't. The Lightborn in charge abuse their power every day. But what if we choose to give it back? Maybe that would stop it all. Maybe that would fix it all."

"Now, who's insane?"

"Hey! That's enough," Mr Parks warned. "I think Anya may be on to something."

We looked at each other and then around the room.

"No more Light means no more decay. Maybe we can balance it out."

"Right, except who will convince the Three of that? You think they're just going to sit there and give all their power back?" Mr Piesch almost rolled his eyes.

"He's right. Plus, they have an army of Lightborn raised to think they're superior. You think they're just going to give that up because we say please?" The man beside me said.

"They will if they know the truth," I said quietly. "If we tell them about the decay and the Brothers' plan to abandon us all-"

"Except, we don't know that's the plan. We have no

proof of any of it!"

"Then we'll have to go find some."

# CHAPTER 13

Anwar was sleeping more and more in recent years. He had been so young and strong when they Ascended, and although their Light kept them looking youthful, he felt ancient.

He'd spent years trying to open a portal to an unfamiliar world and was completely drained. Jumping through time was one thing - it was easy when you had a specific time and place to focus on. But looking for the unknown took so much concentration.

After the last attempt, he felt as though his Light had been completely extinguished. For almost a week after, he couldn't even conjure a sandwich, let alone open a portal big enough to allow their people through.

The Brothers had spent the last week going over plans for the Tournament. New arenas were being built 24/7 and would be ready the week before the start of the games, giving them enough time to travel and place their barriers around each of them.

Once a Lightborn entered through the gates, their power would fade. It would happen so slowly that they would never notice. After a day of competing, it would be natural to feel drained. They would leave, sleep, and regain their strength, only to come back the next day to do it all over again.

Uri decided that most of the Light they syphoned would go to Anwar. He needed the most strength if they would be successful, after all. But he couldn't have it all. Oh no, no, that would be too much. Anwar knew his Brothers were nervous he would abandon their plan and betray them. The truth was, he'd thought about it more than once.

It was close to noon, but the rain made it appear later outside. The house was empty when he finally made his way downstairs. His wife was likely out with her friends at some restaurant or yoga class. She spent very little time at home these days, and the boys were long gone.

They finished school and left to make their own lives away from the Brotherhood years ago. Neither had been gifted with the Light, and Anwar had never quite forgiven them for this. They both lived and worked regular lives and kept their ties to the Brotherhood quiet.

When they visited, it was mostly to see their mother and to endure an awkward family dinner.

His eldest son, Maxwell, had three children: two girls and a boy. The boy was almost at testing age, and Anwar hoped that he would be a young prodigy. Though his father wouldn't be too happy, he knew. His other son, Seth, had a newborn boy. They would have to wait years before finding out if he was special.

How Anwar envied Oran and his son's Light.

Coffee in hand, Anwar looked out through the large window. The rain pounded against the glass, and he could barely see the river beyond the hills. He waved his hand, clearing the skies and loving the feeling of the sun on his face.

That would get him in trouble, he knew.

"We're supposed to be trying to make things better, Anwar!" Uri's voice pestered in his ear. But he didn't care. He needed the sun to make it through the day.

The plans for the Tournament were almost complete. The press had their passes ready and interviews scheduled. Merchandise was almost ready for shipping, and they had sent out invitations to the culinary schools to provide food and drink.

Security was being trained at mass crowd control. Lieutenants and Community Leaders were preparing for the chaos by increasing the number of buses to and from the arenas and ensuring that specific hotels were reserved for Lightborn only.

It was a risk bringing all the Lightborn together like this - it would leave their Townships without their influence or control. With that in mind, they discussed making attendance mandatory. But that brought issues in and of itself.

Where would all those people sleep? They still hadn't decided but needed to sooner rather than later.

Anwar stayed at the window until his coffee was gone, and he felt warmed through. He glanced into the kitchen but didn't feel like food. Unlike Oran, Anwar had lost his appetite of late. Instead, he showered, dressed, and went into the office.

His Brothers were there already, Uri looking mad and Oran eating blueberry pie.

"Can you just, for once, get your hair wet and leave the damn rain alone," Uri spat before he could sit down.

"Right," he said, no fight left in him.

"Anwar, come on, we've talked-"

"Yes, Uri. Ok. No more sunshine. I get it."

Uri looked like he wanted to argue but must've

thought better of it. Instead, he let out a short breath and went back to his files. They worked without speaking for almost two hours before one of the Lightborn from the front desk knocked at the door.

"Sir's?" He said timidly.

Uri waved him in and put down his tablet. "What?"

"Um, you have a message from a Community Leader in Berlin. He is concerned about the crowd sizes at the games."

"And he wants...what?"

"Um, well, he said that maybe they should have a second arena, perhaps in Zurich? To split the crowds and make things more manageable?" Everything this kid said sounded like a question, and it drove Anwar crazy.

"Does this Leader think we haven't thought this through?" Anwar asked with a bite.

"Um..."

"He thinks we made a mistake in our planning and that he knows better?"

"Um..."

"Anwar," Oran said patiently. "He's just delivering a message. Don't take it out on the kid."

The boy stood awkwardly with the message in his hand. He looked like he wanted to cry - or pee his pants.

"Tell whoever this Leader is that we know what we're doing and not to worry."

The boy scurried away before Anwar could add anything.

"Now we have some local Lightborn questioning us? This isn't good, Brothers." Anwar stood and started pacing. "And not just talking behind our backs! No! He's got the audacity to question us directly!"

"Calm down, Anwar. It was just a simple question."

But the frustration was too much. He just didn't have the strength to argue anymore. He had agreed to go along with the plan, and he meant it. He didn't like it, but he would do it because he knew they were right deep down. But that didn't mean that he had to sit there and constantly be torn down by high and mighty Uri.

"I'm done for the day. Whatever you decide is fine by me," Anwar announced as he left the room.

Nobody followed.

His mood darkened further as he reached the gates of the compound. The rain had returned, and it hit hard and heavy, making driving a chore. The lights on his car worked, but he could barely see. Lucky for him, there were no other cars on the road. He drove in the middle and ignored the old signs and traffic lights that were all but useless now.

Anwar was born not long after the Blackout and grew up in a time of change when people still remembered what life was like before the Brotherhood and the Light. Cars were still on the roads, though in much fewer numbers.

He remembered the rebellions and the resistances. When the Dark War started, he was not yet twenty but still a Lightborn under the Elders. He hadn't been there the day someone attacked and killed one of the original Brotherhood and hadn't been sure of his beliefs. But he blossomed into a young man through the fight that followed.

He met Uri by chance. Once Uri saw what Anwar was capable of, he took him under his wing and influence, using his power to become one of The Three. Anwar hadn't minded, and truth be told, he still didn't. Someone had to take charge.

Uri was smart and capable and much more adept at leading. Anwar and Oran had always been happy to follow his lead. Though in recent years, they had been butting heads more. Anwar had ideas and plans, and Uri often refused to even listen.

The car drove well, even after all these years. So few people left in the world knew how to fix them, granting exclusive access to private vehicles. They lived well. Though Anwar hadn't seen his mechanic in some time and made a note to bring the old girl in for a service soon.

He wasn't thinking about where he was going - he let the car take him. The Brothers' compound was far out from any city or Township. Explicitly chosen for its isolation, they didn't want to be running into anyone should they leave the gates. No buses came through, and nobody walked their land or the land surrounding.

It was how they all liked it. But it also meant that they had that much further to go. His wife incessantly complained about her commute to the city - not that she drove herself. She had a driver who was at her beck and call, 24/7. Another privilege that she overlooked. None of her friends were so lucky. He knew they hated when she arrived in her big fancy car when they had to take the bus.

Their compound was a Township all in itself, the surrounding wall being carefully warded against intruders. It was patrolled by Lightborn and Security forces day and night. They couldn't be too careful.

Though they'd had no rebellions since their Ascension, they had to remain vigilant. This was why he never told his Brothers of days like this. His Light blinded anyone to his actions as he snuck away in his car. Anyone that saw the cherry red beamer forgot about it almost instantly.

He arrived at his destination two hours later. The rain slowed him down, and he cursed Uri under his breath. He stopped the car outside of a set of gates and honked the horn. After a couple of minutes, they opened and allowed him in.

The rain parted above him as he got out of the car and walked calmly into the little cottage, without a single drop on his head. It was warm inside and smelled like fresh bread.

"Shoes!" She called from the kitchen.

"You know they're not wet," he replied, bending over to take them off anyway.

"I don't care. We're not savages," she laughed, and he heard the kettle rumbling.

Anwar walked into the cottage and took a seat on the couch in front of the fire. He sighed as he allowed himself the moment to relax. This was the only place he ever felt at peace.

"I'm surprised you made it."

Anwar smiled as she walked into the room. She was holding two cups of tea and a tray with bread, butter, and homemade jam.

And she looked beautiful.

Her hair was half up in a clip, the sweater and yoga pants not too tight, and thick socks to keep the cold out. She knelt down by the table and waited. He took a sip of the tea and did the same.

"You look tired," she said eventually.

"Hmmm. Lots to do with the games coming up."

She nodded and sipped her tea. Her dark eyes watched him in the firelight, and he felt her gaze.

"I'm fine, Kareena, really."

He finished his tea and grabbed some bread. It was still warm, and he realised how hungry he was after not eating all day.

"How is it all coming along?"

"It's coming. We'll be ready."

Kareena stood and moved to sit with Anwar, lifting her knees up and tucking her feet beneath her. She took his hand and kissed the palm before putting it to her cheek.

"You'll make it work - I know you will," she whispered into his ear.

Anwar rested his head against hers and breathed her in. She was the reason he was trying so hard. He wanted to find a way out of all this to keep her safe.

"We'll be away next week putting the barriers up. It should only take a few days. And then I'll try again after the first day is over."

"Just be careful. If they find out you're taking their Light-"

"They won't. There will be so many of them - we'll only need a little from each. They won't notice a thing."

She nodded, smiled, and kissed him on the cheek. He turned to kiss her, but the cry of the baby interrupted them. Anwar laughed and rolled his eyes.

"It's like she knows!"

"She probably does! She's an attention seeker, that girl."

Kareena left the room and collected the baby. She was already giggling as they came back in. The baby reached out to her father, and he took her in his arms with a laugh.

"She misses you."

"I miss her too."

Anwar spent the rest of the day at the cottage and dragged his feet when it was time to go. He hated leaving, especially when he wasn't sure when he'd be back.

The baby was happily picking at the food on her plate as he put his shoes on and kissed his loves goodbye. He opened the door and looked up at the inky clouds. Dammit, Uri, he thought bitterly.

Once in the car, Anwar turned around for one last look. Kareena stood in the doorway with their daughter on her hip. She waved at him and then raised her hand, making a slow arch over her head.

The rain stopped.

Anwar laughed and shook his head as she winked at him and went back inside.

# CHAPTER 14

**After**

Anya had been at the compound for over two weeks, and she so no way of escaping. The Three spent hours on end watching as she opened portals as far as her Light would allow, leaving her completely drained.

Surprisingly, some days, they left her alone to wander the property with Ozzie, understanding that she needed breaks.

Today was one of those days.

What they were asking of her was exhausting enough but added to the stress was having to be always on guard. She only slipped twice with thoughts of the Ludus, but recovered fast, and felt no intrusions.

But Anya did let thoughts of escaping run free, knowing it was impossible anyway. Even if she wanted to try, she wouldn't make it far in her exhausted state.

With every new portal she opened, Anya knew she was getting closer to what they were looking for. She could feel it. They needed a safe place to take their chosen few, but not a place already seen by men. They didn't just want a different time, they wanted a whole other time and space. Anya knew it was possible - not that she shared her knowledge - and it was getting harder to hold back. They chalked it up to her youth and inexperience, but that wouldn't hold for much longer.

Their intrusions into her mind were frequent but random. Sometimes she would feel them as she was building up the strength to use her Light. Other times she would be eating or walking with Ozzie. She never knew when they would invade her thoughts, only that they would, and she had to be vigilant. Twice she considered opening a portal and jumping to freedom, but each time it was as though they were already listening. She was never alone long enough to formulate a plan, and she didn't dare jump without one.

Her only hope was to get a message out to Mr Parks. It was a little over a month until the Tournament, and the Network needed to have a plan in place. Anya tried to get information from the Brothers, but they were all so cautious about what they said near her. They needed a portal, and that was all they would let her know.

She didn't want to give away exactly how much she knew, so she kept quiet. She kept her thoughts as neutral as possible, and she kept her Light low.

Mr Parks would have heard about her capture, no doubt about that. He knew people all over, and word would've gotten to him fast. Had he confronted her mother? Did he even know she was to blame? Could they save her? Would they try?

Anya spent her time alone, not including Ozzie, trying to find a way to communicate. They'd taken her phone that first night, but she assumed the compound was a dead zone, anyway. She knew she had the power to enter another mind, just like the Three could read her own, having done it once, years ago to Alexis. Though her sister had been young and open and sitting right next to her. Anya wasn't even sure where she was in relation to the Ludus. Not to mention the slight snag of them being hidden underground.

Oh, and the fact that the Three were almost always watching and listening. She feared getting a message out would lead the Lightborn right to the willow tree.

The clouds were rolling in, and Ozzie was getting hungry. Anya turned from the river and made her way back to her cell, passing an area she knew to be one of their houses.

That first night, she'd seen a few houses lit up in the darkness, but now, she saw nothing but grass. She could, however, feel a Glimmer, and see it shimmering from her window in the sunlight. Her assumption was that she couldn't see them any more than they couldn't see her. Wouldn't want the family knowing they were holding a young woman hostage.

As she made it to the top of the small hill, another dog came bounding over. He was a handsome border collie with his tongue hanging from his open mouth. Ozzie and the new dog barked, sniffed, and jumped around as Oran moved toward them. This was the first time she had seen him alone since he gave her Ozzie. He was eating a hot dog and offered her one before saying anything.

"Why not?" She laughed.

Oran smiled, and they stood, watching the dogs play. The sun was going down, and the clouds turned the sky a deep grey.

"Anwar won't be pleased. He hates the rain."

"Seems to be a lot of rain recently," Anya commented cautiously. "Does his sour mood bring it here?"

Oran laughed and coughed and laughed some more. "Funny. But no. Just the weather."

"We both know that's not true," Anya muttered as she finished her hot dog. "What's his name?"

"Barney,"

"Barney. I like it."

Oran was the least menacing of the Three, and he had a way of calming her and forcing her guards down. She had to remind herself to stay alert around him. None of them could be trusted.

"We should get back before the rain starts." Anya whistled for Ozzie and started walking without saying goodbye.

"He's taken to you," Oran called after her as Ozzie stopped for a pet and a treat. "You're practically attached at the hip."

Ozzie barked his thanks and chased after his new master. Anya scratched behind his ears and smiled.

"He's all I have," she sniffed sadly.

She didn't look back to Oran before leaving. His words rang in her ears, and she needed to get away from him. She needed to form the thought without fully forming it.

Back in her room, Anya sat on the bed and cleared her mind. She'd learned how it felt when one of them was trying to listen in, and right now, she was alone. Anya looked at her sweet dog and felt the nerves kick in.

This could go so wrong in so many ways: they could figure out her plan and punish her, find her friends or Ozzie could be hurt. It was dangerous, but she had to try.

Anya put her hands on Ozzie's face and rested her head against his. He licked her cheek as she whispered to him. She talked as long as she dared, before letting go. Ozzie stayed on the bed, tail wagging and tired eyes as she stood and shook her hands.

Oran was right, he was basically a part of her now, and she needed him to deliver her message.

Mr Parks had been in Anya's life for years. She knew him and his Light well and knew the Ludus and its walls like a second home. She had to trust that Ozzie would find him.

A tear ran down her cheek as she turned back to her companion. He was, after all, her only friend. Clearing her mind once more, Anya made sure that they weren't trying to get inside. Once she was sure it was safe, she raised her hands.

With her left hand, she drifted to her side, making a decadent burger and fries meal with a thick vanilla shake. At the same time, she lay her hand on her friend's sweet face and sent him into the darkness. She could only hope that the power from one hand would hide the other.

Nobody knocked on her door that night. A few times, she'd felt someone prying into her thoughts, but she watched something mindless that allowed her brain to quiet. Her eyes glazed over as she let the people and the chatter wash over. She wanted to sleep but knew there was no way. Not until she knew he was safe.

They would be at her door first thing, ready to work again. Anya needed to believe that Ozzie would make it back in time.

One thing Anya did let herself think about was the Veil. She thought about it in such incredible detail, it made her sick. But she ran the pictures through her mind, hoping it would shame any prying eyes. She wanted them to see what they had done. She wanted them to know what they would be abandoning the world to.

Eventually, Anya fell asleep. Since that first night, she had no way of knowing that Uri wasn't invading her dreams too. So every night since she used a tiny spark to ensure a dreamless, dull sleep.

When the sun crept in and onto her face, she didn't want to open her eyes. Anya knew the room was empty and feared the worst. They hadn't barged in yet, which meant Ozzie made it away from the compound. But he still wasn't back.

She paced and showered and paced some more. The higher the sun got, the more worried she became. It was only a matter of time before they would come and get her. How would she explain Ozzie's absence? He'd been at her side this entire time. They wouldn't believe that she was just sick of him. They wouldn't-

She heard him before she felt him. Ozzie jumped from the bed and up to greet her. He wagged his tail, licked her face, and danced around. He was happy to be home and proud of himself.

"Oh, sweet boy. You did such a good job. Good boy. Yes. Good boy!" Anya laughed and hugged Ozzie tight. He licked her ear, and she scratched behind his.

He made it out, and she knew that Mr Parks had gotten her message. Around Ozzie's neck was a small collar with a tag. On the tag was a tree and the number eleven.

Township 11. The Ludus would save her. She was sure of it.

# CHAPTER 15

**8 weeks to the Tournament**

The meeting hadn't gone as well as I'd hoped, though I hadn't really thought it would go well in the first place. It was a lot for them to take in, and we had no good options.

We came away with no plan of action or even an idea of what we could do. I felt utterly hopeless and exhausted. We'd been in the astral plane for well over an hour, which in the real world was close to a whole day. I was in for it when I finally got home.

"They really suggested that we just abandon this place? Leave people behind to die?" Miss Turro flinched at the thought.

Mr Parks nodded and sighed. I could tell he wasn't happy with how they had reacted.

"I understand their panic. It was a lot of information at once, and it's a natural instinct to protect the ones you love. Especially when we've given them no real way out."

"Is it really so hopeless?" Miss Turro murmured, choking up.

I looked at Mr Parks, but neither of us had an answer.

"I need to get home," I announced eventually. "Alexis will be going crazy."

The bus ride home was miserable. We were facing something that might be the end of us all, and I felt like that fell onto my shoulders.

I found the Veil, I figured out their plan, and I needed to fix things. But how?

The Brothers would never give up their Light, but what about the Lightborn? I had an image in my head of the Veil cracking open.

Of Anwar standing in front of a vast glimmering portal as he ushered his people to safety.

And the rest of us held back and unable to stop him.

What about after that? Part of me wanted to believe the Lightborn would see sense. But deep down, all I could picture was another war and a new fight for power.

It was well after dark by the time I got back. I'd left around lunchtime the day before and was sure Alexis would be in full panic mode. Not in the mood to be yelled at by her, I dragged my feet. I was also hesitant about being around my Mum. Did she even care that I'd been gone so long?

I got lucky, and the streets were empty. I knew that many of the Lightborn and Security had been taken aside to prepare for the Tournament, so I made it home unimpeded. But as I rounded the corner of our street, I stopped in my tracks.

Alexis was out front, and she wasn't alone. She stood in front of a private car with her arms draped around some guy's neck, giggling like a schoolgirl as he kissed her cheek.

I could practically feel her blushing from where I stood.

Keeping to the shadows, I moved in, but the closer I

got, the more worried I became.

Alexis' suitor was a Lightborn. He was wearing the uniform of the newly initiated, which meant he wasn't a Leader, but a foot soldier, assigned to work with the security forces in local areas.

After a few minutes, the Lightborn kissed Alexis goodbye and drove away. She stood and watched him go with a goofy look on her face. When she saw me, instead of going off on me about being irresponsible, she got jumpy and nervous and hurried us inside. I couldn't believe it. Had she even noticed I'd been gone?

"Where have you been?" Uncle Mark snarled when we came in together.

Again, Alexis seemed nervous as she stammered out an answer.

"What are you-I was talking to your sister," he cut Alexis off.

She sighed in relief, hurrying off to bed.

"I was...with Alexis."

I chased after my sister before he could say anything else. Out of the corner of my eye, I noticed my mother in the kitchen. I opted not to feed my growling stomach and went straight to my room.

The need to be alone outweighed my hunger as I tried to think about what we could possibly do to stop the Brothers. I was sure the Tournament would do nothing but further the imbalance. They would be creating rain and flying around for people's entertainment, and it would just add fuel to the fire.

And then, if they found the right Lightborn, the Brothers would rip a crack in our world and open us up to the destruction they'd been hiding for years.

After a while, the house went quiet. My hunger was

becoming a distraction, so I risked a trip to the kitchen. With the lights off, I stuck my head into the fridge and pulled out some leftovers from dinner. I debated the sound of the microwave vs eating it cold when a voice in the corner startled me.

"Where were you this weekend?"

I almost dropped the plate as I turned with a jump to see my mother sitting in the dark.

"I asked you a question, Anya."

"I was..."

"Don't lie to me."

As my eyes adjusted to the darkness, I could finally make her out. Had she been sitting there since I got home? Had she just been waiting for me?

"What do you want me to say?" I tried to keep my voice low and calm.

"I want you to tell me where you've been."

"You know where I was," I spat, sounding like an indignant tween.

"I thought we agreed you wouldn't go to that place anymore?"

"We didn't agree on anything."

I turned my back and put the plate in the microwave. The beeps rang into the quiet as I tried to keep my cool. This was precisely what I tried to avoid.

"Do you want your Uncle to die?" Her question caught me entirely off guard, and I laughed and stuttered, not knowing what to say. "What about Frankie? You want him thrown in a pit somewhere?"

"Of course not-what are you talking about?"

"You were happy to let your father take the blame for your actions. I just assumed you'd be willing to do the same again."

The wind knocked right out of me. Her sarcastic tone cut like a knife as an image of my father flashed across my mind. Tears came to my eyes as I turned back to the food. I watched it rotate in the light and stood still as it dinged.

"Well?"

"Dad said-"

"Your father spent years rotting in a cell somewhere. That's if they didn't just kill him right away. He was a good man, and they took him from us because you-"

"Stop it!" I sobbed.

I couldn't hear this, not now. I'd spent years feeling guilty, and her disdain for me never made things easy.

"You think it's not your fault?" She asked.

"I was a child. I didn't know!"

"*You didn't know!*" She mocked.

It was then I realised she'd been drinking. I should've known better. She always got nasty when she drank.

"What about you? Are you going to sit there and tell me you didn't know that something was different? I went missing for days at a time! And you just shrugged and pushed the truth aside. Dad wanted to keep me safe! All you ever wanted was to-"

"That's enough!" She yelled.

I was sure we'd woken up the house. We hadn't had a fight like this in quite a while, and the last time Uncle Mark came out early before either of us could say anything too cruel. This time, they left us alone.

"You never forgave me. You wanted a Lightborn. You wanted to be the mother of someone special. The wife of someone special. But you had to settle for us. Admit it! You were happy when they took Dad away!"

She was up in the blink of an eye. Her hand came

down hard across my face, and I reacted before I could think. She flew back and into the table, knocking it over as she crashed to the floor with a thud and a groan.

Part of me wanted to go to her and help her up. I wanted to apologise, hug her, and try to make her love me.

But I knew better.

Instead, I turned, taking the food out of the microwave, and walked back down the hallway to my room.

Behind me, Uncle Mark came rushing out and into the kitchen. As I walked by Alexis' door, I noticed it was cracked open, and she stood, listening. We locked eyes as I passed by, but I didn't stop.

I knew that she blamed me for what happened all those years ago. Though she didn't know all the details, and I was sure she didn't know about my Light, she knew that I had gone missing, and that was the reason the Lightborn came to town. She never said it out loud, but she never defended me to our mother either.

Sitting in my room, I ate, tasting nothing. My cheek was already coming up in a bruise, and I recklessly used my power to make it go away. I didn't need a reminder of tonight looking back at me in the mirror. I listened to the noises coming from down the hall and ignored my Uncle when he came knocking.

"You ok, kid?" He mumbled.

I wanted to answer, but I stayed quiet. He knew I wasn't ok.

# CHAPTER 16

I spent the next week totally distracted. Being in the house with my mother was almost unbearable, and I found it hard to concentrate on anything.

She'd never told me out loud that she blamed me. Though I always knew, hearing it hurt more than I could have imagined.

As a child, I used to open portals and get lost for days at a time. It was fun for me, and I never thought I was doing anything wrong. I didn't know or understand about Light or the Brotherhood, and when I asked my mother about it, she told me that only boys had the Light.

I thought I was normal, but she knew I wasn't.

Looking back, I remember doing things in front of her. She would either ignore me or tell me to stop. Why didn't she make me understand? If I'd known what using my Light would do, I would have stopped completely.

If I'd thought for a second that my Dad...of course I would've stopped.

All this and the stress of the Tournament coming up had me twisted inside. I couldn't focus on a solution or a plan because my mind would keep wandering back to the look of hate on my mother's face after I knocked her down. We hadn't spoken since, and I knew she was going away again in a few days. Maybe after that, I could try to focus.

Still, time was running out. I was afraid to go back to the Veil just as I didn't want to go back to the Ludus. I didn't know how to fix the world, and I needed everything to just stop for a while.

So when the day came for the Brothers to inspect the arena, I called in sick and took a bus to the city. The Tournaments were usually held in smaller sports centres. People would come and go, the arenas being local enough to pull in decent crowds. This time they were building enormous stadiums worldwide in all the major cities so that the Lightborn would have to travel.

People could and would watch the games in their thousands. The Three were visiting them all, checking standards, and giving their blessings to the Lightborn and Lieutenants. It was a stupid formality and nothing more than a show of power, but people were excited to have the Brothers so close.

The bus was much busier than the one I took to the Ludus. It was almost full when I got on, and after a few stops, it was standing room only. I wondered how many people were going to work and how many were, like me, going to see the Brothers.

I hadn't been to the city in years and took in the views from the bus window. It was bigger than I remembered and there seemed to be a lot of new buildings. As we got closer, I saw the arena. It sat on the outskirts, and I wondered what had been there before. I couldn't imagine an empty spot that big so close to the city. Had they knocked people's homes down so they could build it?

I also noticed that security was out in full force. My stomach churned, and I suddenly knew this was a terrible idea. The bus stopped not too far from the arena, and almost everyone got off. I sat weighing my options but jumped off at the last minute. I just needed to stay in the crowd, and I'd be fine.

We walked together until we reached the railings. The arena stood tall and proud, surrounded by people and cars. It was huge. It would hold the entire city and most of the Townships, or that's what I thought. I'd never seen anything so big and imposing.

The people inside the railings were busy and rushing around. I looked and wondered if the Three were already inside but saw no sign of them. I'd heard that they travelled in a big, long car like the rich and famous used to. What were they called? Limes? Lemas? Something like that. Either way, I saw no fancy cars, so assumed I was early.

The other people in the crowd seemed to buzz with excitement. I heard people talking about the Three and their Light, and they sounded totally in awe. A few people kept quiet and rolled their eyes, so I stayed close to them.

I didn't need to be stuck in the middle of a group of Lightborn fangirls. Knowing it was smarter to have a clear exit, I tried to keep to the crowd's edge. But when everyone started chattering and moving in, I couldn't help myself. I slipped between people until I was right at the railing. The big car coming in impressed even me.

Brother Uri stepped out first, and the crowd went wild. They were hooting and screaming as Brothers Anwar and Oran climbed out, joining Uri with their fake grins and waves.

The people seemed to lose their minds, pushing me forward into the railing. I grabbed hold and tried to get my balance as they shoved me from behind.

The second my hands touched the steel, I felt wrong. I lifted my hands but was pushed forward again and had no choice but to hold on. With my hands on the metal, I felt something rush through me and knew that it was a barrier, like the one near the Ludus.

Panic set in as I looked up. Two Lightborn were looking my way and moving toward a few security guards. They spoke quickly, pointing toward where I stood before marching my way. I ducked and slipped between legs, trying to keep my head down and out of sight, desperately trying to find my way to the edge of the crowd.

Risking a look back, I saw the Lightborn at the railing, questioning the closest fans.

Frazzled, I looked around, trying to find an escape. I was *this* close to opening a portal and running home when I saw a large truck pulling up to my left. It stopped barely ten feet from where I stood, and I made my move. Racing behind the big truck, I caught my breath before moving behind a few cars that were parked not too far away.

As I risked a look back, I was relieved to see the truck blocking me from view. Using the truck's cover, I was able to make my way back to the bus stop.

Luckily, they ran on a tight schedule, and I only had minutes to wait. From the bus window, I could see the security guards making their way through the crowd and the Lightborn taking people to the side for questioning.

Why had I been so stupid? What had I expected from going there?

I saw the Brothers. Ok, great. It fixed nothing, and

it almost got me caught. How would that have helped anyone?

The bus drove into the city, picking up and dropping people off along the way. I kept my seat by the window and let the world go by. Part of me wanted to stay on the bus and go to the Ludus. I knew they would be worried, but I just couldn't face them.

I couldn't face the sadness, and I couldn't face any more guilt. So I sat with my head against the window as the city faded and the buildings got smaller.

Feeling desperately hopeless, I just wanted to stop worrying about the Veil and ignore it for another day. I didn't have the strength to go there.

Instead, I allowed myself time to be normal, doing something I hadn't in ages. I got off the bus in Township 4 and went to see a movie. They were playing a couple of recent releases and some older films.

I chose a movie called Shaun of the Dead because they billed it as a comedy, and I needed a laugh. It worked too. For the first time in a while, I thought of nothing other than the zombie apocalypse, laughing at the thought of Alexis playing a zombie. Something I just couldn't picture.

Maybe one day, I would go to the movies, and her name would be on the poster. That would be a good day.

When I left the movie theatre, I was feeling lighter and almost happy. Shaun survived the zombie apocalypse, so we would survive this, right? We would figure out a way, I was sure.

Walking home, it got darker, but just like the other day, I wasn't stopped. Today of all days, I assumed the security guys would be busy in the city.

Having the Brothers in town was a big deal, and we

were the least of their worries. So I dawdled and tried to keep calm as I got closer. I wouldn't let my mother ruin my mood. I wouldn't let her make me feel guilty. She had no right. For once, I let myself believe it wasn't my fault. And even if it was, she was just as much to blame.

The car outside our house made me stop at the corner. Alexis must have liked this guy, but who was he to have access to a private vehicle? I kept walking and hoped to get inside without them seeing me, but stopped in my tracks when another car pulled up. And then another.

The front door to my house opened, and I saw Alexis crying and holding onto a man. Her boyfriend? He shrugged her off, leaving her to scream at the door.

From the other cars, a group of men emerged.

Lightborn.

"No! Please!" Alexis cried.

She left the house and grabbed onto the guy again, pleading with him. Then I saw Uncle Mark and Frankie in the doorway, and my heart sank.

They were being taken, just like Dad.

I ran forward, wanting to stop it. I wouldn't let this happen, not again. "Wait! Wait, you can't-" I started.

"There she is," my mother spat.

I hadn't seen her come outside. She stood in front of my Uncle and cousin, her cold eyes on mine as she pointed me out.

"Her."

To my utter shock, the Lightborn all looked my way. They left my family where they stood and surrounded me. I wanted to do something, but I had no idea what. If it was just the security guards, I could get away easily.

But a dozen Lightborn surrounded me. If I opened a

portal, they were all close enough to follow. I had no way out.

"No! Mum, no! Please!" Alexis was still crying, and I looked to see my mother holding her back.

The surrounding men told me to stay calm and not to move. I couldn't even if I wanted to.

They put their hands on me, tying my hands behind my back. They took me forward toward the cars, the Lightborn ready to strike should I have tried anything.

But I didn't.

I just looked at my family. Uncle Mark was holding my poor crying cousin. He seemed to be in shock as I passed by.

Then I saw my sister. She was on the floor, sobbing and pleading for them to let me go. It brought tears to my eyes, and I had to blink them away.

My mother was standing in front of Alexis, holding her back. I watched her go to her knees and wipe the tears away from my sister's eyes. My mother hugged my sister and shushed her to keep her calm.

As they put me in the car, I watched Alexis struggle to breathe and grab at my mother, screaming for them to stop.

And then I saw my mother clearly.

I saw her stand very still, even as Alexis was hysterical and pulling at her shirt.

I saw her face. Her eyes were cold and unmoved.

I saw them watch me being taken away, and I felt her betrayal deep inside. The hatred she'd been holding back for so long had finally been revealed.

She turned her back to me and took Alexis inside.

I saw her look back to where I sat.

I saw her dry eyes as she pushed my family inside the

house.

And I saw my world end as she shut the door.

# CHAPTER 17

Uri put his tablet down and watched his Brothers working. It was repetitive and frustrating, and they were all close to giving up.

They'd visited one arena the day prior, and at these there, things were coming along nicely. They would spend the next week attending the rest and putting up their barriers. The truth was, he was looking forward to getting away. His wife was driving him nuts.

"I just don't see why you all need to go, Uri. Can't you split the appearances between you?"

Kayla had been bugging him about the trip since the announcement. She thought it was nothing more than a public appearance.

"Kay, we've talked about this. And it's one week! I offered to have someone come help with the babies."

"I don't want some stranger in the house," she snapped.

Uri rolled his eyes. His twins were just six months old, and their young, first-time mother was a little over-protective.

"Not some stranger. I was thinking of inviting Maya to come stay,"

"For the love of the Brothers, Uri. You think we'd survive a week alone? Come on!"

"She loves the boys. She'd be happy to help."

Uri hadn't seen his oldest daughter in some time. She was working in Australia as an ambassador for the Brotherhood. Maya hadn't been thrilled when Uri remarried a woman who was hardly older than her, but he knew she cared about her siblings and would come home in a heartbeat if he asked.

"Just forget it. We'll manage," Kayla said in a tone he recognised.

But he didn't have the time or patience for her nonsense. In reality, he was planning on bringing Maya home anyway for the Tournament. He wanted her close for when they finally opened the portal.

The Three had been looking through Lightborn profiles for weeks but had come up empty. Not one showed any kind of aptitude for time travel. Anwar found the talent in his teens after getting into a fight. Having lost miserably, he went to the bathroom to clean himself up. After closing his eyes in frustration, he found himself standing under the same tree, thirty minutes prior, his bully's fists already raised.

He was too shocked to use his knowledge as an advantage and took the beating a second time. But he quickly realised his power and could soon control it.

If any younger Lightborn had shown anything like it, they would have been informed. But years had gone by without so much as a whisper of such gifts.

With the Tournament approaching, they set guidelines and challenges to test those that entered. Having the Light didn't make you all-powerful, and some Lightborn showed very little control over their abilities.

Uri had seen some that could do no more than control small electronics. In some, the spark was so low they hardly deserved their time at the School of Light.

Those Lightborn would be eliminated during the first couple of rounds but would likely stay to watch and would, therefore, be a source from which they could syphon. Every spark was vital at this point, even if his Brother didn't think so.

“I just don’t see a subtle way of using time control in a game,” Anwar blurted out, bringing Uri’s attention back to the room. “How can we encourage any of them to potentially jump without explicitly saying it?”

This was their newest obstacle. They needed to be sure that if any of the Lightborn in the Tournament had such a gift, they would be found, and not get eliminated in another game.

“There has to be something,” Oran started. “Maybe something less physical?”

“Less physical, how?” Uri asked.

“Most of our trials are asking them to use their power to create fire or move heavy objects or fight toward a totem. Maybe this needs to be a trial of the mind. Set them a task and see if they can figure out how to accomplish it.” Oran smiled, proud of himself.

“A trial of the mind? Sounds a little boring,” Anwar snarked.

Oran stood and sipped at a smoothie while he organised his thoughts.

“Think about it. This isn’t like the other Tournaments. Those were nothing more than Roman Games. We paraded our Gladiators out to distract the commonfolk from their problems, and it worked. Seeing their Light in the flesh left all the plebs in awe. Look at our power! Golly gee, what a display! Some Lightborn got a trophy, and we got to remind people of why we’re superior, right?”

"Yeah, ok. So?"

"So? So now we're looking for someone to join our ranks. We're not just looking for some brute that can knock all the other brutes down. We need someone smart. We need someone level headed that can be another voice in our Brotherhood."

Uri nodded. "He's right. Even if we don't want anyone smart enough to figure our plans out, we can make it seem like we do. Some tests of the mind would do that, and it would help us find who we're looking for."

"And how do we do that?" Anwar asked, mad that his Brothers agreed yet again.

"Oran's right. We need to set them a task. Something that can only be solved by jumping through time or a portal." Uri was standing too now, pacing and trying to think.

"Again, how?"

"Maybe if you helped us think and stopped being so damn negative, we'd figure it out, Anwar."

Uri was losing his temper. They were all responsible for what was going on in the world, but Anwar was so intent on holding them back.

"Ok, ok," Oran began. "We're all a little tense. It's a lot, I know-"

"Don't bother, Oran. I'm fine," Anwar said in a surprisingly calm tone. "Uri's right. I'll try to come up with something."

Uri looked at Oran and then back to Anwar. "Good then. Ok. Let's think."

They didn't come up with anything but agreed to keep working on it. It didn't need to be elaborate, but it needed to be tough enough for a portal to be the only way forward.

Uri found his twins at the kitchen counter when he arrived home. They were strapped in their chairs, watching their mother fret around the stove. She was cooking something and mumbling to herself as she moved. Of course, Uri always told her not to bother cooking, but she insisted.

Before she married Uri, Kayla had been a writer working for a magazine that wasn't always fond of the Brotherhood. But her articles were fair and fact-based.

Anwar wanted total control over the media initially, but Uri convinced him it was vital to have a negative press. They couldn't be seen as dictators, even if that's what they were. They had to give people the illusion of free will.

Instead, they started their own channel and gave people their twisted version of the truth. It wasn't mandatory viewing, but their followers tuned in willingly, their ignorance preventing them from asking too many questions. They absorbed the Three's alternate facts like the blind sheep they were. Never questioning a thing or thinking for themselves.

"Smells good, babe," he gushed as he hugged her from behind.

She jumped slightly before leaning into him. "Well, I figured you deserved something special before you go away."

"It's just a week, Kay. I'll be back before you know it."

They ate with the boys, and Uri helped to bathe and put them to bed. Kayla went up early, leaving Uri in front of the tv. An old movie was playing, and he laughed at the poor CGI.

Now, they had Lightborn working with directors to create anything they wanted - no more green screens and prosthetics.

When his phone buzzed, Uri was just falling asleep, though he knew who it was without looking. He left the phone and got up, moving to meet the caller at the front door.

"Sorry, it's so late. I got held up."

"It's fine, Tim. Come on in,." Uri stood aside and let the man through.

Tim walked straight to the office without asking.

"Anything I should know?"

"No, just some kids being dumb," Tim said as he took a seat on the couch.

"Ok, good. Have you made any progress?" Uri asked as he poured them both a drink.

"Some, but not enough. They're just too good at covering their tracks. But we felt the surge. They met in a sizeable group. Bigger than we've seen in a while. They knew what they were doing, though. They kept their vibrations low, and they were out of the plane too fast for us to find them."

"You've got to be kidding me? They're not all-powerful! We need to find them!"

Uri was frustrated. They had been looking for the underground army for years and always came up a few steps behind.

"Every time we think we're close, they move. Somehow, they know what we're going to do, and they evade us. I've told you-"

Uri waved his hand in dismissal, "I know what you told me, but I vetted your team myself. There's no way you have a leak."

Tim shook his head. He didn't know what else to do.

"Then, all we can do is keep trying. Keep chasing and

hope we get lucky."

"We don't need luck, Tim. We need results! These people are taking young Lightborn every day and training them to work against us!"

"I know, Sir. And we're looking. We'll keep looking, but…their group is practically supernatural. It's big, we know that much. We just can't seem to find them."

Tim looked tired. Ever since they felt a surge of Light no-one could explain, he'd been working tirelessly to find the group responsible. That was five years ago. Since then, they were able to find evidence of a rebel group that took young, powerful boys before they could reach the School of Light. But they could never put a face or name to the group. They were incredibly well hidden, and nobody couldn't figure out how they were communicating.

Uri sighed, "Just keep trying."

Tim left, and Uri returned to his office. When they first found out about the group, Uri worried that they were creating some kind of a rebel army with plans to overthrow the Brotherhood. He figured they would be found and punished quickly, with no one needing to know. But the longer it went on, the more he was convinced they were something else.

When it became clear that the Cloaks wouldn't hold up much longer, Uri made a decision. He doubled down on finding the rebel group, intending to lay all the blame at their feet. They would be his scapegoat, should their plan of opening a portal fail.

Blaming them would mean the Brotherhood could remain in control.

He just needed to find them.

# CHAPTER 18

I'd never been in a car before. As I sat in the back between two monstrous Lightborn, all I could think was what it must've been like to own a car.

They were outlawed not long after the Blackout. It was a way for the Brotherhood to create jobs and keep people under control. Uncle Mark told me that lots of people secretly hid their cars for years and years, letting them rust and rot, just to spite the Brothers.

This car wasn't rusted. The seats were cool black leather, and there was dark wood in the door. I could see that the windows were controlled by a small button on the door and the stick in the front middle controlled... well, something.

The windows were black so people couldn't see in, but I could see them. All of them.

We were quite the spectacle, our convoy of private cars. No one had seen anything like it outside of the city, I was sure. So people were curious, and I wondered how long before the rumours flew.

I knew from school that the Brothers' compound was somewhere south of the old capital. Was that where we were going? The School of Light wasn't far from there. Maybe they were taking me to enrol!

Looking out the window, I didn't recognise much of

what I saw after we passed the city. I'd never been this far in my entire life, and although I knew this road could only end in pain, I actually felt a hint of excitement.

Somehow, I fell asleep against one of the arms beside me. He must have felt sorry for me because he let me sleep, fitfully, against his massive arm. When I woke up, I'm pretty sure he gave me a sad smile before turning sour and looking out the window.

"Two minutes," the driver called back.

I sat up straight and craned my neck to see where we were. The compound's wall was an odd sight in the countryside, and as we came over a hill, I could see inside the border. I recognised the Great Hall from the books in school, but I didn't know what the other buildings were. One looked like an office maybe, and another looked like a house. The others were too far to really tell.

The closer we got, the taller the wall appeared, and I couldn't see anymore. The road hugged the bricks until we reached the gates. These I had definitely seen before. They were in all the books about the Three.

These gates represented them and their secrecy. What was behind these gates was absolute power, and nobody could enter without approval - which was basically nobody. Although I think I read something about tours of the Great Hall in a magazine once.

The gates were massive, and I felt like they were enhanced somehow. They looked like they were looming over us, and the closer we got, the higher they seemed to go. The Brothers' emblem was front and centre, and as we pulled up, I could see it glimmering with no sunlight.

The cars stopped for the briefest moment before the

gates swung open silently, and we made our way inside.

As we crossed the threshold, I immediately felt the power. We'd always assumed that the Brothers safeguarded their land and placed some kind of force field around it, much like that around Township 11.

But I felt strange. I was cold, and the further in we drove, the worse it got. The men beside me didn't seem to feel anything, and I wondered if this was the Brothers' Light or just my nerves.

We drove by the Great Hall, and I tried to not look so amazed. I'd read about old churches and temples, but I'd never seen anything like it in reality.

The building was beautiful and clearly designed to inspire awe in the Brothers' followers. As we passed by, I noticed that our convoy's other cars took a left where we took a right.

The road was lined with flowers I was sure were never supposed to bloom in our colder climate. Despite myself, I smiled and gazed, leaning over the Lightborn beside me. Again, he didn't seem to mind, though he kept his smile hidden this time.

Up ahead, I saw one building I'd seen from outside the compound. The bottom half was old stone, and I wondered what it had been before all this. They'd built a new, all-glass structure on top of the rock - the new and the old. Very fitting for The Headquarters of The Brotherhood of Lights - or so the sign out front said.

“Let's go,” the driver ordered without looking back.

We stopped in front of the doors and found three nervous-looking Lightborn waiting on the steps. They looked young, probably fresh out of school, heads down, feet fidgeting.

I noticed that they kept their eyes low as the men

in the car approached. Nobody spoke when they turned and opened the doors, leading our small group inside, passed a front desk, and to an elevator that we all somehow fit in.

I felt small and powerless, surrounded by men who wouldn't even look at me. They were all tense now, though, I could tell. I noticed clenched fists and shuffling feet. Who could blame them? Considering where we were and what was waiting for us.

The ridiculously large room took up most of the floor. It was filled with a gigantic table, and at least a dozen chairs and the Three were sitting about as far from each other as the space would allow. They each looked furious and impatient.

Anwar had a fowl look on his face. I saw him sigh and noticed a hint of an eye roll. I watched Uri look at his Brother, and I saw him shake his head ever so slightly. Oran was on the end, eating French fries, seemingly oblivious to their frustrations.

He noticed us first, and we made eye contact. His brow furrowed as he scanned the unusual group, and before I knew it, the Three were looking directly at me.

"What's going on?" Anwar asked impatiently as we all entered the room. "Please don't tell me you called us back here for this!"

The three nervous Lightborn scurried away, back to their desks before they had to explain anything.

"Don't tell me this little girl made it over the wall?" Uri laughed, looking me up and down.

"No, Sir. It's something else, Sir."

"We're kind of busy, and we had to come a long way back, so this better be good. Get on with it," Anwar shouted, and I'm pretty sure I felt the man next to me flinch.

The few seconds of silence that followed were excruciating. I steeled a glance up and saw the Lightborn looking to each other, hoping someone else would talk, no doubt.

"Speak!" Anwar's voice boomed across the room, and I took a step back, lowering my eyes as I trembled.

"She…she has the Light, Sir's,"

"She...she what?"

"I got a call, Sirs. From someone in my Township claiming that she has the Light."

"You got a call…" Uri stood and came forward to within a few feet of me. "And you got proof, I assume?"

"Well…no-not exactly. We-we thought it best to bring her to you."

My eyes were still cast down, and I didn't dare look up. But with Uri standing in front of me, I could feel his eyes. My cheeks flushed, and I wondered if he could tell just by looking at me. What if I just refused to show them? Denied it all and pretended I was normal. I doubted that they would just apologise and let me go.

"What's your name?" He asked.

I croaked out a sound and cleared my throat, still unable to look him in the eyes.

"Anya." I managed quietly.

"Anya. 'The one who is bright and shining.'"

I looked up at him, confused.

"The girl who is 'nightless,'" he continued. "Is this true? You have the Light?"

"N-no. No…how could I-" I was stammering and finding it difficult to hear over the sound of my heart beating.

"How could she possibly, Uri?" Oran stood and came

forward.

I noticed he now had a milkshake in his hand, and it made him oddly human. It made me calm slightly.

"Who said she has the Light?" He asked the men around me.

"Her mother," someone replied with ease, but it hit me hard.

I closed my eyes and let out a breath.

"Her mother?" Anwar asked from across the room.

"Yes, Sirs. I have been...well, I mean I was-"

"Spit it out!"

"I was involved with her sister. I met the mother by chance, and she took me aside. She showed me bruises and said that the girl attacked her."

I felt the tears brimming and shook my head. She'd hated me for so long, and this is what it took for her to finally turn on me. Never mind that she hit me first. Not that I had any proof of that.

"Attacked her, how?" Oran asked.

The Three were all standing in front of me now, not inches away. I could smell the milkshake and focused on it, trying to keep my pain hidden.

"She said they argued, and she...well, she said she threw her across the room."

Without warning, Anwar grabbed my chin and raised my head. I felt like a child as we locked eyes, and he searched my face. I didn't know what to do and was embarrassed by the tears that wouldn't stop.

"It's true."

I shook my head, and he took his hand back, squinting his eyes as though he were trying to remember an old face. Nobody spoke for what felt like an hour, and I had a fleeting moment of insanity.

What if I pushed away and opened a portal?

I could get away before they knew what was happening. It wouldn't need to be far, and my Glimmer would be small. Maybe they wouldn't be able to follow...

"Take her upstairs to one of the suites," Anwar instructed suddenly.

"Anwar-"

"Do it now."

Hands were on me again as we trooped out and away. The Three stood where we left them, and I could hear them arguing. Arguing about me. Whether they could force me to reveal my power? Or whether they should just send me to prison, like my father?

My Lightborn guards took me up to another floor, to a suite at the end of a hallway. Not the top level, but close. Were all the other doors suites like this? Who on earth would the Brotherhood be hosting here?

As the door closed behind me, I let out a huge breath that caught in my throat. I fell to my knees and sobbed. Being caught was one thing, but being turned in by my own mother was a betrayal that cut far too deep.

My stomach knotted, and I seethed as the tears fell. But I knew that I had no time to cry. As it stood, I was just an anomaly. A girl with the Light was unheard of, and so I was something they needed to figure out. But if they found out I had the power to open portals, I was toast.

I had to run. Normally, I would need to think long and hard about a time or place I wanted to go, to focus my Light on somewhere specific to make it safely. As a child, it came as naturally to me as breathing. I would think up magical worlds, close my eyes and just find myself there.

As I got older, I became more cautious and less free with my Light. It held me back, I knew. But I hadn't been given a choice after they took my father.

Standing in that room, knowing that the Three were so close, I knew I had no choice. Opening a portal was the only card I had left to play. I doubted that the guards would even know what happened, let alone have the guts to follow me through my Glimmer. And if I kept my jump small, the Glimmer would hopefully be gone by the time the Brothers came running. They would know what I could do, but I would be safe.

The second I was through, I snapped my fists shut, closing the portal. It cracked closed so close behind, I could smell my burnt hair.

It had been such a risk to run, but they hadn't left me with any other options.

Being taken from my home and delivered to the Brotherhood was my worst nightmare.

I'd always tried to be careful with my Light, knowing that if the Brotherhood found out what I was capable of, they would use my power to abandon the world to darkness and decay.

I was what they had been looking for, and I was their ticket out. So when they locked me in that room, I threw caution to the wind and ran.

# PART TWO

# CHAPTER 19

**Way After**

Gabby woke early, knowing it would take most of the day to get there. The sun was beating through the torn drapes and into her eyes, meaning she couldn't sleep even if she wanted to.

She'd packed her bag the night before, and after a quick ration pack, was ready to go. At the door, she took a long, calming breath and nodded to herself.

This was the year.

The rickety tram sped by her door as she stepped onto the sidewalk. At that hour, the streets were mostly quiet, but she knew everyone would be up and out soon enough.

Gabby wanted to be gone by then and took a short cut through the old, demolished condos. The big holes in the stone were jagged and covered in graffiti, so she took her time.

Over the years, most of the glass and rock had been salvaged, leaving the wind to blow from one end to the other.

She'd seen pictures of what the city used to look like, and it always made her sad to see the encompassing desolation. Townships and cities used to be built up and shining. Even before the rise of the Brotherhood, people were building up and up, until skyscrapers started spilling out toward the suburbs.

Apparently, the Brotherhood ordered more buildings to be constructed all over the world, as well as the restoration of older buildings. It was a simple way to provide jobs and keep people in line.

After the Crack, it wasn't six months before they crumbled. Many once stood over a hundred and fifty stories tall. Until the grounds shifted. After that, the tallest building was around sixty floors, and as the rains got worse, the stone began to wear away.

Year after year, the once-grand buildings crumbled under the heat and pressure of the storms.

Further from the cities, the old Townships became just as dangerous. There was less coverage from the weather, and a lot of land was ruined by the decay. Now the Townships were part of bigger Counties and were sparsely populated.

Without Lightborn Leaders, communities had to come together to survive, and most ended up in or around the cities, packing into ruined and crumbling building. Herding together with no other choice.

As she walked through the worn-down city, the sun followed her progress, beating down on her back. It was 6am and already thirty-five degrees. By the time she made it to the station, it would be closer to forty.

And on the Plains, she was looking at temperatures close to fifty degrees. It was always such a challenging trip, but it was too important to miss.

That's why she hoarded cold packs wherever she could find them. They were the only thing that kept her going. Though the heat was preferable to the downpours. Those were so unpredictable these days it was much safer to stay inside.

When Gabby arrived at the station, the line was longer than she'd hoped. She guessed with the rising temperatures, more and more people were starting their days early.

From the back of the line, Gabby watched the slow progress forward. The trams were always packed to the brim, but the trains and buses were more cautious of how many people they took. They didn't want the passengers' weight to cause the vehicle to sink into the soft asphalt or warp the tracks.

After almost an hour, Gabby asked the man behind to hold her position and left her spot in line to visit the vending machines. She had enough for an iced water and an energy bar, and she enjoyed them in the shade of the terminal building. Back in the line, she offered the man water as a thank you. When she realised they hadn't moved an inch, her heart sank.

Good thing she left so early.

Once on the train, Gabby found her seat and opened the window. Standing still, the car was a hot box, and everyone around began removing layers. Gabby took off her two jackets and put them in with her scarf and gloves, and second pair of pants.

People were used to the jarring change in the weather year-round and always carried appropriate clothing should things turn. Gabby had been caught in an ice storm once before, and now she never left home without extra layers.

She thought about removing her boots too but had no idea when she last washed her socks and decided against it. With her head against the glass, she felt the tiniest breeze. She smiled and let herself breathe.

Gabby fell asleep about halfway through the ride. Going to the end of the line, she would feel the brakes kick in. Though she only took the train once a year, it never got any better. She was just happy that it didn't seem worse.

It took years to rebuild the train lines after the grounds moved, and they required constant care. Working on the railroads was a highly sought-after job because there was always work. The ground shifted so often, keeping the trains on their tracks was a full-time job.

"Honey, we're at Southside," the woman across the aisle announced as she stood to gather her things.

"I know. Thanks."

"We won't stop for long. Better get your things," she suggested.

"I'm staying until the end of the line. But thanks," Gabby replied with a slight smile.

"End of the line? What do you have out there? In the Plains?" She looked shocked.

"I'm...meeting someone," Gabby stammered eventually, though it didn't sound convincing.

"It's dangerous in the Plains. You should get off here." She put a hand on Gabby's shoulder. It was warm and clammy.

"It's not my first trip,"

The woman left the train and watched Gabby go from the platform, clutching her collar as the train slowly moved away.

She was alone now; she knew. Nobody ever went further than Southside. Why would they? All that was out there was sand and glass and heat.

Oh, and the Gulls. And they would see and hear her

coming.

Gabby needed to be quick upon arrival. If she hesitated, they would swarm and take everything she had, and she would never make it across the Plains.

The conductor announced a five-minute warning and Gabby used the time to collect her things, make her way to the door, and get ready to run. The train slowed, and she scanned the fields. No movement. No buildings.

The sun beat on the rocks and glass, shimmering in the distance. The sky was clear. That was good. Not even the Gulls liked to be out on such a clear day. Not in the high heat.

But the sun shining meant nothing really. A downpour could start in less than a minute, and Gabby didn't want to be stuck in the Plains when that happened.

The minute the doors opened, Gabby was on the move. She hugged the train to the end of the platform and made a beeline for what was left of the trees. The charred stumps were short but gave her some coverage.

She was through in minutes and made her way to the remnants of an old house. It was down a hill, hidden from the train and missing half its roof. But she knew it was there.

Gabby tried to change her route every year, but there were only so many ruined structures between her and her destination. She would use them as she made her way across the open, desolate fields. It took longer, but she needed to know she had somewhere to shelter if the worst happened.

The area known as the Plains used to be farmland. Just south of the city, it was all sprawling hills and trees and nature. The site of the Crack was right in the middle, and the closer she got, the worse the grounds became.

Any grass that made its way to the surface was burned black until it flew away like embers in the wind. The skies were angry no matter the time of day, and the wind blew humid air in vicious circles. Fire fell from the clouds, and grotesque creatures roamed, looking for food and water they would never find.

The only good thing about getting closer to the site was that the Gulls never came so far.

Gabby came over the last hill and stopped at its peak. The compound stood as empty and burned as ever. The towering walls that once protected the land had crumbled to knee height, and the gates had been blown apart years ago.

Seventeen years of fire and rot had worked to destroy almost all the buildings inside. But the Hall stood tall in the middle. The pictures she had seen were so impressive and beautiful. The green fields, the river in the back, the ornate gates, and the great hall. It had been quite a sight.

Through the darkness, Gabby spotted a glimmer of light on the horizon. She picked up her pace, knowing she had to make it to the hall before the rains fell. If it caught her outside, she wouldn't make it. Her legs ached with the effort, but she ran. She ran down the long road that led to the entrance until the wall became low enough to climb over.

The patches of dull, yellow grass amongst the black always amused Gabby, and she would often take her boots off to feel it under her toes.

But the light was coming up on her, and she didn't have long. She heaved the enormous door closed, and not minutes later, the rains came.

Above her, the skies rumbled and flashed, and the rain poured at a tremendous rate. Gone were the days of light showers.

She closed her eyes and remembered how it felt to go out and dance in the rain as a child. She used to love the feeling of the fresh water on her skin. But she hadn't been able to do that for years. The rains had gotten to the point it would cut through the skin if you stood out in it too long.

Gabby breathed a sigh of relief as she took in the Hall. After seventeen years, somehow, it remained intact. The scorch of the Crack still smelled, and the black line that split the Hall was as prominent as ever. She could just about see the blood on the floor and couldn't help but picture the carnage of that night.

She had felt it her whole life.

It was why she came here on the anniversary every year. Gabby had been so young when the Three abandoned the world, but she felt the pull to this place for as long as she could remember. Though she didn't know why, she knew she needed to be here.

# CHAPTER 20

**4 1/2 weeks to the Tournament**

"She's not even trying!"

"You know that's not true- look at her!"

"It's been three weeks, Oran. Three! We should have our plan ready to go by now, but she's holding back. I can tell." Anwar came upon me fast and grabbed my arm. "You're not getting out of this. You will make this work or so help me-"

"That's enough. Let her go," Uri insisted in a tired voice. "Anwar! Leave her. You've been trying this for years and come up empty, so what makes you think this girl, with only a handful of years experience, will do it in just a few short weeks?"

I snatched my arm back as Uri berated his Brother. This was my new normal. I would try and fail to open a portal to some unknown world, and Anwar would get mad. Oran would stand up for me, and Uri would yell. And then Anwar would yell, and someone would storm away. It was getting exhausting.

"I'm trying my best," I said weakly. "I'm not strong enough to do what you want."

Anwar narrowed his eyes and scoffed. He didn't believe me for a second. "You and I both know that's a lie. I can tell you're holding back. I can feel that you're not letting your mind go somewhere, but I don't know why. You know what will happen to your family if you fail us-"

"I know! You won't let me forget!"

I learned to stand up for myself somewhat over the weeks. They needed me, not the other way around. And keeping my smart mouth under wraps was just too much, given everything else I was trying to hide.

"But like he said, if the great Anwar hasn't been able to-"

He hit me then. Square in the jaw and I fell to the ground. Anwar stood over me, practically vibrating with anger. But I was mad too and reacted without thinking.

Anwar shot back into the wall and then up to the ceiling. I stood with my arms raised, and it gave me such joy to see the look of shock on his face.

When I suddenly closed my fist, he fell to the ground, but Uri stopped him from hitting the stone.

I turned on my heel and left before he could get up and yell at me some more. Still, I could hear him through the walls as I picked up Ozzie and ran back to the main house.

It had been a week since I sent Ozzie to the Ludus with my SOS.

Every day I looked toward the gate, hoping to see them coming for me.

Every day I wondered where they were and what they were planning.

And every day I was disappointed.

A week wasn't that long. I knew that. They would need time to prepare and make a plan. I just had to be patient.

My altercation with Anwar had me all riled up, so I took Ozzie for a walk instead of going back to my room. He was happy to be out, and I needed to breathe. I tried to go in different directions on our walks to get an idea of the compound's size. So far, I'd found two houses hidden from me, and I was sure the furthest belonged to Oran. He and his dogs always came from that direction, closer to the river. But I couldn't tell anything about the other.

After an hour or so, Ozzie and I made our way home. I was hungry, and I figured he would be too. We walked up the little hill that led to the mystery house, and I stopped us both before reaching the peak. A car was moving toward the area with the Glimmer.

As it got closer to where I could feel the Light, it seemed to blur and fracture until I couldn't see it anymore. This wasn't a car I recognised, and my curiosity got the best of me.

Ozzie stood vigil at my side, and I took in a breath, "I need you again, Sweet Boy."

After a quick scratch behind his ears, he bounded forward toward the house. As he moved closer, I closed my eyes and listened. We'd done this a few times over the last week and were getting better. I could hear Ozzie panting and the sound of the wind as he ran, and I felt the warmth of the Light as he breached the border. All I could hope was anyone watching would wave him off.

Muffled voices came to my ears, and I put my whole mind toward them. Ozzie moved accordingly until he must've been standing outside the room they were speaking. But it was hard to focus on them, and I was worried I would miss the whole conversation. Ozzie must have sensed my frustration and lay down to calm himself because suddenly, it all became clear.

"Then why are we talking right now?" It was Uri, and he sounded angry.

"They didn't actually find anyone, but they found their residual energy. A sizeable group was there."

I didn't recognise the second voice, but it still made me nervous.

"Where?"

"Near Paris."

"Paris? Who's in charge there?"

"Boucher. I talked to him, and he had no clue."

"Why would he? He's just the one in charge!"

"I know. But I talked to my men there, and they put me in touch with someone. A Community Leader who moved there around five years ago."

My heart stopped. Paris. Five years ago. I didn't like where this was going.

"Five years?" Uri asked.

"He said that five years ago when he just arrived, he noticed their Security Force wasn't at the same standard as his last post, which had been a smaller area. He noticed that a lot of boys in his area were being sent out to the country."

"Agriculture?"

"That's right. This guy started asking questions, and then a few months later, there seemed to be an influx of students from his area sent to the School of Light."

I felt sick. Five years ago, the Ludus near Paris had to be shut down because some Lightborn was asking too many questions. Did Uri know about them? How could that be?

"So they're taking the boys before they can be sent to our school...teachers?" Uri sounded excited.

"It can only be. Nobody else would have that kind of access." The second voice was calmer now that Uri wasn't so mad.

"And this latest surge. You're saying you can't trace it?"

"This is the closest we've gotten. Normally we feel the power, but we can't pinpoint it. This time, we traced it to Paris. They met in a hurry, that's for sure."

"What could have them so-"

I ran. I called Ozzie to me, and we ran back to my room without breaking stride.

Uri knew about the Ludus.

He knew about all of it.

It sounded like he'd been looking for years, and I might have just led him straight to them. The meeting could only have been about me - they had to meet in a hurry because I was in danger. I'd put them at risk, and I was sure Uri would quickly put it all together.

What happened recently that could cause the rebels to meet so fast?

How did a girl with the Light slip through the cracks for so long?

He was probably already on his way.

# CHAPTER 21

My legs were heavy, and I was weak from the loss of blood. But I ran on, trying to keep the distance between us as big as possible. As the water's edge came into view, I pushed harder and faster, opening my hands and summoning every ounce of strength I had left.

The water rippled as my Light hit, and the portal opened. The purple shimmer was dull, but it held, and I ran and kept running as I reached the beach.

I ran straight into the water and out the other side. The moment I touched dry land, I closed the portal, clutching at my stomach and gasping for air.

My hands came back covered in blood. I needed help and fast.

Looking around, I had no idea where or when I was. When the orange Glimmer appeared, I could smell the air burning behind me.

The Three stepped out together, their hands raised as I sank to my knees and-

I woke with a start, heaving for air. Ozzie shot to the bed to check on me, and I soon caught my breath. The dream was so vivid; I checked my stomach for a wound and sighed in relief when my hand came back clean. After what I'd heard the night before, I had been so sure that Uri was coming for me. So sure that I'd forgotten my spark to ensure a dreamless night.

But he never came. Either he hadn't put it together, which I highly doubted, or he was waiting to speak with his Brothers first. Though, Uri didn't come across as the kind to check in before making any decisions.

It was barely light out, but I knew I couldn't sleep more after that dream. Since the day before had been a long day of using my Light, I assumed I was free. Ozzie and I made our way downstairs to go walk but were stopped at the desk by the nervous trio of Lightborn. Did they ever leave?

"You have to stay in today," one smirked without looking up.

"Excuse me?" I asked.

"Orders from the Three. You are to stay inside until further notice."

I scoffed and moved to the door, which one of them slammed shut with the flick of his wrist.

"We have been told to call security should you not comply."

"He needs to go out," I complained, motioning to Ozzie.

"He's not real. He'll be fine."

I wanted to smack his smug face but held myself back. Ozzie looked sad to be missing his walk, but we behaved. After what happened with Anwar and what I heard from Uri, I figured it would be safer to stay quiet.

So we made our way back to our floor. I left my door open and threw a ball down the hallway, letting Ozzie run around. It made me happy to watch him.

But the hours droned on, and both Ozzie and I felt restless. Had they just forgotten to come get me? Or had that man from the night before found something?

The longer they left me alone, the more panicked I

became.

I started running scenarios out in my head, and they all ended poorly. I could never forgive myself if anything happened to Mr Parks and everyone at the Ludus. They were my family, and they'd met in Paris to discuss my rescue, of that much I was absolutely sure.

It was close to 1pm when I finally lost patience. Ozzie was sleeping on his bed when I snuck out, making my way down to the floor with the conference room. If the Brothers were in the building, I assumed that's where I'd find them.

But the room was empty.

I tried two other floors which looked to never have been used, and they were deserted too. The only people I came across were the three twitchy Lightborn at the front desk. I chose to avoid them.

The building's first floor had a few rooms that I could see. Since I couldn't see any guards around, I opened a few doors. There were lots of boxes and dusty tables and realised that the entire building was just for show.

At the end of the hallway, I found a screening room. It looked like a private theatre with big, plush chairs and a gigantic screen. It was almost comical to picture the Three and their families coming in here for movie night.

I sat in the middle and relaxed into the soft velvet. The seats reclined, and I put mine all the way back. It was almost pleasant. As I moved to stand, I found other controls in the arm, and after pushing some buttons at random, the screen came on.

After flicking through some channels, the news filled the screen. My mouth dropped as I watched the story unfold.

"...unknown what has brought this on. We have been given almost no information and can only report on what we're seeing. According to people inside the schools, the Lightborn simply walked in and took over. Students have been sent home, but teachers appear to be confined to their classrooms. A source at a local elementary school has told NewsNow that they are being held and questioned."

I sat straight up, watching in horror as the news showed images from all over the world. Teachers were being interrogated by Lightborn, and nobody knew why. I thought back to the conversation I'd overheard the night before, but the man said they found nothing. They knew they met in Paris, but that was it.

And Uri's suggestion that teachers were responsible was just a guess. Surely they hadn't found a smoking gun in less than a day? I didn't know how many people were in Mr Parks's Network, but it only took one weak link for it all to come crashing down.

The news kept playing the same story over and over, and I watched it all, my eyes widening as they turned to my school. My colleagues. My friends.

Stuck in my prison, there was no way to help. I needed to get out, and after realising I'd felt no intrusions that day, a plan formed within seconds. There hadn't been a single glimpse from the Three into my mind. That meant the Brothers were busy, and I had a little leeway.

It occurred to me that if I was successful, I would be giving myself away. There would be no doubt about my association with the so-called rebel group. But I was almost positive Uri had figured that out, anyway.

Choosing not to waste any time, I stood in the theatre

room and started pacing. I had never been to Paris, but I'd seen pictures and was confident I could make it. I just had to keep that Tower in the front of mind my and let the rest go.

Taking a deep breath, I allowed myself the time to think. The warmth from my Light filled the room as the portal appeared. It shimmered purple, blue, and pink as it opened, and I breathed a sigh of relief when I saw the base of the Tower.

With no time to waste, I ran. I ran straight through, closed the portal, and then kept on running. Making it to the Eiffel Tower was huge, but I suddenly realised that my plan ended there. A few people around me seemed confused by my sudden appearance, watching after me as I took off toward the city. I wanted to be in the small streets, hidden amongst the locals for as long as possible.

I ran through a park and across the busy streets until I found myself surrounded by people. If the Brothers tried to sneak into my mind, I hoped that my proximity to hundreds of people would throw them off.

They couldn't know yet where I was, so I figured I was at least half safe. Near the Louvre, I sat amongst the tourists while I caught my breath and for a moment, I let myself take in the beauty of the gardens and the river. The sun was shining, and the worry was gone just for a minute.

But my moment of calm didn't last long. Security guards in the area started getting twitchy. No doubt, the local Lightborn felt my Light, and they were putting the word out.

I just needed to stay calm and look like I belonged. When I stood to leave, I took my time, strolling through the park, stopping to look at the flowers as I went. It was hard to keep my cool, but I made it out of sight before running again.

The narrow streets made me feel oddly calm, and I eventually found myself wandering and taking in the city. It amazed me that I felt no one trying to pry into my mind, and I wondered if I was truly safe.

If I was safe, what did that mean? Where were the Three that they would just let me go?

Of course, there was still a high likelihood that they could find me. But what if I made it really hard?

What if I had them chasing me all around the world? They wouldn't know where I was going, or why and would be forced to follow my breadcrumbs.

Maybe I could stop near the Ludus, and they would think it was just another random jump. I only came to Paris because Uri already knew about it and because I was almost sure that there was no Ludus close.

With any luck, they would read into it and assume the rebel forces were nearby, when in reality, it couldn’t be further from the Network.

Maybe they would waste enough time in Paris that I could make it to safety?

But I couldn't be sure. I needed to decide if it was safe to jump again and if I was being followed. With each jump, there would be a small surge in power that the local Lightborn would feel. Did they communicate with each other? Would Paris tell Tokyo? Would London inform Sydney? I doubted it.

If I made enough jumps, I would leave a trail that the Brothers would definitely follow.

And if I played it right, I could double back and make it to the Ludus before they caught up with me.

# CHAPTER 22

By the fourth jump, I was starting to feel weak. I left Paris, knowing they could trace my portal and found my way to Prague. An old movie from my childhood featured the big bridge, and I used the memory as a focal point.

With the portal closed, I ran as fast as I could out of sight. From a small corner street, I watched for Lightborn but saw nothing. With my head down, I got some food and spent a couple hours catching my breath.

The next jump was to another landmark I knew I could focus on. The Leaning Tower of Pisa had been the theme for a pizza restaurant near my childhood home. My parents took us there at least once a month, and the Tower featured prominently all over the walls.

It was getting dark when I arrived, making it easier to get out of sight. But when I noticed a group of Lightborn converging on my area, I had to jump sooner than I was ready for.

As the portal closed once more, I had to reach to the wall for support. The exhaustion was overwhelming, and I could feel myself becoming weaker with each jump. Four portals in as many hours took its toll.

Looking around, the chill of the recent snow seeped into my bones, and I found myself wishing my old pen pal lived in a warmer climate. She used to send me pictures of her home when we were younger, and for some reason, those images came to my panicked mind.

I knew I'd made a mistake as I tried to act casual in the cold. It was a quiet, insignificant town in the north of Sweden, and no doubt the local Lightborn were already on their way. In a Township as sleepy as this, it would probably be the highlight of their month.

As weak as I felt, I knew I couldn't stay. But I took the time to sit, breathe, and figure out a suitable place to go next. I just needed to focus and not go too far.

Though I wanted to, it wasn't the right time to jump near the Ludus. I couldn't be sure I had the strength to jump again, and didn't want to be caught anywhere near Township 11.

While I caught my breath, I felt the smallest note of someone trying to read my mind. It was faint, as though they couldn't quite reach me. But it was there. I squeezed my eyes shut to hide my location and sang a song in my head to drown out any other thoughts. The lyrics rolled over and over in my head until I was sure my mind was free.

But that wouldn't be the last time they tried. The Three were on to me, and they would keep coming until they found me.

With no other choice, I knew I needed to make it to the Ludus as soon as possible.

Feeling stressed, I forced myself to stop and think. How close did I want to get? Too close would be dangerous, but not getting close enough would leave me vulnerable and in the open.

I pictured my home, and so desperately wanted to walk into my room and hide under the covers.

I wanted to open my door and find Alexis and Uncle Mark on the couch.

I wanted to hug Frankie as he came running, happy as always, to see me.

But going home would mean facing my mother, and the pain of her betrayal still hung like a cloud over my head, even all these weeks later.

No. I couldn't linger on my pain. *Think.* A portal - but to where?

For some reason, the pancake place in Township 9 stuck out in my head. It was far enough from the Ludus and close enough to home that it could be explained away. The Brothers would assume I was trying to get home, or maybe meet someone close. Though it would be difficult to get to the Ludus on foot, I didn't dare jump any closer.

Standing in a small ally, the snow falling around me, I set my mind to its task. The town was almost silent, giving me a chance to picture the pancake restaurant and the booth we used to sit at. I could practically smell the syrup as I felt my Light warming me. The familiar restaurant shimmered in front of me, and I stepped through, still nervous but determined.

It was dark, and the restaurant was closed. In the kitchen, I made myself something to eat, keeping as quiet as possible. Surely food would help to keep my strength up.

Back in the dining room, my heart tugged toward our old booth. Slowly, I walked forward, sat in my old spot, and let myself be sad. I didn't have the strength to keep it locked away anymore.

The trauma of being ripped from my home and betrayed by my mother was too close to the surface.

I broke. My head dropped to the table as everything rushed up from where I'd tried so hard to hide it.

The anger I felt at The Three was fierce. I balled my fists, digging my nails into my palms, trying to keep them from my mind. But I was furious at them for all the damage they'd caused and the way they were using me.

Then the sadness I felt at leaving Ozzie behind brought a lump to my throat. If only he could've come with me. If only I'd gone to him.

It all crushed me as I cried like the child I once was, in a place that made me so happy for a time.

My sobs echoed in the empty restaurant. I tried to breathe and calm down, wiping my tears, and willing myself to be strong. Being so close to the Ludus was difficult. It would have been easy to open a portal and walk right out in front of that big willow tree. I could be safe in minutes.

But I knew I couldn't let my trail end there. I needed to lead them away so I could come back when I knew it was safe.

The streets were dark and quiet, and I thought about staying in the restaurant to get some sleep. I was so tired, and my Light was waning. Just a couple hours of sleep would have helped. But not here.

If I was going to be caught, it wouldn't be anywhere near the Ludus or my family. Instead, I plucked a landmark from my mind and prepared myself to jump.

For some reason, the Pyramids had been allowed to remain after the Fall. The Elders destroyed so many older landmarks and buildings dedicated to religion. Still, the Pyramids of Giza stood tall in the bleak desert. Standing at the feet of the Sphinx, I took in the wonder.

It was clear how such structures were revered in their day and why the Brothers felt threatened by the power they held. In school, they told us briefly what religion was and had gone into great depths to explain why it was all nothing more than fairy tales to make people feel better.

There were no Gods in the clouds or spirits watching over us. The only thing we needed to know was that the Brotherhood was all-powerful and always watching. For that, at least, we had tangible proof.

I thought about that as I made my way toward the city. They were always watching, and the Lightborn would likely already be alerted to my presence. All I could hope was to make it to the city to hide. My body and my Light needed rest, and I had no choice but to try to find a place to sleep.

The dark and dusty road ran from the Pyramids to the city, and I followed it quickly, not wanting to be out in the open for too long. I reached the town within a few minutes and hesitated while trying to decide which way to go.

My heart stopped when I heard someone yell.

To my right, I saw three Lightborn heading my way. Panic set in as I turned to run the other way, only to find two more coming right for me.

The only free road was behind, and I took it, trying desperately to wrack my brain for another location.

An image of the canals in Venice popped up, and I didn't have time to think. I shut my eyes as I ran and held my fists tight until my Light was strong enough.

The warmth hit my face, and I smiled, relieved my Light was still strong.

Seconds later, I realised my fists were still tight.

When I opened my eyes, a portal tore through the darkness in front of me, glimmering in orange and red.

To my horror, Anwar stepped out on the path, not twenty feet away.

I slipped in the dust, falling as I tried to stop. Not wanting to be anywhere near him, I scrambled back, jumping to my feet.

But the Lightborn were still coming from the city. As I looked back to Anwar, my heart dropping to my stomach when Uri and Oran step from the portal.

"You're done, Anya. This is done," Uri cautioned in a calm and icy voice.

He raised his hands to halt the Lightborn. They stopped short and moved until they had me flanked. Ready to attack at their leaders' word.

"I'm not going back!" I yelled.

Anwar laughed, flicked his wrist, and I felt the power as he lifted me off the ground. He let me linger in the air, my feet just scraping the floor.

"You're coming back, and you're going to show us a real portal."

He snapped his fist closed, letting me fall to the ground. I landed harder than I should have and felt the air rush from my lungs.

"I...won't..."

"Anya," Oran stepped forward as I got to my feet. "You're weak. You've exhausted your Light. You know that we'll be able to follow you wherever you go from here."

I looked him in the eyes and thought I saw an apology on his face. His brow furrowed slightly, and his lips turned thin in a sigh. He shook his head and took another step forward. Instinctively, I moved back a few too many steps and ran into one of the men behind me. He put his hands on my arms and held me in place.

"Calm down, she's not a threat," Oran said, raising his palm to the man holding me.

I saw red.

Not a threat?

They needed me to open a portal to another world to save them! Something even the great Anwar couldn't do. And they thought I wasn't a threat?

I felt my anger swell, and the Light in my hand tingled. The man holding me stumbled back as the electricity grew.

"Anya, no!" Oran yelled.

But it was too late. I turned to the men surrounding me and raised my hands, letting my power fly. It dove into the sand and came up in lighting shards of glass. The two Lightborn in my sights screamed as they lit up and fell to the ground.

"Oran!" Uri called as I turned back to face them.

He looked shocked and, dare I say, a little scared as I raised my hands once more.

"Stop this!" Uri yelled, rushing forward to stand by his Brother.

Anwar stood still, his mouth open, his eyes unblinking.

I felt nothing but anger as I lifted my hands to the sky. Something brushed at my side but swept it away.

Out of the corner of my eye, I noticed one of the locals flying back into the darkness. Good. One less to worry about.

As my Light grew, I felt stronger and more in control than ever. Sand and wind tore around us, and all I could hear was my father's voice, telling me how strong I was.

When I closed my fists and pulled my hands down, I felt a surge release from inside. My Light hit the men around me, and then a great warmth and energy seemed to encase me.

To my side, I saw nothing but ash and dust. In front, the Three stood unharmed but obviously dishevelled. They looked dumbfounded, and that made me as happy as I'd ever felt.

Their mouths were moving as they came forward, but I heard nothing. The ringing in my ears was too intense. It would take nothing more than a flick of the wrist, I knew. I could kill them then and there.

Determined to end it, I tried to lift my hands once more.

They wouldn't move.

"...be ok. Anya, can you hear me? Uri! Quickly!"

I heard Oran, though he sounded faint.

Somehow, I was on the floor. The Three were at my side as Oran took my head in his hands and spoke to me.

I watched in a daze as Uri moved to my side and felt some pressure near my hip. When he came back into view, his hands were red, and his face was solemn.

Anwar stood back, watching me with a look of absolute disdain.

I felt the pressure again, and then a different kind of warmth spread through me. Oran looked away, worry creasing his brow. He was handsome. That much I couldn't deny. But could I trust him?

The warmth seemed to fade as I lay in the dust, and a chill filled my heart. Oran looked to me again and called to Anwar and Uri for help.

I saw Uri shake his head.

Anwar stayed where he was, watching intently as I

died in his Brother's arms.

# CHAPTER 23

**Way After**

Since her last four trips to the Hall had been relatively smooth, Gabby prepared herself for the worst.

Two years ago, she'd had a close call with some Gulls, and the year before, she almost didn't make it because of a nasty storm. But overall, she'd been lucky.

But as the anniversary of The Crack approached, Gabby started hoarding anything and everything she could get her hands on. She worked extra hours and stored up as many ration packs as she could afford.

She also managed to salvage some protective gear, which would be a game-changer. In the last year alone, the rains had almost doubled in volume. People flocked to what was left of the towers, needing to get high enough to escape the flooding, but not too high that the pounding of the rain would destroy their roofs.

Because of the downpours, trains and trams were far less frequent, and whole industries had shut down, leaving people without work. Things were getting worse and worse, but Gabby felt that she could do something to stop it all.

And it started with her annual trip to the Plains.

This year, she was up before the sun. Having packed the night before, she was out in a matter of minutes. The city was eery in the dark, so Gabby pulled her hood up and kept her head down.

Every snap or clap had her on edge as she tiptoed through the streets. Most of the short cuts she used to take were now full of homeless people, and they would fight her tooth and nail for even half a ration pack, let alone the stockpile she had.

That left her with the long way around, staying out in the open but on guard as she moved.

Unsurprisingly, Gabby was the first in line for the train. Given that the schedules were unreliable these days, and the frequency of the downpours had increased so much, she left two days early.

The train from her County no longer went straight to the Plains, and she would have to go pretty far west in order to head south. But it didn't matter. She just needed to be standing in the Great Hall on the anniversary, even if that meant getting there a day early.

The first train arrived right as the sun was coming up. The balmy 30-degree shade quickly changed to a humid 35 at first light. Within an hour, the temperatures would quickly rise, and she knew that this year would be the toughest yet.

Gabby had already removed a couple of layers while she was waiting but didn't want to be caught in a freeze should the snows roll in. It was months since the last big storm, and they predicted the weather to turn any day.

The weather was the first to turn erratic after the Crack, and Gabby remembered the first big freeze vividly. At first, the sun would stay out for days on end with no sign of darkness on the horizon. On the other side of the world, they would be lost in the endless night until something decided to shift.

Sudden drops in temperature became normal: a day going from a pleasant 25 degrees down to zero in less than an hour. And then right back up again. But once the decay spread further and seeped deeper into the earth, things changed fast.

Days in what should have been the dead of winter would be so hot, people could fry eggs on the sidewalk. Heatwaves became everyday life, and the rain would often evaporate before hitting the ground. The sun got hotter and hotter until one day, the earth couldn't take it anymore. Thunder as loud as a rocket launch boomed around the whole planet, and the world experienced its first real downpour. The rains were so hard, and so heavy people were told to stay inside. Floods destroyed homes and killed thousands as the water continued to pour.

The downpour lasted almost a week before letting up, and it took months to repair the worldwide damage.

But the storms didn't stop. Six months later, Gabby was playing in the yard with her brother when the sun seemed to fade in the blink of an eye. She was wearing a pink sundress and running around barefoot when the first snowflakes fell. Amazed and enthralled in the beauty, neither child understood the danger it brought.

The ground froze in a matter of minutes as her mother screamed for them to come inside. Gabby's barefoot stuck to a patch of ice, and she cried when the skin tore from her heel. They made it inside and grabbed blankets just as the whiteout began. It was three months before they were able to leave the house again. They almost starved to death.

Since that day, Gabby had never been caught out unprepared. And after so many years, she had her routine perfected.

The first leg of her journey took her slightly north and west. The line she used to take had totally washed away during a downpour, and they hadn't been able to rebuild with rains being so frequent.

This train took her through Counties she had never seen before, and it was a little more crowded. She fought through the crowds to jump off at her stop and found the platform to be just as full.

Since so many industries closed down, because of the destruction of their plants during storms, many people now worked in the further out Counties. Agriculture and railroads were always looking for workers, even though work was often shut down for days and weeks on end when the storms came.

People just had to take what they could get.

The next train was going north, to the fields, and the platform quickly emptied. Gabby looked around as the train whooshed past and quickly realised she was alone. Being further from the city, she knew the Gulls would be lurking somewhere.

People told her that in the last year alone, their numbers had significantly increased. She wasn't sure if they would come this close to the tracks during the day, but she kept her eyes out anyway. Everyone was getting more desperate these days, so she couldn't be too careful.

When the train going south finally arrived, Gabby was twitching with nerves. She heard the chirps and laughs from the burnt-out land behind the station, and was sure that they would attack at any minute.

The train slowed, and Gabby jumped up the stairs, slamming the door closed before it stopped. Looking past the building, she was sure she saw movement. Small dots flitted through the brush and blackened tree stumps.

More than a dozen.

A chill shuddered up her spine despite the heat as she waited impatiently for the train to go.

This train took her south and a little east, but it was slow going. The heat was all-encompassing, and the slow speed meant low airflow through the car. Gabby was just glad there were so few people on this train. The only people going south these days were railroad workers and traders heading for the sea.

Gabby felt out of place and tried to keep her head down. She hugged her bag to her body and sat with her knees up. No way she was falling asleep here.

It was getting dark as they approached the station and the thought of arriving in the Plains in the dark made her heart race. She still had another leg of her journey, but too soon, the clouds rolled in. She wasn't sure whether she should curse her luck or thank the unknown. Either way, she wouldn't be going anywhere.

The rain fell as the brakes squealed, and the conductor told the passengers it wasn't safe to leave their cars. A collective groan filled the air around her as the rain slammed down on the train's roof.

If they'd made it before the rains, they would all have been fighting for the rooms at the station motel. But the minute the first few drops hit the train, the driver put on the brakes and brought everything to a stop. As frustrating as it was, they'd all seen what happened to trains that got washed away on floating tracks.

Gabby could see the station up ahead and sighed. All she could do was hope that the fortified roof would keep them safe and that the storm didn't last long.

# CHAPTER 24

**Way After**

"Hey, are you gonna go?"

Gabby jumped to her feet when someone put a hand on her shoulder.

"What the-" She muttered, yanking her arm free.

She looked down to find her bag, seemingly untouched. It was dark outside, and the rains had stopped.

"Calm down. We're at the station. You getting off or just here for the ride?"

"How long was the downpour?" Gabby asked as she grabbed her belongings.

She peeked inside her bag to make sure nobody had snooped and took out the thick scarf, wrapping it around her neck.

"Just finished a little while ago. We sat for over five hours."

Gabby cursed under her breath. They sat, not a hundred metres from the station for five hours. Somehow she fell asleep and hadn't felt the train move. But she was angry at the wasted time.

"The train south?" She asked as they moved to the door.

"Doubt you'll see it today. Too dark."

Standing on the empty platform, the train left the

station. She had never been stuck out in the open like this, and a nervous energy washed over her. The open fields seemed to loom around her but saw no movement in the dark. All she could hope was for the downpour to have sent the Gulls back to their caves.

Luckily, the motel had a room left that Gabby happily paid too much for. The clerk told her that the next train south would be in the morning, so she found her room, locked the door, and took a cold shower.

She thanked the universe for the shelter, knowing how dangerous it would have been to try to sleep on the platform. Between the Gulls and the rains, she wouldn't have made it through the night.

When the sun hit her window the next morning, Gabby shot up and gathered her things. She ate a ration pack and chanced a trip to the vending machine for a cold coffee and a water, keeping her eyes on the bush and the movement that wasn't there.

She practically ran back to her room, feeling the heat of eyes on her. By the window, Gabby looked out across the tracks and gathered her wits for what lay ahead. As she waited for the train, she kept her things in hand, not wanting to be a target on the tracks. Letting the train stopped for a few minutes before she left her room, Gabby made her run for the doors.

At the early hour, the platform filled quickly, and she felt safe amongst the workers. No way the Gulls would attack such a sizeable group.

They were scavengers that preyed on the weak, and whether she liked it or not, she was the weak. She travelled alone and knew the risks. She always had. But she also knew that what she was doing could change things. Would change things.

Her last train journey brought her further south but a little closer to the site of the Crack. This train continued toward the sea, and Gabby was the only person to leave the train when it stopped. Having never been to this station before, she needed to double-check her map.

There was a plan in her mind, but she had no way of knowing if there was anywhere to shelter on the way to the compound. Six months ago, she considered making a dry run but quickly dismissed the idea as an unnecessary risk. There was just as much chance of being attacked then as now.

It took a few minutes to get her bearings, but Gabby wasted no time once she did. She'd worked silently to listen for any dangers and heard nothing. The smell of the rain suggested it had been through recently. Hopefully, that meant the Gulls were still in hiding.

She just needed to get to the compound, or close to it, as fast as possible. Once she got close enough, and the skies turned dark, she knew they wouldn't follow.

A few hundred metres from the platform sat a cluster of sad-looking trees. The Plains were as sparse as ever as she ran for cover, keeping her backpack held tight across her chest. To the south, Gabby saw nothing but open land. She was heading northeast and was grateful to see some kind of structure on the horizon - she just had to make it there.

At the trees, Gabby ducked down and tried to slow her breathing. She stuck to the edges, looking through the thin trunks for any sign of life. Needing cover from potential downpours was important, but she also knew that this was a perfect place for the Gulls to hide.

She saw nothing.

She heard nothing.

Maybe this area was safe? Nobody came out here, so why would the Gulls lurk so far from potential prey?

Gabby slowly edged her way around the trees until she was facing the right direction. The ground had a gradual incline, and on top of the hill, she could just about see a building. Knowing she was within a few miles of the compound, Gabby hoped to reach the top and find the skies beyond darkening.

At the old compound, she could relax. For now, she feared the Gulls more than the grotesque creatures that roamed under the flames in the sky. Half of them were blind and the other half too weak to give chase.

Several deep breaths later, Gabby made her move. She clutched her things and ran like hell for the hilltop. The ground was hard, and the gravel made it difficult to keep a fast pace, but she pushed on.

When she heard laughter behind her, Gabby turned briefly. Out of nowhere, several people were suddenly moving toward her. Not as fast as she was going, but fast enough to know they were hunting her.

Gabby pressed on, her legs burning from the effort. She kept a tight hold on her bag as the gradient worsened and pushed herself to breaking point. Bile rose in her throat as she dared another glance back.

The Gulls were flanking her now, splitting up and moving to the sides, so she had fewer places to run.

When she reached the peak, Gabby's heart sank. The inky skies of the compound were much further back than she hoped. The structure she had seen was to her left, but she couldn't stop. They were too close, and she needed to make it to the Hall.

Her survival instinct took over. Gabby reached into her bag, pulled out two ration packs, and a jacket before turning the bag upside down and trailing her things behind her.

She could only hope the Gulls would take the bait and leave her alone.

Behind her, she heard whooping and the rustling sound of ration packs being torn into. She smiled and increased her speed, happy her plan worked.

Shaking the bag empty, Gabby looked to her hand to check she still had some food and a jacket. If she were caught out without them, she was dead.

When her foot caught on a rock, she tripped, tumbling her way down the side of the hill. She dropped her things and tried to shield her head as she fell before coming to a painful stop against a small stump.

Her head hit the burned bark, and everything went black.

# CHAPTER 25

**3 1/2 weeks to the Tournament**

"It's been a week, Oran. We can't sit on our hands any longer," Uri sighed as he paced around the compact room.

"She's alive. Right now, she's alive, and we still have a chance. But if we try anything, we could lose her." Oran was sitting in the chair beside Anya's bed, Ozzie at his side.

One week earlier, they had been too distracted to notice Anya's escape.

Uri had come to his Brothers with news of a rebel group of Lightborn. A resistance. He claimed they were stealing away young boys before they could be taken to the School of Light.

Once Uri shared this, they got caught in the middle of a witch hunt of sorts. Apparently, Uri had had such suspicions for years but no proof to back up his theory. When he came to them a week ago, he seemed reluctant to share.

"Wait, where exactly is this coming from, Uri?" Anwar asked.

"I've heard...rumours of rebel groups. Nothing concrete, just-"

"Rumours? Why is this the first we're hearing of this?" Anwar was mad. It was clear Uri had been lying to them for some time.

"A few years back, there was a surge of power in Paris. One of my team-"

"Your team? We have our own teams now?"

"Are you going to let me finish, Anwar?" Uri was getting frustrated.

"Don't you have anything to say?" Anwar turned to Oran, who had been quiet the whole time.

He shrugged and looked to Uri to continue.

"Paris. Power surge. I had someone look into it, but they couldn't pinpoint anything solid. Over the years, we've seen other events similar but haven't been able to locate the source. That was until last week. This group has been meeting for years, and they've always been so careful. But they slipped up. And think I know why."

"Why weren't we told?" Anwar asked, furious at being left in the dark. "You're saying some rebel group has enough power to hide from us for years, and you didn't think we needed to know?"

"Why?" Oran asked before Uri could respond. "They slipped up, why?"

"Anya," Uri said, taking a seat at the table.

Anwar stopped pacing and looked at his Brother, confusion on his face. "Anya?"

"That's right. We think her being taken caused the group to meet in a hurry. They needed to discuss her rescue, most likely. Or figure out if we could find them through her."

"The timing fits, I guess. And it would explain how she stayed hidden for so long," Oran commented as he lifted a milkshake to his lips. "You're saying it's some kind of rebel group. Is that just you guessing, or?"

Uri sighed and looked away. He was obviously not enjoying filling his Brothers in on all his lies. He should've been honest with them from the beginning, he knew.

"The information we've gathered has led us to believe that this group has been taking young boys. Somehow they've managed to find and hide young Lightborn before our people can get to them."

Anwar lost it then. He went into a long-winded rant about the Brotherhood and their connection, and how they couldn't keep things from each other.

He yelled at Uri, and Uri yelled back.

Oran sat between his Brothers and thought about a rebel group. He thought about them taking these young boys and training them to be soldiers. He thought about another Dark War.

"So, what's your plan, Uri?" He asked just loud enough to get their attention. "You haven't come to us with this because you felt bad about lying. You've come to us...because you think Anya can lead us to them?"

"Actually, no. We need her. We've already threatened her family, and she already hates us. This would be the last nail in the coffin. She would refuse to work with us, and we'd be back at square one," Uri answered, surprising Oran with his level of calm. "I think these rebels are teachers. Who else would have access to these kids before their Light can truly shine?"

"Teachers?"

"I'm not saying every teacher on the planet is conspiring against us, but yes, I think the key players are working in the schools. They see glimpses of Light, and instead of reporting it, they move the boys away. Five years ago, a Leader in Paris found that a lot of boys were being sent to the Agricultural Townships. As soon as he raised his concerns, the number of boys being admitted to the School of Light almost doubled."

"So they're seeing signs of Light and moving them to the lesser guarded and lesser watched areas?" Anwar calmed down, and he finally took his seat.

"Smart," Oran noted.

"Treasonous is more like, Oran. This is serious!"

"Ok, but why are we focussing on this now? Don't we have enough to worry about? And if Anya finds us a place to go, we won't have to worry about rebel groups at all."

"If Anya, if Anya...we can't rely on her. We can't just assume this will work-no Anwar, I'm sorry. But we need a plan B."

"You think I'm going to fail?" Anwar was on his feet again.

"I sincerely hope that you don't. I want this to work and for our people to be safe. But, we can't be so naïve as to think it will be a happy ending. And should the day come that the cloaks fall and the rot is exposed, we're going to need a fall guy."

Oran looked to his Brother and laughed, "You want to find them and make them our patsy?"

Uri rubbed his forehead. "If the cloaks fall, people will revolt. They will forget about how much they fear us, and they'll take to the streets."

Uri's words of warning had been playing in Oran's mind all week. They had been so focussed on interrogating teachers; they let Anya slip through the cracks. She jumped through three portals before they were even aware she was gone.

Her jump to Paris reignited the search there, Uri now sure that was the rebels' primary hub. Her other jumps had been easy enough to track, and it was Anwar that put it together using the landmarks.

Anya was smart to lead them on a chase, but she was choosing such obvious locations. It made it easy to predict her next move. She hadn't been in Egypt for more than a few minutes before the local Lightborn sent word of a power surge. The Three were on her before she knew it.

"We should've moved faster," Oran lamented as he looked at Anya.

She'd been unconscious since that night in Egypt, with no signs of waking.

"We've been through this," Uri sighed. "They thought they were protecting us."

"Protecting us," Anwar scoffed.

He'd been quiet by the doorway, never wanting to come all the way in. "As if we would need protection from her."

"You saw what she did, Anwar. She turned five seasoned Lightborn into dust with a flick of her pinky. I don't know about you, but I definitely felt her power."

Anwar rolled his eyes and walked away. If it were up to him, he would've used his Light to force Anya awake days ago. He didn't care if it killed her.

"Not just her power," Uri recalled as he looked out the window. "She took their Light. That local attacked her, and she reacted. But even injured, she was able to take them down, and she actually absorbed their power."

Oran looked to Ozzie, who had stayed by Anya's side since they brought her back. "I've never seen anyone do that before. Not like that. Not since-"

"Regardless, she needs to wake up soon. We only have a few weeks until the Tournament. You know the kind of damage that it will cause. We won't be able to wait."

Oran nodded his agreement, "I know. But I'm worried if we push her, she'll fall further. Taking in that power overwhelmed her. Her body wasn't ready for it, and she's paying the price. She's trying to adjust to all that Light, and I'm worried if we wake her up, she'll lose all of it."

"If this goes on much longer, we won't have a choice," Uri stepped forward and put a hand on his Brother's shoulder. "I can't even see in her mind. It's just dark."

"The Light she absorbed wasn't taken willingly, and it was taken in anger - a dead man's Light. You and I both know what it's like to feel the darkness inside. I just hope she's strong enough to hold it." Uri patted his Brother and left.

He would continue to pry into Anya's mind, but Oran knew it was no use. Wherever she was now, they couldn't follow.

During the Dark War, Oran fought with Uri and the younger Lightborn. He helped lead the charge, standing beside Uri, fighting for their freedom. They stayed off the battlefields, for the most part, Uri insisting they needed to survive in order to lead.

But when they did join the fight, Oran brought his Light forward in ways never before seen.

Sitting with Anya, he thought back to a particular battle. The Elders fought hard to keep their power. They had a loyal following of Lightborn, who were steadfast in their beliefs and willing to give their lives to ensure the survival of the Elders and their ways.

When Uri got word that two Elders had entered a particularly gruelling battle in the snowy fields of Russia, he and Oran jumped at the chance to take out their opponents. They used Anwar, who had not yet become one of their inner circle, to open a portal and take them to the battlefield.

When they arrived, it bolstered moral for their soldiers. It encouraged the Lightborn to show their potential new leaders what they were capable of.

Things were looking up for the Usurpers as the Elders, and their people seemed to fall back, running from their enemies to hide.

Uri raised his hands in victory for only three-seconds before Anwar grabbed him and Oran, pulling them through a portal. They landed hard on the ground, and Uri was furious. Until he realised that Anwar had saved their lives.

The enemy Lightborn had not been hiding. They were making their way to safety, to allow the Elders a last strike. Every single man and woman left in the fields fell to their knees as their hearts stopped in an instant. Anwar had seen the Elders step forward and reacted as quickly as he could. He opened a portal, and they landed not two miles from the fight. By the time they made it back to the field, their people were dead, and their enemy was gone.

But that wasn't everything.

Oran never told his Brothers the extent of it, but that day he felt his Light slip. He hadn't noticed the Elders stepping forward, but he felt their power. He turned in time to see a flash and wave of Light moving over his army but was yanked away by Anwar before it reached them.

Still, he felt it. He felt his Light slipping away, and he knew where it was going. As he walked amongst the dead, he found the Lightborn laying within the bodies and saw scorch marks on their palms. He knew that the

Elders had somehow stolen their Light.

With all that power, the war raged on. Oran was sure it was the reason it lasted so long, Uri and his people being unable to overpower the Elders and their loyalists. But as the years went by, he heard rumours of two Elders losing their way.

He was told by spies that these Elders snapped and lost their minds. They would attack their own people and even killed one of their Brothers. All that power was too much for even the greatest of them, and they eventually were lost to darkness as their minds corrupted. It was the beginning of the end for them. In taking in dead men's Light, they were lost into madness, and it cost them the war.

Oran took Anya's hand and looked at the scorch mark in her palm. She had only taken in the Light of five, but she wasn't an Elder. She had hidden her Light for years, instead of using and strengthening it. He was afraid she would be sucked into the darkness, unable to ever find her way out.

And he was afraid that if they tried to bring her out before she was ready, they would be dragged down with her.

# CHAPTER 26

Anwar left Anya's room and made his way to the lobby. He was frustrated and sick of Oran standing guard over the girl. She got herself into this by running, and he wouldn't feel guilty if she didn't make it.

But Uri and Oran were determined to keep her safe. They still didn't think he was strong enough - or trustworthy, apparently. Uri had been lying to them for years, and Anwar would not forget that quickly.

"Brother Anwar! Do you…need a car, Sir?" The boys at the desk jumped to attention as he appeared from the elevators.

He wasn't sure if these were the same Lightborn that let Anya open a portal, not fifty feet from where they sat. Taking them in, he tilted his head, looking them over for something familiar. He genuinely couldn't tell either way.

"No. I don't need a car," he brushed them off and walked to the door.

As Anwar stepped outside, his mood fell further. The ominous clouds on the horizon would hide the sun within the hour. He wanted to lift his hands and send the clouds away and hated himself for not just doing it.

To hell with Uri and his rules.

The weather seemed to pick up on his mood, sending a faint rumble from over the hills. A storm was coming, and he wanted to make it to Kareena's before it arrived. It had been too long since his last visit, and the guilt was growing with each day. She would understand, of course, but he missed her. He missed his daughter and how at ease he felt in that house.

Looking back into the building to the three Lightborn at the desk, he rolled his eyes as they hovered, unsure of what to do.

More than ever, he needed peace.

But just two steps from the door, Anwar hesitated. He turned again to look through the doors and watched as one of the boys came running.

"Sir? Is there something I can get you?"

Anwar considered him. He had never actively tried to take the Light from another, even during the war. Though he hadn't felt the effects, he was there the day the Elders stole the Light from a field of dead Lightborn. It had been a titanic battle, and many of their followers had come to their aid and perished. After that day, he heard about the effects on the Elders, which instilled in him a great fear.

Their plan for the Tournament was to syphon power from the Lightborn taking part. He could take it in and use that extra power to open a secure enough portal to allow their people through. But they weren't taking all their Light, and they weren't killing anybody.

Anwar was sure it was the act of killing that turned the power dark. He and his Brothers had killed during the Dark War, but they never stole a dead man's Light. It was something not even Uri was willing to do to win.

But standing in the sun with the storm rolling in, Anwar's mind went hazy. He glanced up and thought about the girl in the bed. His Brothers put all their faith in her and weren't prepared for her failure.

She might never wake up. She could be lost forever, and all their time working with her would have been for nothing. Or she could wake and still fail. No matter what his Brothers believed, she was weak.

"Come with me," Anwar demanded of the three Lightborn who were now standing in the doorway, confused and scared. "All of you."

They followed quickly, not wanting to keep him waiting, and to their credit, they didn't ask where they were going. They knew better. Anwar marched toward the storm and the Great Hall, his mind racing through possibilities.

He had been in Anya's mind, and he was sure her success with opening portals to other worlds was her youth and innocence. After she arrived, he'd grabbed at a memory of her father before she caught him sneaking around, and it was incredibly telling.

She'd been doing this from a very young age - much younger than any of The Three were when they first found their Light. She blossomed at an age in which she was free and clear of life's burdens. She could simply close her eyes, dream up a wonderland, and *poof*, she was there.

He'd never been able to do that. His mind was always weighed down with worry, even from a young age.

In the Great Hall, Anwar had the three Lightborn stand in a line in the middle of the room. He ordered them to stay quiet while he thought and focussed. They stood, nervous and flustered as one of The Three wandered around them muttering.

"Quiet!" Anwar yelled suddenly. "Quiet your minds. It's distracting."

He paced around, talking to himself, and trying to find a clear place in his subconscious. Dream up a fantasy world was hard enough, let alone finding it out in the universe.

The last time he tried to open such a portal, he lost focus, and his mind fractured. He became stuck somewhere between here and there, and the portal closed before he was ready. Oran barely managed to pull him clear and save his arm from being stuck in limbo.

Anwar hadn't tried since.

But today, he was determined to make it work. He had the three desk jockeys sit in a circle and grasp each other's hands as he stood in the middle and closed his eyes. Anwar stood silent for a long while before he felt it.

His mind calmed, and he felt the warmth of their Light on his legs. With his palms open their Light to washed over him, creeping up from his toes to his fingertips. If they felt anything, they kept it to themselves.

Focussing on their Light, Anwar let his mind stray. He thought about the books he read his daughter and of the magical lands in their stories. He pictured grass as far as the eye could see, blue skies and sunshine playing over crystal clear water, and trees that almost touched the clouds.

It was a place untouched by man and undamaged by the Light. Feeling his own Light coming to life, he kept his focus on this place. The warmth of his portal filled the room, and he hesitated before opening his eyes. One of the boys gasped as the air split open, no doubt in awe of the power.

Anwar sighed and opened his eyes. He saw in front of

him what he had seen in his mind. The grass, the sun, the water. It was perfect. When he felt the connection wavering, he ignored the strained noises coming from the Lightborn as he took in more and more of their power. It was so close he could smell the flowers.

"Anwar!"

He heard his name, but he couldn't stop. This was it. This was their Oasis. Their Salvation. He finally found it, and he couldn't walk away. Not now. He just needed a little more-

"Stop!"

Someone grabbed his arm and whirled him around. As he turned, he felt his connection break, and the portal closed in a cold snap.

"What did you do!" Anwar yelled at his Brother. "I had it!"

"What have you done?" Oran shouted, taking a step back, his eyes wide and confused.

"I found our new home, Brother! Didn't you see?"

"All I see is death." Oran cast his eyes down to their feet.

Anwar didn't understand. It had been so bright, how had Oran not seen it? He moved to take a step, but his foot caught, stopping him in place. Frustrated, he looked down, and suddenly he knew.

At his feet were the dead bodies of the three Lightborn.

"Anwar, what were you thinking?" Uri gasped from behind.

"I..."

"They're dead. All three," Oran snapped as he reached down.

Anwar watched him take their hands, running a finger over the scorch marks on their palms. His mind flashed back to that day, all those years ago.

"I just needed more power. I didn't mean to-"

"To murder three of our kind?" Uri snapped. "You brought them here, and you knew what could happen. And after what we just witnessed with Anya!"

"Anwar, how could you-" Oran began, but Anwar cut him off.

"Enough! Both of you. I did what was necessary. They gave their lives so we can live on. And it worked! I found it!"

"Anwar-"

"You found it? Found what?" Uri moved around the bodies and stood beside Oran. "You're saying it actually worked?"

"Yes, Brother. Yes! All I needed was that extra push, and it worked. And oh, it was perfect. It was beautiful!"

"How do you know it's what we need?" Uri asked, ignoring Oran's attempts to scold.

"Well, if you hadn't pulled me back, I would've gone through and seen for myself."

Oran groaned and began pacing.

"Oran, relax. It's not ideal, but-"

"Not ideal? The dead boys at his feet aren't ideal?"

Uri sighed and waved a hand. The bodies vanished into the ground in an instant. "There, happy?"

"Uri, I'm telling you. I found it. I found a new home!" Anwar stepped forward and embraced his Brother. "We're going to be ok."

Uri patted Anwar on the back, avoiding Oran's glare. "That's good, Brother. That's so very good."

"We don't need her. I told you, we never did!" Anwar was excited. He bounced and laughed and pumped his fists.

"We still might," Uri said, raising a hand to calm his Brother.

"Why? I just-"

"We can't leave anything to chance. You found it! That's amazing! But the portal will be stronger if you both work at it. We need it to be as stable as possible if we're going to get all our people through. It's not just us, you know that." Uri put a hand on Anwar's shoulder and squeezed. "But you did it! You really did it!"

Anwar nodded, unhappy with Uri's insistence of using Anya. He had just shown them he didn't need her help. All he needed was the Tournament and the Light. He was sure that after day one, he would have syphoned enough Light to make a portal strong enough for the whole world to walk through.

"Where are you going?" Uri called as Oran walked to the door.

"To find us some new desk boys. Let's try not to kill these three, hmm?"

# CHAPTER 27

Since Anya's escape, Uri had focussed on finding possible rebels. He and his team had personally spoken to hundreds of teachers at the public schools, looking for any signs of deception. But they kept coming up empty. Uri could more or less read their minds, and he knew that they were telling the truth.

Though he didn't like it, he and his Brothers agreed to postpone putting up the rest of the barriers - for now. Oran was distracted with Anya, and Anwar was busy trying not to kill anyone.

For his part, Uri knew finding potential insurgents was more pressing. He'd spent days in Paris speaking with teachers from every public school in the city and then another two days in the country's smaller schools.

Anya's first jump had been to Paris, and Uri was more sure than ever that it was where the rebels were based. Why else would she risk that jump?

When he'd finally arrived home, Kayla has been furious. He'd initially said he would be gone a week, and now he was saying it would be longer.

"You've not been here all week, Uri. And I didn't see a thing on the news about you all visiting the arenas,"

"Plans changed. We're going to be making the rounds next week. I'm needed elsewhere," Uri kissed his sons and moved to the stove where Kayla had soup waiting.

"Where were you?" She asked, slapping his hand away from the pot.

"You know where I was. You've seen the news," he replied, frustrated and hungry.

"Paris? The teachers?"

Uri nodded and grabbed a bowl. Kayla stepped aside, watching him with dark eyes. When he turned, she looked frightened.

"Don't worry-"

"Don't worry? You're rounding up teachers and doing Brothers knows what. Why, Uri?"

Kayla's sister was a teacher, and no doubt, she'd been in touch about her treatment.

"We've been given some information, and we're investigating a viable threat. I can't tell you more, but you know that everything we do is to keep our people safe."

"How is my sister a threat?"

"I know she's not a threat, but my Lightborn have their orders, and they're following them to the letter. If Jamie has nothing to hide, then she'll be fine."

Kayla stormed out of the room, and Uri rubbed his temples. She'd gone to bed early, and he knew better than to follow. Instead, he used the time to visit Oran and check on Anya. With no change, Uri was beginning to really worry about their plan. Oran seemed hopeful, but he'd looked into her mind and saw absolutely nothing. If she was fighting, there was no sign of it.

So even though it took the death of their Lightborn gatekeepers, knowing Anwar found a place for them made it all worth it. Maya was due to arrive the following week, and they would be ready to go.

But he still needed to find the rebels, just in case. That meant he had to leave again.

Kayla wouldn't be mad after they made it through the portal. For now, she would just have to cope.

He'd left Anwar in the Great Hall, high on his accomplishment and giddy with power. Oran stormed away, angry but on board. That left Uri with the rest of the day at home before he was due back in the field for interviews.

His people did the initial interrogations and held back those they felt were suspicious. Most of his team had been chosen because they followed orders and were good at seeing through people. They couldn't read minds, but they could read people and body language. He trusted their judgement to weed out the innocents.

Deciding to avoid his still angry wife, Uri went back to their office to look through the files of the Lightborn that would take part in the Tournament. With everything else going on, they had all let plans slip. He knew Anwar wouldn't take charge and made a mental note to give the work to Oran, who was mad at being lied to, but he would stand by their Brotherhood, as he always had.

He made it through almost a dozen files before he felt it - a mind splitting pulse that seemed to shake the walls. The rush came upon him so fast, and for a second, he saw nothing but bright, searing light. It seemed to go as quickly as it hit. Hands to his temples and fire in his eyes, he raced out the door.

He knew what he would find, and he just hoped he wasn't too late.

Uri walked off the elevator but picked up his pace when he saw Anwar on the floor of Anya's room. Ozzie was barking, and Oran was nowhere in sight.

"Anwar? Can you hear me?" He yelled, shaking his Brother by the shoulders.

Anwar was out cold. Uri stood and looked to Anya who seemed unchanged but for Ozzie, now in a protective stance at the foot of her bed. He took a step forward and hesitated slightly before taking Anya's hand.

Electricity pulsed from her palm, and as he was knocked backwards, an image flashed across his mind.

He saw bodies and fire and scorched earth.

He saw a stone building and angry skies full of ash and flames.

And he saw Anya at the centre of it, her arms raised high as Light whirled around her.

"Uri..." Anwar groaned weakly.

Uri got to his knees and went to his Brother. "Anwar, what happened?"

Before he could respond, Oran came running in. He took in the scene: Anya still unconscious and two of the most powerful Lightborn on the planet on their knees.

"What the...what did you do?"

"I didn't-"

"Don't lie, Anwar!" Oran yelled as he tried to calm Ozzie.

When he went to touch Anya's hand, Uri cautioned him.

"I wouldn't. How do you think I go down here?"

Oran looked confused. "What are you talking about?"

"You saw it too?" Anwar gasped.

Uri nodded and helped his Brother to his feet.

"Saw what?" Oran demanded.

"I just had a flash. An image-"

"I saw it all," Anwar mused, his eyes glazed over. "I saw us standing in the Great Hall, a portal open and ready for us. People came rushing in - the rebels. There was a fight, and the portal closed. I saw her die! She died, but then...she wasn't dead. She was-"

"In the Light," Uri finished.

"What do you mean, in the Light?" Oran snapped, clearly frustrated.

"I don't know, Brother. I can't explain it, but...she's powerful."

"We should kill her now," Anwar suggested, moving toward the bed.

Both Uri and Oran got in between.

"We can't kill her. We don't know what we saw," Uri warned.

"I know what I saw. I saw her end us. She had her army of rebels and some girl by her side, and they ended us!" Anwar yelled.

"Ended us? You're not making any sense." Oran kept his hand on Ozzie as the dog appeared to calm.

Anwar glared at Anya, but Uri looked at her with genuine curiosity. Had they been shown a vision of the future? He heard rumours about this kind of power, but nobody had ever stepped forward. They had seen nothing like it in the School of Light or during the Tournament.

Was it possible that this girl, the one who could open portals, could also see into the future?

"She showed me our future. You saw it, Uri!" Anwar was still amped up, his wild eyes glaring at the girl in the bed.

"You think she can see the future now?" Oran almost laughed.

"It would make sense," Uri said, surprising even himself. "She can open portals to the past and present, why not the future? If she can jump forward in time, maybe her mind can too. With all that extra power, maybe she can see ahead without needing to jump at all."

"So you're saying...what? We're going to open the portal, and then she's going to kill us all? It was probably just a dream. Think of what she's been through! She's stuck in the dark and having a nightmare. That's what you both saw." Oran shrugged.

"How could it be possible? She's not that powerful-"

"You and I both know that's not true - especially now. She was powerful before Egypt. We can't know what her Light is like now. Not until she wakes up." Uri moved to her side.

He hoped she would be the missing piece in their puzzle. That she was young enough and strong enough to stand beside Anwar. That they could come together to find their new home.

A safe place.

She was resistant, but she would do it to keep her family safe. And Uri still believed that they needed her, even after seeing Anwar kill those Lightborn and open the portal. His Light was too unstable. He was too emotional, and Uri couldn't trust him to hold steady.

"She might never wake up," Anwar noted with a glint in his eye.

"Then we'll make her," Uri promised, looking to Oran.

"Uri...we can't. It could kill her-it could kill us!" Oran pleaded.

"We have to try, Brother. Before it's too late."

# CHAPTER 28

**Way After**

The cold hit Gabby before anything else. Her mind was fuzzy, and she struggled to open her eyes, but she felt the cold. Her whole body hurt, and moving her stiff fingers was a chore. When the pain in her head kicked in, she turned slightly and raised a frozen hand to the site of her wound. When her eyes finally opened, she could just about see blood on her almost blue fingers.

"I don't know how this is taking so long. Is it your first day?" A voice asked from somewhere close by.

Gabby couldn't feel any snow falling on her, and the darkness surrounding suggested she was sheltered. But where? How? She tried to clear her mind and vision while thinking back.

The train. The Plains. The Gulls.

Her mind raced as she sat up, eyes still unable to focus. Scrambling back, her hands ached, and she cried out when she ran into, not a wall, but a person.

"Don't bother. Nobody's going anywhere," the voice said, hands on her shoulders.

"Who are you? Where am I?" Gabby slurred, stumbling away and rubbing at her eyes.

"Ok, I got it!" Another voice announced.

"Finally," the first voice sighed.

The movement in the flickering light made her

flinch, but she was too out of it to fight back as someone grabbed and dragged her toward the fire. The heat pricked at her skin as she felt it seep into her clothing. After a few minutes, her hands loosened up, and her eyes cleared a little. She looked around carefully, trying to keep her movements small and indistinct.

They were in some kind of cave. It was small, maybe two metres by five. The dirt walls didn't look to be structured in any way, and Gabby suddenly felt trapped and as though there wasn't enough oxygen.

There were only three of them in the compact space, and the other two seemed to pay her little attention. She tried to keep her breathing under control, but the panic set in when she remembered why she was there in the first place.

"How long was I out?" She asked loud enough to stop their quiet conversation.

"Does it matter?" The smaller of the two asked without looking.

"You can't imagine how much it matters," Gabby replied, her icy tone causing the tall man to turn and look at her.

In the firelight, she took them in. The smaller, a boy of maybe sixteen, was hunched over the fire, his hands out front and rubbing together. The larger, a man of well over thirty, was stooped in the small space, and she saw her bag in his hands.

"That's mine," she huffed defiantly.

"Not anymore. Don't you know who we are?" He asked with a grin.

"You're Gulls. Vultures is more like," Gabby spat, trying to hide the shake in her voice.

The big man laughed and put his hand in her bag. He

pulled out two ration packs and gave one to his companion. He kept the second and tore into it, keeping his eyes on Gabby.

"We saved your life. You should thank us."

"I don't think so. I wouldn't have needed saving if you'd left me alone."

"We all do what's necessary to survive these days," he said, putting her things down and crouching to the fire. "We just wanted your stuff. We could've left you out in the snow, ya know."

Gabby looked up and shuddered. She would've frozen to death, and nobody would have known a thing.

"So why save me? You people aren't exactly known for your hospitality."

"Nobody really knows what our people are known for."

Gabby laughed. "You're scavengers. Hunters. You rob and murder innocent people. You stalk out in the Plains until you find a target weak enough, and then you jump at the chance to hurt them. You're pathetic!"

The man smiled and laughed and nodded along. "Ok. Accurate."

"How long was I out?" Gabby asked again.

"Not long," he answered, his curiosity showing. "The snows came almost right after we got to you. We made it here before the whiteout hit."

"I need to go." Gabby moved to stand, but he held out a hand.

"You won't last thirty seconds. Where were you going anyway?"

"Does it matter?"

"I guess not. We already know, more or less. Our people have been tracking you, and the boss is intrigued. You've been seen out here a lot. Once a year. Every year. You rush off the train to the old Brotherhood compound and...what? What are you doing there? You some weirdo Light-worshipper or something? Waiting for the almighty Three to return?"

Gabby's eyes bulged as he spoke. How could they know so much? How long had they been on her tail?

She averted her eyes, wondering what to say. The truth was too much.

"Why do you care?"

"I don't. I would've left you out there to freeze. But I got orders." He shrugged and finished the ration pack, grabbing at another with his free hand.

"I need that stuff-"

"So do we."

"I need to go. I need to-" she stopped short.

The man sighed and shook his head.

"Go check outside," he said to the kid.

The kid nodded and made his way around a corner Gabby hadn't noticed. She felt a gust of freezing air come into the space, and the fire flickered and lowered, almost going out. She hugged her knees to her chest and waited.

She needed a way out. She still had time.

But if this whiteout was anything like the last, she might miss her window completely.

"Still white. Still cold," the kid said as he came back to the fire. "No sign it's gonna let up."

The man nodded and sighed again. He looked at Gabby and tilted his head, taking her in. He was curious, but she believed him when he said he would've left her to die.

"Baz," he said out of nowhere.

Gabby furrowed her brow. "What?"

"I'm Baz. This is Charlie." He looked at her expectantly.

"Gabby," she said through clenched teeth.

"Why do you need to go there? Just tell me."

"I don't get why-" she started before he cut her off.

"The only reason we're out here is because of you. Because our people have been tracking you for years and nobody can quite figure out what you're up to. Because everything is going to hell, and the boss is just...entertained by you, I guess. She sent us way off our path, so we'd be here to get you because she just needs to know why you go there every single year."

It made Gabby sick, and her head spun slightly. The thought of being watched for years made her skin crawl. Had they tried to catch her before? Had she been lucky, or had they left her alone? And who was this 'boss'? She thought the Gulls were just the downtrodden of society - a rag-tag bunch of criminals that were a law unto themselves.

The way Baz was talking, they were more like an organization. An army.

"I go to the Great Hall. The site of the Crack," she mumbled, her eyes to the flames. "I go to...to try and find a way out of this mess."

Baz cocked his head and chuckled. "A way out?"

"I can't explain it. I've just always felt this...pull. I need to be there. The day of the anniversary, I need to be there,"

"For what?" Charlie spoke up for the first time, his interest peaked.

"I don't know."

"Oh, you know. Come on. Don't hold out on us now,"

Baz laughed, though she saw he was less amused and far more worried about her answer.

"Really! I don't know. I didn't know what it was when I was younger, and then I read a book about the Brotherhood and the Crack and everything that happened, and it just hit me. I just felt this pull to that spot. And when I'm there, I feel connected somehow. Like I have to be there, but I don't know why," Gabby stopped and blushed.

She'd told no one about this before and felt embarrassed. She knew she sounded crazy.

"Do you…have the Light?" Charlie gulped.

"What? Me? No. No way. I don't- I don't! I promise!" Gabby cried.

If they believed she did, this wouldn't end well. When The Three and their people jumped through that portal, they left behind a broken world. After the Crack, the Lightborn were hunted down. They were persona non grata, and she'd seen what people had done to any that were found.

"Then what? What draws you there?" Baz asked, looking to have tensed up at the mention of Light.

"I have no idea. I don't even know what I'm waiting for. I just know, deep down, that I have to be there and that one day, I'll know why."

They sat in silence for a while, watching the fire and each other. Charlie looked anxious, as though she would shoot lasers from her fingers at any moment. Baz just looked sceptical.

After a few minutes, he reached behind and pulled out a walkie talkie. Clicking the top dial, static and white noise spewed from the small speaker. He adjusted the volume and turned the dial, his frown as dark as his eyes.

"Sutton Park, come in," Baz spoke into the receiver.

He waited a beat and repeated himself.

"Sutton Park. You all good, Baz?"

"Yeah. I need you to get a message to Carlsberg."

"Go ahead."

Baz looked to Gabby before he spoke. "We got her,"

"Ok. That all?"

"For now. I'll come back in an hour," Baz said.

"Sure thing. Stay warm,"

"You too."

Baz turned the dial off and put the walkie back in its clip. Gabby was stunned. They were organized. They communicated and planned, and they were here for her.

She couldn't risk the storm. Even if they let her run, Baz was right; she wouldn't make it thirty-seconds in the cold.

"Carlsberg's really coming?" Charlie asked.

"Yeah, she's really coming."

"Who's coming?" Gabby asked, afraid of the answer.

"The boss. She wants to meet you."

# CHAPTER 29

**2 1/2 weeks to the Tournament**

Oran persuaded his Brothers to give Anya another week. They weren't happy about it, but they knew it was right - not for Anya, but for them. If Uri really believed they needed her, then they would need her at her strongest. Pulling her from whatever darkness she was stuck in could kill her, or it could leave her completely powerless.

Uri took the week to continue his search for the rebels. His men held more teachers than he could believe, and he was exhausted after just one day of interrogations. They were all jumpy, nervous, and in complete denial of any wrongdoing. Going into their minds was tiring but essential. Uri searched through their memories for any indication they wanted to defy him and his Brothers.

But day after day, he found nothing. Sure, many didn't like the Brotherhood and hated their local Lightborn Leaders, but that wasn't unusual, and it wasn't a crime. He was beginning to wonder if he was wrong about the rebels being in public schools. Maybe they had another way of getting to the young boys.

At home, Kayla refused his calls. She was furious at his leaving again and became irate when he told her

Maya was due to arrive. Their animosity could get tiresome after a while, but Uri knew he needed his daughter close. As soon as the Tournaments began, they would be syphoning Light in preparation for their departure, and he needed his people close so they could be the first to jump to safety.

And if they failed, he wanted his daughter with him. She would be a target for the public once they inevitably revolted. With only two weeks until the Tournament, his nerves were on edge.

Anwar went from riding high to dark and sombre overnight. The images he'd seen when he touched Anya haunted him, and he refused to go back into her room. From the very beginning, he'd known that she was bad for the Brotherhood. He hated how much faith Uri put in her Light and despised the way Oran bonded with her. Too often he let himself daydream about killing the girl and having it be done with, but he knew that would cause too big of a rift between them.

And deep, deep down, he liked the idea of having her to blame should he fail.

The deaths of the three Lightborn was unfortunate. He hadn't meant to kill them, but he wasn't sorry either. Their sacrifice gave him the strength he needed, and he was grateful. Anwar knew that having the Light from the Tournaments would give him the boost he needed.

His wife had been gone for weeks now. She was visiting their youngest, Seth, and helping with the new baby. That left Anwar alone in the house and free to visit Kareena whenever he liked. Part of him wanted to bring her home to the safety of the compound, but he knew it was a foolish thought.

Neither Uri nor Oran knew about her or their baby,

and he wanted it to stay that way until they had to leave. When they found out what he'd done, they would be furious. She needed to remain hidden until the very last minute. It was safer that way.

Anwar spent most of the week away from the compound. Nobody asked or wanted to know where he was going since - no doubt they knew they wouldn't like the answer.

Oran left Uri to his witch hunt, not convinced of any rebellion himself. He didn't see a point in putting their energy into finding them. Instead, he made the trips to the arenas alone, doing away with the public appearances and focusing on the barriers.

Declan had been worried initially, when the interrogations began. He had friends in the public schools and was concerned he and his colleagues would be next.

"What's going on, Oran? The news is-"

"Don't worry about the news," Oran said, trying to keep his tone calm. "This doesn't concern you or your friends."

"I have friends in public schools too. I've heard things, Oran. About their treatment at the hands of your men."

"Uri's men," Oran clarified. "I didn't start this. But it's necessary right now. You'll just have to trust me."

Declan put a hand on his husband's face. "Talk to me. What is it?"

Oran always tried to keep Declan and Tyler out of the Brotherhood drama. He wanted to appear powerful in his husband's eyes and never wanted his family to worry. But he also hated lying to them.

"We've been given information about a potential threat, and we're dealing with it. I can't really go into it, but you don't have to worry. Our men know who you are - they won't bother you. And if they do, believe me, they'll be dealt with accordingly."

"I'm not worried about that. I'm worried about what this means," Declan said, his eyes wide and concerned, "What this means for you and the Brotherhood."

"You don't need to worry. Uri does enough of that for all of us."

He hadn't been satisfied, but Declan let it go. He trusted his husband and never pressed him too far. It was one of the many things Oran was grateful for.

When the day came to try and wake Anya, a storm brewed overhead. As if mother nature knew their plan, the sun was overtaken by dark grey, rumbling clouds. The rain started early and persisted throughout the morning. The Brothers sat in their respective homes with only one thing on their minds: the darkness.

"We can't put it off any longer," Uri thought.

"I know," Oran replied.

"Then let's get it over with. We still have things to do before the Tournaments start." Anwar's apathetic tone was apparent even in his thoughts.

They convened in the meeting room, nobody quite sure where to start. Anya was showing no signs of improvement, and Uri was still unable to enter her thoughts. She was stable, medically speaking, and appeared to be in some kind of coma. But her heart was healthy. Her breathing was even.

Oran had gone back after the incident with Anwar and hesitantly took her hand. Bracing himself for impact, he laughed with relief when nothing happened. Whatever happened with Anwar, it was because he tried something.

"We need to find her and bring her back to the Light," Oran said eventually, after too many minutes of silence. "She's lost. The dead men's Light corrupted her mind somehow, and she's stuck in the corruption. She just needs help finding her way back."

"And if we get lost in there with her?" Anwar snapped. "Is she really worth it?"

Uri let out a deep, exhausted exhale. "Anwar, we can't keep doing this. Yes, you opened that portal, and that's amazing. But, you also killed three Lightborn in the process. You know, as well as I do having Anya there will strengthen the portal and give us the time we need to get our people through. I'm sorry, but you're too-"

"What, Uri? I'm too, what?"

"You're too emotional. You let things get to you, and you lose focus."

Anwar stood and slammed his hands on the table. "Emotional?! I'm the only one of us with this power. Me! You don't know what it takes-"

"Exactly! But you do. And you know how it drains you. You were a teenager when you first found this power - Anya was a child. She was jumping to dream worlds at four years old! This comes as naturally to her as breathing, and we need that consistency if we're going to hold the portal open for long enough to get everyone through."

The room fell quiet again, the Brothers lost in their own thoughts. Sick of having the same arguments, Oran stood and walked to the door.

"We don't all have to go. I'll do it. I'm strong enough to find her and bring her back. And if I'm not, well, you'll know that all of this is on your shoulders, Anwar."

He walked out and to the elevator without waiting.

Uri and Anwar stayed back, watching him go, not wanting to volunteer themselves. After a few minutes, Uri stood and followed. Anwar stayed where he was.

Ozzie was asleep at her side when Oran entered. He stirred and looked up but kept his place in the bed. Oran scratched the loyal pup behind the ears and gave him a treat. He looked at the dog and tilted his head, moving his eyes between Ozzie and Anya.

They were connected, he'd said as much not too long ago. Maybe Ozzie was the key to finding Anya and bringing her back safely.

"You don't have to go alone," Uri said from the doorway.

"I won't be alone. Ozzie will come along, won't you, boy?"

And with that, Oran put a hand on Ozzie and the other on Anya's forehead. Uri watched as his Brother's head tilted back and he took a deep breath, before falling to the ground, limp and unconscious.

"He's gone," Uri thought.

"Let's hope he finds her," Anwar replied from the room below. "It'll take all of us to finish this. We're going to need his Light no matter how this all ends."

Uri nodded and moved to Anya's bedside. Ozzie was splayed out at her side, his tongue hanging loose from his jaw. He bent down and lifted Oran, moving him to a more comfortable position.

He was warm, and Uri could see his eyes moving beneath the lids. He put his hands to his Brother's temples and was able to extract a half dozen images, none of which were pretty.

"Be careful," he whispered before leaving the room and heading home.

# CHAPTER 30

"Alexis! Where's your sister?"

"Where did she go?"

"She can't be far..."

"She was right here."

"Alexis, you were supposed to be watching her!"

"Mum, she was right behind me!"

"Get your jacket, we need to find her."

"Why would she just run off?"

"You know she didn't."

"She just got lost-"

"We won't find her out there."

Anya, fully grown, watched as her family became frantic in their search for her. In the strange, unfinished place that was supposed to be her home, she stood as they argued and became upset.

Alexis cried.

Her mother, hands on her hips, shook her head and furrowed her brow. Her father grabbed his jacket and went out of sight.

The scene changed. The brightness was overpowering, and Anya had to cover her eyes. Squinting, she saw herself.

Little Anya was only two, sitting in the forest and picking at the grass. She was laughing and singing to herself, oblivious to her situation. From somewhere far, her father's voice rang through the trees. Little Anya looked up, smiling and expectant. She got to her feet and trotted around, looking for Daddy. He called out again, and Anya clapped her hands.

The trees changed to tall grass. The bright skies were now cloudy and grey. Her father came running, scooping her into his arms, and hugging her tight. She laughed into his shoulder.

At home again, Anya watched her three-year-old self making a mess in the kitchen. The flour covering the floor and her new dress. Alexis came in to help clean up the mayhem. Her mother found them and yelled. Little Anya, head hung, closed her eyes and was gone.

The kitchen went to black, as blue flames surrounded her mother and sister while they searched. The back door opened to a long room that seemed to go on forever.

Alexis ran inside, screaming for her sister. Anya followed until they found her, sitting in the corner, crying in the shadows.

Outside again, Anya could see her father. He was working on a car, music blaring. She saw herself sitting in the driver's seat, smiling and pretending to drive. She would have been no more than four in this memory.

The ground seemed to swirl beneath their feet, and Anya watched herself vanish from the seat. Her father, not seeing a thing, continued to work.

The clouds came in fast and sinister, and the rains started. He looked for his daughter only to find the car now empty. Lightning overhead drew his attention, and he saw his daughter sitting on the roof. He cried out her name and ran for a ladder.

She was back in the forest now. Little Anya playing

in the grass once more, only this time there were other creatures. Big, gnarly things with horns and giant paws. They lumbered forward, surrounding the small child.

Anya cried out and tried to run, to save herself, but the ground moved, and she couldn't get close to the child. She watched in horror as the beast tore into the little girl. Her screams echoed around them, and Anya could do nothing but turn and run.

Six years old now, Anya was picking flowers for her mother. Her father was only five feet away. Alexis was trailing behind. Grown Anya looked on as the family made their way home.

When the ground beneath them shook, her father turned to check on his girls. But Anya was already gone. Hands in his hair, he called out her name. The tears fell in thick, black streams down his face, which he wiped away in menacing streaks across his cheeks.

Alexis sobbed deep, guttural sounds. The pair stood, night and fire encompassing them in their pain.

"Anya!" She heard from afar.

Behind her, she saw nothing but the shadows.

"Anya?" The voice again. Her father?

Afraid to venture into the void, she turned back to her family only to find them gone. Replaced by her mother, drunk in the kitchen.

No need for a younger Anya this time. This memory was fresh in her mind. The rage on her face, the hatred in her words. It was all so raw.

The surrounding kitchen may have been blurred, but the memory of that fight was as clear as day. She watched her mother struggle to stand before coming at her, fast and wild.

This time, she had a knife. This time, she plunged the

dagger into her youngest daughter with glee in her eyes and stood over Anya as she bled to death.

"Anya! Where are you?"

The voice was following, but she couldn't figure out where it was coming from. It felt familiar. It gave her a glimmer of hope in the gloom, but she just couldn't find it.

Young and carefree once more, Anya watched herself roaming a field of flowers. They swayed in the wind as she skipped and laughed. Birds sang overhead. At the edge of the field, she found a lake. It was so pure she could see the bottom and the fish swimming around.

She tiptoed in, feeling the chilly water on her bare feet. In the sky, two suns shone down and warmed her face. She walked in, letting her summer dress get wet and heavy.

But it got too heavy.

"Anya!"

The little girl turned too this time. Both Anya's looking for the voice but seeing nothing.

Her dress was getting heavier, and her feet sank into the sand. Anya tried to move forward to help the girl but, again, she couldn't get close.

Little Anya screamed when she saw something big coming upon her. Through the clear waters, a monster hurried forward, leaving thick blood in its wake. Both Anya's screamed as the creature broke free, jumping high over the water, coming down, teeth first into the child.

Running from the water and the monster, Anya found herself in her old back yard. She saw her mother in the kitchen, dancing and playing with Alexis as they cooked dinner. Anya, seven years old, was helping her father weed the plants.

She tugged at the stubborn roots and laughed when she sprayed dirt on her father's clean shirt. He laughed too.

Grown Anya closed her eyes. Grown Anya knew this memory all too well and didn't want to have to relive it.

She turned and ran but came full circle on the happy family. She could do nothing but watch as her mother and sister brought food out to the small table on the grass.

She watched her young self race into the house to wash up.

She heard the cars before she saw them.

They came from the void behind, big and menacing with flames trailing behind. The men that came forward had black eyes and were hunched and broken.

Demons.

They invaded her space, bringing their wickedness into the no longer peaceful garden. The sun disappeared, replaced by a menacing green ball of fire.

Her father stood and moved upon them, arms raised and angry. Little Anya returned, her smile dropping as she watched the demons beat and break her father. He struggled until they struck him with a large bat.

She saw blood and tears and the end of them all.

Little Anya ran after the men, clawing at their boots, begging for her father to come back, but was kicked away. The young girl cried and ran for a mother that couldn't even look at her.

"Anya! Can you hear me?"

Now the house was empty. Their things sold or given away. The pictures taken off the walls, and their lives boxed up.

Anya watched as Uncle Mark appeared, young and sad looking. Her mother, dark and unforgiving, moved to the doorway.

"Anya! Anya!"

Little Anya cried on the floor as mother hugged Alexis and Uncle Mark goodbye.

"Anya! I see you! Anya!"

The big car waited outside. The demons standing vigil.

"Anya! Look behind you!"

Her mother looked down at her youngest daughter. Anya reached out for comfort.

"Anya! We're here!"

Mother turned and left without a word. She walked to the demons and gave them her hands. They bound her and put her in the car.

She was ready to serve her own prison sentence. Her punishment from the Devils. Her daughter's fault.

"Anya!"

A bark brought her out of the memory. The house and her family faded as she turned, furiously scanning the dark for signs of the sound. The black turned to grey, and she could see something in the distance.

Low and fast, it moved toward her. She feared another monster and made to run, but his bark held her still.

"Ozzie?"

The dog answered and picked up his pace. She matched him and ran forward, arms out, tears streaming. The dog jumped into her arms, licking and wiggling in his greeting.

Anya fell to the ground, sobbing and laughing as Ozzie ran around her, barking and snuggling close.

“Anya,” the voice said from close by.

As she looked up, Oran came into view. He seemed hazy, like looking through weathered glass. But she could see him. He was the voice.

“Can you see me? Anya?” He asked, coming close but stopping short.

“Are you really here?” She said, her voice breaking.

“Yes. And we have to move. We have to go home."

Ozzie barked and left her side. He moved to Oran, turning hazy as he got closer.

Around them, the darkness receded, and the scene changed.

“No, Anya! You need to focus on us. Only us!” Oran yelled, sounding distant.

“I can’t...” she replied, her mind drawn to the little girl in the woods.

Little Anya was collecting pine cones. She and Alexis had on their warmest clothes and were going to paint the cones and hang them in the house.

The snow was coming, and Alexis was ready to leave.

“Anya, look at me." Oran was further away now. Ozzie too.

She reached for him, and he came to her, leaping over the black ground. He licked her cheek and put his head on her leg. Anya looked back to her sister and felt the pull.

“I need to-”

“You need to keep a hand on Ozzie and move with him. Don’t let go, no matter what. You hear me?”

Anya nodded and stood, her eyes still on Alexis and herself. But she kept her hand on Ozzie as he moved.

The trees blurred, and the ground shimmered like asphalt in the desert sun. Beneath them, the dirt of the forest turned to rusted steel. With her hand firmly on Ozzie, she looked up and saw a train heading their way.

It was coming fast. Around the tracks, she saw nothing but a wasteland: burned trees and desolate fields.

A movement behind drew both their attention. She saw a figure coming forward, but the train was approaching in front. Oran stood on the tracks, shouting her name, and Ozzie's.

Ozzie barked and tugged. Anya picked up her pace and started running toward Oran and the train. She tried to slow, but Ozzie was determined to make it back.

She looked behind and saw an army of demons heading their way. The train loomed ahead, black and dirty, and grinding on the tracks.

The ground shook.

She couldn't hear Oran anymore. The steel on steel screeched so loud, even Ozzie flinched. But they persisted. They ran, head-on, into the oncoming train, and Anya screamed upon impact.

"Anya?"

Ozzie licked her face as she opened her eyes. She saw Oran, worried but happy. She shot up, looking back for the demons, but found herself in a bed.

Her bed, in her suite at the Brothers' compound.

"Is this real?" She whispered.

Oran sighed and brushed his hand over Ozzie, dust coming away in the air.

"It's real. You're back. You're safe."

# CHAPTER 31

**Way After**

"Sutton Park, come in. Sutton Park?" Baz said into the receiver.

"Here, Baz. Carlsberg got your message. She wants you to go to the Hall. Take the girl. She'll meet you," the voice on the other end replied.

"My team?"

"They should be safe in the Hollows. We're sending the Burlak to get you and Charlie. The rest will just have to wait for now. If the cold doesn't let up, we'll send someone back for them. I assume they left with rations?"

"Yeah. They'll be fine for a few days."

"Ok. The Burlak should be there soon. Listen out," the voice instructed.

"Yup. Out." Baz clicked off the walkie talkie before he got a reply. He seemed mad.

"Who is that?" Gabby asked again.

The first time he'd told her to mind her own business, and she hadn't pushed it. But now, they were talking about going out during a whiteout. Were they insane?

"Who's Carlsberg?"

"You'll find out when we get there," Charlie remarked.

"I'm not going out in this! We'll die!"

"Not likely."

Gabby frowned. They were taking her to the Great Hall, and she was partly grateful. Knowing she was running out of time, it was essential to make it there on time. But how would they cross that distance in the snow?

After half an hour, she got her answer when the ground above rumbled, and dirt fell from the unsecured ceiling.

Charlie stood and put out the fire as Baz gathered their things. He threw Gabby her extra layers, and she got dressed as quickly as possible. He kept her bag as they made their way around the corner where Gabby saw some kind of canvas across the exit. They'd pinned it into the walls, which let in only a fraction of light from the outside.

When he pulled it back, they were hit with icy air and snow. It whipped around as they climbed out, and Gabby watched as Charlie hurried to cover the hole once more.

"Our ride's here," Baz yelled over the wind.

He pointed over her shoulder, and Gabby almost fell back as the massive truck came into view.

Through the blizzard, she saw a grey tank making its way over the ice and snow. It looked massive - bigger than any of the buses she had been on.

The tires, all six of them, were taller than her, and there was a ladder on the side to climb in. The side door opened, and Baz lifted her into the arms of another man. She pulled herself free and moved to the corner. To her surprise, the cab was warm.

Baz and Charlie jumped in, and the door slammed shut with a thud. They were on the move before she had time to think.

"Hey, thanks for the lift," Baz called, shaking the hand of the man in the back. He leaned over and patted the driver on the shoulder.

"You guys are always in the wrong place at the wrong time!" The driver joked.

"Who's the girl?" The man in the back asked.

"Brendan, Gabby. Gabby, Brendan," Baz said, waving his hand between the two. Neither responded.

"Hey, it true Carlsberg is coming down?" Brendan asked.

Gabby couldn't tell if he seemed nervous or excited.

"She wants to meet our new friend here." Baz nodded toward Gabby.

"What's so special?"

"Nothing from what I can see."

Gabby rolled her eyes and looked out the window. She couldn't believe what was happening. Not only were the Gulls a highly organized group, but they also had a truck that could make it through a whiteout. She thought most vehicles had been destroyed by the Brotherhood almost a century ago.

The monstrous truck quickly made it over the icy terrain, and it was a matter of minutes before she saw the angry skies over the compound. As they got closer, the snow seemed to let up and turn to rain. It pounded on the hard roof but had no effect. The immense wheels covered their distance within an hour.

"Ok. Let's go," Baz said, opening the door.

He jumped down, followed by Charlie and Brendan. Gabby got to the door and grabbed for the ladder. It was easily a six-foot drop to the slippery ground, so she ignored their sneers and took the safer route.

Inside the Great Hall, Gabby wasn't sure what to expect. With how she used to view the Gulls, she half expected to find a group of dirty, animal-like creatures. She'd always thought they were violent and dumb and acted on impulse. That all the time spent in the Plains had turned them into something more primal.

But the people she'd met proved her completely wrong. When she walked through the old door, she froze in shock.

The Hall was filled with some two hundred people. They were talking and trading and packing bags. One table held dozens of walkie talkies. Others had goods to trade and clothes to disburse. It was loud, but she could see the organization. They were a team, whether they knew each other or not.

Baz walked in, leaving Gabby in the doorway. She watched him walk to a table and place his walkie down, taking another as he spoke. He grabbed some food from the next table and nodded his thanks. The driver of their big truck brushed by and followed Baz to the table. She shook the man's hand and traded her walkie for another. She then spoke to Baz briefly before making her way into the crowd.

Baz turned back and motioned for Gabby to follow. She had no other option and stayed with the only person she knew.

It wasn't long before the men and women surrounding started eyeing her suspiciously. Gabby was new. Gabby was why they were here. She heard mumblings and whispers and tried to keep her head down, not totally convinced the stories of violence hadn't been exaggerated.

"You made it," a man near the main doors called.

“Just about,” Baz laughed. He hugged the man and turned to Gabby. “Here she is.”

The man nodded and looked over his shoulder. A woman with cropped hair and a scowl looked up. Her eyes narrowed as she took Gabby in before sending the girl she'd been speaking to away.

“Gabby?” She asked.

Gabby nodded, afraid her voice would shake if she spoke.

“You're why we're all here,” she said, looking around. “Why is that?”

“Uh, I'm not-” Gabby started before being cut off.

“You've been coming here for years. My people have seen you, so don't lie. Always on the same day." The woman looked to a watch on her wrist. “Today, to be exact. Tell me why.”

Gabby looked at Baz and down at her feet. She'd felt foolish explaining it to him and Charlie and didn't really want to go into it with so many people around.

“She claims not to know,” Baz offered.

“Is that true? You come here once a year, every year, on the anniversary of the end of the world…and you don't know why?”

The woman sounded surprised more than angry. Gabby looked and saw the curiosity on her face.

“She claims to *feel a pull*. She said she'll understand it one day." Baz's tone was casually offensive, and Gabby scowled.

“I can't explain it. I just…I need to be here in case-”

“Who are you waiting for?” The woman asked suddenly, stepping forward. As she did, thunder cracked overhead.

“We should finish up,” the man near the doors said,

putting a hand on her arm.

The woman held Gabby's gaze before turning and nodding. "You're right, Tony. Start making arrangements."

Tony took her arm and kissed her hand before leaving her side. Gabby watched him, and his people move between the tables, and the whole room started shutting down.

Trades were made.

Stories were swapped.

It was time to go home.

"The factions don't get to gather like this too often. We have people all over the country, and they work as one, but rarely do they get to meet up," the woman told Gabby as they watched everyone move. "The Gulls. We started out so small - just a group of people trying to survive after the Crack. We were outcasts and given little choice but to swoop in and take what we could. The stories have been embellished over the years, but our numbers haven't. Every day people come out to the Plains because they have nowhere else to go."

Gabby watched as the last of the tables were put away, and people said their goodbyes. She saw families and children and laughter. It was amazing.

"But you steal. You hurt people!" She refused to feel sympathy for the group she'd feared for so long.

"We steal, yes. We hurt...when necessary. As I said, the stories have been embellished."

Someone came to the woman and told her they were all ready to go. Gabby glanced out the tall windows and saw the driving rain. She was sure the snowstorm was still raging outside of the compound. How many of those vehicles did they have?

"We'll send everyone here home, except Baz, Charlie and Gemma. They can go collect the team still in the Hollows," the woman instructed.

Tony returned, three walkie talkies in his hands. "I think they're ready, but are you sure about this? Maybe we should keep some of them back?"

"That's why I have you," the woman said, laying a gentle kiss on his cheek.

"They won't survive the snow!" Gabby cried suddenly, genuinely worried about the people around her.

Tony laughed. "Everybody ready?"

The room filled with confirmations. Gabby looked to the children and became nervous. They weren't dressed right. They would freeze if they made it passed the rains. How could they-

A loud snap filled the room. Gabby looked toward the sound to see Tony. His arms were raised, and she saw Light at the tips of his fingers.

Back in the Hall, the people were gone. Their bags and tables, everything had vanished. Her mouth fell open as she turned back.

"You're...Lightborn?" She gasped, taking a step back.

The woman laughed and nodded. "Handy to have around, in a pinch."

Behind them, Baz and Charlie made their way back outside with Gemma, the driver. The woman told them to find the rest of his team and return to the Hall. Tony would then send them home.

"What about you?" Baz called before he left.

"Tony and I will wait here with Gabby. Today's the day, right? I'm dying to see what will happen!"

Gabby moved back. She was in shock. She'd never seen anyone use Light before and felt woozy. The Lightborn had been run out of society years ago. But the Gulls were led by one?

"Can you bring in some cots, Tony? It's late. I doubt whatever we're waiting for will mind if we take a little midnight nap." The woman stretched and smiled at Gabby.

Three cots appeared, with blankets and pillows. Thunder cracked overhead as Gabby sat down, trying to unravel the mess of the last couple of days.

"You hungry?" Tony asked, holding out a sandwich.

Gabby shook her head and looked back to the woman. She was on her cot, eyes closed, and a blanket over her legs.

"What about you? Alexis? You hungry?"

Alexis opened her eyes and smiled. "Always."

# CHAPTER 32

**2 weeks to the Tournament**

For me, all that time lost in the dark felt like months. Watching my life play over and over, my mistakes and regrets consumed me in the black void. I was utterly lost.

The darkness had been vast and disturbing. Looking into it, I often saw flashes and movement and was sure something was stalking me. And the nightmares had been so real. My memories were distorted but still brought out the guilt in my gut. I watched my father get dragged away over a dozen times before Oran and Ozzie found me.

The first couple of days back in the real world, the Brothers left me alone. I stayed in my room with Ozzie and spoke to no-one. My mind was so consumed with the nightmares, I didn't even try to stop Uri's intrusions.

But on the third day, I took a breath and opened the curtains. I got dressed, ate some food and took Ozzie for a walk. Being out in the open was daunting at first. I had been in the open in a sense, my dreams surrounding me in the abyss. Walking in the grass under the sun, I had to remind myself that I wasn't lost. Ozzie stayed close, sensing my hesitation.

"You look better," Oran called from behind.

I turned to see a beautiful Australian Shepherd come

running for Ozzie. He looked at me for permission before running to play.

"I don't know that I feel better."

"You will. I know you feel lost, but you're not anymore. It will get better."

"How much did you see?" I asked, eyes to the ground.

"Enough. Enough to know how hard that must have been for you. I can't even imagine-"

"Thank you for finding me," I blurted out.

I'd wanted to thank him for days but wasn't ready to see anyone before now.

"I know you only did it so I would help, but-"

"That's not true, Anya. I went in there because..." Oran stopped and tugged on his ear.

He ran a hand through his hair and looked at me with kind eyes.

"Anya, I know you feel trapped here. I know we brought you here, and you hate us for everything. But you're not just a tool. We want you and your family to come with us."

I raised my eyebrows and let out a sharp breath. "You want me to come? To abandon everyone and everything I've ever known? You all know what will happen after we open that portal. The world will crumble in on itself and everyone-"

Oran raised his hand to stop me. "That will happen no matter what we do. You've seen it. We can't stop it. Maybe it won't happen next week, but it's coming. Don't you want a chance at something better?"

"Better? This is all your fault! You and your Brothers and this need to be all-powerful. You did this. You! The decay I've seen...why didn't you stop? When you first noticed it, why didn't you stop?"

I tried not to yell, but I was scared to hold in my anger any longer. Afraid I would be consumed with the darkness all over again.

"You're right. We were arrogant. We thought we could fix it, and we were wrong."

I didn't know what to say. Hearing Oran admit to their wrongdoing was refreshing but frustrating. I liked Oran, even with everything that had happened. He was kind to me and had shown me his heart was good. But he'd stood by for too long, and he was just as responsible as the others.

I looked back to the dogs and smiled as they ran around, barking and jumping. Ozzie was happy to be out again, and I felt yet another pang of guilt for keeping him inside for so long. Oran moved closer, and we watched the dogs together. I could sense he wanted to say something more, but he held back. When I turned to speak, he had a strange look on his face.

"Uri and Anwar would like you to come to the Hall," he said, seemingly out of nowhere.

I looked around, confused. "How do you-" I stopped short as he tapped his temple and shrugged.

"I don't know if I'm ready."

"They know that. But Anwar thinks he's found the right place. Uri wants you there."

Shaking my head, I sighed and turned to Ozzie. Both dogs came running as we all turned back. Oran stayed quiet, but my mind was suddenly racing.

"How did Anwar find the place? What happened? Are you saying he actually opened the portal? Why do you even need me if-"

"Slow down. It's a little complicated, but he thinks he's found the right place. It happened while you were...

gone. But it took its toll. He opened the portal but didn't go through. We need your strength to be sure it's safe."

"And if I don't have any strength?" I said, looking at my hands.

I hadn't used my Light since being back, eating only what they gave me and using the clothes I'd already conjured. The idea of being powerless was crippling, and I wasn't ready to find out.

Oran stopped and took my hands in his. He looked down and put his hand on the ugly black marks on my palms.

"Do you feel weak?"

"I don't know," I confessed.

"You're not. I can feel your power."

I took my hands back and shoved them in the pocket of my hoodie. When Oran told me about the men I'd killed and the Light I'd stolen, I almost threw up. Just the thought of taking in their Light made my skin crawl. I had a nasty mark on my side where the Lightborn attacked, and Uri tried to heal me. But I remembered little of that night in Egypt. Was the power still there? Or did I leave it behind in my dreams?

As we approached the Hall, I turned to Ozzie and told him to go play. He happily ran off with the Aussie, and I suddenly felt cold without him. Inside, Uri and Anwar were arguing.

"...to the slaughter. How would that look?" Uri yelled.

"What does it matter, Uri? We are in charge. They do as they're told!" Anwar raged back.

"Do they ever not fight?" I quipped to Oran.

He rolled his eyes, and I could see how much it drained him. I wondered how long he had been in the middle of the two.

Oran cleared his throat, and his Brothers went quiet. Uri smiled when he saw me. Anwar clicked his tongue and turned his back. Nothing had changed, apparently.

"Anya. Nice to see you out and about. How are you feeling?"

"Fine."

Uri nodded and looked to Oran. They didn't speak out loud, and I wondered how often they communicated this way. Anwar didn't seem to react.

Their dynamic always intrigued me. Uri was undoubtedly in charge, but I could tell they each had a say in things. Being a trio, they voted when they couldn't all agree. But the way Anwar behaved, it was obvious he lost the vote one too many times.

"I know this is a lot to ask so soon," Uri said, turning to me, "but we're under a time crunch here. It's only twelve days until the first day of the Tournaments, and we need to be ready."

"Right. Why put off the end of the world?" I provoked.

Uri moved to speak, but Anwar turned and interrupted. "Can we just get on with it?"

Oran sighed quietly and moved toward Anwar. "What do you need?"

"We don't need anything," I answered, moving into the middle of the Hall. "If he's found the place, then he just needs to find it again. I can follow his Light."

I stood tall and confident, and they each looked surprised at my arrogance. After seeing my childhood self open a portal with such ease, I suddenly felt incredibly self-assured. It came so easily to me once, and I knew I had it in me. I just needed to stop holding back.

Anwar definitely wanted to comment on my sudden bravado, but I saw Uri hush him. Wishing I could hear what they were saying, I knew I should've spent more time practising the mind-reading schtick. To be privy to their private conversations would make life a lot easier.

"Ok. Fine. Just don't hold me back," Anwar warned as he came to join me.

We stood toe to toe and hesitated. The idea of holding his hand and sharing my Light was nauseating, and I could see he felt the same. Taking the high road, I held my hands out, palms up. He let out a sharp breath before placing his hands on mine.

The electricity was immediate, and we both flinched. I didn't want to look him in the eye but knew it was the only way. One deep, deep breath later, I looked up and locked my eyes on his. His whole face made me angry, and the longer I held his gaze, the angrier I got.

After a few minutes, Anwar stepped back abruptly, breaking our connection.

"This isn't going to work. She's too hostile!"

"I'm hostile? Is that a joke?" I laughed as the grown man threw yet another tantrum.

It took both of his Brothers' encouragement before he came back to where I stood.

This time I tried to keep my feelings inside. I let my mind go to the unknown and used Anwar's Light to guide me to what he wanted me to see. It was obvious he was struggling and, truth be told, his Light felt weak. Weaker than my own, even. Was this due to him opening the portal already? Or was he just not that strong to begin with?

I was almost ready to give in when I saw it. His mind was stumbling through the stars, drifting aimlessly, it felt, until he seemed to fixate on something. His mind jumped and locked on as warmth spread from his hands, up to my arms. I let him take me where he wanted to go, his orange Glimmer leading my mind along with his. The sound of a portal opening to my side was unmistakable and filled the room as I saw what his mind was seeing.

We opened our eyes, and I took my hands back, wiping them on my jeans. Anwar turned to the portal with tears in his eyes. He covered his mouth and looked to his Brothers, who stood in awe of the beauty.

I kept my eyes on the unfamiliar world in front of us and groaned. I didn't want to be the bearer of bad news, but I knew that Anwar had failed before the portal opened.

"I did it!" Anwar yelled, fists in the air, moving forward.

"Wait," I said, putting a hand out to stop him. "You didn't. Sorry-"

They looked at me, brows furrowed. Anwar wiped his eyes and turned on me.

"What?"

"It's not what you're looking for. It's not a new world."

Anwar moved, his arm raised aggressively, but Oran got between us.

"Whoa. Calm down. Anya, what are you talking about?"

"Look. In the distance? That's a bridge. I can see the cars. He didn't find an alternative world. He found...I don't know, Switzerland, maybe? Probably old Switzerland given the lack of houses, but still."

The Three turned their attention to the portal. They looked closer, eyes squinting into the distance. I watched as each of them slumped, shoulders rolling forward and eyes dropping to the floor.

"I'm sorry," I breathed, moving a few extra feet from Anwar, sure he would blow up at any minute.

"She's sorry," Anwar said under his breath. "She's sorry." He looked at me and pointed right in my face, "You did this! You held me back!"

"Don't, Anwar," Uri warned, his icy tone cutting through the tension. "She's right. You failed."

The argument that followed was the worst I'd witnessed. They yelled, getting into each other's faces and screaming insults. They seemed to let out every frustration each of them had ever felt. They'd been together for decades, and it showed. I was just amazed it didn't turn violent.

My eyes drifted back to the portal, and I briefly considered jumping through. Instead, I waved my hand and closed the broken wall, thinking back to the memory of myself as a young child. It had been so easy for me once. Coming up with imaginary worlds was second nature. My poor family would be frantic, thinking I was lost, but I was having the time of my life.

One particular place always stuck out in my mind, even before I'd seen it again in the darkness. I'd been dreaming about it for years, even all these years later. It was filled with strange flowers and open fields. There were two suns, and the waters ran pink. I couldn't be sure I hadn't created the place myself, but it stood vividly in my mind.

The yelling behind me echoed around the hall. Closing my eyes, I let the sound wash away and tried to focus on the little blue flowers that grew from the trees. Instead of angry men, I heard birds singing and felt the sweet breeze on my face.

The suns were warm, and I could feel the soft yellow

grass under my toes. When I opened my eyes, I saw my Light glow and open the air in front of me. The purple-blue Glimmer lit up my face and opened to show me what my three-year-old self had imagined.

It was real, and it was right there.

"Hey," I said, keeping my eyes on the pink and orange sky. "Hey!"

The Three finally calmed and turned their attention to me. I heard a gasp and whispers from behind as I waited for them to join me. Oran was first at my side. He nudged my arm and smiled as the suns warmed his face. Uri appeared on my left, mouth open, and a hand reaching out. Anwar stayed back.

"How did you..." Uri trailed off and took a step forward.

"Don't!" Anwar yelled. "You don't know where that is. She could trap you in there!"

I let out an exhausted breath and looked at Uri. He was standing two feet from the portal, and I could see he wanted to go through. Without asking, I moved forward, passed Uri, and let the Light wash over me. Looking back, I motioned for him to join me. Both he and Oran came willingly, but I closed the portal before Anwar could make up his mind.

"He won't like that," Oran laughed.

"Who cares?" Uri said, eyes wide like a child as he took it all in.

"How did you do this?" Oran asked, moving toward the water.

"I just needed to remember what I was capable of," I said, watching the men invade this precious space.

It felt wrong having them there, but I knew it was the only way. This was going to happen whether I helped or not. They would never stop, and I knew deep down they would do anything to escape. All I could hope was that we could work with the remaining Lightborn to fix their mess once they were gone.

# CHAPTER 33

Though in awe, Oran and Uri didn't want to spend too much time in the alternate reality. I could see they were uncomfortable in the unfamiliar world and were anxious to get back. I obliged, eager myself to get them out. The Great Hall came to me with ease, and we were back on familiar ground after twenty minutes.

Anwar was nowhere in sight.

"Don't worry about him. He'll get on board." Uri answered the question nobody asked. "Well done, Anya."

I smiled, despite myself, and blushed slightly. Oran patted my shoulder as he passed, a smile on his face and a skip in his step. I felt proud. I didn't want to, but I couldn't help it. I'd done in an instant what the great Anwar hadn't been able to in a decade. No doubt he was off sulking somewhere.

"What are you thinking?" Oran asked his Brother, out loud this time so I could hear.

"That we're going to need to send a team to check things out. We only saw a fraction of that world. We need to know more."

"We're running out of time, Uri. The games start in less than two weeks."

Uri put a hand on Oran's shoulder and smiled. "But we're so close. Finally."

"Then let's do it tonight. We can get a team together

and send them in as soon as possible. We can give them a few days to explore and report back." Oran looked back at me. "Can you handle that?"

I nodded, but my heart beat faster as they kept planning. The place I took them - the wonderland of my childhood - was precious to me. I feared what these men would do to it. They would send Lightborn, and how could I know what their power would do? It was so close to destroying this world, and we had no way of knowing how it would affect things through the portal.

I spent the next few hours in my room with Ozzie snoozing at my side, exhausted from his playdate. I watched an old movie I'd seen a hundred times, letting my mind relax and lose focus. I needed to recharge. Finding the world had been easy, but the Light it took to get us there and back was significant.

Outside my window, I saw lots of movement. Cars came in and out of the gates, moving from the main building to the Great Hall. I wondered how they would choose the team.

Would anybody really volunteer to be sent to another time and space? I wouldn't be first in line, that much I knew.

Somewhere during the movie, my mind wandered to my home. I thought about Alexis and my mother. I missed Uncle Mark's cooking and Frankie's laugh.

Did they miss me?

My mother was the reason I was gone, but I was the reason my father was gone. Could they forgive her like they forgave me? Alexis would graduate soon, and Frankie was coming up on the testing age. Had they just gone on with their lives?

That night, I sent a team of twelve Lightborn through

a portal to a whole new world, and they didn't even hesitate. Their leaders asked them to go, and they went blindly into the unknown. Their loyalty frightened me, and I thought back to the meeting of the Network.

We wanted to make the Lightborn understand what the Brotherhood was responsible for. But if they were all this obedient, I doubted we would be able to get through to them.

With each crossing, I felt my power wane. Finding the world and opening the portal required power, but holding it steady enough for twelve Lightborn and their equipment to make it through took all my focus. When the last of them was through, I let out a breath and snapped my hands shut. My head spun, and I reached out for stability. Oran took my arm and held me steady.

"Good job," he said, squeezing gently. "Doing this on your own-"

"Where is Anwar?" I asked, breathless.

"We're not sure," Oran admitted, looking to Uri.

He seemed pleased with my work, but I could see an inner fury. No doubt, they expected Anwar to be here to help.

Over the next few days, they had me open the portal at noon every day. The team leader was waiting in the same spot they'd jumped through, ready to report. I knew it was just as much about the reports as about my ability to open the portal again. But Uri and Oran seemed happy at what they were hearing, and I could feel my power strengthening the more I used it.

With only ten days until the Tournament, I was feeling a sickness deep down. From the moment of the announcement, I'd felt it, and now it was worse than ever. We all knew what kind of turmoil the games would bring.

After all the power used at the last Tournament, the earth fought back with a bang. A long-dormant volcano in Italy erupted with no warning, throwing a cloud of ash over most of Europe. The ring of destruction spread out to almost a hundred kilometres, and thousands of lives were lost.

The memory of this had taken me back to the Veil. It took me to the Ludus to ask for help. Even then, I knew that things would end in disaster, and I couldn't help but wonder what Mr Parks was planning. Many of the Lightborn at the Network's meeting seemed sceptical.

And why shouldn't they be?

Who was I to suddenly announce that I knew what the Brothers were planning?

But even without that knowledge, they knew what destruction the Lightborn would cause in the pursuit of a damn trophy. I could only hope that they were still planning to help - not me, but everyone else.

I'd sent Ozzie to Mr Parks over three weeks ago, confirming the Brothers' plans. I hadn't expected an answer necessarily, but it was hard to not think about them coming to get me. Looking at things now, I wasn't even sure what the best plan would be. If they tried to stop the Tournament, they would be outnumbered and thrown into the prison camps. The Games would go on, and nothing would change.

Even stopping the Brothers from jumping through my portal seemed futile. Oran was right: the Veils dropping was inevitable. So how could we fight this? Deep down, I knew the damage was already done, and our only course would be to try to contain the decay and keep as many people safe as possible.

It was still early, the sun low and cool. I wasn't expected at the Hall for a few hours and spent my morning walk with Ozzie making up my mind: I needed to risk getting another message out. Uri and Oran had been distracted the last few days, no doubt planning their great escape. I hadn't seen Anwar, and that was fine by me.

Nobody came running when I sent Ozzie away. I stared at the food I'd made as a distraction, but couldn't face it until Ozzie was back and safe. I knew the message would be difficult to hear, but they needed to know everything. When he came back to me, I gave him a bone and let out a sigh.

The daily check-in went according to plan, and they released me for the rest of the day. Ozzie was loving having extra time for walks, and I felt better being with him outside. Our usual route took us to the river and into the small woods. Today though, we walked the other direction, away from the houses I couldn't see and toward the part of the compound I ordinarily avoided.

It was where Anwar lived, I was sure. I could almost feel his anger as I got too close. For some reason today, I was drawn to the end of the property. I neared the wall, throwing a toy for Ozzie to collect and put my hand on the stone. The Light barrier was clear as day, and I knew they would be checking on me.

Ozzie and I followed the wall further back into the compound. The gates and the Great Hall faded as we made our way parallel to the wall. I could feel we were closing in on the third house, but we pressed on, moving passed the hidden area and toward the water I could see in the distance. The lake sparkled in the fading light, and I sat on a hill watching Ozzie roll around in the grass. After a while, he came and sat by me, happy to rest a beat.

We sat for a few minutes before I felt it. Ozzie felt it too, his ears perking up and his head tilting. We both looked around, unsure of what we were feeling. Looking back toward the gates, I wondered if Anwar was back and angrier than ever.

"Anya? Can you hear me? I don't have much time." The voice surprised me, coming from nowhere in particular.

"Mr Parks?" I gasped, looking around.

To my left, Ozzie was sniffing the air. He jumped back when Mr Parks materialized in front of us. Ozzie barked and went to him, rubbing his nose on his leg.

"I have to be quick. I'm sorry it took so long-"

"Oh, my Elders! You're here-Wait, they'll find you!" I said, suddenly afraid the Brothers would descend upon us at any second.

"It's ok. I made arrangements. Just listen. We got both of your messages. But after this morning, we talked again, and we're getting ready. The entire Network is coming."

Mr Parks seemed to flicker in and out, his urgent voice holding steady in the air.

"But Uri is looking-"

"He won't find anything. We're careful. But I needed you to know that we're coming. We've got a plan, and we're coming. Just keep doing what you're doing."

I couldn't believe what I was seeing. I wanted to tell him everything. More so, I wanted to take his hand and go with him, but I knew I couldn't.

"What I said this morning about letting them-"

Mr Parks waved his hand and cut me off. "It's ok. I

know this must be so difficult for you-I have to go. Just know, you're not alone."

He was gone before I could speak. Ozzie sniffed the ground and came back to me, licking my hand to comfort us both.

Reluctantly, we made it back to our room. Thoughts of the Network and the rebels were constantly on the periphery of my mind, and I tried harder than ever to keep them at bay. The last thing we needed was for Uri to see my meeting inside their walls with Mr Parks.

The next couple of days were total chaos. Without asking too many questions, I found out there had been a series of inexplicable events around the world. I snuck into the theatre room at night to watch the news and was in awe of the risks they'd taken to get a message to me.

Apparently, when Mr Parks told me he'd made arrangements, that meant he'd asked people in the Network to use their Light to draw attention away from the compound. With all the events happening simultaneously, it would have been impossible to pinpoint them all. He came and went unnoticed.

But with eight days until the Tournament, my nerves were fraying. Mr Parks hadn't told me details about the plan, and I woke up every day wondering if today was the day. I tried to keep my mind neutral, but I couldn't help looking to the gates. If they came for me, I wanted to be ready.

The team of Lightborn had been exploring for days. Each daily report seemed better than the last, and I could tell Uri and Oran were getting excited. I brought the team back with only a week to go until the Tournament. Uri was more than happy with their findings, and

I could see his mind plotting.

They had a week to get themselves ready. Just seven days to prepare their families to abandon the world they'd ruined.

That gave me a week to figure out what to do. I needed to decide once and for all if I should go forward with the plan and let them go. Oran was offering my family and me a place with them, and I would be lying if I said it wasn't tempting. But my heart pulled me back to the Ludus and Mr Parks.

I thought about all those young boys and their families, and what it would mean to leave them behind. They were my family too, and I knew I couldn't just abandon them.

I didn't know what the Network was planning. In my last message, I'd told Mr Parks it would be best to let the Brotherhood leave. I'd already made things worse by opening the portal every day, and I knew the scale would be much more severe when the day finally came.

The damage I could cause frightened me, though I had finally come to terms with it. It was the only way I could see us moving towards healing.

Though I couldn't know when to be ready or what to expect from the Network, I knew that I couldn't rely on them to succeed. The odds were against them at every turn, and I needed to be ready for their failure.

I felt the weight of the world on my shoulders and just hoped they listened to my plea and would be ready to help pick up the pieces.

# CHAPTER 34

"Good morning, and welcome everyone to Day 1 of The Tournament of Light! I know you've all been itching to get inside the arenas since the Brotherhood made their announcement, and it has been a long three month wait. But it's finally here! We will be with you throughout the Tournament, bringing you coverage of all the games and entertainment, so don't worry if you can't make it. Brother's Dispatch has you covered!"

"Cut, I think we got it."

Audrey let her smile drop as the camera's light went out. She wasn't in the mood for a fifth take. As her producer checked the footage and spoke with his assistant, she lit a cigarette, taking in the crowd with tired eyes.

It never ceased to amaze how many people came to these things. It was as if they forgot about the disasters that always followed. Of course, she was part of the Brotherhood's spin team, so it just meant that she was good at her job.

"Yeah, that's great, Aud. Let's grab some people, and we'll do a couple of interviews. I'll try to get some excited fans, and then we'll head in to talk to the workers and the Lightborn."

Audrey smiled and nodded obediently. She wanted to sneak a pull from the flask in her jacket pocket but resisted. It would be a draining day, and she knew she would need it later.

"Ok, this is-"

"Audrey Kemper! Oh, my Elders! We watch you all the time!"

Her producer always managed to find the most enthusiastic fans.

"Oh, thanks. That's wonderful to hear. We're just going to ask you a few questions, and then we'll let you go. I know you must be excited to get inside."

Audrey smiled her best fake smile and got herself ready for the show.

"We're here now with Daniel. You seem pretty excited for the games to start?"

"Oh yeah! The Tournament of Light is, like, the best thing ever. I've been going since I was a kid and was so pumped when they said they were holding it early!" Daniel was practically jumping up and down as he spoke.

"What's your favourite part?" Audrey asked, trying to look sincere.

"Oh, the fire rounds, for sure. I mean, I love seeing their Light and what they can do, but the fire, man...it's awesome."

Audrey threw Daniel a few more softballs before thanking him and sending him on his way. He insisted on getting a picture and an autograph, and she obliged, as always.

The next three interviews went mostly the same. It wasn't often that people opposed to the Brotherhood came to the games. But when she saw her last interview coming forward, she got a grim feeling.

"Hi, I'm Audrey."

"Yeah. I've seen you on TV," the girl remarked, eyebrows raised and judgemental.

"You are?"

"Laura."

Audrey smiled and looked to her producer. Sometimes, even Steve missed the mark, and she knew that they wouldn't be showing Laura in her footage.

"So, Laura, you're here nice and early. Is this your first time at the Tournament?"

"Oh no, I come every time. We all do." She gestured behind her to a group of equally somber looking people.

"Family outing?" Audrey asked, keeping the sarcasm in her head.

"We're here to protest. These Tournaments do nothing but cause destruction to our already fragile world. You people worship the Lightborn like they're gods, but we know that they're not! And shame on you for preaching their propaganda. You spread their lies to the masses, and they just lap it up."

Laura looked proud of herself. She stood, hands on her hips, no doubt expecting Audrey to fight back.

"Well, it's a free world, so I won't keep you." She motioned for Laura to leave.

Confused, the girl went back to her angry friends. They all looked around to Audrey, cold eyes, and mean stares. They hated what and who she represented. Truth be told, she hated them too.

Being press meant Audrey and her team were allowed in through the back doors. She nodded to the other reporters and smiled at those she knew to be friendly. They all worked together, covering anything and everything newsworthy, but that didn't mean they were friends.

Oddly, the Brotherhood allowed the other news channels to continue their negative press, giving people the choice of what to watch. At first, she didn't understand why they would allow their criticizers to continue - being all-powerful, they could've put a stop to it decades ago.

But after so many years covering the Brotherhood, she knew how simple it really was: being all-powerful meant any criticisms were futile and irrelevant.

"Audrey? Hey!"

To her left, she saw Timi Lawrence coming her way. Audrey held in a groan and used all the strength she had to keep her eyes from rolling back into her skull.

Timi was a Brotherhood fanatic, drinking in whatever they said without questioning a thing. Audrey had met her once, briefly, and hadn't been impressed. Timi was shallow, small-minded, and not too bright. She was also small time, with very few followers. But her followers were just as mindless and easily led as she was, making them loud and dangerous.

"Hi! Wow, how cool is this?" Timi grinned and flicked her too blond hair.

"Yeah, it's something."

"This is my first year here," Timi whispered behind her hand, as though divulging some big secret. She tried too hard to be noticed but always fell short.

"Oh, well, I won't keep you then. Lots to see," Audrey said dismissively, but Timi didn't get the hint.

"You know, I grew up watching you. You're my total idol. I was glued to the screen during the Tournaments, wanting to be just like you."

Audrey smiled and looked at Steve for help. Timi was blabbing at her side about the importance of the Tournaments, and how the Brotherhood were stronger than ever. She'd been raised not to question them and was playing the part of ignorant sheep perfectly.

"Oh, Timi, hi. Nice to see you here," Steve said, finally doing his job.

"Hi, Steve. You know, I meant to thank you for the advice you gave me. I've really been working on my voice, you know. I want to make sure my followers get the truth - the real truth - from me first. If we let them go to the...other press, I mean...can you imagine. The lies they tell!"

Audrey was fuming. At Timi and her total lack of character, but also at herself. She was the reason people like Timi existed. They'd sat and watched Audrey tell the Brotherhood's lies for years and accepted it all as fact. It didn't occur to them to look anywhere else for the news. If they did, they would get a very different side to things.

The flask in her pocket was calling, and Audrey needed to get away.

"Aud? You listening?" Steve teased, he and Timi looking at her expectantly.

"What? Sorry no, I zoned out," she admitted taking a step back.

Timi moved with her, putting a hand on her arm. "Oh, I get it. You must still be furious over that whole thing with the teachers. I couldn't believe it when I saw your broadcast. How could those people complain about the Brothers? It makes me sick. They were protecting us, obviously. And people are mad because they're not being given all the information? As though they're entitled to it!"

"How do you know they were protecting us? And from what exactly?" Audrey said, stopping suddenly and turning on the young puppet.

Timi's smile faded as she looked on Audrey's serious face. "I don't know what you mean. Of course, they were protecting us. Why else would they-"

"Hold teachers hostage and interrogate them? What threat do you think a bunch of teachers could be? To the Three, no less?"

"I mean, I don't know. But if the Brotherhood says they're a threat, then we have to believe them. Why would they lie?"

Timi was glitching. Audrey smiled as she watched her struggling to answer the simple question. But it went against everything she was. Timi would never admit that the Brothers could possibly be wrong.

Steve appeared then, a smile on his face but a tight grip on Audrey's arm. "Timi, sorry, we need to get going. Lots to cover."

Timi's smile returned on cue. She thanked Audrey for her time and made her way down the hall. Audrey shuddered at the thought of what she would be broadcasting. Brotherhood propaganda full of lies and alternate facts - just like she would be doing.

"Hey. What do you think you're doing?" Steve reprimanded, pulling her close.

"What? I can't ask a simple que-"

"Shut up. You know your job. Smile. Ask our questions. Read our scripts. That's it. If you can't do that, you know where you're welcome."

Steve let go and stepped to the cameraman. The two talked briefly before turning and walking away.

The day dragged on as Audrey was forced to smile during countless trivial interviews. She spoke to some workers responsible for building the arenas and the staff inside, getting ready for the big opening. She talked to the man in charge and had him explain the schedule for the games. She even spoke to half a dozen Lightborn about their excitement to take part. Each interview more mind-numbing and misleading than the last. Audrey started drinking not long after lunch.

"Have you taken part in the games before...?"

"Oh, Joe. And no. This will be my first year. I came of age the year after the last Tournament."

Audrey nodded and looked past the camera to the large holding room. It spanned half of the arena and was filled with Lightborn and their people. Staff ran around, getting food and drinks. The press and their cameras took up their fair share of the space, getting their own interviews for those who couldn't attend.

"So, you must have been thrilled when they announced the Tournament early?" She said, not looking at him as he replied.

Along the back wall, the Lightborn were each given a cubicle of sorts. They could leave their things or use them for privacy. Audrey knew that each arena around the world looked the same. In Australia and Canada and Spain, to name a few, Lightborn were preparing for the first of the games. It didn't matter the time of day; they ran on the Brotherhood's schedule.

"I can imagine. And what's your secret weapon? What are you bringing to the floor today to prove your worth to the Three?"

"Well, I'm pretty good at controlling water, so..."

"Oh, how exciting. I always love water games!" Audrey feigned a giggle and looked to Steve.

He made a 'cut' sign with his hand and moved in to thank Joe for his time.

"You look tired," Steve said as he came back to Audrey. "Let's break for now. There's time before the first game. Come back looking fresh, ok?"

She smiled and nodded as though she could control the dark circles under her eyes. He left her alone, no doubt looking for Timi. Maybe Audrey would get lucky, and the Three would decide she was too old for this gig. Timi would jump through fire at the chance to be their new mouthpiece.

Outside, the sun was shining, and the crowds were getting more notable. The staff would let everyone inside soon enough, but they were happy to eat and drink outside for now. Music was playing, and everyone was in high spirits.

Once the doors opened, they would file inside, buy souvenirs, and more food, before finding their seats. The gigantic screens would play action shots from the last Tournament, and the Lightborn would be warming up in the middle. Camera flashes and chattering reporters would be her life for the next week as the games went on.

The first day was nothing more than a welcome. There were fireworks and songs and a display of Light to leave the crowd in awe. None of the tests were difficult today, and Audrey couldn't recall anyone going home on the first night.

Her flask was empty, she was out of cigarettes, and Audrey hardly noticed as the music blared from the arena's speakers. She rubbed her arm where Steve grabbed her. It wouldn't bruise - it never did. But she felt it, and a heat from inside swept over her.

She lifted the hair off her neck and tried to breathe. He'd been her producer from the beginning and always had a nasty streak. He was more of a prison guard these days. He would be looking for her, but she just needed five more minutes. The spectators moved as one, like cattle, as they chirped and laughed their way inside. Audrey hung her head. Another Tournament.

Another hurricane or tsunami.

Another fake smile and twisted set of 'truths' to dish out.

They had sentenced her to thirty years of servitude. She'd been spewing their lies for thirteen years, though it felt more like fifty. The guilt she felt for peddling their deceits for so long was weighing her down and keeping the smile on her face was becoming almost impossible. Only the thought of her family kept her going.

Losing Andy almost broke her. Raising the children without their father had left her bitter and resentful, and she felt guilty for that too.

Recently, however, it was a pang of different guilt she felt in her gut. Since the night they took her youngest daughter away, Audrey had felt a pain in her stomach that she couldn't shake.

It hadn't been an easy decision, but she'd told Anya again and again that she had to stay under the radar. She told her that using her Light would bring the Lightborn down on them, and she wouldn't have Alexis paying the price for Anya's selfishness.

When she found out she'd been visiting that school again, Audrey knew she had no choice. If she didn't turn Anya in herself, the Lightborn would have found out for themselves, and they would all have been punished.

Audrey had spent so many years paying off her daughter's debt to the Brothers because of Anya's power, and she refused to let Alexis fall to the same fate.

# CHAPTER 35

Steve fixed a piece of hair, frowning at the dark circles under her eyes. He grabbed the concealer and dabbed at the bags in silence. The camera was set up, and they were ready to go.

Down on the floor, they gave the press specific locations depending on the network: the less favourable the coverage, the worse the spot. Audrey was given prime real estate in the dead centre. She looked on as the Lightborn flexed and stretched and let out little sparks to keep the restless crowd intrigued.

"Ok, let's get an intro, and then we'll cover the welcome." Steve spoke to the cameraman, but she knew he was talking to her.

Audrey cleared her throat and took a deep breath before working her features into something that resembled a smile. It felt wrong on her face, and her brow furrowed. Steve raised an eyebrow, so she worked a little harder at being human.

The thought of Alexis gave her peace, and she let the calm seep in. She smiled, all the way to her eyes, and began.

"Welcome to the arena. What a sight! Can you believe what the Brotherhood has accomplished in just a few short months? Look at this place! It's more spectacular than any of the previous arenas, and I can already tell that these games are going to be on another level!"

She gestured around, her hands elegantly moving so the camera would follow.

"Any minute now, Lieutenant Phillip Osbourne will make his speech. And around the world, trusted Lieutenants in every major city will do the same. As you can see, the Lightborn are already inside and ready to go. I, for one, can't wait to see the show."

Steve cut across his neck, and Audrey stepped to the side, letting the camera get some shots of the crowd. She looked up in awe at the number of people inside. When the roof opened, the crowd cheered, whistled, and applauded. Balloons fell into the arena, and music blared across the field.

The Lieutenant made his way to the podium, flanked by his underlings and local Leaders. On the screens above, there was footage from around the globe, of the exact same image. Only the Brothers' most trusted Lieutenants were put in positions of genuine power. These men stood tall and proud as the Brotherhood's banner flew behind them.

The speech was everything Audrey expected - bold claims of power mixed with fawning compliments of the Three.

The Brotherhood is strong.

The Brotherhood is powerful.

The Brotherhood is here for you.

She almost laughed at the spiel. It was one she was all too familiar with, having touted it herself for so long. But the crowd was eating it up. They raised their arms and hooted their allegiance at all the right places. Over the years, she'd read books about these kinds of things. People blindly following someone with perceived power. Religion. Cults. It was all the same.

When the fireworks went off, Audrey jumped and cursed under her breath. She hadn't really been listening, and the speech was shorter than she expected. The crowd watched as the sky lit up, and Audrey watched as the Lightborn got into position. The first game was about to start.

With eyes trained on the fireworks, many people missed the obstacle course that materialised in the middle. As was tradition, the first game of the Tournament was nothing too strenuous. They wanted to show off their power without sending anyone home.

Although it changed with every Tournament, the course was mostly the same. The Lightborn lined up at the far end of the arena and waited for their cue.

Moving three at a time, the game commenced. One young Lightborn looked barely of age, but he moved quickly and effortlessly. The first group ran up the ramp and came face to face with a wall of water.

One tried to blow a gap and jump through, but wasn't strong enough. He hit the floor, and the crowd groaned and cheered.

The younger of the group took in the challenge and closed his eyes. The water turned to snow in the blink of an eye, and he cartwheeled through with a grin on his face.

The next three to go were faced with a wall of wind, and each had unique ways of getting by. The wind turned into funnels sporadically, pulling up debris and balloons. It was comical and silly, and the crowd went wild.

Eventually, two of the Lightborn stood side by side, crossed their arms, and jumped into the blast. They swirled around but held steady until they were spat out the other side.

The next challenge was pretty simple, but always a favourite. The ground opened up into a fiery pit, and if anyone tried to go around, it got wider and deeper until it reached their feet. Above the pit, a bridge hung in the air.

One Lightborn used a running jump and a little spark to get himself onto the platform. Unfortunately, flight was not an easy thing to master, and very few Lightborn had the ability.

The next contestant was struggling to find a way up. As the others approached behind, he panicked and conjured a staircase. When he was halfway up, the stairs turned flat, and he slid back to the ground.

The Brothers wanted a show, not a boring solution.

An older looking Lightborn turned his lower half into a kangaroo and sprang up with ease. Another lifted his hands and created a hot air balloon. He blew into the void and was soon rising up to the bridge.

Those that fell into the fire pit were transported back to the start and had to wait their turn to try again.

Further on, the young Lightborn from the first group was making excellent progress. As he approached the tank, he didn't hesitate. The colossal glass enclosure reached the top of the arena and inside swam various deadly creatures.

The Lightborn had to enter the water from the ground and make it to the surface. Simple enough.

He opened the door and put a hand to the water, which stayed in place behind some kind of barrier. It allowed him to enter, but Audrey couldn't make out what he had done. The young man swam gracefully to the surface, shaking the water from his hair and taking a slight bow with typical Lightborn arrogance.

"He got a name?" She asked.

"Uh...yes...it's...Anar Jones," Steve said, looking through the information package they had all been given.

Audrey nodded. She didn't care but assumed she would need to know for later.

Just behind Jones, the next man approached the tank. When he stepped inside, the water split around him as if he were in his own pocket of air. But it was clear this Lightborn didn't possess any talents for flight. He stood on the ground, frustrated and unsure of what to do.

Another raced thought the doors and conjured a scuba tank onto his back without breaking stride. He waved as he ascended, leaving the resentful man still on the ground.

The man in the bubble looked furious as he conjured a tank for himself and was visibly nervous as he let the water come crashing in on himself. He whirled around, drawing the attention of a shark. Halfway up, the shark got a little too close, and he had to turn and defend himself. Panicking, he kicked his feet, frantic to make the surface. At the top, he almost collapsed.

Back in the tank, it was getting crowded. The Lightborn entered one after another, using weird and wonderful magic to make it to the top. The children all seemed to like one guy who turned his head into a pufferfish. He crept up the side, puffing out when anything came to investigate.

An older Lightborn gave himself sea-star-like suckers on his hands and climbed up the tank's side like a spider.

At the next obstacle, the Lightborn were confronted

with a tunnel. It was clear so the audience could see, but the dangers were hidden. Inside, the Lightborn were faced with various obstacles, such as flying arrows and shooting spikes.

Audrey had seen things like this in old movies and knew that they had been the inspiration. Though these men defended themselves by turning the arrows to birds or the falling rocks to confetti.

It was clear after just a few hurdles which Lightborn would go far and which would burn out on the first real day. They presented themselves as better than everyone else because they were blessed with the Light, which made them high and mighty. At least that's what the Brotherhood wanted people to believe. In reality, most of the Lightborn weren't trained for combat of any kind. They were given basic training and honed their power to a degree. But they didn't know how to control their power in the face of danger or distraction. Many struggled to focus, and their Light failed them.

Audrey kept an eye on Anar Jones leading the pack with ease, not faltering at anything so far. Most of the men behind him had struggled with something and lost ground, but this young man was a powerhouse.

He could conjure as he ran, not overthinking things, and making his way quickly through the course. These were the Lightborn that would draw the attention of the Three.

In the past, they had given the winners trophies and the honour of becoming a high-ranking lieutenant. They were put in charge of multiple, high profile Townships and seen as untouchable. Of course, the Brothers were the only true authority. But this Tournament would birth a new Brotherhood. Was this young, inexperienced Lightborn ready to take that monumental step?

He ran forward to a challenge Audrey had never seen before. The big black box stood alone in a space surrounded by water. The young Lightborn didn't hesitate, crossing the water with ease and walking through the box's wall. No handle or windows were visible. Audrey couldn't see him coming from the other side, and there was no footage on the screen.

"What is that thing?" Steve asked from beside her.

She shrugged and kept her eyes on the shining black surface. After a few minutes, another Lightborn caught up and paused before going inside.

"Where are they?" She wondered aloud as the screen showed nothing from inside the box.

A collective gasp from the crowd drew her attention. She watched as people looked and pointed up. Suspended in the sky, she saw the Lightborn. They were fighting an invisible enemy, and none seemed to be winning. She found Jones and was shocked to see blood on his face. He had lost his cool now, his eyes wide and frantic.

"What is that?" She asked Steve, knowing he didn't know either.

"No clue. But we better find out. That's gonna stand out for sure."

A loud bang rang out, and Jones fell from the sky, followed in sequence by the others. The crowd called out as they fell, many genuinely worried.

Audrey stayed quiet, watching them all try to come up with something. At the last minute, Jones' hands shot out, and the floor gave way, depressing like a trampoline as he hit. He flew up and landed on his feet, stumbling slightly.

Jones looked shocked and war-torn before gathering himself and moving on. Above, others were released with a bang, falling to the ground faster than they could think. Those that were unable to stop themselves were suspended by the Light of the Brothers. Not a good look.

For the first time, Anar Jones seemed to struggle. Whatever he'd faced in the black box had shaken him, affecting his performance.

The last challenge was another favourite - the enchanted wall. It stood as tall as the arena and tested a Lightborn's creativity and speed. If they conjured a rope, it would eventually stretch or break, and the man would need to change tactics. If they created footholds to climb, they would soon fill will spiders. Any Lightborn that simply tried to fly over was met with pounding hail that caused them to fall.

As he looked up, the young Lightborn tried to calm himself. He glanced back to see his competition getting closer and quickly moved, wanting to keep his advantage.

At first, he created small steps on the surface, climbing slowly up. Jones jumped back and hovered in the air just as the steps disappeared. Reaching up, he grabbed at a rope and swung into the wall.

Moving as quickly as he could, he shimmied up a few more feet before he felt the line becoming brittle. As he let go, his hand turned a dark grey colour. The crowd gasped as he punched into the wall and held on, resting a beat while trying to think of his next move.

At the base of the wall, four Lightborn were slowly creeping up. Jones kept his focus on his own climb, reaching out to grab a platform. He left the wall and stood still. His breathing was ragged, and Audrey could tell he was struggling.

When Jones put his hands on the wall once more, she thought he was giving up. Any second, his platform would disappear, and he would fall. The crowd clapped along, cheering and shouting out to their favourites. It was deafening.

All at once, the young Lightborn stepped off the platform and into the wall. He was holding onto something, and as everyone watched, he started turning. Holding only with his fingertips, his body twisted in the air until his feet were above his head. Audrey looked closely and saw his hair flop up, and his feet rest on a new step.

Then, faster than anyone could follow, he fell. He fell *up* until he reached the top of the wall. Looking down the other side, he was back to his arrogant self. Jones stepped off the ledge and behind the wall, the winner of the first game and one to watch going forward.

# CHAPTER 36

**Way After**

Despite everything, Gabby managed to sleep. She'd arrived at the Hall just after midnight on the anniversary of the Crack and was grateful that this Alexis woman was letting her stay. She felt uncomfortable sharing her yearly pilgrimage but knew she had no choice.

And the Lightborn! Her mind was still racing after witnessing actual magic.

At some point, Baz and his team came into the Hall. Gabby stayed in her cot, pretending to sleep, watching them through half-closed eyes. They all kept looking over, though nobody approached. The group talked for a few minutes before Tony sent them away. Gabby held in a gasp, once again entirely in awe of the magic.

The next time she woke up, a little light was peeking in through the windows. She was alone in the Hall and wondered if the leader of the Gulls had gotten bored and left. Fat chance, she knew. The rains had stopped, but the skies remained as dark as ever.

She tiptoed to the big doors and peeked outside. In the distance, she could see the snow on the hills. Over the Hall, the fiery clouds grumbled.

She couldn't see Alexis or Tony but knew they wouldn't be far. Her things were by her cot, and she moved, stomach growling, for a ration pack.

"Oh, come on. You can't eat that," Alexis called from the small door at the side.

She smiled and walked inside with Tony. He waved a hand, and a table of food appeared.

"Help yourself."

Gabby held back. It looked and smelled amazing. Better than anything she had ever seen, and her mouth was watering. But something was nagging inside.

"Isn't this what caused the Crack?" She questioned, waving her hand toward the food. "Weren't the Brothers just as frivolous with their Light? They caused all this-"

"Isn't it a little late to worry about that now?" Tony laughed.

He grabbed a sandwich and took a bite. Alexis followed, her eyes on Gabby.

"You're right. The Three and the Lightborn abused their Light. They took and took until the earth couldn't give anymore, and it all came crashing down. I was there, you know. I remember when we were a group of Townships under the rule of Local Leaders and Lieutenants. I remember before the Crack."

Alexis moved to a chair and sat. Tony brought her a hot drink and made himself a seat.

"If you were there, shouldn't you be...I don't know. Shouldn't you hate the Lightborn?"

"Oh, I do. I always have, truth be told." Alexis looked around the Hall, letting her mind wander back in time. "The day of the Crack, I should have been home with my Uncle and cousin. It was the first day of the Tournament, and Frankie was excited to see the magic. My Uncle and I knew better. We knew the games would bring nothing but destruction. But what could we do?" She let the question hang in the air as she tilted her head. "How old are you?"

"Twenty," Gabby said, moving to the table where she picked up a sausage roll and closed her eyes as she chewed.

"Twenty. So you were just a child. Shame you didn't get to see this place before. It wasn't so bad, even under the Brothers' rule."

Alexis stood and grabbed another sandwich and an apple from the table.

"My sister tried," she said so quietly Gabby wasn't sure if she was supposed to hear. "She was special. She tried to stop them, and they killed her for it."

"I'm sorry." Gabby looked down. She didn't know why Alexis was telling her all this. "What happened?"

"Too many things. Bad blood. Bad memories. Bad timing." Alexis shook her head as she thought back. "She was so strong. I always knew it, but I never said anything. I feared her strength and had my head in the sand. After she died, I...well let's just say, I lost my way. Until I met Tony."

She smiled and reached her hand out. He beamed at her and took it.

"He saved me. And now, here we are. In this place. On this day."

"I told you, I-"

"If you don't know why you're here, why are you here?"

Gabby stood and paced, grazing at the food, and trying to find a way to explain herself without sounding crazy.

"My mother used to remember this day, like everyone else, I guess. I remember going to the memorials and watching people cry. Like you said, I was a baby, so it was all still raw, even four or five years later. We would go and cry, and people would lay flowers down and make speeches. I never understood, obviously, but I was there. And on those days, I would always wake up feeling...off. Not ill, but not right. My stomach would be in knots, and my head felt thick. My mother waved it off. She never connected that it was always this day. But I did. As I got older, I figured it out. And then I started dreaming." Gabby sat back down and kept her eyes on her food. "I read a book about the Brotherhood and the Crack, and I started having these dreams. Most were nonsense. I saw lights and people blurring in and out and weird flowers. I couldn't make sense of it all. But one dream, one dream always stood out, clear as day. I'm in the Plains, near the tracks. I can see someone standing there, and the train's coming. Then I hear barking, and I see a dog. Then I see...well, I see Gulls, only they're different. They look twisted and evil. They're moving in, faster than I've ever seen. And the train's getting closer and closer. I see a man, and he's calling out to the girl on the tracks. The Gulls are coming, and the train is coming and, bam! I wake up."

Gabby looked up to Alexis, and to her surprise, she was sitting forward, on the edge of her seat.

"You saw a dog?"

Confused, Gabby nodded.

"What kind of dog?"

"Does it matt-"

"Obviously, or I wouldn't be asking." Alexis stood, brow furrowed and sharp tone in her voice.

"I have no idea. Medium-sized, black and white."

Alexis turned to Tony and motioned him to the side. "Have you seen this dog anywhere else? In any other dreams?"

"How did you-"

"So you have? You've seen it again, in different dreams?" Alexis came close, her voice sounding oddly hopeful.

Gabby stood and moved back. She raised her hands and shrugged her shoulders.

"Look, I told you: I don't remember most of the dreams. I see things, and it's all blurry. Yes, I've seen the dog, but I don't know a Terrier from a Bulldog."

A bark from behind made her jump. Gabby spun around to see a medium-sized, black and white dog rushing forward. She flinched as he reached her - most dogs became far less friendly after the Crack. Many grew extra limbs or ears, and their owners sent them away.

"This is Ozzie," Alexis said as she moved to pet the dog. "He was my sister's."

"But I thought…she died twenty years ago, so-"

"He's very special." Alexis threw Ozzie a treat, and they watched as he ran around.

Ozzie sniffed at the scorch mark and pawed at a spot on the ground. When he sat, Alexis took in a breath and turned her face. Gabby watched her wipe her eyes but said nothing.

"He's been here before. He remembers," Tony said, putting his arm around Alexis.

Ozzie moved forward and went to Gabby. He put his head on her leg and looked up at her with sweet, innocent eyes. She squatted in front and scratched behind his ears.

"He's cute."

"He likes you," Alexis smiled. "He senses you're a good person."

Gabby looked back at Alexis, who was smiling. "I really don't know why I'm here. I don't know what I expect, I just-"

"It's ok. I have a feeling we were meant to meet."

Ozzie didn't leave Gabby's side for the rest of the day. Tony gave her some toys to throw, and she had fun, actual fun, chasing the dog around. Alexis seemed happy to watch, and Tony never strayed from her side.

Even without the sun, Gabby knew the day was drawing on. Alexis kept looking at her watch but said nothing. Gabby felt ridiculous. Nothing would happen; it never did.

"It's almost time."

Alexis turned to Tony, and the pair stood shoulder to shoulder, eyes on the old spot on the floor. It was darker now, the sun having gone down behind the black clouds.

"You should move."

Gabby looked up and watched as Ozzie left her side. He trotted over to Alexis and sat obediently between the pair.

"Time for what?"

"You've been coming here all these years without knowing why. You would sit in the Hall, alone, waiting for nothing and everything, right?" She waited a beat, and Gabby nodded her head. "Wouldn't it stand to reason that whatever you're waiting for in here, whatever it is, it's connected to that day?"

Looking around, Gaby stood and moved closer. She looked at the black scorch, totally confused.

"Eight minutes," Alexis said to Tony.

"Eight minutes?"

"In eight minutes, something will either happen, or it won't."

Alexis put a hand behind Ozzie's ear and scratched. He sat patiently, looking at Gabby with his head to one side.

"I don't understand. Do you know what's going to happen? Do you...do you feel it too?" She asked, coming closer, genuine excitement in her voice.

"No. I haven't been back here since that night. Not since Anya died."

She looked at the black marks and the stains on the floor. Gabby could see the pain on her face as she relived something private.

"What are you saying?"

"Six minutes," Alexis continued, looking down at her watch. "In six minutes, it will have been twenty years since the Crack. Twenty years since my sister opened a portal to another world, and the Three left us all to rot."

"Wait, your sister-"

Ozzie stirred at Alexis' side. He whined quietly and shifted his feet. Tony tried to calm him, but the dog became agitated. He barked at nothing and started pacing in front of them.

"Stop. Wait. I can't- you can't just..." Gabby ran a hand through her hair and looked at Ozzie. "What's wrong with him?"

"Three minutes." Alexis took a few steps back and motioned for Gabby to follow. "Ozzie, come here."

The dog obeyed but stayed alert.

"Anya was a good person. A teacher. She just wanted a normal life. But they found her, and they made her help them. They threatened us, her family. She had no choice."

Gabby could see the tears in her eyes. What was she saying? Her sister had the Light? How was that possible?

"Alexis, you said your sister, Anya-"

"That's right. I don't know how, but she had the Light, and they killed her for it."

Ozzie was barking now, non-stop. He ran up and down, growling into the air, sensing something strange.

"One minute."

"Why did they kill her? What happened? What's happening?"

The surrounding air shifted. The doors were closed, but Gabby could feel a warm breeze. Overhead, the thunder boomed louder than ever.

"She was the only one strong enough to do it. They needed her to open the portal. They needed her to escape all the damage they caused. And when she did, they walked away, leaving all that power and all that carnage to come crashing down on her. We tried to help, but we were too late. She died in my arms and faded to nothing as-"

An intense burning filled the centre of the room. They stopped and waited as a small light flickered in the air. It started out tiny, a glittering speck anyone would have missed had they not been looking.

But as it grew, the wind picked up around them, and the sound roared with the thunder.

Out of nowhere, a blue and purple light cracked open the space in front of them, until all at once, it went quiet. Gabby was frozen in place, but Ozzie moved forward. On the floor, in the centre of the Hall, lay a girl, bleeding, but alive.

# CHAPTER 37

**Opening Day of the Tournament**

I avoided the news on the opening day of the Tournament. I didn't want to risk watching my mother smiling and spewing the Brothers' lies. Although I knew she didn't believe in any of it, it still hurt to watch. Especially now.

All day the Three had been in the Great Hall. Slowly and quietly, they took in the power of the Lightborn in the arenas across the world. Anwar had shown up that morning, stubborn, solemn, and spiteful as ever. I avoided him, choosing to stay inside with Ozzie for most of the day. But I could feel the power emanating from the Hall. The thing practically glowed, and it made me sick to my stomach. I had taken in the Light of others, and it almost killed me. How would this be any different?

Oran said they wanted me there. He said I needed to take more power to strengthen my portal. He was right, in theory. It would take so much energy, and I couldn't rely on Anwar. But I feared the power and the consequences I knew would follow.

The clouds rolled in early in the day, and I took it as a bad omen. I knew the games had begun, and Light was being used all over the world. In their attempts to win the Three's favour, Lightborn would be frivolously conjuring, with no thought of what could happen after.

My fingers twitched. I wanted to jump to the site of the Veil to see if it was holding. How could any of us know how it would be affected?

My mind was also consumed with thoughts of Mr Parks and the Network. Ever since his visit, I'd been on the lookout for them. With no idea what they were planning, all I could do was wait, and it was killing me.

I feared for their safety. The Three would be more powerful than ever, and I'd told Mr Parks as much in my last message. Had he listened? I was so afraid that people would be killed at my expense. I worried that Alexis and Uncle Mark would be punished if I didn't help the Three.

"Anya? They're calling for you," a voice said through my door with a slight knock.

I sighed and stayed where I was. He knocked again and called my name, but I didn't answer. My heart was pounding, and my palms were sweating. I had no good options. No way out.

"Anya?!" The Lightborn burst in, worried I'd escaped again. He looked angry when he saw me sitting on the bed. "Didn't you hear me?"

"I heard. Sorry." I motioned to Ozzie, and we dragged our feet down the hallway.

Oran was waiting outside the Hall with a handsome Border Collie. He and Ozzie ran off to play, and as I got closer, the warmth from the Hall hit me. The Lightborn escorting me held back, keeping his distance from the Hall and the Three. I wondered if he knew what was happening. I could feel the power, and so could he. It was overwhelmingly intoxicating.

"Thanks for coming. I know you're hesitant-"

"I almost died last time, so yeah."

Oran nodded and opened the door.

"It's different this time."

He walked in and waited for me to follow. I looked back to Ozzie one last time before following Oran inside.

The Great Hall was filled with sparks and Glimmers. It was a little kid's dream, and I half expected to see a unicorn trot by. As I moved inside, my arm touched a green streak, and I immediately felt the power move inside.

I shuddered as a chill filled me, despite the warmth. It felt uncomfortable and foreign. And that was just one.

In the middle of the Hall, Anwar and Uri sat in large chairs. They both looked zoned out as Light swam around them. Oran brushed aside a few sparks and took his seat, gesturing to his side where a chair appeared for me. I sat down and kept my head low as the power moved around us all.

"Beautiful, isn't it?" Uri slurred. He was smiling and looked goofy. "It's just small bites, but they can pack quite a punch."

He reached up and grabbed a yellow streak. His hand moved through the Glimmer, and it followed down into his fingertips.

"It's like they're drunk," I whispered to Oran, not trying to hide my disgust.

"It's a little like that, yes. I told you this was different. The Light you took, it came unwillingly - from dead men, no less. Of course, you were damaged. But this," he lifted his hands into a cluster of sparks that bounced around in the air. "This is different. The Lightborn are happy. They're strong-"

"They don't know they're losing their power."

"Enough!" Anwar screeched from opposite me.

He didn't look my way, but I could see the anger on his face. He hated that I was there. He hated sharing this with me. The feeling was mutual.

"You should feel honoured that you're even in here. Just shut up and accept it. You know you don't have any other choice."

His words stung because they were true. So I sat quietly in the Hall as the Three became literally high on power. I tried to avoid it, but it soon became impossible. Lightborn from all around the world were in the arenas, and their energy was being funnelled back to us.

Looking up into the clouds of Light, I found myself in awe of it all. There were so many. The Lightborn had increased their numbers, that much I knew. But I'd never stopped to think about it in terms of physical people. And now here I sat, in amongst them. I felt like I was violating them, and they me. I reached my hand toward a pink-ish Glimmer and wondered if he could feel my presence.

After a while, I was feeling drunk too. My head was spinning, and I couldn't stop myself from reaching for the Light. The warmth around me was cut by the chill I felt as the power absorbed. When I finally cleared my head, the sun was long gone, and the Hall was back to normal.

"That's enough for today. Get some sleep. We're going forward with the plan tomorrow." Uri looked severe and sober.

"What happened?"

"Nothing to concern you-"

"The cloaks are failing. The decay's seeping out, and

we don't have much time." Oran stepped in with the truth that made my heart sink.

"You're sure?"

"Oran, no," Uri warned.

"We all know she knows. She's in this now. Why lie, Uri?"

I rubbed the fog from my eyes and felt tears on my cheeks. "How bad is it?"

"Not terrible, but it's only day one. The obstacle course is the light intro. Hardly any Light is required to make it through. Tomorrow will be much worse."

Without thinking, I reached out and shoved Uri. He stumbled back, managing to stay on his feet.

"How could you? All of you! You moved the Tournament forward, and you've brought this down on us all!"

"Calm down, Anya. It's done," Uri said, ice in his voice and fire in his eyes. "You're smart enough to know that you've lost this fight."

He walked away, leaving me with Oran.

As the door opened, Ozzie came rushing inside. He wagged his tail and looked up at me with his big brown eyes. I hugged him and put down a bowl of food, wanting to focus on him and him alone.

"Anya," Oran breathed. "I know how this all looks. I know you're upset. But," he sighed and moved away. "You know we have no other options. Yes, we moved the Tournament forward, and yes, we caused this. But you didn't see the other spots. Many are far worse than the one near your Township. They were on the brink long before today."

"So why, then? Why not try to fix things?"

He almost laughed, but the look on his face gave away the sadness inside.

"You know we can't fix this. It's too late."

"What if we can?"

I hadn't mentioned my delusional idea of returning our collective Light to the Earth because I knew the Three would laugh in my face. But looking at Oran, I took a chance on his humanity.

"We got our Light from somewhere. And when we abuse it, mother nature fights back. So what if we all put our hands down and gave it all back? Maybe we could actually fix things."

To his credit, he didn't laugh out loud. "You're kidding? You must be because I know you're not crazy."

"I'm neither. I really think it could work!"

"Anya! Come on! You've been here for long enough to know us. To know them. Can you really stand there and tell me you think Uri would be willing to be a mere mortal? Anwar?"

I hung my head. He was right, I knew.

"Would you do it?" I asked without looking at him.

"I'm one of them, Anya. I've been one of them my entire life. I fought with and for them, and I've been by their sides for decades. Everything they've done, I've done. Everything you hold them responsible for, I'm responsible for. I could have-should have stood up years ago, but I didn't. I know you think we're monsters for wanting to go through that portal, but you need to know that it's really the only option left. Once the cloaks fall, the rot inside will seep out into the world and twist it into something uninhabitable."

"People will die. Good people," I mumbled, sounding weak and pathetic, even to my ears.

Ozzie raised his head and licked the tears from my cheeks.

"Many people, most likely. But you and your family don't have to be amongst them. Think about it, Anya. You could save Alexis, Frankie, and your Uncle. Even your mother."

I bristled at the mention of her. Oran put a hand on my shoulder before leaving Ozzie and me alone in the Great Hall. I looked around and took it all in.

Tomorrow was the day. It was decided. I would open the portal for the Three and their people so they could escape the coming apocalypse.

# CHAPTER 38

I couldn't sleep. I tried for a while, tossing and turning, annoying Ozzie with my sudden movements, but after a while, I gave up and made myself some tea. At the window, I watched as cars came and went. I saw lots of people I'd never seen before and suddenly noticed the sounds around me.

There were faint footsteps above and muffled voices through the walls. The Three were bringing in their chosen people, preparing for the big jump. I wondered what they'd told them.

Did any of them know what was going on?

I doubted the Brothers would have shared their plans. It was more likely that the Brothers simply gave an order, and people followed.

Ozzie and I snuck out as the sun was coming up. I could see rain clouds in the distance and felt the cold in the air. We walked all over, for hours it felt. As we neared the house I assumed to be Oran's, I half expected him to appear with a happy dog at his side. But I was surprised when I saw another man walking toward me, over the damp grass, two coffees in his hands.

"Hi," he called, hesitantly, when he got close enough not to yell.

"Hi," I replied, holding Ozzie back.

"This is for you. I saw you before and figured you

could use it."

The coffee smelled amazing, and I held it in my stiff hands. I thanked him and looked past to the empty land behind, wondering what their house looked like.

"I'm Declan. Oran's husband."

I knew I recognised him.

"You're Anya?"

"Yeah. Yes. This is Ozzie."

Declan laughed. "Yes, I think we've met. My husband has always loved dogs."

I nodded and sipped my coffee, no idea what to say to the husband of one of my captors.

"Listen, I need to apologise to you," Declan blurted out. "I had no idea about any of this. Oran kept us completely in the dark. He just told me everything and... well, I don't even know what to say."

His face was so genuine it hurt. His compassion and empathy brought a lump to my throat, and I felt a sudden urge to hug him.

"I just can't believe it. All the lies- for years! And now he tells me we have to leave everything we've ever known before the world ends! Oh, and he kidnapped some poor teacher, by the way, and threatened her family."

"I know it's a lot."

"A lot? My Brothers, are you ok? Please tell me they've at least treated you...with kindness? I feel absurd even saying that, I'm sorry."

I moved forward, closing the gap and smiled weakly.

"Oran has been kind. I promise."

Declan sighed in relief before catching himself.

"You can leave. Right now. I'll walk you out myself and by the Elders, if they even try and touch you I'll-"

"It's kind of you, but I can't. I have to do this."

"You don't. This isn't your responsibility. They did this. All of them."

I nodded and cleared my throat. My coffee was finished, so I refilled our cups and tried to keep my tone calm.

"I'm one of them, like it or not."

I could tell he wanted to ask how, but he kept his curiosity inside.

"You're not them. And you don't have to do anything. I'll take you home myself."

"I won't have a home, not after today. They'll go ahead with their plan, with or without me. Today you and your family are leaving this place. If I don't help, Anwar will kill any Lightborn he can to gain enough power, and even then, I doubt he'll find what you all need. I have to help. You and your family, their families, you don't deserve to die because of their mistakes. With my portal, you'll at least make it to safety."

"What about you? What about-"

"Everyone else? Yeah, that's something I'm gonna have to live with. But at least this way I know they can never come back. They'll be gone, and then maybe we can try to fix their mess."

Declan's mouth dropped open. "You're willing to risk everything to save my family? Their people?"

"I've spent months going over this in my head. I've thought about trying to expose them and their damage. I've thought about mobilising an army against them and removing them from power. But what would that look like? I've seen their followers, and we wouldn't last a day. We're outnumbered, and they've got their loyalists willing to die for them. And even with every other scenario, it won't change the basic fact: the earth is dying. Oran told me himself there are spots all over the world. They're getting bigger, and the Light that's holding the rot inside isn't strong enough. With or without the Brothers, that decay is breaking out."

Declan almost dropped his cup. He looked out of breath and sweaty.

"Are you ok?"

"I just…I can't…" He sat on the floor, and Ozzie went to him.

"I know it's a lot. Believe me, I know."

We sat together for a while as the grass dried in the sun. Ozzie rolled around some before putting his head down and falling asleep. I could tell Declan was overwhelmed and in shock. I'd known for months and was still in shock.

"You're not obligated to save my family. I can't ask you to-"

"You're not asking. They're telling. And I've made my peace with it."

# CHAPTER 39

The rains came just after noon. Ominous clouds rolled in, and the skies opened up to a torrential downpour. I looked out my window and wondered if Anwar would do anything about it, or if that would just be a waste of power.

I could feel the Light inside of me now. It hadn't been a lot the day before, but I was acutely aware of its presence. On my way to the Hall, I felt itchy inside and nervous at the thought of taking in more.

The Great Hall was full of Light once more. The Three were in their chairs, arms up and welcoming. The Tournaments were well underway, and the power was being funnelled right here. Before the door closed, I was hit with a wall of sparks. The Light was coming from so many places at once, it made my head whirl. I reached out and held onto the door handle, trying to keep a clear mind.

"Anya, let's go. We need you to take in as much Light as possible before our departure tonight," Uri called, speaking as though they were just going on vacation.

"It's too much," I said, making my way over.

"You're strong enough. Just let it in. Stop fighting."

Oran nodded to me and closed his eyes. I watched as a cluster of sparks bounced around his head before disappearing into him.

We spent the next few hours in the Hall, taking in every little Glimmer that came to us. I could see Anwar greedily seeking out the more significant streaks, no doubt wanting to prove his worth.

When the time came, my hands were glowing. I felt warm and full and powerful. The Three were acting no different than usual, and I wondered how often they had stolen Light in all their years. I was struggling to stay upright.

They left me alone, leaving to collect their families and chosen few. Ozzie came in and sat by my side, aware of my tension. With a hand on his fur, I closed my eyes and thought about what was going to happen. I'd told Declan I'd made my peace with it all, which was true to an extent. I knew there was no going back from the destruction and decay.

But as I sat alone with my thoughts, part of me wished I'd tried harder to escape. I should have jumped further or smarter. I should have been faster and made it to the Ludus. I should never have lost my temper with my mother or even gone to the city that day. I should have kept my power secret and stayed away from the Ludus. I should have done so many things differently, and as I looked around at the mess I was in, I felt the guilt deep down in my gut, cold and heavy.

"You had no other choice," Oran said from nearby, though I was alone in the Hall.

"Really? You're really invading my thoughts right now? Now?" I said out loud.

"I wanted to check in on you. Declan told me you two spoke and-"

"Yeah, he's not too thrilled with you. Good luck with that in the new world."

I heard him laugh a little. "It won't be easy, that's for sure."

Ozzie looked up to me, and I leaned down to him. He licked my face, and I scratched his ears. I knew I would need to send him away when it all started. I would not risk his safety.

"Anya, you know there was nothing you could have done. We broke all the rules and let things get to this point. We brought you here, held you here. You tried to run, and we caught you. There was nowhere you could've gone that we wouldn't have followed. You can't blame yourself for your Light. It's a gift, Anya. A great gift."

"Stop. Just don't."

I could hear cars coming, even over the rain. The headlights flashed in the windows, and I knew that it was time. Their people were ready to go.

They filed in, looking confused and upset. I saw children and women and Lightborn. How had they chosen the Lightborn?

No doubt, I was looking at the families of the Three, their spouses and kids. But the Lightborn? What made them special enough to be saved?

I noticed that nobody would look at me. I was back in my chair with Ozzie at my side. Did they know why I was there? How much had they been told?

When the Three came in, they each joined their respective families. Oran tried to speak with Declan, but he turned away, angry and defeated. Their son was apparently in the dark and stood confused.

Uri had a wife and two little boys. There was another girl there, around my age, standing slightly apart. Uri's wife looked angry and fed up.

Anwar was the surprising one. I saw more people looking at him than anyone else. I thought I recognised his wife from some magazine article, and the men were his sons. They had children of their own and stood protectively in a tight group. But standing nearby was another woman and baby. I could see the woman looked uncomfortable, and Anwar's wife looked furious.

Tut tut, Anwar.

The Lightborn all seemed to be clued in, moving around and bringing in gear and bags. They moved the luggage closer to me, and a few of them spent time going over the equipment. I counted forty. Then there was a smattering of other people. Extended families, I guessed.

I took in the group. There were close to a hundred people. In the entire world, they chose to save one hundred people. I felt sick and angry. With all the power I had now, I knew I could save more.

"Anya, we need to start this," Uri said, rushing forward and pulling me from my chair.

"Ok, ok."

"Everyone is here. Let's go," Anwar shouted, making his way toward me.

"Anwar, who is that?" Oran demanded, looking back over his shoulder.

"Don't worry about it."

"Is that where you've been disappearing to? You have to be kidding?" Uri asked, incredulous.

"I said, don't worry about it."

"We limited this group for safety. We're going through a portal to a new reality, and you're bringing your mistress?"

Anwar stepped forward, into Oran's face. "Leave it

alone, Brother."

I looked back at the woman and the baby. She didn't seem nervous or scared, and when we locked eyes, she scowled at me. She knew exactly what was going on and who I was.

"Let's just start," I snapped, moving between the men. I was sick of their arguing and just wanted it all over with.

Uri gritted his teeth and turned from us, speaking to the people at the end of the Hall.

"Ok, everyone. I know you're all scared and confused. We're sorry for all the secrecy. But right now, we just need you to trust us. What's about to happen might be a little scary, but you're with us, and we'll make sure you're all ok."

Anwar ignored his Brother and took my hands, yanking me into the centre of the Hall.

"Wait, Ozzie."

"Forget the dog," Anwar said, raising his hand up.

Oran stepped in. "Anwar, don't." He turned and pet Ozzie until he faded away. "He's running around outside with a few friends. He's fine."

I nodded my thanks and turned back to Anwar. The hate I felt for him was overwhelming me. Being this close made my stomach turn, and I just wanted him gone.

As I closed my eyes, I focussed on the new world with ease. I'd had so much practice, it was like opening a portal to my own bedroom. As my Light lit up the room, I could feel the warmth on my face. With all the extra power, it was easier than ever.

I didn't even need Anwar's help.

Gasps and cries filled the room. Some kids yelled and

ran forward, wanting to see. The Lightborn held them back as the Three moved forward.

"There it is," Uri said, wistfully.

"What's wrong?" Oran asked.

"Nothing."

Uri turned back and called his Lightborn forward. The group I originally sent stepped up and walked through with their equipment. I felt them cross over, but my Light held true.

One by one, the Three ordered their people through. A few more Lightborn went first, showing the others it was safe. I tried to keep my mind calm as I focused on the portal and nothing else, but after a while, I could feel my Light fading.

"We need to hurry," I stressed to Oran.

"Already?"

I nodded, and he moved to hustle more people through. In the back, I noticed Anwar's mistress staying clear of the others. She scowled as his family stepped forward and rolled her eyes when Anwar hugged his wife.

More than half made it through before I felt it. The sharp stabbing in my gut came out of nowhere, and as I doubled over, I felt the portal weaken. Oran put out a hand, holding the line back.

"Anya, what's happening?"

"I don't...oh. I don't know."

I couldn't stand up straight. The pain was incredible, and I had no choice. I looked up to make sure nobody was close before closing the portal.

"No! What did you do?" Anwar came rushing to me, fury in his eyes and fists balled.

Again, Oran got in front of him.

"Can't you see she's in pain? She can't focus like that."

"The cloaks are hanging by a thread. The cracks are too big, it's affecting her," Uri whispered so the others couldn't hear.

"Get up! We need to finish this-"

Anwar was cut off by a crack of thunder so loud I crouched down and covered my ears. The ground shook, and the surrounding walls trembled.

"Open it!" Anwar yelled, grabbing my arm and dragging me back to the middle.

"Anwar! Stop, give her time."

"We don't have time!"

The thunder sounded as though it was in the room. The skies flashed, and when I looked out the top windows, I thought I saw flames in the sky. We were too late.

"Anya, can you try again?" Uri asked.

"I don't know what happened, but I'll try."

"Leave her, Oran. Let her go home." Declan suddenly was at my side, a hand under my elbow. "She's done enough."

I'd noticed him staying back. He wasn't on board with the plan and held their son aside as the others jumped through.

I smiled at him. "It's ok."

I didn't wait for Anwar's help as I stepped forward. Ignoring the pain, I found the place in seconds and opened the portal once more. But as soon as we could see the people on the other side, the pain got worse. Through the Light, I could see the Lightborn conjuring up structures and food.

"They have to stop. I can't do this when they're using their power."

I had a sudden sinking feeling in my gut. I could feel the Lightborn using their power, and it was dark and painful. What would happen to that world after a year of the Light?

Uri yelled through the portal, and the Lightborn stopped their work. The pain subsided, allowing me to focus on the portal. The Three rushed their people through while they still could, but I felt my hold waning with each crossing.

"Hurry!" I yelled.

Declan was still at my side. Oran hustled their son through before turning back to call his husband forward. He stopped in his tracks, eyes wide and mouth open.

I watched him turn and yell to his Brothers. The Three looked in my direction, shouting and calling to the Lightborn still in the room.

I saw a flash in my periphery and looked up when a ball of electricity flew over my head.

Behind me, I felt the wind and rain whip into the Hall. I turned around and came face to face with Mr Parks. He raced forward, shouting my name and waving his hand, motioning for me to duck. Behind him, the entire Network came rushing into the Great Hall.

# CHAPTER 40

My mind was split in two. On my left, Declan crouched down, hands on his head and terror in his eyes. In front, Mr Parks was yelling in my face as the force of the Network burst into the Hall. Over my shoulder, I could see the Three and their Lightborn scrambling to get the last of their people out of harm's way.

"Anya, you need to go. Get out!" Mr Parks shouted as he stood tall.

I watched as he threw a ball of light at the Lightborn. It hit one and erupted into a thousand spiders. The Lightborn screamed and ran into the wall.

The sounds from the Network seemed to silence all at once, and I spun my head to see the Three moving forward. I stood and took a step toward my freedom, but was held back by an invisible wall. The Network was in front of the big doors, sending all kinds of things forward, but nothing was getting through. The Three and their people were at the other end, holding back the attack.

"Anya, come with me," Oran yelled as he grabbed Declan's arm.

"Where's Tyler?" Declan cried, looking around frantically.

"He made it through."

I looked over his shoulder and saw my portal still open. It was fading, but I could see through to the other world.

"Declan, go! You need to go now before I can't hold it."

Before he could reply, the earth shook once more. It was so violent, nobody stayed on their feet, and the invisible wall fell.

Mr Parks and the rest were on their feet fast, charging forward before the Three could react. My portal closed as I got to my feet, unsure of what to do.

I wanted to join my people, but a Lightborn came forward and grabbed me. I reacted quickly and, with my hands on his arm, let some of my power seep out. It burned his skin, and he jumped back. I reached out a hand to open a small portal beneath him. He tumbled back and disappeared.

Standing in the chaos, I was torn. Mr Parks and the others had come not only to save me but to stop the Three. I knew they were too late - the Veils having cracked already, and before long, they would fall entirely. And then there were the innocents at the other end - the last few of the Three's chosen travellers. Uri was standing in front, his arms raised in protection.

"Anya!" Mr Parks called to me again.

He turned but was stopped by a huge Lightborn. They each raised their arms in defence, locking wrists in a crash of Light. The Lightborn towered forward, pushing down on Mr Parks, who was struggling to fight back.

I didn't need to think. Rage in my heart, I grabbed at the enormous man with an invisible force, tearing him away and into the wall. He smashed through, leaving a gaping hole in the thick stone.

By now, the Hall was a mess of people and anger. The

Network was toe to toe with the remaining Lightborn, and it was hard to tell who was winning. I could see chains and restraints being used on one side, where the other fought with knives and weapons.

A cry filled the Hall, and I saw Anwar's mistress and her baby in the corner. Anwar tried to get to them, but the Network was now blocking his path. The woman was struggling to hold the baby as it cried and kicked. The noise must have been defeating to the child.

The ground trembled again, and thunder shook the walls. I could see the rain outside subsided, but the skies were darker than ever. The fire was coming.

I ran to Uri, blocking anything that came flying my way.

"We need to get them out!" I yelled as he sent a familiar-looking man flying.

"Are you serious?"

"I can do it. We just need to get them to safety."

I knew I couldn't stop the fight. I knew Mr Parks and the others had come here to stop them - to stop me. And I knew they would probably never forgive me. But getting these people out was the only thing I knew for sure was right. They didn't deserve to die in this fight.

I moved behind Uri and his protective wall.

"I'm going to open the portal again. You have to be quick!"

"Take her!"

The woman stepped forward and shoved her baby into another woman's arms. I could do nothing as she ran into the Hall, arms raised. My mouth fell open when sparks flew from her fingertips. She attacked the people blocking Anwar with what looked like spears.

Anwar used the distraction, and I gasped when he

snapped his fingers and broke the closest adversary's neck.

"Anya!" Uri shouted, but I was too angry.

With one hand I reached out and opened the portal once more, allowing all the extra Light to flow from my hand. With the other, I sent a shock wave to Anwar. The ground shifted, cracking slightly, and he fell back into a table before finding me with his eyes. His fury was palpable, but he knew he couldn't touch me, not yet anyway.

The few people left scrambled through the portal. The woman with the baby panicked and almost threw it into my arms. I waved my hand and put the child in the small crib, keeping my eyes on Anwar as he yelled at his mistress, pointing to the portal and pushing her my way.

But she stayed back. She wouldn't leave his side.

I put a protective shield around the child and moved to join the fight.

"Anya, close the portal!"

Out of nowhere, a girl came running through the fight, grabbed my shoulder, and yelled in my face.

"Do it now! You can't let them leave."

I pushed her aside as a Lightborn sent a wave of water our way.

Now the only people left were the Lightborn and the Three. Their people were safe.

"Uri, go!"

"Anya, no!"

The girl pulled me away again, clawing at my arm and forcing my focus away. She grabbed my face, and I felt the portal fade.

"Anya, please. I'm here to help. You sent me to help!"

It was too much. The girl wasn't making any sense,

and I didn't have time to hear her out. I heard Uri yell to his Brothers before turning and darting to safety. When he ran through, it felt like a dagger to my chest, and the earth shook once more.

The Hall was a battlefield. The Network was small but enraged and ready to fight. The Lightborn had been taken by surprise and weren't trained for this, not like the Ludus. I watched in admiration as my people fought to capture, not kill. They used bindings and traps to subdue their enemies and fought with non-lethal magic. They were clustered at the entrance, spilling out into the rain.

Some of the Lightborn that were still free gave up and ran to the portal. I let them go, knowing the world would be better off without them.

"Help!" I heard Declan cry as the Network rushed him.

I'd forgotten he was still there, trapped by the fighting. They had him wrapped up in vines, and he could do nothing as they dragged him away.

Instinctively, I turned to Oran. He saw his husband, bound and terrified, and reacted without hesitation. A growl escaped his lips as he knocked back the men in his way, stepping forward and closing his fist.

The Lightborn from the Network let go, putting their hands to their heads and crying out in pain. Declan scrambled to his feet and ran to his husband.

"Oran, no!" I yelled.

He was going to kill them, I could see it in his eyes.

He looked to me briefly and then back at the men, his hand still raised. Locking eyes with me, I felt what he felt. He was furious that his husband was in danger, but he knew it was his own doing.

I opened my mouth to shout a warning, but he held up a hand. With a slight nod, he turned and ran to the portal with Declan. The men were released from his hold, and I let out the breath I'd been holding.

"Enough!" Anwar's voice filled the Hall, and I felt the ground disappear from beneath me.

We were floating, unable to do anything as he held us in limbo.

"Just go! Be with your family," I pleaded.

He smirked at me and closed a fist. One man closest fell into a heap on the floor. Beside him, his mistress smiled.

"Anwar, I'm warning you! If I close that portal, you'll never make it out."

"You think I need you?!" He killed another man without so much as a sigh.

The rage inside me almost blew out when I felt a hand on my ankle, and the ground rushed toward me.

The girl helped me to my feet and yelled, "Anya, you have to jump. Jump forward before it's too late."

"What? Who are you?"

"I'm a friend, trust me."

I didn't know this girl, and I could tell she didn't have the Light. Was she with the Network?

"Anya, please. Go, now, before Anwar jumps."

I heard a cry and watched as the Network fell to their knees. Anwar was standing in the middle of the room, arms raised, and lightning firing from his hands. He was drunk on power, and I needed to stop him.

When he lifted his hands once more, I took a step forward, but the girl grabbed me and held me back. Before I could react, Anwar clapped his hands together, and the Network disappeared.

He stumbled and fell to his knees, his Light fading fast.

"Anwar-" I tried, but the crack overhead stopped me.

I flinched and could hear ringing. The girl at my side was bleeding from her ears. Even Anwar was clutching his head. He grabbed at his woman and pulled her to where my portal had been. But the wall closed when he was just steps away. He had nowhere to go.

Someone called my name, another girl. I looked up and saw Alexis. She was running my way but stopped short, fear in her eyes.

"Open the portal," Anwar said calmly, "or she dies."

"No! Stop! I'll do it!" I cried, rushing to my feet.

"No, no. Stay right there," Anwar warned as he pulled Alexis closer to him. When she stopped, I saw roots come up from the concrete, wrapping around her legs and pinning her arms down.

"Don't do it! Wait, I have something to show you." The girl behind me pleaded.

She was fumbling in her pocket for something, but all I could focus on was my sister. Alexis looked to be in pain.

"Anya, now."

I looked at my sister, raised my hand, and the portal opened in a blurry Glimmer. I couldn't focus. It was as though I could feel the decay seeping into my skin, distorting my mind, and keeping me from seeing what I needed to.

The woman ran forward, taking the chance and rushing through the blur. I could feel she made it, but only just.

"Just go while you still can!" I yelled. "Let her go!"

Anwar smirked again and moved to the portal. He

tilted his head and stepped backwards into my Light. I had half a mind to close it there, cutting him off from both worlds. But I let him go.

As he stepped through, Alexis fell to the ground. The girl at my side cried out, reaching a hand toward me.

I raced to Alexis, taking her hands in mine. "Alexis, what are you doing here?"

"Anya, you have to listen to me. You have to jump!" The girl cried again as she raced forward.

I wanted to scream at her to leave me alone.

"Anya!" Alexis pulled a hand free and pointed to my portal.

I saw Anwar coming closer. He was reaching out and shouting, rage filling his face. I stood and clapped my hands closed with a smile, locking him and his people away.

The second my Light was out, the world cracked. Everything went quiet as I flew back into the wall. The room seemed to fill with smoke, and I could barely see Alexis on the ground.

It was as though someone had stepped on a mine. As my eyes cleared, I could see an enormous black line, cutting the Great Hall in half. It ran from one wall to the other and up to the windows. The floor had tiny cracks reaching out from the still smoking crack in the earth.

The fire in the sky was angry and loud. I looked through the door and knew it had finally happened.

The Veils had dropped.

Alexis called my name, but she sounded too far. I felt a hand on my arm and looked to see her kneeling at my side. I couldn't hear and tried to stand, but a pain in my chest held me down. I fell back, my head rolling to one side.

There was something in my hand. Through the tears, I could see an old photo of my father, torn and crinkled. I kept it in my jacket pocket, so he was always close. This was the same but looked worn somehow.

A movement to the side drew my eye. I watched as the girl I didn't know reached into the crib and lifted out the baby.

The baby.

That was what Anwar was shouting. I'd forgotten she was still there. They've must've thought she was through already. He was coming back for his child, and I stopped him.

The girl took the baby and ran to the main doors. She stopped and looked up to the angry skies, hesitating in the threshold. As she got there, Mr Parks and the Network came racing in from the night.

He rushed to my side, calling for help and telling me it was all going to be ok. But I kept my eyes on the girl as she turned back.

Before she left, I somehow heard her say, "Jump."

It was then I realised we were wearing the same jacket. I put a hand on my chest and found the pocket. Inside was my father's picture.

Through the pain, I called for Ozzie. His bark found me, even from afar. I could see the tears in Alexis's eyes and tried to tell her I was ok, but I had no strength.

My arm was weak, and I dropped the photo the girl had given me. In my other hand, I closed my fist around the same picture from my own pocket.

I shut my eyes and felt the last bit of power inside warm through me. I felt weightless as I faded into the light.

# CHAPTER 41

**July 3011**

Everything felt warm and cosy. I smiled as I sank into the covers and slowly woke up. Even from that first crazy night, I'd appreciated the bed at the compound. It had to have been enhanced somehow. It was so soft and warm, and I always seemed to fit perfectly no matter how I was positioned.

Ozzie licked my arm and nuzzled my face as I let the nightmare come back to me. It had been so vivid: the portal, the fight, and the crack of power. I had no clue who that girl was or why Alexis was there. Probably just the thought of what I had to do haunting me. I was doing it all because of Alexis, after all. Alexis, Frankie, and Uncle Mark. Maybe the girl was my conscience?

The curtains were closed, but I could tell it was still dark outside. I felt like I'd slept a week, but it could only have been a couple hours. Today was the day. The first official day of the Tournament and I would have to go steal a bunch of Light and send the Three and their people away. Weirdly, I couldn't feel any of the excess power I'd taken in the day before.

An image of Declan crossed my mind as I rubbed my eyes and sat up in bed. Why had I dreamed that? We'd never met. He'd seemed so kind in my dream, and I wondered if he was as empathetic in real life.

As more of the dream came back to me, I started to feel tired. Obviously, my mind was trying to work through my feelings.

"What do you think, Sweet Boy? Am I just crazy?"

Ozzie wagged his tail and tilted his head. I gave him a treat and made myself a tea. After a few minutes, I stood and stretched my legs. They felt weak and heavy. From my toes to my hips, I felt stiff and tingling.

As I raised my arm to grab the curtain, I felt a sharp pull in my chest. Brushing it aside as stress, I pulled the curtain back, hoping to see the sun peeking in the distance.

When I dropped my cup, Ozzie jumped to his feet and rushed to my side. I felt his nose nudging my hand, but I couldn't move. I couldn't speak. I couldn't comprehend what I was seeing.

The sky was black and angry. Fire rolled around in the clouds, dropping flames to the ground. The grass was gone, burned, and bare, along with what used to be trees. I could see movement in the darkness. Gigantic lumbering creatures roaming in the dark, and the wall that surrounded the compound had crumbled to nothing.

I lurched back to the bed. Ozzie barked, trying to pull me out of my shock.

"What happened?" I asked the poor, confused dog.

"Anya?"

A voice from the doorway made me jump. I turned to see a woman standing and watching me. She had tears in her eyes and a hand on her chest. Behind her stood a man and a girl-the girl!

"You!" I cried, jumping to my feet. "Who are you? What's going on?"

The woman in the doorway held out her palms to calm me. To my surprise, Ozzie went to her and sat at her side.

"Anya, calm down. I know this will be a lot to take in. Maybe you should sit?"

"Don't tell me to sit. Who are you? Where's Oran? What happened outside?"

The woman sighed and moved into the room. "You always were stubborn, you know that? It drove me crazy."

She sat on the bed and looked at her hands. I watched as she ran a finger over something before holding it out to me.

"Just like him."

She handed me a picture of my father. I kept it in my jacket pocket. It was the same picture I'd seen in my dream. I looked at the girl and then back to the image. The woman on the bed sat patiently as it all clicked in my head.

I looked at her again, taking in every inch of her face. Her long curls were cut short, almost shaved. She had lines around her mouth and eyes, and the years showed. But her eyes were the same. Big and brown and beautiful. Our mother's eyes.

"Alexis?" I whispered, not wanting to believe it.

The woman nodded before standing and pulling me into a tight hug. I felt her shake as she let the tears fall. I cried too, for both of us and for the world outside.

Alexis stepped back, put both hands on my cheeks, and wiped away my tears.

"Oh, Anya. I thought I'd lost you."

"I don't understand. How is this-"

"I know. I was confused too, believe me." She looked over my shoulder and motioned for the girl to join us.

"This is Gabby. We're here because of her."

"No, no, not really. I just-"

"You brought me here. You brought me here to my sister. After all these years."

Gabby blushed and looked to her feet.

"How about some food? Anya, you must be starving?" The man came to the doorway and smiled.

"Anya, this is Tony," Alexis said, not taking her eyes from mine.

"Um, yeah. Yes, I think I am hungry."

More shock hit me as Tony waved a hand and created a table, chairs, and delicious looking meal.

"You're…" I stammered.

Tony nodded and shrugged, embarrassed of the attention.

"We have a lot to catch up on," Alexis began, taking a seat and feeding Ozzie some bacon from the table.

They started to fill me in on everything, but I held my hands up, stopping them. My brain just couldn't accept the information. I needed answers to all the questions burning through my mind.

Where were the Three?

What happened to the skies?

It's been how long?

I just appeared?

Why were you in the Hall?

What about Mr Parks?

"I just don't know how to make sense of this. You're saying I opened a portal and jumped forward twenty years? The Brothers left, and everything came crashing down? Because of me?!"

"Slow down, Anya. You're weak. You've been asleep fo-"

"Four days. Yeah. Another coma. Great."

Alexis gave me the same look she had when we-she was younger. The raised eyebrow and pursed lips. I knew it well.

"And I just do not get where you come into this," I said to Gabby, who was quiet for the most part. "You were there! I saw you. You talked to me, and then...you had my jacket. That jacket!" I pointed to the chair where it hung and looked back to the picture of my father.

"I don't know what to say. I've never met you before. And like I told your sister, I don't-"

"Don't know why you were there. Right."

I was trying to take in twenty years of information all at once, and it was giving me a headache.

"What...what about Mum?"

Alexis sighed and cast her eyes down. She pet Ozzie a little and seemed to work herself up to the story.

"After what she did, I was furious. All those years, I knew the truth about you and what-who you were. I don't know why I didn't say anything. It scared me, I guess. I was scared they'd come for you - for all of us. I kept my head in the sand, but it was the reason I was always so protective."

I put my hand on hers and squeezed.

"But her turning you in like that? That was it for me. For Uncle Mark, too. I told her to leave. I couldn't even look at her. The way she blamed you was disgusting, and I'm sorry I let it go on so long. She played the victim for too long, and I wasn't going to stand for it anymore. After she left, I got on the bus and went to see your Mr Parks."

"Wait, what? How did you even know?"

"I followed you," she smiled and looked at me, proud

of herself. "You made it a little too easy, An."

We both laughed, and it felt good. After the weeks with the Brothers, the stress and worry, it felt freeing to be able to laugh with my sister.

"I'd seen you going off, getting the bus, and I just followed you one day. I watched where you went and figured out why. After they took you, I knew they were the only people that could help. I stood by that damn tree for hours before someone finally came and let me in. I felt like an idiot, talking to the leaves."

"You told Mr Parks about me? You told him I'd been taken?"

"Mmhmm. He was furious and scared. He sat me down and told me everything about the Brothers, the Tournaments, and the Veils. Knowing what you had been dealing with just broke my heart, Anya. I wished you'd come to me."

"I couldn't. You know that."

"Still, I wish I was better to you. Anyway, I was frustrated. I wanted to storm the castle, but they told me we had to wait. It was torture, knowing they had you, forcing you to help them. Oh, and then we got your message from Ozzie here. Oh! I felt relief like you can't believe."

She turned and kissed Ozzie on the nose. He was loving being the centre of attention.

"I couldn't attend the Network meetings, but Mr Parks kept me in the loop. After Paris and the investigation that followed, we had no choice but to lie low. It was killing him, you know. He cared about you like a daughter. That much was obvious. We both struggled with the wait."

I stood up, moved to the window, and let the tears fall

as I thought about them trying to save me. The burden they must have felt.

"Is he..." I was afraid of the answer, but I needed to know.

"He survived the Crack. He helped me get you back to the Ludus. But the years after, there was so much destruction. He didn't make it."

"What about you? How did you make it?" I asked, wanting to change the subject.

I noticed a look between Alexis and Gabby but didn't comment. I knew there was a lot more going on that I didn't know. I would find out eventually.

"I stayed with the Network. We tried to help people but...they didn't want it. After the Crack, everything changed. The earth was broken. People lost their homes and their humanity. People like you, the Lightborn, they were ostracised. Somehow they were weakened and couldn't fight back. We outnumbered them and drove them away. They have a community somewhere up North, and it's the same in other countries. Once they grouped together, they became stronger, so people tend to leave them alone."

"But the people from the Ludus? The others?"

"Unfortunately, people couldn't really distinguish between the good and the bad. They only saw the Light."

Tony shifted in his seat.

"It wasn't an easy time. But then, it wasn't for anyone. The weather went haywire. Fires broke out, and flash floods took out entire towns. The ruin spread from the point of the Crack, infecting everything as it went. The areas you called the Veils, they were the same. Creatures like nothing I'd ever seen came out from there. Crops were lost. Families were broken. People turned away from each other instead of banding together."

"Uncle Mark? Frankie?" I'd been afraid to ask but couldn't wait any longer.

"We tried to stay together initially, but after a few years, they moved away. Uncle Mark needed work, and he wanted to get away from the city. I haven't heard from them in a while."

Yesterday (or what felt like yesterday), I had been so sure sending the Three through my portal was the best option. They were the reason for all the corruption. Their way of life, using their Light and encouraging others to do the same, was the source of it. Getting rid of them felt like the only option. But now, here I sat, listening to my sister tell me about the end of the world and how it was my fault.

"I never should've helped them."

Ozzie came over and put his head in my lap. He'd been with Alexis for twenty years, but I could see the love in his face. It made me happy knowing they'd had each other.

"You had no way of knowing. And what other choice did you have?" Tony said.

He lifted his hand as if to pat my arm and then thought better of it.

"Exactly. And they would have found a way, regardless. This was always going to happen."

"So, what then? If this was always the only outcome, why am I here? Why did you tell me to jump?" I looked at Gabby, and she shrugged.

She had nothing to add.

"I can only think of one way to change things."

Alexis stood and moved to the window. She put a hand on the glass and watched the flames fall from the sky.

"Care to share?" I asked in a tone she was all too familiar with.

I saw her laugh in the reflection before her eyes turned dark.

"We have to kill them.

# CHAPTER 42

Gabby's head had been spinning for days. After so many years of coming to the Hall, she finally knew why - though she was still confused. When the girl, Anya, appeared, her mouth fell open, and she collapsed to her knees. Everything seemed to fade as she'd watched Ozzie run to her side. Alexis followed, shouting instructions at Tony.

Anya had been bleeding and looked near death. Gabby worried they'd waited all this time just so Alexis could witness her die again. But Anya stayed alive. Tony fixed some of what was wrong, and she stayed asleep for four days. Ozzie never left her side.

Now she was awake, asking questions and claiming Gabby had told her to jump! What? She had to be mistaken. Anya had jumped from the very moment after the Crack. Obviously Gabby hadn't been there.

After their awkward meal, she left Anya with Alexis and took Ozzie outside. They had too much to catch up on, and Gabby felt intrusive listening in. Instead, she stood under the fiery sky and wondered about Alexis' plan. She wanted to kill the Three? How would that even work?

"Hey."

Gabby turned to see Anya coming her way.

"Oh, hi. Where's Alexis?"

"Inside. We both needed a break."

They stood and watched the dog run around. He was happy as ever, not showing any signs of the twenty years he'd been waiting for Anya to come back.

"Look, I know this is all crazy," Anya started out of nowhere. "It's crazy for me too. I thought I was dead. And looking around here, hearing about the world now...it breaks my heart to think I'm responsible."

Gabby turned to argue, but Anya waved her away.

"Don't. I don't need you all babying me. This is on me. I made the wrong choice, obviously."

Gabby nodded and stayed quiet.

Anya looked up at the building and laughed. "Elders, this place used to be impressive. They brought me here against my will, and even then, I was in awe."

"I've heard about it. Hard for me to imagine what the world looked like before all this," Gabby shrugged.

She didn't want to make Anya feel worse, but she wasn't willing to lie either.

"I live in the city. The high rises are some of the only safe places left."

"What about your family?"

"It's just me." Gabby tried not to let the sadness through. "Has been for a while."

She watched as Anya hung her head and wiped an eye.

"This was always going to happen." Gabby put a hand on her shoulder and smiled. "From what I hear, it was only a matter of time."

The pair went quiet and watched Ozzie. Above, Gabby could just about see Alexis through the window. With Anya at her side, Gabby noticed a feeling of calm wash over her. She'd been waiting so long for this, and even though it made little sense, the tightness in her stomach was starting to unravel.

“What are you thinking?” Anya asked.

“Just that, I’ve been coming here for years without knowing why. And now you’re here. So…what now?”

“Good question. But I have no clue. Alexis wants revenge. I want revenge, and I’m sure you feel the same. But my power is practically non-existent. I won’t be jumping through a portal any time soon.”

Gabby watched her look to her hands, noticing a black mark on her palm. She could only imagine what Anya had been through, and though she had questions, she decided to try to keep things light.

“So…tell me about you. What was life like before the world ended?”

Anya laughed. She sounded just like her sister, but Gabby could see where they differed. She’d seen the picture Alexis had given Anya, and it was clear she took after her father. Gabby had been curious when they spoke of their mother but thought it better not to ask.

“I was a teacher. I worked in the culinary school up in Township…I guess it doesn’t matter anymore. But I liked it. I met friends there and my ex-boyfriend. He taught too.”

“What was his name?”

“Joshua." Anya smiled as she said his name. “He was a good guy, but we were too different. I found out after a while, he was far more pro-Brotherhood than I ever realised.”

“Not a brilliant match, then?”

“No, but we stayed friends. I liked my life. Alexis was going off to be in movies and plays. My cousin Frankie wanted nothing more than to drive trains. We were happy, more or less, even without all our freedoms. Even living under their rule. We went shopping and to the movies-"

"I've never seen a movie," Gabby admitted.

"Oh, they're amazing. I'm sorry you've had to live... like this."

"What about your Mum?" Gabby asked tentatively, keeping her eyes on Ozzie as she spoke.

"She worked for the Brotherhood. They took my father away when I was little, and they forced her to work for them. It was that or go to prison herself."

Gabby was still confused but didn't want to pry. They fell quiet again and started walking the grounds. Ozzie ran ahead toward the Great Hall. Flames fell from above, burning the rooftop. In the distance, Gabby could see a storm brewing.

"We shouldn't go too far. We don't want to be caught out when the rains come."

She could see Anya wanted to ask, but she stayed quiet, looking up to the sky.

"This is what I saw under the Veil. I was so young when I first found it, and it looked just like this. The sky was angry, and fire flew around. The winds were biting, and they'd thrown in their mutated creations. I don't think even they knew how many spots there were in the end. I guess the Light used in the Tournaments and the power it took to have the Three cross over was just too much. I felt the Crack, deep down inside. It was as though an avalanche crashed down on me. I think I knew then that I'd made a mistake."

The rains started, and the pair hustled back to the main building. They stood in the lobby and watched as the flames whirled in the skies and joined in with the droplets. Thunder cracked overhead, and lightning flashed behind the deep clouds.

"This is normal now?" Anya asked, mouth open and eyes wide.

"Pretty much. I used to play in the rain, but now...it would kill me. If you're caught out, you don't have a lot of time to find shelter. But the rains are nothing compared to the snow. One minute you're walking down the street in a T-shirt and then next you're scrambling for cover. The whiteouts come in so fast, and everything just freezes. That's why most people carry extra layers now. I remember one-"

Gabby stopped when she heard Anya sniffle. She was trying to hold back the tears, but they were flowing anyway. Gabby wanted to try to apologise - to reassure Anya that it wasn't all her fault, but she knew it would do no good.

Looking to Ozzie, who was already at Anya's side, she smiled, took a step and put an arm around Anya, pulling her in until her head rested on her shoulder. Anya turned into Gabby and cried, letting it all out.

She noticed Alexis standing near the elevators. She nodded and wiped a tear away of her own. Gabby put her arms around Anya and waited until the rains stopped.

# CHAPTER 43

Anya seemed to get better after the storm. The rains washed away the dirt and ash, just like her tears washed away some of the guilt she felt. After that day, she seemed to stand a little taller and worked harder to regain her strength.

Gabby was sure she still felt the pain inside, but now she was using it as fuel. It was impressive to watch.

Tony could snap his fingers and send an entire room of people to different locations. He'd conjured beds, food, and toys for Ozzie. Every time, Gabby was in awe. So even though Anya was frustrated with her little progress, Gabby was happy to watch her re-learn how to use the Light.

"Try over there," Gabby called, pointing to the stump of a burned up tree.

Her grin was bright in the low light, and she felt like a little kid.

Anya smiled and focussed in on the scorched wood. She raised her hands and breathed out, letting her Light fly. The sparks fluttered around the stump, bringing it back to life before their eyes. Flowers appeared around the base, and it looked wholly out of place in the burned and barren wasteland of the compound.

Gabby clapped, and Ozzie barked. Anya looked proud of herself, even as the magic faded and the darkness washed back over the tree.

"Better than nothing," she said with a shrug.

Gabby was impressed at her positivity. She could see how frustrated Anya got sometimes, but she was always able to stay calm.

"You're doing great."

Anya raised her hands to try again when the sound of a vehicle drew their eyes to the main building. They were on the hill near what Anya said was Brother Uri's house, but the sound of the engine was unmistakable. Ozzie was first to go, racing across the dirt and dust toward the noise. Anya held back, looking to Gabby to take the lead.

"It's probably one of Alexis' men. She's been here for two weeks, I'm sure they're just worried."

When Anya asked Gabby about her sister, she hadn't known what to say at first. It wasn't her place to tell Alexis' story, and she didn't want to taint Anya with stories of the Gulls. But she'd known when Alexis finally told her. She could see a slight change in both of them. The stories were probably as hard to hear as they were to tell.

As they rounded the corner of the main building, they saw the big Burlak parked by the steps. It was wet, and Gabby could see frost on the windows. It was hard to tell from the compound, but the snows persisted beyond the Crack site.

"Gabby."

She jumped as he said her name.

Baz laughed and clapped a hand on her shoulder. "Nice to see you too."

"What are you doing back here?"

"The boss calls, we answer." He looked passed Gabby

to Anya and raised an eyebrow. “Is that who we were all waiting on?”

Anya stayed where she was, eyes on the strange man and machine.

“Don’t worry about it,” Gabby said dismissively. “You need me to get Alexis?”

Baz shook his head and walked inside. Gabby watched him go with Charlie and the same driver as before, Gemma. They stood together, looking nervous and glancing back at Gabby and Anya. Two new, mysterious girls. Probably the most excitement they’d had in a while.

“Who are they?” Anya asked quietly.

“Your sister’s people. He said she called them here." Gabby took a step toward the Burlak, keeping her eyes on Baz. “We met just before you got here. I haven’t decided if I like them or not.”

They watched as Alexis and Tony entered the lobby. The group talked a little before heading into the building. Tony made the elevator rise, and they disappeared from sight. Gabby just hoped they weren’t staying long.

“Hey, you ok?” She turned to Anya, who looked nervous.

“I don’t know. My sister...she’s not the person I knew. It’s not her fault, I know that. But these people...”

“The Gulls.”

“Gulls." Anya breathed out sharply and rolled her eyes. “I’m sure I didn’t get the total truth, but what she told me didn’t sound great.”

“No, I guess it wouldn’t.”

“So, how bad are they?”

Gabby had been dreading this for days. She and Anya had become close, talking all day and into the night.

They were the same age but had lived such different lives.

Gabby loved to hear about before the Crack and what it was all like. They talked about Ozzie and how he'd saved Anya in her darkest moments. Gabby shared all about the dreams she'd had and growing up in the aftermath of it all. But she'd purposefully avoided any mention of the Gulls. Even when recounting her past visits to the Hall, she never explained why she had to hurry or what she might have been afraid of.

"Gabby?"

"Honestly, I don't know. I've heard stories my whole life and thought I knew exactly who they were. But after meeting them, I don't know what to believe."

"The stories had to come from somewhere." Anya was looking up, picturing the building as it once was.

Gabby looked to her feet and tried to figure out what to say. She was quiet until Anya looked back at her and tilted her head.

"I've heard lots of things. The Gulls are like the boogyman. People talk about them like they would come and get you in the night. As I got older, I found out that they never actually go into the city. They stay out there, in the Plains, but they would attack near the train stations. If they get someone alone or a smaller group, they swoop in and grab whatever they can before running back to their holes." She stopped herself. It sounded bad. "I mean, I don't know where they live. It's just what we always said."

Anya nodded, "It's ok. I can hear it."

She put a hand on Gabby's arm and smiled, encouraging her to go on.

"I've heard about them hurting people. People going

to work and not coming home. Some people found cars and stuff over the years, and I heard stories of them being attacked out in the middle of nowhere. I always thought the Gulls were nothing more than ruthless scavengers. Every trip I made here, I was afraid. I would always run off the train, and my legs would burn with the effort, but I just knew I couldn't be stuck out there."

Anya shuffled her feet. It was one thing to hear stories about a group of random people, but quite another to hear that your own sister was in charge of them.

"Did they ever hurt you?"

"Me? No. I mean, they caught up to me this time - they came out of nowhere and chased me up the hill. I tried to distract them with my ration packs, but I tripped. Actually, Baz saved me. The snows rolled in, and he could've left me to freeze. Only Alexis said she wanted me alive."

"What about your family? Was it them?" Anya looked up, fear in her eyes.

"No. The Gulls didn't kill my family," Gabby said with a tight mouth. "It was just...this place."

Anya took Gabby's hand and squeezed. "I'm sorry."

"I've told you, you don't have to keep apologising."

"I know, but I can't help it. I look around and see all this destruction, and I see the pain in you. I can't help but feel responsible."

Gabby squeezed back and nodded. "I get it. But I don't blame you."

She heard Ozzie whine to their side but couldn't look away. Anya was holding her stare and her hands, and she felt a sudden flicker in her stomach.

"Ahem. Not interrupting, am I?"

Gabby could feel Baz's smirk before she turned to face

him. He had an eyebrow raised, and she could feel the blush on her cheeks. She let go of Anya and took a step back, hands clasped behind her back.

"You all done?" She asked, trying to act casual.

"Hardly. You two should go pack. We're leaving in the morning."

"Leaving?" Anya asked, moving past Gabby and up the steps. She glanced inside, looking for Alexis.

"Yeah. No time to waste."

Anya looked back to Gabby, who shrugged and followed her inside. They found Alexis and Tony whispering near the elevator.

"Alexis, what's going on?"

"Oh, hi. You saw Baz, I take it?"

Gabby nodded, her mouth turned down in an awkward frown. She looked from Alexis and back to Anya, not wanting to get in the middle of a sister fight.

"He told us to pack our bags. What's going on? Why are we leaving? I need to be here, 'Lex, I need-"

"Power." Alexis interrupted with a simple word.

She crossed her arms and let out a sharp breath as Anya's brow furrowed. "You need power. And there's none left here."

Gabby looked back to Baz and the Burlak outside. She knew the mighty machine would make it over the snow and ice with ease. But if the storm had persisted since they arrived, surely it would be too dangerous to attempt a long journey now.

"We can't make it that far." She kept her eyes on Alexis as she spoke. "It's been snowing for two weeks, right? It's not safe. And no offence, but I'm not sure I wanna be 'snapped' anywhere."

Tony laughed and shook his head. "It's not as hard as

you think."

"Can someone tell me what's going on?" Anya stepped forward, frustrated at their seemingly coded conversation.

"We're going North. My people found the Lightborn colony, and we're going up there. We can't have Tony send us because we don't have an exact location, and in this weather, we can't afford to be left out in the cold for even a minute. Besides, after bringing our people together and getting them home, he's spent. The Burlak will make it. And even if Tony could get us close, we'd need the truck to go the rest of the way. We've got stops along the way for fuel and supplies."

"But...why?" Anya asked, though her face suggested she knew the answer.

"You need power. They have it."

Alexis walked away before Anya could reply. She walked out to Baz and the big tank and began giving instructions. From a room down the hall, Charlie and Gemma came out holding bags. They nodded as they passed but said nothing.

"She wants me to take their Light. I'm weaker than I've ever been, and she thinks I can just steal power?"

"Can't you?" Gabby asked, genuinely curious. "I heard that was what the Three did back then."

Anya nodded and dropped her head. She spoke to her feet, ashamed of her reply.

"We all did. It was the only way to open a portal strong enough to allow them all through."

Gabby tried to hide her shock. The way she'd been told, the Lightborn at the Tournaments suddenly went weak, their power stripped away as they played silly games. They were left too vulnerable to defend themselves. The regular people overpowered and kicked them out of society.

"I'm not proud of it. But I'm getting stronger. You've seen!"

"I know. I don't know what the rush is, but…I don't know that we have any other choice."

Anya balled her fists and let out a groan. "Why am I always backed into a corner?"

She withdrew into the wall, her back sliding down the dark wood. She hit the floor with a thud and brought her knees to her chest.

Outside, Alexis and her people were preparing the Burlak for the journey. Anya didn't understand the life her sister had been forced in to. The life they'd all been forced in to. Anya had only been there two weeks, and she'd seen nothing of the real world.

Gabby's heart went out to her, but she understood where Alexis was coming from. She didn't want to live in this world any longer than she had to, and if going North meant changing things faster, then she was on board.

Ozzie brushed his head against her thigh as she turned and sat next to Anya. He curled at their feet while Anya rested her head on Gabby's shoulder and took a deep breath.

"I know you don't want to go. But your sister- all of us, we've been living in this place for so long. You can't imagine what it's like. Alexis just wants what's best for her people."

"I used to be her people," Anya murmured. "But I get it. She's right. It could take months for me to get my Light back, and even then, jumping through time will be exhausting. I'm gonna need power when I get back to...wherever we decide. The more I have going in, the safer I'll be on the other end."

Gabby lifted an arm around Anya's shoulders and pulled her in close.

"I'm sorry this is all on you."

"Me too."

# CHAPTER 44

Being with Alexis was bittersweet in so many ways. In my mind, I'd been gone around a month and had missed her every day. I did what I did to protect her and the rest of my family. There wasn't a single day at the compound I didn't dream about jumping home and seeing them all. But I stayed away and did as I was told because I knew what would come of them if I didn't.

Seeing her in the future, as a harsh, dangerous leader of, well, criminals, was jarring. She had been tall and beautiful with flowing curls and perfect skin. I wouldn't have called her shallow, per se, but she paid a lot of attention to her appearance. Still, she had a kind heart.

She watched over me and helped me with homework as a child. When I doubted my skills before becoming a teacher, she yelled compliments at me until I agreed. With Frankie, she was like a mother, comforting and sweet. I never told her about the Ludus or my Light, partly because I was afraid she'd blame me like my mother had. Mostly, I kept her in the dark to keep her safe.

The first few days after I arrived, she'd been the Alexis I knew. We talked and laughed and were sisters for a while. But then she seemed to come to her senses, and a wall went up. The woman before me barking commands at people was severe, intense, and intimidating.

I had to remind myself that she'd lived for twenty years without me in a world of ruin.

I wasn't thrilled about the trip, and I didn't hide it. Baz and his people milled around, mostly keeping their distance, though I saw the way he looked at Gabby and wasn't too thrilled about it. She'd become a real friend to me, and I leaned on her for support. She was good and kind and just wanted to help.

But there was something more there, for me at least.

We set off from the compound the next morning, all cramped in the back of the mammoth truck. Charlie told me it had been a Russian snow-mobile once upon a time. The Gulls found it in some old museum, and Tony got it moving again.

As we left the gates and moved away from the Hall, my mouth fell open at the sight of the Plains. Just a month ago, I'd been driven through the greens and flowers to the big, imposing wall. The grassy fields spread out far and wide, and the sun shone down.

When the fiery skies of the compound receded, we were met with thick grey clouds and snow as deep as the truck's windows. We stood over two metres off the ground but still had to carve a path through the ice and snow.

"The whiteouts are becoming more and more frequent. It used to be two or three a year, but now." Alexis shrugged and looked out the window. "Now, you can't go anywhere without a few extra layers and a plan to hide."

Gabby nodded, her face turning sad. She had a bag with her, the same bag she'd carried to the Hall for years. Inside, I knew she had extra sweaters and scarves. I could feel the chill as we hit the snow and couldn't imagine anyone surviving outside.

We ambled, the driver ever cautious of what lay ahead. Burned tree stumps were the most pressing concern, so Alexis had Tony map a course. He could somehow put himself ahead of the truck and navigate us around obstacles. I thought about using my Light to melt the snow away, but the clouds above us were too persistent.

Mostly we stayed quiet. I think Baz and Charlie were intimidated by Alexis and opted to keep their mouths shut. Ozzie snoozed at our feet, happy to be coming along. Gabby and I sat in the back, jostling around as the enormous tires pounded the ice.

I wanted to talk to her, to try and go through my feelings about stealing power from other Lightborn, but it wasn't the time. So we sat. We watched the snow and kept our thoughts to ourselves.

When they did speak, it was through walkie talkies. Baz talked to a place called Sutton Park and told them of our impending arrival. As we moved up what I assumed to be a driveway, my mouth fell open once more.

"It was a prison, once," Baz announced.

I looked to see Gabby equally in awe.

"I wouldn't mind doing some time here."

Sutton Park was a vast, red-brick manor. It looked more like a castle than a prison.

"The Gulls live here?" Gabby breathed as we rounded a fountain.

"Some," Alexis smirked.

"How is it still standing?"

"The prisons were all shut down after the Brotherhood took over. Prisoners were either brought back into society or sent to the camps-"

"Camps?"

Gabby turned from the house. I wondered what she really knew of the Brotherhood's Awakening.

"Truthfully, nobody ever really knew what happened. People were taken and never seen again. But places like this - mansions and castles - they were given to the Brothers or higher ranking Lightborn. It was the same all over the world. We just happen to have a lot of these to go around. Anyway, most people flocked to the cities after the Crack. Nobody wanted to be caught out here during a storm or whiteout. These places were just abandoned, but she's stayed strong over the years. Some parts around back have shown wear and tear, and they lost a whole portion of the side to decay, but mostly, it's sound."

We pulled into a garage, and everyone got to work. Gabby and I jumped down and moved aside to stretch our legs. I watched in silence as Alexis jumped out and rushed into the big house.

People hustled in and out with supplies, throwing them inside to Baz and Charlie. Nobody talked to us, but they all looked our way. Before long, we were back on the road.

We skirted the city, keeping to the East to cross the river. Baz called to 'Friern' this time, and after an hour or two, we arrived at another manor house.

Covered in ivy, its light bricks showed more wear than the last place. I could see some of the building had crumbled away, and a prominent crack was making its way up the middle. I doubted it would be safe here much longer.

Over the next few days, we stopped at various places on the East coast: Railway Sleeper, Highpoint, Fuggle

Bunny, and Crayke, to name a few. Alexis explained that as the cities became more full, places out in the fields were emptying. The Brotherhood had kept strict limits on Townships when they took over and moved people where they saw fit. After the Crack, the outer Townships were mostly abandoned.

The fields to the south were destroyed, and agriculture moved to wherever the plants would still grow. Other people wanted to be closer to the cities and trains. It was their best chance of finding work, so the old prisons, breweries, and manors sat empty. As more and more people were forced to leave the cities behind, they came to the Plains, and to the Gulls.

With each new location, I heard Gabby gasp. She'd used the word 'holes' when speaking of the Gulls' home. I was sure seeing them living like kings was eye-opening.

"You ok?" I asked as we left yet another grand house.

"I don't know. The towers in the cities are falling apart. People are living in cramped rooms, sharing beds, and communal living. And they're out here with entire castles to themselves."

"Hey, don't get mad at us for being smart," Baz snarled. "Nobody made you live in the city."

"We didn't know we had any other options."

"It's not all dinner parties and buffets out here, you know. We can't grow food or find work. Having a roof over our heads doesn't make us royalty. We struggle like the rest. Most of us lost jobs and family and were left with nothing else."

Baz looked genuinely upset, and I noticed Gabby take a breath at his scowl. She reached out a hand and touched his lightly.

“Look, I’m sorry. I didn’t mean anything, I’m just shocked. That’s all.”

Baz nudged her with his shoulder, and they both laughed. I tried to hide my pout as I watched the snow melt.

We’d started out at the compound, south of the city. Creeping up the coast, we avoided any populated areas and stopped only for some rest and fuel. It was eight days before Baz announced we were close. I was ready to jump out and run, but Alexis held me back.

“The snows might be melting, but it’s still freezing. We should head to the overnight and see if things warm-up tomorrow.”

She’d told me there were no Gulls this far north, but Tony found us a place to sleep. I could just about see the words ‘Glenkinchie Distillery’ on a faded and battered sign.

Charlie and Baz got the doors open while the driver pulled us into an enormous warehouse. Charlie hauled the doors closed, and Tony was quick to make a fire, the stone walls holding very little heat.

“How can anyone survive this far North?” I asked, peeking out the tall windows.

“North or south doesn’t matter anymore. It’s cold everywhere, and then it’s hot everywhere. There's no more rules with the weather,” Charlie said without making eye contact.

“When they were cast out, they regrouped and made for a place with fewer people. You remember the maps from before?” Alexis asked me. “The way they redistributed the Townships, a lot of the North was empty. And then with the decay and everyone flocking to the cities, the people left up here couldn’t stay any longer.”

"What about the others? Around the world. The Lightborn were weak for a day or two, but surely they could come back once they'd regained their strength. Didn't any of them try to lead?"

Baz laughed out loud. Charlie sniggered into the fire, and Alexis sighed. She looked to Tony for an explanation.

"The Three took almost all the Light from the Lightborn at the Tournaments. They left us practically human. And when the Crack happened, it was like…the rest sort of seeped away. I couldn't so much as make a coffee for months. So when they were driven out, there was nothing they could do. Obviously, the Light came back," he added, holding his hands out as if to show something. "After a long, long time, I felt it. But the rot in the world corrupts the power. I know you've seen it, with the trees at the compound."

I nodded. "But then how are you able to…do what you do?"

"Practice and lots of it. Wherever the power comes from, its depleted. It finds its way to us little by little. I've been lucky to have what I have. I know I make it look endless, but I have to rest for weeks in-between use."

I looked down at my fingers and let a couple of sparks fly. The Brothers told me we were taking an insignificant amount of Light. They said the Lightborn wouldn't even notice. Why was I so surprised at the lie?

"The Lightborn here, some never regained their power. But they were kicked out of the cities anyway. It's the same all over. People felt the Crack, saw the destruction, found out the Brothers left, and they just lost it. Without the Three, without their Light, they threw even the higher ranking Lightborn from their homes.

People were marching in the streets. There were riots."

Nobody had told me any of this. I looked to Gabby first, searching her face for the truth. She kept her eyes down, no doubt reliving the memories. Alexis had her eyes on me. I could feel them and knew she was waiting for my reaction.

"So who's in charge now?"

"The Counties came together organically after the Crack. Neighbours and families tried to stick together for safety. I don't even know how the leaders were chosen. I think someone just decided to take charge." Tony shrugged and looked to Baz for confirmation.

"Yeah, that's pretty much what I heard. I did hear that some old military families took charge in the States. The generals or whatever from before raised and trained their kids to be ready for war. I don't know. Probably true. Why not, right?"

The chaos I'd left behind was devastating. The guilt in my stomach threatened to come rushing up as I thought about what I'd done. Before we left the compound, the idea of stealing more power was repulsive. I hated myself for doing it once and thought I would refuse Alexis this time. But the longer I spent in this world and the more stories I heard, the more I knew Alexis was right.

I thought sending the Three away was for the best. In reality, they took so much Light with them that the balance on earth shifted. I didn't know what they had become in their new life, and honestly, I didn't care anymore. It was time to put this world first and put an end to the Brotherhood, for good.

# CHAPTER 45

I didn't sleep much. Deciding to steal a bunch of power and actually doing it are two very different things. I was still weak and couldn't exactly waltz in on a bunch of disgruntled Lightborn and ask them for their power…could I?

Alexis was right in the end. The cold let up slightly overnight, and we were finally able to go outside and breathe in the fresh air. The melting snow glistened on the hills, and the sun felt warm on my face. Ozzie was thrilled to finally run free.

"Careful, it'll heat up fast," Gabby laughed from the doorway, two coffees in hand.

"What do you mean?" I took the coffee and sipped with my eyes closed.

"The heat will come roaring back, it always does. One minute you're layered up with scarves and coats, and the next, you're tearing it all away and searching for shade."

"The weather could be unstable before too. We saw a lot of crazy events, but nothing like this. Nothing this persistent."

We went quiet and looked out over the shining hills, enjoying our coffee and the peace. When she finally spoke, the calm I was feeling disappeared.

"What's going to happen today?"

"I can't say for sure. But I think I'm going to start with 'please.'"

She laughed and nudged my arm a little. Her coffee was almost done, so I topped it up. Her smile worth the Light.

"It's not a portal to the past, but it's handy."

"I bet. I can think of a lot of mornings where I would've liked to have you there."

She sipped her coffee and glanced my way. I smiled back, wanting to say something more. As if on cue, Baz appeared from inside.

"Hey, you should eat. Both of you."

"What is it today?" Gabby asked, turning her back to me. She walked up to Baz and looked at his plate. "No!" She ran inside before either of us could say anything.

"It's just a bacon sandwich. Probably been a while for her," he explained, taking a mouth full and avoiding my eyes.

"I guess it's the simple things you miss most."

Baz was already a sandwich down and working on his second when Gabby appeared with two plates. She looked practically giddy.

"You don't understand what this is like for me. It's like I forgot what bacon even was! How have I been this close to a Lightborn for two weeks and not requested a bacon sandwich?"

She grinned and took a big bite. I laughed, delighted to see her so happy over so small a thing.

"Anya? We should talk."

Alexis broke the mood, and I reluctantly left Gabby with Baz. Inside, the team was getting ready to go.

"We need a plan. How did you steal the Light before?"

She was so matter-of-fact it was unnerving.

"I didn't. They had...I don't know, barriers placed around the arenas. When the Lightborn entered, their power seeped away. It gathered in the Great Hall, and we just kind of..." I hesitated, ashamed of my actions, not ready to share.

"Kind of, what?"

"Kind of took it in. Like I ran my hand through the air, and it...absorbed into me."

"Sounds gross," Charlie sneered as he walked by.

"But without the barriers, how would you do it?" Alexis looked worried.

"How are you just asking me this now? We've been on the road for more than a week, and you didn't think to ask?"

"I assumed you had a way."

Alexis turned and shooed away the driver. Tony faded into the back until it was just us. Things had been tense the whole ride, for both of us.

I took the private moment and said what I thought she needed to hear, "'Lex, I'm sorry. I'm sorry I left you."

She actually looked shocked.

"What? You think I'm even thinking about that right now? Anya, I've spent the last twenty years living in the aftermath of the Crack. This isn't about you! I'm not mad at you. I'm not frustrated or disappointed in you. I'm just worried about my people - about all the people. Look, I hate putting this all on you. I know what you've been through, and you haven't had twenty years to adjust, but we need you."

It stung a little to hear that she wasn't thinking about my feelings. Her focus was on her new family, but I couldn't blame her. I'd been dead for twenty years after bringing this mess down on their heads. The happiness and relief she'd felt when she first saw me had melted away to something else. Something cold.

"I want to go in alone," I said, changing the subject back to the Lightborn.

"No. Not an option."

"Alexis, I'm not strong enough to walk in there and overpower them. Not in any way, with or without Light. At my strongest, maybe I could do it, but it would be wrong. I want to give them a choice."

"Choice? You think a bunch of Lightborn are going to, what? Hand over their power?"

"That's exactly what I think."

The door opened. Gabby walked in, her plate empty, and Ozzie munching on something at her side. I wanted nothing more than to take her hand and walk Ozzie over the sunlit hills. But, once again, I couldn't do what I wanted. Once again, the weight of the damn world was on my shoulders.

"That's what's happening. So tell your Gulls to stay back. I won't have any more deaths on my conscience."

We set out on foot as a group and walked for almost an hour before Alexis stopped her people. She nodded to me and put a hand on Gabby's arm as she tried to follow. Ozzie nuzzled against her, calming both their nerves. I left with Tony at Alexis' insistence, not wanting to say any goodbyes.

The closer we got, the more I felt the Light. The Gulls found them using word of mouth and stories from locals, but Tony and I could have found it alone. Even in the heat, I could feel the warmth from their Light spreading out.

Though they were apparently weak, someone had

managed to put up a barrier. They knew we were coming. When a group of men appeared from out of nowhere, I tried to keep my cool.

"We're here to talk," I said, holding my hands up.

I motioned for Tony to do the same. They knew what he was the minute they saw him, but I was sure they hadn't figured out my power just yet.

"Who are you?" One of the younger men asked, his hands raised and ready to fight.

"Her name is Anya," a voice from behind said slowly. "Bring them in."

I looked back but saw no-one. Tony and I were checked over before being pulled forward and escorted toward their base.

The property was a lot like the Brothers' compound. The surrounding wall was shorter, but as we entered through an archway, I saw what used to be a sizable garden and an impressive red brick manor. The wall had crumbled away in parts, and the once lush grass was faded and yellow. This place looked almost vibrant compared to the rest of the country, and I wondered how much Light they used just to keep the decay away.

"The Royal Musselburgh Golf Club," one of the Lightborn said with a grin. "Something, isn't it?"

I nodded and kept my eyes open for more men. It had obviously been beautiful once, and I wished Gabby could see it with me. Tony and I stayed quiet as we entered the house and were taken to a large room with old furniture and a fireplace.

"Not exactly roughing it, are they?" Tony scoffed and rolled his eyes as the Lightborn left the room.

"How exactly did you manage to keep your place in society? Why weren't you cast out like the rest?" I whispered.

He was around Alexis' age, if not slightly older. He would have been under the Brotherhood's influence back then.

"I wasn't with the Three. I was with the Network. My Ludus was brought here to help you. We stayed together after the Crack and kept hidden when the worst of it started."

Before I could say anything more, the door opened, and three men walked in; two older and one relatively young. I doubted he'd been alive to see the Crack.

"Anya, nice to see you again."

One of them stepped forward and motioned for us to sit. As I took in his face, I tried to place him.

"I look a lot different to you now, I'm sure. I also don't have any of your friends holding me down, so."

I didn't recognise him. He hadn't been in the original group I sent through the portal, which meant he was one of the Lightborn chosen to follow. He must have been taken captive by the Network, unable to make it to safety.

"You were there when..."

"That's right. I watched it all with wonder in my eyes. The New World! The promise of a new life! How naïve I was. Both of us, actually."

The Lightborn sat, and so did Tony. I stayed on my feet, nervous this would turn bad quickly.

"Relax, I don't blame you. You were practically a child."

I bristled at the word but said nothing. His face was utterly unfamiliar to me. That day, I was too focussed on the Three and the portal. The truth was, I'd hardly looked at any of them.

"Look, I'm not here for trouble, and I'm sorry about-"

He held up his hand to stop me. "My name is Jackson. This is David and Patrick. We're the de facto leaders of this little ragtag group. I'll admit, when I saw you, I was floored. You look remarkably well considering it's been twenty years. But I'm guessing it wasn't as long for you?"

I shook my head and glanced at Tony. He was letting me take the lead, which I appreciated. But the younger of the Lightborn, David, his eyes were burning into me.

"Let's not beat around the bush. Just tell us why you're here."

I drew in a deep breath and closed my eyes as I took a seat. I knew this was a long shot, but I was determined to try.

"After the Three left, I jumped here. I was basically half-dead, and I just jumped. In the last few weeks, I've learned about what happened after. They've told me about the destruction, the rains, the creatures. I'm sorry for what happened to you all. Like it or not, we're the same, and I feel such guilt over what followed."

"That's nice. How does it help us?" David spat.

I watched Jackson give him a look and realised quickly who was really in charge.

"I came here accidentally. But it's opened my eyes to the truth. What happened, it was always going to happen. We ignored all the signs for too long until it was too late. But I think I know a way to fix it. I think I can go back and change what happened and prevent the Crack. But I'm going to need your help."

"Ok, I'll bite. How exactly can you fix this?" Patrick asked, his eyes slight and suspicious.

I reached into the bag I had with me and pulled out

the dead branch. It was dark and twisted, worn from years of exposure to the harsh weather. With it firmly in my hands, I closed my eyes and let my Light flow into the wood. I felt it twitch and change, and as I opened my eyes, I saw the wood return to its natural state.

“Nice trick. But any of us could do that."

“I know. That’s not the point,” I said, putting the branch down on the table, watching as the darkness seeped back in. “I gave this branch my power, and it healed itself. Right now, I’m not strong enough to do much more. But..." I looked up and balled my fists, ready for their laughter, or sudden anger. “But, I truly believe that if we all came together and returned our Light to the earth, we could heal it.”

The room was silent. Nobody laughed or made any sarcastic comments. For a moment, I wasn’t sure I’d spoken aloud until David stood and grabbed the branch from the table.

“You’re dumber than the Three were. You think we can just kumbaya the world back to normal? Have you looked outside?”

“No, not now. It’s beyond too late *now*." I let the word linger in the air. Jackson caught it and looked me in the eye.

“You want to go back and do it?”

I nodded, keeping my eyes on Jackson as I spoke.

“If I go back to before the Crack, I can try to fix things before it all goes to hell. It’s worth a shot!” I added as David scoffed and groaned. “Don’t you think it’s worth a shot?”

“A shot? You’re insane."

“I’m not. Think about it! Where does our Light come from? We’ve been taking it for granted, and the earth has suffered because of it. Doesn't it stand to reason that we would never have gotten here without all that abuse?"

Jackson shouted to David to sit down and keep quiet. He threw the branch in the fireplace before retaking his seat, scowling like a scorned child.

"Let's just say you're right about this. What's your plan?" Patrick asked, ignoring David.

"If I can jump back in time, to before the Three left, I think I can..."

I couldn't say the words. I knew what Alexis wanted, and I more or less agreed. But Oran's face always came to my mind when I thought about killing them.

"I think I can persuade them to do the right thing. And if I can't, then...I'll kill them."

"So in this little fantasy world of yours, why don't you just jump back and do this yourself? Why do you need us?"

David turned to me, pointing his finger in my face. I wanted to reach out and snap it off, but I stayed calm.

"You don't have the power. You need more Light." Patrick breathed out, a hand in his hair.

"You mean our light?" Jackson said with a smirk. "You want us to give you our Light so you can jump back in time and defeat the three most powerful Lightborn of all time?"

I was losing them. Even Tony was looking at me funny.

"You don't understand. I knew them. Anwar was bad, no doubt about that. I don't think anybody could bring out the good in him. But Oran was kind to me. His husband, too. And Uri...I think if I can give them all a vision of what's coming, I can get at least Oran on my side."

"And then?"

"He can help me bring down the others. I thought about jumping back to way before, but I don't think that would work. I can't go back to before the decay started because nobody knows when it started, and I don't have the strength to just jump around in time." I was up and pacing now, trying to get my plan out before they could stop me. "If I were to jump back to before they took me, there would still be all the other Lightborn in the world. Nothing would really change. But if I can jump back to just before I opened that portal twenty years ago, I would be jumping back to a time when the vast majority of the world's Light was in one room. Imagine what this place could be if the Crack never happens. If the decay went away and the weather wasn't so crazy. Imagine not having to hole up here, ostracised from your family and friends."

David wasn't impressed with my speech. He laughed and clapped his hands, rolling his eyes and standing to leave.

"I'm not buying, honey." He put his hand on my cheek and winked.

With a tilt of my head, David suddenly found himself upside down. He screeched like a small goat as I lifted him to the ceiling. Jackson let out a little chuckle, and Patrick looked mildly amused. I let David go near the door, not bothering to cushion his fall.

"You-"

"That's enough, David." Jackson dismissed the young Lightborn with a casual wave of his hand. David stormed from the room, slamming the doors behind him.

"I thought you said you were out of power?"

"I said I didn't have much power."

"Do you genuinely believe you can bring Oran to your side?" Jackson asked.

He'd known the Three too, though I doubted Oran had ever shown his softer side to the help.

"He was good to me. His husband was good to me in the end. With Declan's help, yes, I think I can convince Oran to see reason. Uri will be a tougher sell, but I saw signs of humanity in him. It's Anwar that will be the biggest issue. But if I can get Oran to work with me, I'm sure we can overpower even two of them."

"And this idea of, of, giving our Light back. Why would we want that?" Patrick held out his palms, and I watched little sparks fly from his fingers.

"I know how intoxicating this can be. I know it must have been beyond difficult to lose your Light the way you all did. But, if it's a choice between living in the here and now, or potentially saving the world...living without your Light but in a better place with the people you love?" I was laying it on thick, but I felt like I was getting through to them.

"We're going to need to bring it to the group. It's not our decision alone."

I nodded and thanked them for their time. Tony was getting twitchy, probably ready to fight when the rest of the Lightborn found out my plan. I was putting all my hopes on these men and knew it was a risk. But if they came back to us with a 'no,' I was ready to do what was necessary.

# CHAPTER 46

Anya and Tony had been gone a while. But according to Alexis, the Lightborn base was another hour or so away, and she just needed to relax.

“You’re pretty concerned about her, huh?” Baz asked, with a stupid grin on his face.

“Actually, I am. I’m worried the Lightborn will kill them, and we’re all stuck in this hellhole,” Gabby snapped, her tone sharper than she meant it to be.

“I’m sure your little girlfriend can handle it."

“Enough, Baz,” Alexis warned. She looked to Gabby, her face serious. “She’ll be ok. I trust them both.”

The sun was going down when Charlie finally pointed them out. The heat caused them to seek shade under an old bus stop, but they raced into the road as Anya and Tony approached, red-faced and grim.

“What happened?” Alexis asked, moving to Tony’s side and offering him water.

Gabby gave hers to Anya, who smiled her thanks.

“We met with them, and I laid out my plan. It wasn’t received well...at first." Anya’s face broke into a grin.

“She did it, ‘Lex,” Tony said, pulling Alexis into a hug and spinning her around.

“You did?”

Anya nodded and laughed. “They took it to their people and, I don’t know. They just agreed. All of them-well, most of them. A couple were reluctant, but majority won."

"You're telling me they handed over their Light, just like that?"

"She was pretty convincing." Tony playfully punched Anya's arm and nodded his approval. "She was great."

Alexis stepped forward and hugged her sister. Gabby stepped back and watched their embrace go from tense to loving. They had both been noticeably cold the last week or so, and Gabby knew it was just the stress of everything.

"I'm proud of you," she gushed, taking her sister's face in her hands. "Dad would be too."

Anya let a tear fall before Baz ruined the moment. "We should get going. It's a long way back."

"No." Tony shook his head. "I can get us back."

"You can open portals?" Anya turned in total shock.

"No. Not exactly. I can send people places. They have to be thinking of it, their minds totally blank but for the location. It has to be a place they know better than anywhere. We've trained our people. They know how to do it-"

Anya opened her mouth to reply, but Alexis jumped in.

"Wait. You kept your power?" She turned to him, brow furrowed, and anger in her eyes. "She needs everything she can get!"

"But I thought-"

"That you were exempt from trying to save the world? Hardly!" Alexis cocked her head. Her eyes were wide as she put her hands on her hips.

Gabby looked to Anya, watching the awkward moment unfold.

Tony sighed and nodded his head, moving to face Anya and offering his hands. She tried to protest, but Alexis was having none of it.

"It's all or nothing, An. Take it."

Gabby watched in awe as Tony put his hands to Anya's. Little yellow sparks flew between their palms before his Light fully emerged. They all watched, mouths open, as his Light dispersed in brilliant streaks across Anya's palms, and up her arms. Gabby could see she was glowing and wondered how it felt.

"Is it enough?" Alexis asked, ignoring Tony, who looked weak and unsteady on his feet.

"Definitely. They had a lot more than any of you thought. I also think I can take my own Light when I jump back. I'm going to need as much as possible if I'm going to subdue the Three."

"Wait. How would that even work?" Baz asked, looking interested for the first time.

"If I'm going to jump back twenty years, a version of myself will be there. Theoretically, the other me will have done the same things I did. So she, along with the Three, will have taken in all that Light from the Tournaments. She'll be there, ready to open the portal. If I can take her Light too, that will make me even more powerful."

"But what about her?" Gabby asked.

"Well…I guess she needs to jump forward, right? She needs to come here, or to the new here."

"How will you get her to do that after you've rushed in and taken her power?" Charlie moved forward, a curious grin on his face.

"I guess she can't. I'll have to send her."

Gabby shook her head and laughed. They were talking about magic and time travel. How was any of this real?

"Is everyone coming back to the compound?" Anya asked, changing the subject. "I can get us back, and it won't take too much. No point in wasting a week on the road."

"Baz and Charlie will take the Burlak and head home." Alexis motioned to her people to collect their things.

The driver was waiting with the truck. Baz hesitated slightly, looking to Gabby with an awkward smile. She smiled back but looked to Anya. She was going back to the compound to see this through.

As they prepared themselves, her heart started pounding. She'd seen the Light in the last few weeks and understood what they could do. But she'd never been touched by it. She was scared, unsure of how it would feel. Even coming from Anya, she felt the nerves.

"It's ok." Anya took her hand and squeezed. "Just walk through the Light like you're walking through a door. You'll see the Hall on the other side."

As she spoke, she waved a hand in the air, and her Light lit up their faces. It sparkled in the fading sun before opening to reveal the Great Hall. Gabby looked around, feeling foolish when she saw the road and bus stop behind the portal. She gasped when Ozzie barked and ran through, followed quickly by Tony. Alexis was next, but Gabby held back. Her arm went stiff as Anya tried to pull her forward.

"Just keep hold. We'll go together."

Her mouth went dry, and she could feel the sweat down her back. She knew it was safe. She knew Anya was strong and could even see Ozzie running around on the other side. But it took a lot of coaxing to get her feet moving.

To her credit, Anya didn't laugh. She stayed patient at her side, giving her all the time she needed. When they finally breached the Light, Gabby felt a warmth like she'd never experienced. It seemed to move inside and swirl through her body. The sparks tickled her skin as they moved until it all washed away, and her feet touched the stone floor.

Anya let go and moved into the hall, leaving Gabby frozen in place. Her heart was beating out of her chest, and she felt adrenaline coursing through her veins. A chill washed over as she tried to move.

Alexis and Tony were unfazed and on edge. She was mad at him, and he didn't know how to fix it. Anya went to Ozzie, calm as ever. Gabby suddenly realised she didn't know what would happen next or where she fit in.

"Anya, how soon can you jump?" Alexis called eventually, breaking the silence.

"The sooner, the better," she replied, not taking her eyes from Ozzie. "I don't want to risk the Light fading."

"What do you need from us?"

"Nothing. I think I'm going to go outside, jump near the doors. I know what time it all went down, so they should all be inside. I can take them by surprise."

Gabby stood, watching the cold exchange between sisters. "Wait, you don't mean right now?"

"Why wait?" Alexis shrugged.

"No, you can't just-"

"Gabby, it's ok."

Anya stood and puffed out her chest. She looked confident and ready. But Gabby wasn't. It all happened so fast.

Alexis and Tony said a few words. They went over the general plan, Anya talking over what she needed to do. She kissed Ozzie goodbye and hugged Tony in thanks. When she turned to Alexis, Gabby could see the tears in her eyes. As they hugged, she saw Alexis' lips moving but couldn't hear their exchange. She just hoped they were words of sisterly love and not coming from the leader of the Gulls.

Anya was in front of her before she knew it. She wasn't focussed and missed her words, grabbing her hand in panic.

"Anya, wait. We should wait. This is all too fast."

"I know. I'm sorry. I wish we had more time, but... well, time is the issue, isn't it?"

She hugged Gabby, holding her a beat longer than expected. When she turned her back, Gabby felt the tears.

"Ok, wish me luck," Anya said as she turned and made for the doors.

She looked back one last time, waving goodbye through the tears. When the doors closed behind her, Gabby's heart sank. She watched Alexis fall to her knees, the sobs filling the hall. She'd stayed strong for her sister, but couldn't hold it in any longer.

Ozzie licked Gabby's hand, and she turned to the sweet dog. He pawed at her leg, and she stooped down to hug him. Then it hit her.

"Wait!" She called, running for the doors, hoping she wasn't too late.

Outside, the portal was open, and Anya was a step away. Gabby rushed forward, her hand outstretched. Anya disappeared into the Light, and this time, Gabby didn't hesitate.

# CHAPTER 47

**July 2091**

It was pouring outside the Hall. I waved a hand over my head, creating a shield to stay dry. Coming from the other side of the wall, the Three, their Lightborn and families were rushing inside, ready to jump through my portal. I was a little early, but that would work-

"Anya!" Gabby whispered from beside me. She grabbed my arm and spun me around.

Was I seeing things? I took her hand and pulled her to the wall, out of sight.

"What are you doing?"

"After you left, I realised I had to come. I was there before, right? You said I was there!"

I couldn't process what was happening. But she was right. I'd seen her. She'd tried to convince me to jump.

"But I don't need you this time," I started, feeling a knot in my stomach at the harsh words. "I mean, I don't need you to convince the other me-"

"Maybe not. But you shouldn't have to do this alone. I waited for years for you, and I couldn't just wave you off to do this by yourself."

My heart just about exploded. I wanted to kiss her, but I needed to stay focused.

"Ok. They're just walking in. We have a few minutes. I need to stop the other me before she opens the portal.

We can't let any of them cross over."

"Just tell me what to do."

"Ok. I'm going to rush in and...stop time."

Her mouth dropped. I hadn't mentioned this in my plan because I knew how crazy it sounded.

"Just listen. I know I can do it, and I'm not actually stopping time, I'm just slowing it. But it will be so slow they won't be able to do anything. I'll steal the Light from the other me and send her to the future. Then I can give the Three a vision of the future. I need to show them what happens."

"This is insane." Gabby laughed.

She smiled and looked at the sky, her eyes holding when she realised there were no flames. The rain was pounding on the barrier above us, but we could still see the clouds. There were small breaks through which we could see a few stars. Her face turned down as she looked at the grass. The green was visible even in the dark. My heart leapt out of my chest as I saw her wipe away a tear.

"It's beautiful," she gasped.

"Let's keep it that way. Come in with me. I'm going to need you to get everyone out. The Network is already on its way. They'll keep the Lightborn busy, but I'll need you to help me with their families. Just get them out of harm's way."

She nodded and swallowed hard. I was sure she was regretting her choice, even just a little.

We moved to the big doors, and I cracked one open slightly. We couldn't see, but I could hear them speaking.

"Leave it alone, Brother."

"Let's just start."

Gabby looked to me, expecting me to rush in, but I held up a hand. When Uri spoke, and I pictured the scene from my memory.

"Ok, everyone. I know you're all scared and confused. We're sorry for all the secrecy. But right now, we just need you to trust us. What's about to happen might be a little scary, but you're with us, and we'll make sure you're all ok."

"What are we waiting for?" Gabby asked, keeping her voice low.

I held up a hand and turned my ear. Ozzie's bark brought a smile to my face, and I knew it was time. I wanted him out of the picture, and the Three distracted. Right now, Anwar was pulling me to the middle, and I was focussing on the portal. Oran and Uri were staring at our hands, waiting for the Light to appear. They wouldn't see us coming.

"Let's go."

A last glance over my shoulder made my heart jump as I saw lights in the distance coming our way. Mr Parks and the others were so close.

My hands were full of sparks before I opened the door. I wasn't willing to risk a thing, needing to be as fast as possible. But when the doors flung open, I couldn't help but freeze. Just for a second, my mind got stuck.

Looking at myself, hands with Anwar's, Uri and Oran peering over our shoulders, it was a lot to take in.

The other me looked up first. The confusion on her face was almost amusing as I raised my hands. In an instant, everything stopped. I raced to myself and grabbed her hands away from Anwar. She came out of the magic, totally confused.

"What-"

"I'm sorry!" I said as I pulled the Light from her hands.

It shot up my arms and settled inside like a rock in my stomach. Before I could stop myself, I opened a portal to the future and pushed her through. I could only hope that if we failed today, she would follow in my footsteps and try again.

The rest of the room was still semi-frozen. Everyone was moving at such a glacial pace, I could've run around and bound all the Lightborn with ease. But I needed to focus.

Everything seemed to blur as I frantically turned to my next targets. The Three tried to move, but I was working too fast. I grabbed their hands, yanking them to me, but keeping them under control.

The vision I gave them was dark and upsetting. I showed them the decay, the snows, and the heat. I took the memories Alexis had given me before I left and played them big and bold so they couldn't see anything else.

It hurt my heart to see what she'd been through, but I needed that pain.

Behind me, Gabby was held in time like the others. But I could see the lights of the Network coming at normal speed. I just needed a little longer.

When I felt the pull, I let them all go. Most of the Lightborn fell to the ground, their momentum catching up too fast. Oran stumbled back, a hand on his head and tears in his eyes. Even Uri looked shell-shocked.

"I need you to see what you're all doing. We have to stop this!" I pleaded to them, hands clasps to my chest.

"What was that? Where did you come from?" Uri shouted, coming to his senses.

"You know who I am, and you've seen where I came from. I know you think you can just jump away to a new life, but that is what you're leaving behind."

Anwar stepped toward me and lashed out. His hand struck my face, and I hit the ground hard. I heard Gabby yell and rush to my side. Anwar raised his hand to her, but she cried out, and he stopped.

"Kareena?" He said, arm still raised.

He looked back to where their families stood in fear and repeated her name. His mistress and baby were where he'd left them. I watched as she handed the baby off and raced toward us.

"Anwar, we can't wait any longer," she cried, reaching for him.

We all looked from Gabby to Kareena. They could have been twins.

"Oh, my Elders." I put a hand to my mouth and looked at a confused Gabby. "You were the baby."

Anwar looked back to the baby, screaming at the other end. Kareena didn't seem to catch on, taking Gabby in like she was nothing.

"What are you talking about?" Gabby asked, helping me to my feet.

"You're…" Anwar stepped toward her and put a hand to her face. She stepped back, leaving his hand in the air.

"Anya?" She turned to me, but I didn't have time to explain.

"Oran, I know you don't want this." I looked him in the eye and could see his doubts. "You know this is wrong."

From out in the rain, I heard them coming. The Network had arrived. Suddenly I wished we had more time. How could I get through to them when they were fighting so hard?

It went down much the same.

The Network rushed in, and all hell broke loose. The Lightborn, who initially held back having no instruction from the Three, suddenly came back to life.

Mr Parks called to me to retreat as the Network flung fire and hail to their enemy. Oran and Uri stepped forward and raised the barrier down the centre of the Hall, protecting us from the Network's assault.

The difference this time was Anwar. He rushed to Gabby, pulling her away from the danger and putting himself in front in a protective stance.

Thunder rumbled overhead, and the floor shook. Like before, it knocked us all to our knees. Even without the power of my portal, the Veils were cracking. I could feel it and knew I had to be quick.

With the protective barrier down once more, Uri rushed to the back and put up a field around their families. Anwar moved Kareena and Gabby back as the Network rushed them. I wanted to stop it all. I could see Oran was close to coming around and, miraculously, even Anwar wasn't fighting. If I could just get them to all stop, I knew I could talk them round.

"Oran!" I yelled, trying to keep him with me. "Oran, please!"

But he looked angry. His eyes moved back to his family, and their fear seemed to fuel him. Declan and the others were huddled behind Uri, heads low, and tears in their eyes. I found him and spoke in a low voice, sending my message across the carnage.

"Declan, you need to get them out. Get everyone out now." I pointed to the side door, which I swung open.

He looked up to me and nodded. Grabbing Tyler's

arm, I saw him shouting instructions. Oran grabbed my arm, but it was too late. Uri couldn't hear them as he blocked any attacks that came their way. The families hustled out the side door and into the rain, leaving Uri protecting an empty corner.

I heard the baby cry and looked to Gabby. Kareena raced to the empty corner and found her child alone on the floor. Anwar looked torn, his eyes on the baby, but his hand on Gabby. She looked terrified and confused and was trying to pull herself free.

How hadn't I seen it?

With the Three distracted, the Network subdued most of the Lightborn. I caught a glimpse of a young Jackson being dragged from the hall, a shining rope around his wrists.

But with their families gone, the Three came together once more. I'd taken away their chance at a new life, and I could see the fury in their eyes.

Uri and Oran moved forward and raised their arms. I took a breath, raced to the centre of the hall, lifted my arms, and let my Light shine. The people from the Network flew to the big doors, while the Lightborn were dragged to the other end. I stood tall in the middle, holding back any attacks from either side. But I knew I couldn't hold it for much longer.

"Stop, Anya. You know you can't win this," Uri called.

I felt them move closer, their power trying to penetrate my own. But I was much stronger than they knew, and my Light held.

Uri looked amazed and shot a confused look to Oran. I thought that was it as the two turned on me, but Declan's voice rang through the hall.

"Stop, Oran! Just stop!"

As he turned, I felt his Light fade. Uri held true, his eyes on his Brother. He looked to Anwar, who was dragging Gabby toward Kareena.

"Anya!" She screamed my name, and I broke.

I let my Light slip for just a second, but it was enough. The Lightborn raced toward the entrance and the Network.

With my hands up, I tried to reason with the Three once more, but they were too far gone to hear me. I risked a glance back to the big doors and saw the fight was ongoing.

The Network and the Lightborn were locked in a heated battle. I saw Light, fire, and fists flying. Someone had conjured snakes, while another was using daggers. It was utter chaos.

In that instant, I knew I had the power to stop it. Bringing my hands together in a hard clap, the Lightborn disappeared from the room. I'd sent them to the other end of the property - not far, but far enough.

I heard Gabby cry out as she broke free and ran to me. She stood at my side defiantly, her head high, and her heart racing. I took her hand and looked at the Three.

"You know I'm right."

"No, you're not," Anwar snarled, moving toward us.

"Yes, she is."

Oran left Declan by the door and walked toward me. His eyes found mine, and I couldn't help but look to Declan. Whatever he'd said had been the end of it. Oran had come around like I knew he would.

I heard Mr Parks call my name, but I held a hand up as I looked to Oran to do the right thing.

"We all saw that future. We can't leave the world to that."

He stood on my other side, and I could've squealed with glee. He was the man I thought he was. With him on our side, my plan would work.

"Come on, Brother, you can't be serious?" Uri mocked. He looked back to Declan and laughed. "You're going to let your husband guilt you into this?"

"No, Uri. I have enough guilt of my own."

"Anwar, we can't stay here."

Kareena slowly walked toward us, the baby fussing in her arms. I looked back at Gabby and knew what I had to do.

"Look at your daughter, Anwar."

He looked to the baby.

"Not her. Her." I put a hand on Gabby's shoulder as he looked over. "Everything I showed you, she went through. You both left, and she was alone in the world. In that world. Come on, you know I'm right!"

Kareena tried to pull him aside, but I wouldn't let up.

"Here, both of you see." I took Gabby's hand and looked her in the eyes. "I need your memories. I need to show them what became of their daughter."

She looked so many things but pushed back the fear. She closed her eyes and let me in, and as I watched her life playing out, so did Anwar the rest.

We saw baby Gabby in some kind of home for orphans. Then in a small house with a brother and a new mother.

We watched her have nightmares and run from a coming storm. I watched her pain as her mum died from what looked like heat stroke. And then her brother not coming home after a building collapsed in the city.

I saw her sitting in the Hall, sobbing in the darkness. All around her was darkness and pain and decay. Immense worry overshadowed any light in her memories. Her life had been harder than I could ever have known.

I turned and pulled Gabby into a hug, holding on tight as the last image faded away. We both had tears in our eyes when we pulled apart.

“Anya?”

The sound of Alexis’ voice was almost unsettling. She sounded so different from the Alexis I’d just left, but it was so familiar. I turned and let out a cry as she walked through the Network toward me. In all the madness, I’d forgotten she’d been there.

“Alexis, I need you to wait. All of you." I called to her and the Network. They looked unsure and on edge. I didn’t have much more time.

This time I looked to Anwar. The pain on his face was unmistakable. “Anwar, that’s the life your daughter lived. The pain and suffering she endured. But you can stop it. Right now, you can make that choice.”

“Come on, Anwar, you know it’s the right thing to do. We’ve caused too much pain."

Oran put a hand on his Brother’s arm. Anwar hung his head, tears spilling over his cheeks.

“Anwar, no, we can’t-” Kareena started, but he stopped her.

“She’s our daughter, Ree.”

“No, this is our daughter.”

I looked to Gabby again and felt more guilt than ever. I wanted to tell her I hadn’t known, and I was sorry for using her like this. I couldn’t imagine how she felt finding out her father was Anwar. Not after years of hating them all.

“They both are Kareena.” He looked at me and nodded. “I won’t do that to either of them.”

The relief that spread over me was extraordinary. I wanted to fall to my knees and sob. Somehow, it worked. Oran hugged Anwar, and I looked back to Declan. He stood in the doorway with a hand on his heart and a smile on his face.

When the flash hit, Declan flew back into the night. My legs buckled as I was tossed aside, my head hitting the stone. When I finally regained some sense, the room was filled with smoke and Light.

The bodies of the Network were spread around, and I had no idea if they were dead or alive. Gabby was a few feet away, and I scrambled to her, my hands on her face looking for signs of life. When she blinked, I almost lost it.

In the middle of the hall, Uri stood, arms raised and lightning at his fingertips.

# CHAPTER 48

Oran coughed my name from close by, and I searched through the smoke for any sign of him. He was bleeding from a head wound and looked to be in total shock.

He made his way to me before turning his eyes to Uri. Without a word, I watch him reach a hand up and snap his fist closed. Uri was lifted from the ground and started clawing at his neck.

I saw Anwar stand and rush to Kareena. She was unconscious, and the baby was bawling. He picked her up and hushed her, his angry eyes turning to his Brother.

Uri broke the bond and landed on his feet. But Anwar was faster. He snapped his fingers, wrapping Uri in a thick and heavy chain.

The smoke cleared a little, and I helped Gabby to her feet. A cough near the doors jerked me back, and I raced to Alexis. She was bleeding from her nose and ear and wasn't waking up. Mr Parks crawled to us, severely wounded himself.

"Anya, I've got her," he said, putting a hand to her chest.

"Mr Parks, I'm so sorry," I cried, knowing he had no idea I wasn't the Anya he knew.

"You're the bravest Lightborn I've ever seen. Go finish this."

He squeezed my hand and turned to my sister. I didn't want to leave her, but I knew I had to.

Back inside, Anwar was now beside Gabby. He handed the baby over, and I could see her mind melting. She was holding herself, and herself was screeching.

Uri was stuck in the middle. Oran and Anwar approached him like lions stalking their prey. The chains grew barbs, and I could see them getting tighter. He was no match for them.

"You attacked us?" Oran took a couple steps forward and looked to the open door at the end. "You attacked our families?"

"You were being weak," he snarled, struggling against the chain.

I could see his Light through the gaps and moved in.

"They're not weak for wanting to save the people they love."

"That's what we were doing!" He exploded from his restraints and stood like a boxer, his fists raised, and his feet light.

"We're not going to fight you, Uri," Anwar said, keeping his distance but moving away from his daughters.

I turned to Gabby and motioned for her to leave. She nodded, running out the big doors, and I flashed back to the last time I was here.

"Anwar!" Kareena's yell came from the other end, and we all turned.

She raced forward, arms reaching out and Light shooting from her fingertips. I watched in horror as Uri lifted a hand and flicked his wrist.

Kareena flew into the wall with a sickening thud. I didn't see how anyone could recover from such a blow.

"Did you really give your mistress your Light?" Uri

mocked as he turned back to his Brothers.

He hadn't seen Anwar coming his way. He hit like a truck, and the two went down.

It was odd to watch two Lightborn fighting with their fists, and I wasn't sure what to do. I raced around the room to Kareena and checked for a pulse. She had a nasty head wound, and her chest wasn't moving.

"Is she alive?" Oran asked in my head.

I touched her neck and leaned in. Nothing. Oran stood waiting, and all I could do was shake my head. She was gone.

"No!" Anwar screamed, his eyes on his dead girlfriend and me.

Uri was on the ground when Anwar raised his fists high, yelling out in pain as he brought them down. I heard Uri beg, and I screamed as Anwar made contact. The crunch of bone rang around the Hall.

Oran stood still, mouth open in shock. We watched Anwar stand, blood dripping from his hands.

Uri was dead.

Light began swirling around, and Anwar reached out, taking it in as he breathed in deep. He now had more power than any of us.

Fear ripped through me. Oran stepped back, giving Anwar a broad reach. I scrambled away from Kareena's body when he turned to us, not wanting to be anywhere near him.

"Oran," I whispered, knowing he would hear, but he held out a hand to stay me, his eyes locked on Anwar.

"Brother," he whispered, taking a tentative step forward. Uri's blood was pooling around and would hit Oran's shoe any minute. "Anwar?"

Without warning, Anwar fell to his knees. He took

Kareena's face in his hands and kissed her head. I saw him looking for Gabby and assured him they were both safe.

"Anwar, what-"

"Let's get this over with." He stood abruptly and looked me in the eye. "She died so you can have your way."

His words bit into me, but I didn't react. I needed to keep him on our side, which meant not insulting the most powerful man in the world.

"Anwar, it wasn't her fault. It was Uri and his greed."

"You don't think I know that?"

The tension was too much. I wanted to slip away and find Gabby, check on Alexis, and Mr Parks. But I forced myself to stay. To stay and speak up.

"I know you want to do the right thing. For Gabby. What Uri did-"

"Uri paid for what he did. And I'm not going to let my daughter grow up in pain. So, how do we do this?"

His calmer tone threw me. Even Oran looked confused and unsure of what to do. When I'd shown them Alexis' memories and visions of the future, I'd also entered their minds and told them of my plan to return our Light. It was now or never.

The Two followed me outside and into the rain. The Network, those still alive, were helping their wounded. Alexis was leaning against the wall, taking slow breaths. Gabby was nowhere in sight, but I took comfort in knowing she was safe.

"We need to release it all. Touch the ground and let it flow. Give it back willingly."

Oran looked around at the mess and put a hand through his hair.

"How do we know it's not already too late?"

"Trust me, you'd know. But we can't wait - it has to be now."

I went first, kneeling on the wet grass and pressing my palms deep into the mud.

At first, I felt nothing. Closing my eyes, I tried to concentrate to no avail. Oran and Anwar looked sceptical but soon joined me on the ground. The minute their hands touched the earth, I felt the power.

"It's working," I stammered.

Oran let out a laugh, his smile as strong as the Light in his hands. I could see the ground beneath us coming to life. The green grass seemed to grow and shine. I could see the Light flowing from my hands in a kaleidoscope of colour.

The wind came from nowhere. It swirled around us, whipping the rain into a frenzy, and I felt the heat before I saw the flames. When I looked at Oran, I could see the fire reflecting in his eyes. We were surrounded, the fire and wind whirling in a circle as our Light poured into the ground. Suddenly, it didn't feel right.

I heard Oran yell but couldn't make it out. When I looked down to his hands, my heart fell. The grass under his palms was turning black. I watched in horror as it seeped into his veins. The inky decay shot up his arms and into his neck until his eyes were nothing but black.

His body fell back into the wet mud with a splash.

Anwar's laugh chilled me to my core. I yanked my hands free of the dirt, but I knew it was too late. I saw the Light spreading across the ground, moving toward Anwar. He wasn't giving anything back - he was taking it all in.

"You can't do this!" I yelled over the wind and fire.

"Why not?"

"What about Gabby? What about her future?"

"She won't have that future. She'll have me, and anything her heart desires."

The storm overhead screamed at us, until all at once, the wind and fire subsided. Thunder cracked, and lightning rushed to the ground. Anwar stood tall, his hands raised, taking in the power.

I jumped to my feet, summoning everything I had, and threw a wave of energy at him, but he brushed it aside like it was nothing. I knew I had no choice. With my hands clasped together, I drew from what was left in the earth and thrust it out, sending every dark thought in my mind his way. I watched it go, expecting his death to be swift and painless.

But before the Light could leave my fingertips, Anwar sent me flying.

I landed in a puddle of mud, my head hitting a tree trunk. I tasted blood in my mouth and could feel pain in my back and abdomen. From somewhere far, I heard someone call my name.

All at once, Anwar loomed over me, a crazed smile on his face. I saw him turn and groaned when Gabby came rushing forward. She still had the baby in her arms as she dropped to her knees at my side.

"No, stop! Please!" She begged the father she never knew.

When he raised his hand, I closed my eyes, ready for the fatal blow. But it never came.

I heard her voice in my ear, "It's ok. I'm here."

She moved back to look at Anwar. He couldn't do it, not even in his madness. He leaned forward and tore the child from her arms.

"I'm sorry, Gabby. Truly. But this is my daughter, and I will keep her safe."

Lightning hit from overhead as he let out a wolf-like howl and I felt the pulse before I heard the Crack. He was gone. The scorch left in his wake ran as far as I could see, cutting through the Hall and the wall of the compound. I cried out, anger bubbling inside at my failure. I tried to stand, but something felt wrong.

"Anya, stop. You need help."

"I failed. It happened anyway."

The blood was getting worse. I needed to cough and could feel it running down my chin. Gabby called for help, but she sounded fuzzy.

"Gabby." I got her name out, and she turned to me.

Her big, beautiful eyes were full of tears, and all I wanted was to take them away.

"Wait, Anya? Wait, they're here. You'll be ok."

I reached a hand through the pain and touched her cheek. I couldn't feel my toes and the pain in my stomach was getting worse. It was getting harder to breathe, and I knew I needed to be quick.

"Gab-" was all I could manage.

I pulled her in and kissed her, tears streaming from my eyes as I said goodbye.

# CHAPTER 49

Gabby was frantic. She could see Anya fading and didn't know what to do. She couldn't believe Anwar had betrayed them.

Inside the hall, he really seemed to be coming around. Her father! How was that possible?

In her arms, Anya cried out in agony as she tried to move.

"Anya, stop. You need help." Gabby put a hand to her cheek and felt the cold.

"I failed. It happened anyway," Anya muttered through the blood.

"Please! Somebody help, she's dying!"

"Gabby."

She welled up as she looked down. Anya was waning, and she couldn't stop it.

"Wait, Anya? Wait, they're here. You'll be ok."

Anya lifted a shaking hand to Gabby's cheek. She let the tears fall when Anya said her name and pulled her in. The kiss was heartbreakingly sweet, and it was all she could do to not grab her face and hold tight. When Gabby pulled back, she knew it was too late.

On her lips, she felt a tingle. In her periphery, she saw Light sparkling around her, and a warmth appeared in her stomach. Anya went limp in her arms as Gabby felt the Light spreading through her body.

"Anya?" She sobbed. "Anya?"

She waited for her to disappear like she said she did before, but it didn't happen. Anya didn't jump forward. Gabby pulled her lifeless body into a hug and sobbed like she never had.

Behind, she heard a commotion and turned to see Mr Parks and Alexis racing their way. Gabby gently put Anya down and made way for her sister.

Alexis scooped Anya into a tragic hug, and she screamed in agony. Mr Parks fell to his knees, sobbing into the rain.

Gabby looked to her hands and felt the pain welling up inside. Twenty years ago, Alexis held her sister in her arms and watched her die. She really thought they could change things.

Above, the rain subsided, but the clouds deepened. Sparks turned into flames as the fires stretched across the skies.

To Gabby, it was just like being back home.

# ACKNOWLEDGEMENT

Thank you so much for reading. Lightborn is the first of a trilogy, the second of which will be coming out later this year.

If you enjoyed the book, I hope you'll consider leaving a review.

# PRAISE FOR AUTHOR

*As a first novel, this is exceptional.*

*- AMAZON REVIEW - LIGHTBORN*

*The narrative holds plenty of twists and turns, right to the last action-packed page. The climax of the story may be guessed at as the pace picks up but the final twists will surprise you, tug at your emotions and leave you wanting more.*

*- AMAZON REVIEW - LIGHTBORN*

*Lightborn feels so relatable and timely, with its themes of climate apocalypse and displacement, epic rebellions led by public school teachers, and powerful selfish men who are trying to find a scapegoat for problems they've created.*

*- GOODREADS REVIEW- LIGHTBORN*

# BOOKS BY THIS AUTHOR

## An Easy Target

Grace works for Nico & Associates as a professional fixer, and having just closed out a case, she's ready for a vacation. But when Nico calls, it's time to work.

It's just a search and rescue.
Find the girl. Bring her home.

Only, it's not that simple.
The girl ran away for a reason, and she's not alone.

Pretty soon they all have blood on their hands, and they're nowhere near finished.

Made in the USA
Middletown, DE
27 August 2021

47027856R00219